Y0-BCM-980

# *Treason*

## Meredith Whitford

BeWrite Books, UK
www.bewrite.net

Published internationally by BeWrite Books, UK.
32 Bryn Road South, Wigan, Lancashire, WN4 8QR.

© Meredith Whitford 2004

The right of Meredith Whitford to be identified as the author has been asserted in accordance with sections 77 and 78 of the Copyright, Designs and Patents Act 1988. All rights reserved.

A CIP catalogue record for this book is available from the British Library

ISBN 1-904492-72-X

First published in Australia by
Jacobyte Books, 2000

**Also available in eBook format from www.bewrite.net**

This book is sold subject to the condition that it shall not, by way of trade or otherwise, be lent, resold, hired out or otherwise circulated without the publisher's or author's consent in any form other than this current form and without a similar condition being imposed upon a subsequent purchaser. No part of this publication may be reproduced, stored in a retrieval system, or transmitted in any form by any means electronic, mechanical, photocopying, recording or otherwise without the permission of the publisher or author.

This book is a work of fiction. Any similarity between the characters and situations within its pages and places or persons, living or dead, is unintentional and co-incidental.

# About the Author

Meredith Whitford lives in South Australia. She is a freelance editor and writer, and director of Between Us Manuscript Assessment Service. Meredith has a degree in History, Classics and English from the University of Adelaide. Her interests are reading, history, sleeping, watching too much *Red Dwarf* and listening to Queen and Mozart. She is married, with two children and three cats. When she isn't editing other people's books she tries to find time to write.

She can be contacted at meredithwh@yahoo.com

# Reviews of *Treason*

"... a sublime historical novel ... it flows, it's real, the characters are honest, and their actions are consistent with their belief systems and their deepest feelings ... a joy ... Whitford's writing is impeccable... historical fact melds seamlessly with historical fiction.

### *Historical Novel Society Reviews*

"Sweeping, grand, ambitious ... I was literally breathless once I got into this book. The descriptions of London, of dress of the day ... recollections of the fears before a battle, and of the time-stop effect a battle has on a man. The plot – the rise and fall of a king – is almost incidental next to the fascinating life of a pre-Elizabethan England, complete with in-fighting, treachery, honor, and friendship. A fascinating historical novel, a wonderful work of fiction, and a romance of ages."

### *Kara L Wolf*

"The Wars of the Roses ravage the peace of Martin's life again and again ... the tragic revolutions of the Wheel of Fortune (to which the medieval world made almost pagan obeisance), never ruin his innate good temper. I can't say how much I enjoyed spending time in Martin Robsart's head."

### *Juliet Waldron*

# Dedication

For my nearest and dearest: Rex, Annabel, and Julian, some of whom have read some of this book.

# Acknowledgements

I am grateful to the following people for reading *Treason* in manuscript, making helpful suggestions, and encouraging me by liking it:

In New Zealand: Frances Grattan, who read it first. In Australia: Kevin Clarke, Darry Fraser, Nick Grant. In Great Britain: Lorraine Pickering, Geoffrey Richardson. In the USA: Ellen Ekstrom, Rania Melhem, Trace Edward Zaber (who published an excerpt in 'Of Ages Past'), and Barbara Zuchegna.

Thanks also to everyone on the Later-Medieval-Britain email list for information, help and advice, and some wonderful differences of opinion.

Thanks, all of you.
Meredith Whitford

# Main Characters

*Henry VI was descended from the Duke of Lancaster. Thus, in this novel, 'Lancastrian' refers not only to Henry and his wife but to all the people of the same descent and their supporters. 'Yorkist' refers to the York family and their supporters. 'Plantagenet' was the family name of the descendants of Edward III, and principally used by Richard, Duke of York.*

### York

**Edward**, Earl of March, Duke of York, Edward IV (b. 1442). Eldest son of Richard Plantagenet, Duke of York and his wife **Cecily** Neville.
His siblings:
Anne, b. 1439 (Duchess of Exeter)
Edmund, b. 1443 (Earl of Rutland)
Elizabeth, b. 1444 (Duchess of Suffolk)
Margaret, b. 1446 (Duchess of Burgundy)
George, b. 1449 (Duke of Clarence)
**Richard**, b. 1452 (Duke of Gloucester, Earl of Cambridge. Later King Richard III)

Edward's wife **Elizabeth Woodville**, formerly Dame Grey.
Their children: **Elizabeth** (Bess); Mary; Cecily; **Edward**, Prince of Wales; **Richard**, Duke of York; others.

*__Martin Robsart__. Cousin of the Duchess of York
*__Innogen Shaxper__.

Richard Neville, **Earl of Warwick**, nephew of the Duchess of York.
His wife Anne, née Beauchamp.
Their daughters **Isabel** and **Anne**.
His brothers **John Neville**, Baron Montagu, later Earl of Northumberland then Marquis of Montagu; George Neville, Archbishop of York.

Elizabeth Woodville's sons by her first marriage: Thomas Grey (later Marquis of Dorset) and Richard Grey.

Her parents: Richard Woodville, Baron Rivers, later Earl Rivers and his wife, Jacquetta, previously Duchess of Bedford.
Her siblings: Anthony, Lord Scales, later Earl Rivers; Catherine, Duchess of Buckingham; John; Edward; Lionel, Bishop of Salisbury; others.

John de la Pole, Duke of Suffolk. Married Elizabeth of York.
Their eldest son John, **Earl of Lincoln.**

**William**, **Lord Hastings**.
**John Howard**, Lord Howard and later Duke of Norfolk. His son Thomas Howard, Earl of Surrey.
**Henry Stafford, Duke of Buckingham**. Married Catherine Woodville.
**Francis, Lord Lovell**. Married Warwick's niece Anne Fitzhugh (called Anna in this novel, for clarity).
Robert Percy, friend of Richard III.
Henry Percy, Earl of Northumberland.
William Herbert, Earl of Pembroke, later Earl of Huntingdon.
Elizabeth ('Jane') Shore, Edward IV's mistress.

### *Lancaster*
**Henry VI.** His wife, **Margaret of Anjou.** Their son Edward, Prince of Wales.
**Margaret Beaufort**, married 1) Edmund Tudor, Earl of Richmond, half-brother to Henry VI; 2) Humphrey Stafford; 3) Thomas, Lord Stanley.
Her son Henry Tudor, later Henry VII.
Jasper Tudor, Earl of Pembroke, uncle of Henry Tudor.
**Thomas, Lord Stanley**. Married Lady Margaret Beaufort. His son George, Lord Strange.
His brother Sir William Stanley.

**\* = fictional character**

# *Treason*

*Winner*
*Sime~Gen Reviewers' Choice Award*
*for Historical Fiction*
*EPPIE Award for Historical Fiction*

# Prologue

1505, the twenty-second day of August.

*Edinburgh*

Twenty years ago tonight I was riding for my life through England. Riding blind, most of the time, from the head wound I'd taken in the battle, and only Lovell's hand on the bridle kept me going. Riding to tell York's Duchess that the last of her sons was dead. The last true King of England.

I still keep the anniversary of his death. It is one of the few times I attend Mass, for I no longer believe, except when I pray for my dead. When we returned from the chapel tonight I fell into maudlin mood, drinking too much of what passes for wine here in Edinburgh. (To think I've ended my days in Scotland – twenty years ago I helped conquer the place.) My wife offered to sit up with me, but she was heavy-eyed with her own memories and I sent her up to bed. My children too offered to bear me company, but they have heard all my stories and they have no wish to live in the past. It was my daughter-in-law Mary who asked why I did not write my story down. The others agreed with suspicious readiness; anything to save listening to another repetition, no doubt.

But I shall do it. I'm fifty-three, but with luck I've a few years left, and I need a pastime. Perhaps my writings will amuse my grandchildren, should they ever read them. I daresay I'll prove no author, not like Thomas Malory with his glamorous tales of King Arthur, but it seems important to record my story. Perhaps my mark on history is small, but I am at least an honest man, which in the company of monarchs has the charm of rarity. All I can tell is my own story, and there is much I never knew – but I was there, I saw it all, the quarter-century that changed England and the world forever. And, after all, it's not everyone who can say he grew up with two kings.

# PART I

## *One*

## *1461*

There being nothing duller than the tale of someone's happy childhood, I shall start with the day that childhood ended. The day the Lancastrians came. January, 1461. I was eight.

I had been at the priest's house in the village for my Latin lesson. Snow had fallen in the night, but the day was sparklingly clear and the air so crisp that despite the cold I dawdled on my way home. In the next year I would go to some nobleman's household for my knight's training, and I was wondering if the country would come to peace in time for me to go to the Duke of York – or, even better, his son Edward, Earl of March. Mother had written letters about the matter, but we could expect no answers until summer. So, with my mind a whirl of plans and the Latin subjunctive, I pottered home.

As I crested the hill I had a clear view of our manor. The courtyard was full of horsemen. My father was back! Whooping with delight, I ran the rest of the way.

But these were not our men. Too late I saw that they wore the Queen's livery badge. There were a dozen or more of them, and they were loading their packhorses with our barrels of wine and salted meat. One was stuffing our precious silver plate into his baggage roll. I looked frantically around for my mother, and saw two men bundling her into the house. Her gown was torn right down the front and there was blood on her face.

She saw me and screamed to me to run. Perhaps I would have

obeyed, perhaps I would have tried to fight the men, but as I started instinctively towards her I tripped over something. It was one of our dogs. Its throat had been cut. As I stumbled, one of the men grabbed me and twisted my arms up behind my back, jerking me off the ground. I squealed with the pain of it, and my mother broke loose and brought her knee hard up between one man's legs and hit the other in the face with her fists. It was useless, of course; she was a small woman, and there were too many of them. My mother went very still then. She said, 'Let the boy go.'

'Who is he? Your son?'

'No. A servant's child. He is no one. Let him go.'

The man holding me wrenched my arms until I thought my joints would rend apart. 'Who are you, boy? What's your name?'

Mother's eyes fixed wide and hard on mine. 'I'm the steward's son,' I said, and somehow I found the wit to use the country accent I picked up from the village boys. 'I work for my lady.'

'This is the Robsart manor. Robsart has a son. Where is he?'

It's said that necessity is the mother of invention; well, terror makes a kindly stepmother. 'Master Martin's away at school. At King Henry's new school near Windsor. Who are you? Where's Sir Martin?'

'Dead and carrion, like his master York and the rest of the traitors.'

I heard the words, but they meant nothing. My mother gave one breathless sob, and the men holding her shoved her down onto the ground. She said quietly, 'Not in front of the boy. Please,' and, laughing, they hauled her up again and into the house. I heard her scream a few times, then there was no more sound.

I don't know how long it was before another man came, a man on horseback, in better clothes than the others. Dismounting, he kicked idly at a lump in the snow. Blood trickled out, and I saw that the lump was our steward, Robert, his eyes open and with a great wound in his head. A sword lay by his hand – he had done his best for us.

'Find anything?' the newcomer asked.

'Meat and wine, a few beasts. They've got the women inside. If you're quick you can join the queue to have your sport with Robsart's wife.'

With a flick of his eyebrow the newcomer went into the house. He came back in a moment, shaking his head. 'I've no stomach for this work. Who's this boy?'

'The steward's son.'

The new man looked me over, and I knew he recognised that my clothes were too fine for a servant. But he had more Christian feeling than his fellows, for he said, 'Let him go.' My captor protested, but this new man had authority. 'Go,' he told me. 'Get out while you can,' and he gave me a slap on the backside that sent me stumbling forward. He shouted again, and I ran for my life. As I reached the top of the hill I saw smoke rising from our house.

The village was deserted, silent, every door shut. Not a dog barked as I stumbled by. Obeying some age-old impulse I ran for the church. As I wrenched hopelessly at the latch the door opened a crack and a masculine arm snatched me inside. I screamed, then the smell of incense and unclean flesh told me it was Father Anselm who held me.

'We saw the soldiers come – Martin, what's happened?'

'They're the Queen's men, they're hurting my mother, the house is burning – please help, make them stop, go and help my mother!'

I got that much out, then the smith's wife swept me up in her arms. Most of the villagers were there, huddled down by the altar. Vaguely I heard the gabble of voices and saw Father Anselm and the smith leave the church.


Memory erects its own defences, and I remember almost nothing of the next few days. Were I an artist I could draw every vein, every age-spot, every swollen joint of the priest's hands clasped in his lap as he told me that my mother was dead and my home destroyed, but I can't remember the words he used. Nor do I remember Mother's funeral.

I suppose a full week had passed when Father Anselm sat me down in his parlour and asked what to do with me.

'For you've no kin nearby, if I remember rightly?'

'None, Father Anselm. My father had a brother but he died when I was little. Mother was an only child and her parents are dead.'

He stared worriedly at me, biting his lip. 'Not so much as a cousin?'

The word broke through my apathy. 'Yes!' I cried. 'Cousins! The Duchess of York is – was Mother's kinswoman; I used to live at Fotheringhay. The Duchess is in London, I'll go to her!'

Of course I had no idea what I was asking. It was the dead of winter and we were at least four days' ride from London. There was no one to escort me. The Queen's army was on the rampage, looting and burning its way south through England; that much news had made its way to us. The country was virtually at war. However, when it was put to an impromptu village parliament the smith said that a man what'd brought a horse for shoeing had said as how the Earl of March, young Edward of York, had his army not far away, two days' ride at most; why shouldn't Master Martin go there? Father Anselm could go with him, not even the Lancastrians would harm a priest. The little lad's dad was one of the Duke of York's men, it was right he should go to my lord.

So it was decided. That night, as I snuggled into my makeshift bed in the priest's house, some of my shock began to lift. Grief for my parents still gripped me, but there was hope now, and the prospect of comfort. The Duchess of York awed me less than she did the rest of the world because I'd grown up in her household. I had the right to call her cousin, for she and my mother were connected through two marriages. Mother had been lady governess to the Yorks' daughters Elizabeth and Margaret; that was how she met my father, accompanying the Duchess and her children when the Queen exiled the Duke to Ireland back in '49. So yes, there was comfort in the thought of the Duchess – and in the thought of seeing Richard again. He was the Yorks' youngest son, and my own age to within three months; his mother had helped deliver me, and mine had helped deliver him. I remembered him well; after all it was not two years since my grandparents' death had meant my mother had to leave Fotheringhay to manage our family manor. I liked Margaret and George, Richard's next oldest brother, but Richard and I had grown up like twins. He had written to me once after we left Fotheringhay, carefully penning a postscriptum to his mother's letter. Since then he had gone to Ludlow, the Duke's castle over in the west, and met his elder brothers Edmund and Edward. He too had suffered from the Lancastrian outrages, for the Duke had been betrayed, men had gone over to Queen Margaret, and the Duke had had to disperse his army and flee for Ireland. My father had gone with him. The Duchess and her children had been taken prisoner. They'd only recently been safely released; my father had brought that news when he and the Duke returned from Ireland three months ago.

Remembering my father like that made me cry; I pulled the meagre blankets over my head so as not to awaken Father Anselm. A soldier's son sees his father rarely, but I had loved him. He'd been as handsome as my mother was pretty, and his visits had meant fun, merrymaking, with Mother in her best clothes and happy. When he came back from Ireland Father had ridden in unannounced, a troop of men-at-arms at his back – for he was on his way to Yorkshire with the Duke – and when I forgot my manners and ran to hug him he swept me up in his arms and held me for a long time. That night, the only night he could stop with us, he told us of the flight from Ludlow, the urgent conferences as they decided that Edward and his uncle and cousin should go to Calais while the Duke and Edmund made for Ireland. To me it had been an adventure more exciting than any legend, and I'd been disappointed when the talk became serious and my father spoke of the Duke claiming the throne. Evidently that was a shocking matter, for my mother made a dubious mouth and spoke of the Duke's loyalty to King Henry. Father had said, *Yes, but* ... and went on to speak of the King's unfitness to rule while his wife led the country to ruin: '... after all,' he had said, 'York has the right by descent.' It was dull stuff to me, and I fell asleep on my father's lap while they were arguing.

Remembering that little domestic scene made me sharply aware, as if for the first time, that the world I'd known had ended. My parents were dead. My home was destroyed. All because Queen Margaret was a vindictive, foolish woman who'd made an enemy of the Duke of York. Quite how or why she had done so was beyond me. It was simply knowledge I had absorbed with my wetnurse's milk. Queen Margaret had come here from France sixteen years ago to marry our king and, ignorant of England, had made friends with the wrong people. The Duke of York was the king's cousin and the mainstay of the crown, yet the Queen had feared and hated him from the outset. He had been a kind man, and now he was dead. And, with him gone, Queen Margaret was laying her adopted country waste.

But Edward would stop her. He had already won a battle against her army, back in July, at Northampton. He was eighteen, and, although I had never seen him, I knew he was tall, and clever, and a brilliant soldier, a hero like – like – I groped sleepily for the tales my mother used to tell me – like Alexander, or Sir Galahad, or … In a confused blur of armoured figures I fell asleep.

Well, on the next day a horse was found – perhaps better not ask where from – the villagers lent a few coins, and we set out the following morning. Down the road I asked Father Anselm to stop at our manor. He said we should not, that it would distress me, but I insisted.

There is nothing so sad as a burnt-out house. It had been a snug manor, not large or particularly grand, but handsome enough. It had been built some hundred years before, laid out on the usual plan: hall and stillroom, a solar on the southern side, kitchen and buttery behind, and four rooms above. My mother had put glass in the front windows, made a knot-garden, added the luxury of a stool-room. All gone now. The main walls still stood, and the chimneystack and the central beam of seasoned oak, but the roof and staircase had burnt away; only a shell was left. The outbuildings and stables had been of wattle and daub, and must have burned like tinder. Of course our horses had gone, and the house cow, and Mother's hens and the pigs.

Passing through what had been the front door, I shuffled through the ashes to the chimneypiece. There I moved a certain brick, and saw with a surge of triumph that the Lancastrians hadn't found this hiding place. The little coffer was intact. Inside was a bundle of letters, my father's emerald ring, my mother's jewels and a purse holding two gold nobles and a handful of silver coins; finally, in a paper: a curl of fine baby hair which must have been my own. My inheritance.

I tugged the lacing cord from my shirt, threaded it through Father's ring, and hung it around my neck. Then I hitched the coffer under my arm and let Father Anselm help me back onto the horse. I didn't look back as we rode away.

Being on the road to Edward cheered me, for I had no idea how foolhardy the scheme was. Only a child and a naïve country priest could have tried it, or had the blind luck to succeed.

But succeed we did. By evening of the second day our tired horse shambled into the outskirts of a market town, and it was clear that we'd found Edward's army. The streets were full of men-at-arms in the Falcon and Fetterlock badge of York, or Edward's Sun in Splendour. I'd never heard such noise: men shouting, horses whinnying, townsfolk crying their wares, bedraggled children screaming with laughter as they got underfoot, a man in half-armour swearing like, well, like a trooper as he detailed a group of archers. There were a lot of pretty ladies about, and although my mother had worn a little face-paint on grand occasions I'd never seen such rouged lips or darkened eyes, or such vivid shades of blonde or red hair. One lady, sidling past in a gust of violet scent and bouncing bosoms, winked and said something about *Half price for the Church, big boy.* I thought it a very kind offer, whatever she was selling, but the back of Father Anselm's neck went scarlet and he spurred the poor horse quickly on.

The problem now was to find Edward, but Father Anselm displayed a worldly wisdom that made me realise he hadn't always been a poor country priest. 'The thing to do, Martin, is to ask at the best inn. If Lord March isn't lodging there, someone will know where he'll be. Now sit up straight and don't look about.'

The inn was not at all like our village alehouse. I looked in surprise at the handsome, spreading building with its timbered front. Light shone cheerfully from every window, and I heard singing and gales of laughter. We went into what the Father called 'the ordinary' – a room like a hall, with long tables and booths where men sat with more pretty ladies like those outside, and with the unexpectedly domestic touch of copper pans on the walls and settles pulled up to the fire. The entrance of a priest and a child brought a hush. Some hundred men stared blankly at us for a moment, and the ladies' laughter stopped. A serving maid, her hands full of a dozen mugs, bobbed a curtsy, saying, 'Can I help you, Father?'

'I seek the Earl of March – the young Duke of York. Is he lodged here, or could someone tell me where to find him?'

A man who'd been warming his feet by the fire rose stiffly and came over to us. He wore a soldier's leather jacket over a woollen jerkin bearing the York insignia. His face was square and kindly, and he looked as if he hadn't slept for a week.

'You want His Grace the Duke of York? May I ask your business?'

'It is private business, sir; a family matter.'

The man's eyes moved with impatient courtesy from Father Anselm to me. A frown pleated his brow, then he snapped his fingers as at a puzzle solved. 'Surely you are Sir Martin Robsart's son?' All my life people had remarked on how much I resembled my father. I nodded. Father Anselm murmured something, and the man said, 'Yes, Edward lodges here. Look, we'd better speak in private. I'm Hastings, by the way, William Hastings, a friend of His Grace's as well as one of his captains. Come through.' He led us out into a staircase passage, gesturing kindly for us to sit on a bench. 'Now, what has happened? What does Sir Martin's son here?'

Father Anselm told him, and his tired face took on deeper creases. 'That whoreson Lancastrian bitch – saving your cloth, Father; my pardon – we're hearing this tale from everywhere. The Queen's letting her army run riot, she's treating England like conquered territory. You'd think she *wanted* to turn people against her, and against the King in whose name these things are done. They have even sacked and despoiled churches!' Father Anselm exclaimed in shock. 'Oh yes, Father, nothing is safe, nothing is sacred. Women – women and children killed, houses burned, towns pillaged … Martin, you poor boy, you have my sympathy; I knew your father well, and I believe I once met your mother.

'Now, Edward is lodging here, as I said, but whether he's come in yet or is still at the camp … Wait here, please.'

Tired, and content to have reached journey's end, I leaned against the priest, and he had to shake me awake when Hastings returned and bade us go upstairs.

The panelled bedchamber was full of light. Branched candlesticks stood everywhere, the light shining on the metal of armour, on the crimson-hung bed, on the golden hair of the man who rose to greet us. I had never seen him, but I knew him at once. He was just as I'd been told, his handsome face the image of his mother's. He was the biggest man I had ever seen, a full handspan more than two yards high, and with a deep, strong chest. We had interrupted his toilet, for servants were emptying a bathing tub, the ends of his hair were wet and he was fastening the buttons of a dark blue gown.

'Your Grace –' Father Anselm began, but Edward hushed him with a gesture and knelt down in front of me. He put his hands on my shoulders, looking gently into my eyes. His were grey, with little golden flecks.

'So you are Martin. Yes, you've a great look of both your parents, may God assoil them. Welcome, cousin.' He kissed my cheek and then my mouth. And that did it – to my utter shame I burst into tears. Edward lifted me in his arms and sat down by the fire, cradling me on his lap. After a while he put a handkerchief into my hand, saying, 'At Ludlow I had some practice looking after boys. Richard often spoke of you, he missed you when you left Fotheringhay. Do you remember him and George? And Margaret?'

'Oh yes,' I whooped. 'I missed Richard too. All of them, but he was my special friend.'

'So he told me. Come on, big blow then we'll talk.' I had a big blow, mopped my eyes, and babbled out the whole story. Edward had heard it from Hastings, of course, but he listened gravely, patting me from time to time.

'A horrible thing,' he said at last. 'Never before in England have innocent people had to pay the price of great men's quarrels. I'm sorry, Martin. There's nothing I can say – except that your mother is in God's keeping. Cling to that.'

'Yes. Yes. But ... Your Grace? Edward?'

'Yes?'

'Why did Mother say to the soldiers, "Not in front of the boy"? They took her inside then, what did they do?'

Hastings made a sound in his throat, but Edward said flatly, 'Those men weren't soldiers, Martin, except in name. They were cowardly brutes, scum who'd run from an armed man but can be very brave with a woman and a child. They wanted to rob your house, loot it and burn it. Your mother didn't want you to see that.'

'Oh, I see. Yes. Edward, I mean Your Grace, sir –'

'Oh no, cousins need not be formal, you shall call me Edward. What is it?'

'The Queen's men said my father was dead, and the Duke, your father ...'

I knew, of course; there was no hope left to die when he said gently, 'Yes, I'm afraid it is true. They were up at Sandal Castle, near Wakefield, you know? There was some sort of Christmas truce agreed between the Queen's force and my father's, but the Lancastrians swooped down on the castle when our men were out gathering firewood or something. Your father died with mine, fighting bravely like the good soldier he was. He is buried at

Wakefield with all honour, that I do know.' He swallowed, and tears filmed his eyes. 'My father was killed, and my brother Edmund, and my uncle Lord Salisbury and his son Thomas. A royal fellowship of death.'

Greatly daring, I put my arms around his neck and kissed him. He returned the hug, holding me tightly, then set me on my feet.

'You were right to come to me, and I thank this good Father for seeing you safely here. But I'm moving south tomorrow, the enemy army is reported not far away – I think I had better send you to my mother, hadn't I?'

'Oh yes please, Edward. If Her Grace won't mind? I've no one else now, you see.'

'Of course she won't mind! Had she known, she would have sent for you; you're our kinsman and your home is with us now. Well, let's see. I'll dispatch you tomorrow, with a troop to see you safe. And you, Father? Are you for London too, or will you return home?' The priest looked wistful for a moment, but said he had to go home. 'Tomorrow, then, and be sure I'll send you with an escort. And I'll take it kindly if you'll allow me to make some small gift to your church? Excellent! Now, you'll sup with me? It's almost time.'

In fact the servants were carrying the meal in as he spoke, and with greedy eyes I watched the damask cloth being spread and the bread cut for trenchers. Despite winter shortages the town was doing its ducal guest well: there was a big raised pie, an almond soup, winter salad, fritters, a whole baked fish, braised beef, wafers, cheese. I hadn't tasted demain bread, fresh and white, since I left Fotheringhay. I could have wolfed the lot, but for Mother's sake I was careful about my manners, using my knife daintily and taking care not to drip juices in the spice-dishes. After one incredulous look at the food, Father Anselm too cast the sin of gluttony into the category of tomorrow's penance and ate till his ribs squeaked.

After the meal Edward had the bathing-tub brought back, and I bathed there before his fire; long overdue, I may say, for I'd had no more than a cat-lick wash since Mother died. I had no clean clothes, but the squires wrapped me in one of Edward's shirts, which came down to my ankles, and lent me a warm furry gown. Edward had carefully given me two cups of wine with supper, so I was sleepy and content when at last he rose saying he had to meet with some of his commanders. I managed to thank Father Anselm (both of him; perhaps I should have watered the wine), and say farewell to him properly and then the squires pulled out the truckle bed and I knew nothing more till morning.

The next day I was despatched to London, riding lordly with a guard of a dozen men in York livery. Travelling at cavalry pace – walk a mile, canter one, gallop three, then canter and walk again – meant that the journey wasn't too long or too miserable, but despite seeing country new to me I was bored by the time we reached London.

I loved that city from first sight. That Scottish rhymester, Dunbar, who visits me to punish the wine, hit it off when he wrote, 'London, thou art the flower of Cities all'. The city holds some fifty thousand people, and it seemed they were all out in the streets, and all talking at the tops of their voices. They're a confident lot, the Londoners, and they swing boldly along in their fine clothes. They wouldn't call the king their cousin, as the saying goes. The houses are jammed in higgledy-piggledy, their upper storeys leaning out over the narrow streets; fine, big houses, many of them, for London is the richest city in Christendom. I'd never seen such shops, the great, opulent shops of the mercers and grocers and gold- and silver-smiths. And the people, surely they were all courtiers, earls at least, in their furs and jewels and gold – but no, these were quite ordinary folk, rich citizens of a rich town. Of course there were poorer people, and noisome warrens where you wouldn't keep a dog, but even they were gilded with London glamour in my eyes.

One thing there was no ignoring was the smell. London stinks. Well, all big towns do, but London has the extra, and fortunately unique, smell of the Thames. Nightsoil, stagnant water, animal dung; the stench of tanneries, of hogs being scalded, of the shambles, of the flocks of sheep and cows being driven through the city to the markets; of unwashed humans, of mud. And, more pleasantly, the smells of spices, pepper, herbs, turpentine, cooking food; scent from a passing lady.

And the noise. Church bells, pealing all day long for the Offices, for month-minds and year-minds; passing bells, bells for warning or for celebration. Street cries: 'What d'ye lack? Cherry ripe! Get your strawberries! Fresh fish here, selling now, no better food than here!' Shouts of 'Make way, there!' as some important person tries to force a path. Arguments and brawls, news being shouted the length of the street. The bleat of sheep, the lowing of cattle, the squealing of pigs, the gabble of strange languages, the clank of weapons and the thud of marching feet as a troop of soldiers passes.

I longed to see it all right then and there, but the day was drawing in and the sergeant made haste for Baynard's Castle. This stands right on the river, its feet in the water as they say, but of course we approached it from the city side, riding from Thames Street into a rather grim courtyard. This was bustling with men in scarlet livery with the Bear and Ragged Staff badge; I'd seen such uniforms all through the city, and knew these for the Earl of Warwick's men. Edward had explained that while he was raising troops in the west his cousin Warwick was holding London; the capital is a great prize, and the Queen was expected to attack at any moment. I might in fact have been safer staying with Edward, not that I thought of that.

An outrider had come on ahead, so the Duchess's steward awaited us on the castle steps. At once I was whisked inside, my cloak taken, and I was conducted upstairs to the solar.

Here everything was gay with colour and beautifully warm. Familiar tapestries covered the walls, the Duchess's precious Indian carpets the floor. Familiar too was the smell, the rose pot-pourri we children used to help make. A fair lady sat on the window-seat, sewing by the light of a branch of candles. A blonde girl of about my age was inexpertly playing a lute. Watched by another blonde little girl, George and Richard lay before the fire playing chess. And, coming to greet me, their arms outstretched, were the Duchess and Margaret. In truth, I knew it was Margaret only from her pale auburn hair, so much had she changed in the past two years; she was fourteen now, grown up and remarkably tidied. To my embarrassment she had a bosom now. The women were in mourning, and the Duchess wore the widow's barb and wimple covering her chin as a sign of her rank. Black suited her, but I missed the pretty clothes I remembered. She had favoured blue, which made her eyes the colour of sapphires, and once I had seen her dressed for a grand party in cloth-of-gold and ermine with her hair in a pearled net, and I had thought that the Queen of Heaven must look like that.

She said, 'Martin, my dear boy!' and put her arms around me and kissed me, and I knew I was safe. I had prepared a little speech of thanks and condolence, but the words dried on my lips; what could I, a little boy, say to a woman who had lost husband, son, brother, and nephew in one fell swoop? And words didn't matter; as I fought back my tears the Duchess laid her finger across my lips and said, 'You are truly well come, Martin. We are your family now, and we are united in grief. Edward sent a letter, and his man has told me everything. Martin, your mother was my dear friend as well as my cousin, and your father my husband's trusted companion. You know our hearts are with you.' She gave me another gentle kiss. 'Now, greet your friends, Richard's been anxious to see you.'

Richard hugged me. 'Martin, I'm glad you have come, I've missed you. I am so sorry about your parents. But I'm glad you are here. Are you well?'

'Don't chatter so, Dickon.' George gave me a manly buffet on the shoulder. He was eleven now, plumper than I remembered, and his pale hair had darkened to honey-colour. 'Welcome, Martin. My condolences on your parents' death. I suppose you've heard what happened? About our father?'

I said yes, and that I was sorry, and Margaret guided me gently over to the fair lady. 'Cousin Nan, may I present our kinsman Martin Robsart? Martin – our cousin's wife, the Countess of Warwick.'

I bowed, murmuring the right things. Smiling, the Countess said that in fact we had met – 'Though you won't remember, Martin, for you were only three at the time. You have all my sympathy, my dear.

Now, this is my elder daughter, Isabel, who is a year older than you and Richard. And this is Anne, our baby.'

'I'm not a baby!' The younger girl bounced furiously up, her stubby plaits flying. 'I'm four, Mother, I'll be five in summer, I'm not a baby, I can play chess and everything!'

'Moving the pieces to make pretty patterns isn't playing,' George said. 'And you're the littlest, you *are* the baby. You haven't even greeted Martin.' With a mutinous shrug she rattled off a greeting, caught her mother's eye and did it again properly, and this time shot me a sweet, sunny smile.

'You're not a baby, Anne,' Richard said, 'but they'll go on calling you that because you're the youngest. They call me the baby of the family, and it's worse because I've got so many brothers and sisters. And don't call me Dickon, George, you know I hate it. Come on, Martin, I'll show you our room, there's just time before supper. If you will excuse us, Mother, Madam?' The ladies nodded. Seizing my hand, Richard raced me out and up a flight of stairs and along two galleries.

'You'll soon learn your way about. That's the garderobe, by the way. And here we are.'

The room was full of shifting light reflected up from the river. There were two beds, their woollen curtains striped in the York colours of blue and murrey. The only other furniture was a washstand and three clothes chests, one of which was placed under the windows with cushions to make a seat. A tiny sea-coal fire sulked in the hearth. (It wasn't that the Duchess was mean with coals, more that, bred in the far north, at Raby, she thought anywhere south of York a paradise of Mediterranean heat. Lady Warwick must have been responsible for the warmth of the solar).

'That's my bed,' said Richard, 'and I'll be glad to have you to share it, I get awfully cold. George has become very grand now he's eleven, insists on his own bed.' He perched up on the chest under the window, wrapping his arms round his knees. I joined him. 'I like our room being on the riverside, I like to watch the boats. Look, if you lean right over and peer sideways you can see London Bridge.'

I took an unenthusiastic look, for how interesting could a bridge be? Then I was transfixed, staring with delight.

The whole world knows of the glory that is London's bridge. Nineteen stone arches span the Thames, the greatest thirty feet high. Shops and houses crowd its length yet leave room to hold a joust, so broad is it. St Thomas's chapel clings to one of the piers, only just above the water. I shouted aloud when I saw the drawbridge being raised to let a ship through into the Pool of London, and I nearly fell off the chest trying to watch the barges and count the ships.

Steadying me, Richard said, 'Martin, I'm very sorry about your mother, I liked her so much. And your father. Everything's horrible now.'

'Yes.' Shying away from the subject I asked him about Ludlow. 'For we had your mother's letter saying you were going there, then no news till my father wrote from Ireland. What happened?'

'Well,' he said, 'we went there, summer of the year before last – often it seems no time ago, often years and years. I liked it, it's beautiful. It was a military camp when we got there, for Father mustered his army there, the soldiers' camp filled all the meadows around the castle. We used to watch the men drill and often I would go to watch the fletcher making arrows, and the armourer ... And there were Edward and Edmund ... It was a wonderful summer.'

As he turned to me I saw tears shining in his slate-blue eyes. 'I loved Edmund. He was – was kind. Merry. Rather quiet, but fun. The day we arrived he said, "Oh, hooray, another dark one, you're like Father and me."' He ran his hand through his dark reddish-brown hair. 'It was true, Edmund and I take – took after Father. My sister Anne does too, I think, but I can't remember her, she got married before I was born and I've only seen her twice.'

I had no interest in the Duchess of Exeter. 'Remember how we used to talk about Edward? Richard, he was so kind to me; and he's as wonderful as we used to imagine.'

'Yes, he is.' Richard smiled, his face glowing with hero-worship. 'That first day he lifted me up onto his shoulders, and he said, "How odd to have a brother one has never met." He and Edmund are –

were both soldiers, of course, they were preparing to lead troops for Father, so they were busy, but most afternoons they gave time to me and George and Margaret. They took us riding and fishing, and taught us to shoot, to arm a knight for battle, oh, all sorts of things. And chess and tables and tennis.' I felt a pang of envy, for this was what I had dreamed of when I heard he was going to Ludlow. 'And most days if it was fine we'd go down by the river and Edmund and Edward told us stories or read to us from books, Chaucer and Xenophon and Caesar, or they'd tell us about battles, real ones, I mean – Henry V, and the great Edwards. My ancestors. I suppose yours all fought in those battles too. And there was this one old fellow there, Old Pete they called him, and he had fought at Agincourt!'

'Truly?'

'Oh yes. And he would talk to us about it. Actually, he said it rained most of the time and what he best remembered is mud. He said it's very bad terrain for battle, around the River Somme. But he talked of the battle, and when he told us of the speech the King made his voice would change and suddenly we were listening to Henry the Fifth himself! It was wonderful.' His voice flattened. 'But then it all changed, of course. My uncle Salisbury was bringing his troops to my father, and the Queen sent a wing of her army to intercept him and there was a battle at Blore Heath. My uncle won, and he came on safe to Ludlow. But that made it real to me, if you understand? Seeing the wagons full of dead and injured men, hearing them … seeing my mother and Margaret help the surgeons … It's as if it had been a game before that, and then suddenly it was real. Father and Edward and Edmund were going to have to fight and they might be killed or might come home like those wounded men in the wagons.'

As his voice died away a bell sounded distantly. On its echo a manservant bustled in with hot water and towels. 'Supper time,' said Richard, and we were both glad of the interruption. Feelings are hard to talk about when you're eight.

The Earl of Warwick had arrived while we were upstairs.

Warwick is very important to my story, so it is a pity I cannot now remember my first, unbiased impression of him. I suppose he dazzled me as he did most people, for although he lacked the imperious Neville height he was a stocky, well-made man, and the blue Neville eyes gleamed in a handsome face. He wore black for his father and brother, but it was elaborate, perfectly tailored black, with a quiet embroidery of pearls here and there, and jewelled spurs to his boots. He was England's richest man, a famous sea captain, head now of the great Neville clan; authority and self-confidence shone from him. He also had the charm of all that family. Later I knew him for a man of great pride, arrogance if you like; one who could never be in the wrong. But that first time, I suppose, I took him at his own evaluation.

The Duchess must have told him about me, for he embraced me and spoke very kindly, with great tact, about my parents. He had known my mother well, he said, speaking of her as Cousin Dorothy. 'And of course I met your father at Ludlow; a fine man from a fine family. The fact that our fathers died together for our cause makes us more than kinsmen, Martin.' He smiled at me, and I decided I admired him almost as much as I did Edward and my father.

Worn out from travel, I fell asleep the moment my head touched the pillow. Nightmares woke me, however; in the dead of night I jerked from horror to find Richard shaking my shoulder.

'Martin, ssh, you're dreaming, ssh, wake up now, it's all right, you're safe.'

'Sorry. Was I talking?'

'Rather. Whimpering and kicking. Wake up and the dreams will go away.'

I was all twisted up in the bedclothes, my pillow down the side of the bed. Richard helped straighten me out, and moved the hot brick to warm my feet. 'It's cold – cuddle up. That's right.' We were young enough to hold each other without embarrassment. I lay with my head on his bony shoulder, realising I had been crying in my sleep.

'What were you dreaming?' he asked.

'About the Queen's men – about my mother.'

'That was horrible,' he said. '*Horrible.* And they say it's happened all over England, the Queen is letting her army do what it likes; perhaps she is telling them to do it. They did it at Ludlow too.'

'Do you want to tell me about it?'

'Yes, now I do. I told you about my uncle Salisbury – well, just after he arrived so did Cousin Warwick, from Calais.'

'I know, my father told us – with the Calais garrison under Sir – sir –'

'– Andrew Trollope. We thought they were fine men. Well, the Queen's army moved gradually down on Ludlow and in October, not long after my birthday in fact, they camped about a mile away and we knew it would be battle in the morning. Father's men had built defensive earthworks across the valley, all that sort of thing.

'We children knew nothing till they woke us in the small hours. Trollope and the Calais men had deserted to the Queen. It meant her force outnumbered ours, and Trollope knew all our plans and defences. So our men had to flee. Martin?'

'Mmm?'

'I thought it seemed – well, seemed rather like – like running away. I was ashamed at first. But then Edward explained that it was a – a strategic withdrawal and that in a situation like that you can't afford false pride. And the Queen would have killed them if they hadn't died in battle, and she might have killed us. So they went, in the night.'

'Mmm, my father told me. What happened to you? We heard you had been taken prisoner?'

'Sort of. In the dawn my mother took us down to the castle courtyard. We waited on the steps of the keep. We heard the enemy army coming on. They moved on us slowly; suspicious, I suppose, at meeting no resistance. We saw flames from the town. Heard noises. A group of men rode into the courtyard, and Margaret told us the leader was the Duke of Somerset. Mother went forward. She had told us to stay back, but George went after her and took her arm – and I think that was brave of him, not letting Mother face the enemy alone.'

I thought so too, and I felt a vicarious pride in George. 'And what happened?'

'Well, Mother talked to Somerset; he is her cousin, you know? And then we waited there. And Martin, the Lancastrians sacked the castle and Ludlow town, stripped them bare. They stole everything from food and wine to our clothes and books. What they couldn't carry away they smashed or ... They broke Mother's Venetian looking-glass and – and I saw a man shitting in the corner, and he was wiping his arse on pages from Edward's copy of *Historia Regum Brittaniae*. That book cost over a hundred pounds. But even if it hadn't been so costly, well, I mean: *a book*!'

'And ... we had a little guard with us, just three or four men, all pensioners. They'd been ordered not to fight but when they saw what was happening, they did ... They were all cut down, all killed. One of them was Old Pete, the Agincourt veteran. He had fought for Henry the Fifth, then under Henry's son he was cut down in an English village by an English army. I saw him lying there, and he had his bow in his hand, and it might have been the one he used at Agincourt.' He was crying now; we both were. I hugged him closer, patting him awkwardly. After a moment he sniffled, and went on, 'Well, then the Queen came.'

'What's she like?' I had always pictured something along the lines of Medusa.

'Quite pretty. Plump. Very dark, very French-seeming.' He giggled suddenly. 'She had the Prince of Wales with her, perched up on her saddlebow. Martin, he's near our age but he was cuddling up to her like a baby and he was wearing *white velvet*! With silver embroidery. The Queen called him "*mon Edouard, mon ange*".' His voice flattened again. 'She cursed Mother and slapped her face.

'Well, soon after that they took us to the royal camp at Leominster – and we met the King.'

'What's he like? I've seen pictures of Henry Five.'

'So have I. He's not like that. He looks old. Tall, very thin, a big nose. Rather moth-eaten. When he came in I thought he was the Queen's confessor and I thought he should tidy himself up, cut his hair and put on a clean robe. But it was the King. He was kind to us, though, and he called Mother "Cecily, dearest cousin", and took a great interest in us. Then he asked where Father was, and said his "dear Cousin of York" had no reason to fear him, he trusted Father's loyalty. Then he went over to his prie-dieu and began to pray and you could tell he had forgotten all about us.

'Then later we were taken to Coventry, the Queen had called a parliament there. They sent Mother and us to her sister the Duchess of Buckingham, whose husband is – was – on the Queen's side; he died in battle at Northampton. Mother and my aunt loathe each other, they squabbled all the time. Then a letter came from the Archbishop of Canterbury, he is our cousin and Edward had written to him asking him to care for us. George and I were sent to him. He was kind, but it was very dull.'

Suddenly we heard the rattle of curtain-rings and George said furiously, 'Will you two shut up! A fellow can't get a wink of sleep!' (I might say he'd been snoring all this time). The rings clattered again, and we heard him tossing, then a moment later his snores were shaking the rafters again.

'Better be quiet,' Richard whispered, 'he's like a baited bear if he's woken.

'Well, that's about all there is to tell you. In July Edward and Warwick and my uncle landed, and came to London, and won the battle at Northampton. Then Father and Edmund arrived from Ireland – and your father, of course – and although I didn't understand much of it, my father claimed the crown ... While we were waiting for Father, George and I were put to lodge at Sir John Falstolf's house over in Southwark. Mother was at Fotheringhay once Edward got her and Margaret released. And, Martin, while we were there Edward came every single day to see us! He never, ever forgot. He was busy with government and raising an army, but he never once forgot us.'

I heard his lashes brushing the pillow. 'Martin, I hope I'm not a coward but I'm afraid of what might happen. The Queen is besieging London, Edward is over in the west with the army – and if he – if anything happens to him, George and I are the only ones left, the only males of our family. The Queen would try to kill us, I think.'

'Surely not. Not even Lancaster could. You're just boys.'

'Take us prisoner, then. A lifetime in the Tower. Or Pontefract Castle, where the King's grandfather killed Richard II. I could not bear that.'

'Edward won't fail, you'll see. And there's Lord Warwick.'

'Yes. But I can't help being frightened. I'm glad you are here because I can tell you things like that. We're still friends, aren't we, like we used to be?'

'Yes. Best friends. Forever.'

'Good. Martin?'

'Yes?'

'I wasn't supposed to know, but I heard Cousin Warwick telling Mother … The Queen took my father's head, and Edmund's and my uncle Salisbury's, and stuck them up over the Mickel Gate at York, as you do with traitors. She said Father had been a traitor, and he wasn't, he wasn't!' He rolled over, burying his face in the pillow. I could feel his body shaking with sobs. I managed to get hold of his hand, and after a moment he laced his fingers into mine. There was nothing I could say. Soon he turned towards me again and went on, 'And the Queen made her men put a straw crown on Father's head, in mockery, because she said he had wanted the Crown of England and a straw one was all he deserved … And I keep wondering if the people of York have taken the heads down now the Queen's left, or whether they are still there. For I've seen traitors' head up like that here in London, and I loved my father and Edmund, and Uncle Salisbury was kind to me … What if their heads are still there? Although Father's dukedom was York, the *city* of York is Lancastrian.'

Of course I hadn't a clue, but I said in a voice ringing with authority that naturally the citizens of York would have acted properly, of course there had been a decent burial.

'I hope so. That didn't happen to your father or the other men who died.'

'I know. I'm sorry, Richard, I'm sorry, I'm sorry, I'm sorry.'

'And so am I, for your mother and father and everything that happened.'

We lay open-eyed for a while, silent for George's sake, then, sure we wouldn't sleep, we began to recite the opening to the Canterbury Tales, line after line in turn. No disrespect to Master Chaucer, but after a dozen lines we were asleep.


While I can recall every detail and word of that first day at Baynard's Castle, little of the next few days remains. I know I grieved sharply for my parents, and I suppose that like Richard I was afraid of what might happen, but I was content to be with people I knew, I was secure in love. Why should I remember more?

What I do recall, vividly, is the news of Mortimer's Cross.

We boys were fooling about in the courtyard when there was a cry in the street outside and the porter sprang to open the gates. Pushing hesitantly forward we watched a troop ride in on lathered horses. The men wore the badge of York. Sliding wearily from the saddle the leader saw us, and grinned. 'Good news. There has been a battle – a great victory! Now, I have letters for Her Grace the Duchess –'

She had heard already, she was there on the steps. 'My son is safe?'

'Safe and well, Madam, and victorious.'

Her shoulders slumped with relief, and the sudden flowering of colour in her cheeks told how fearful she had been. Smiling, she said, 'Then come you in and tell us.'

Edward had been leading his army towards London, the man said, when he had word that the Earls of Pembroke and Wiltshire were closing up behind him with a mighty force. Edward had therefore swung about and formed up his men in battle array near

Mortimer's Cross, defending the east-west road crossing the River Lugg.

'It was bad weather,' the man said, 'icy cold, snowing – and, Madam, my lady, God sent a miraculous sign! Three suns shining in the sky! Some of the men were afraid, they thought it an ill omen, but Edward, I mean His Grace, he got up in front of us and shouted that it was a sign of heaven's favour – for the Sun in Splendour is his badge and he's one of three sons. That put us in new heart, I can tell you – and surely he was right, for we won the battle. His Grace said later he'd heard of such signs before and there's a name for it –'

'Parhelion,' the Duchess murmured. 'Yes, I've heard of it. A Greek word, I believe. But yes, it was a sign of God's favour.'

'Indeed it was. The Lancastrian leaders escaped, but some four thousand of the enemy were killed. Few on our side, and your son and his leaders are unharmed.'

'*Deo gratias*. And now?'

'His Grace is marching for London.'

'Good. And the Lancastrians?'

Some of the messenger's exuberance ebbed. 'Madam, the Queen leads her army down on London.'

'Then I,' said Warwick, who'd been listening with his chin on his hand, 'shall deal with her.'

On the twelfth day of February, Warwick mustered his army to march against the royal force. I recall that day, the flurry of goodbyes, Lady Warwick weeping when she thought no one was watching, and Warwick's brother John, Lord Montagu, coolly seeing to the last arrangements while Warwick strode about in half-armour shouting instructions. The Duke of Norfolk was waiting at the head of a troop in his silver lion badges, and George pointed out the Duke of Suffolk, who was married to their sister Elizabeth, and the Earl of Arundel and Viscount Bouchier. With nearly ten thousand men under leaders like these, Lancaster was done for.

It was time. Warwick kissed the ladies, hugged his daughters, spoke cheerfully to us boys. The banners cracked out overhead, the word of command was given, the gates were opened, and in tidy file they rode away through London.

Those were days of stretched nerves and silly quarrels over nothing. We boys were supposed to do our usual lessons, but the chaplain released us when we couldn't so much as conjugate the Latin *amo* correctly. Nor did the Duchess insist. On the fourth day news came that the royal force was at Dunstable, and that Warwick had made camp at St Albans. Tomorrow it would come to battle. Poor St Albans, I thought: there'd been a battle there before, back in '55. I took heart from the omen, because that time York had won. And Warwick had all the modern weapons, he had cannon and Burgundian gunners, and calthorps – the metal star-shapes that will lame a horse or an unwary man – and he had spearsmen, pike-men and archers.

Eleven o'clock dinner on Shrove Tuesday was a silent occasion of crumbled bread and food pushed around trenchers. Battles begin early in the day and it might already be over. The slightest sound had us springing to the windows. Once, going to my room for something, I saw the Duchess pacing silently up and down the gallery, her clenched hands pressed to her mouth, and for the first time it occurred to me that an adult could be afraid.

It was the Lord Mayor of London, Richard Lee, who brought the news. We tumbled into the hall to see him standing before the ladies, an awkward figure in half-armour, turning his sallet round and round between his hands.

'Your Grace, my lady, I've had a message. Lord Warwick brought the royal army to battle at St Albans this morning.'

Lady Warwick gasped and put her hands fearfully over her face. Isabel burst into tears. Anne sidled close to her mother, clutching her skirt.

'And?' said the Duchess.

'Lord Warwick is safe and unhurt, my word on that. But – but he lost the battle.'

'Lost?' faltered Lady Warwick, and George laughed in disbelief. I was watching the Duchess, and although her face didn't change I saw a cool, speculative glint in her eye. I thought, She's not surprised! Shocked, but not surprised.

'Yes. I gather ... the royal army took Lord Warwick unawares. They came down before dawn, and my lord was changing the positions of some of his troops; the scouts had brought some wrong message, Lord Warwick did not understand the Queen's army was so close. The archers held the royal army off, but there was some sort of flanking attack ... and although Lord Warwick fought most valiantly, of course, his forces were split ... and the Kentish men went over to the Queen.' He seemed to be finding the brim of his sallet of absorbing interest. 'And Lord Warwick lost the battle. They reckon three thousand died, mostly on Warwick's side. His brother Lord Montagu and some others of his leaders were taken prisoner.'

The Duchess flinched, for she was very fond of her nephew John. So too was Lady Warwick, who was weeping silently. The Duchess put her arm around her, and looked back at the Mayor. 'But why, sir, do you bring us this news? Where is Lord Warwick?'

'He has fled westward to join up with your son Edward. He feels that the two armies should join up, and under his command Lord March – your pardon, Madam: His Grace of York – will march back to London.'

'Leaving London defenceless meanwhile?'

That brought the Mayor's head up. 'London is not defenceless, Madam. The Watch is out; you see me in armour, a military captain. The apprentices are armed and patrol the city as we speak, each Guild has its armed troop. We have barred the gates against the Queen. London will hold.'

'Of course,' the Duchess apologised. 'No one can doubt London's spirit. But without my nephew Warwick there is no military man to command an army. And the Queen's forces ...'

'Are already besieging the city,' the poor man admitted. 'Refugees have been pouring in for the last hours. But, Madam, London is for York – for your son, now. We will hold.'

We were sent upstairs to our room then. We perched on the

beds, no one willing to be the first to speak. At last George said, 'Well, I admit at first I thought Cousin Warwick was wrong, but when you think of it, it makes sense. You should not split your forces. I don't know why Edward went to the west in the first place.'

'Because much of the Queen's support is in the west,' Richard said. 'Wales and everything. The Tudors.'

'Who are they?' I asked, more for something to say than because I cared.

'Remember the messenger said one of the men executed after Mortimer's Cross was a Welshman called Owen Tudor? Well, when King Henry the Fifth died the present King was just a baby, he was brought up at Court by his uncles and the Royal Council. Queen Katherine wasn't very important any more and she was given a household over in the west, in Wales I think. And she had, well, she …'

'Had an affair with Owen Tudor,' George said impatiently. 'Oh come on, you two are eight, you must know about such things. They went to bed together like married people do. Actually, some say they were secretly married; I don't know. Anyway, Martin, Queen Katherine had three children before anyone knew. Well, that means they're King Henry's half-brothers. One married Mother's cousin Lady Margaret Beaufort, but he died years ago. Jasper Tudor, he's Earl of Pembroke, has thousands of men.'

'And as I was trying to say,' Richard said between his teeth, 'that is why Edward took his army to the west. It's not only Jasper Tudor, there are many others over there who are for the Queen.'

'Yes, well,' said George in triumph, 'that's why Cousin Warwick was right to go to him.' This did not seem to follow, to me. I was a soldier's son, I had grown up hearing military talk. I thought: Warwick is a grown man, an experienced soldier, the senior man of the York-Neville connection. England's capital city and its government were entrusted to him. He should not have fled. He should have fallen back on the city, disposed his forces, and defended London to the last man. To the last drop of his own blood. Edward is a week away: London could hold, had Warwick stayed.

Would have to hold, regardless. Chilled, I remembered the night-time fears Richard had confided to me; remembered what I had heard of the dishonourable treatment the Queen had given York and his men. Remembered what her army had done to my mother and my home. I had heard of sieges: could Baynard's Castle hold out if the Queen came to get York's two last sons? It was a castle, built to be defensible. Bar the gates, and its walls stood sheer to the river. What of the city side? But we had no men. The City would send men to protect us. Or would it? History was full of cities that had saved themselves, and prospered, by yielding quickly to an enemy ...

And in fact Mayor Lee had lied to us. Oh, to be sure, the city was for York, but the Mayor and magistrates, some of the merchants, were for the Queen. No doubt they were concerned to protect the city from the outrages that had made the Queen's army infamous, but against the will of the people they sent a group of ladies to treat with the Queen. If they let her into London, ran the offer, she must promise to hold her troops back from plunder or any attack on the citizens.

It says much for the people of London that they dealt with this clever scheme as it deserved. Perhaps they were spurred on by the Queen openly declaring Edward a traitor, or by the news that she had made a pact with the Scots to give them the northern fortress of Berwick in return for support. Anyway, the citizens took charge of their own affairs – they armed, they formed troops, they forced the magistrates to bar the city gates against the Queen, and they refused to admit her emissaries. At that, her troops began to pillage the suburbs. That was the last straw for the Londoners – and, no doubt, for the Queen, for London was now truly under siege.

We boys were making ready for bed, trying to pretend we didn't hear the guns half a mile away, when the Duchess came in. 'My dears, I have something to tell you.'

Richard turned white as bone. 'Edward's dead?'

'No. Nothing like that. Listen.' She went over to sit on the cushioned chest, tucking her skirts around her. 'You're old enough and have seen enough to know that I cannot trust Lancaster to be merciful to children. You are York's sons.' Normally a serene woman not given to fidgeting, she was twisting her rosary tightly around her hand. 'So I have decided to send you away. Abroad. To Burgundy.'

'Why Burgundy?' said George. 'Why not Calais? France?'

'Because Duke Philip of Burgundy is well disposed towards England, our two countries depend on the trade between us. And Louis of France is cousin to both King Henry and his wife; the moment you set foot in France he would deliver you up to Margaret of Anjou with a garnish of parsley. No, Burgundy is the only safe place. Besides, there is a large colony of English there.'

'I see. When do we go?'

'Now. On the next tide. I have arranged your passage on a trading ship. My squire Master Skelton goes with you, he is in charge of you.'

'And when do we come back? When Edward's here?'

'As soon as it is safe. A few weeks, perhaps. Come now, gather your things.' She stood up, clapping her hands to hurry us.

'But Mother,' Richard said, 'what about you and Margaret? And Lady Warwick and the girls? If we're in danger, aren't you too? The Queen could use you as a hostage to make Edward and Cousin Warwick surrender?'

'No, my dear. It is different with women. Not even Margaret of Anjou would dare harm women.' Despite her certainty, I thought of my mother. 'And Edward and I agreed long since that he must not be swayed by our safety. But you boys are politically important, you are the last heirs of York. You too, Martin, you are my kinsman and at risk. So you will go, as I say. We will be quite safe. Now, George, you're the eldest: I put your brother and cousin in your care.'

'Of course. Mother, you didn't have to say that.'

For a moment she looked at him, then gave him a kiss. 'I know. I'm sorry.'

She packed for us with her own hands. We changed our house shoes for boots, found our travelling cloaks and a few favourite things. Downstairs Master Skelton awaited us, a dark, stocky man who looked exactly the sort you would entrust with this venture.

Lady Warwick and the girls fluttered around us, all saying goodbye at once, but there was no time for more than a quick word.

The Duchess and Margaret came to the landing stage with us. It was already dark, and very cold, snow threatening. Margaret hugged and kissed me as she did her brothers. The Duchess embraced me, blessed me and said, '*Au revoir*, my dear. That is all it is, a brief parting. Not farewell but *au revoir*.' She knelt down then and took her two sons in her arms. It was too private to watch; I let Master Skelton guide me down into the barge that would row us to our ship.

I have now crossed the Channel six times, and every time was a torment of seasickness. That first time I was puking before we were out of the river, and soon I thought I would die, then feared I wouldn't. George was nearly as bad until he found his sea-legs, but Richard proved to have the cast-iron stomach of the true sailor, and he held our heads and passed us basins, puzzled throughout that we should feel poorly. And I'll say this for George – seasick or not, he did his best to care for us. When we were bundled off to lodgings at Utrecht it was George who insisted we were given decent rooms, who made Master Skelton buy us clothes and secure a tutor (we had hoped for a holiday from lessons) and who in general saw we were comfortable by reminding people that for the moment we were unimportant refugees, but one never knew …

We had no news. Rumours floated our way: London had held; London had fallen. The Queen had won; she had lost. Edward and Warwick were dead; they were flourishing. Battles were reported from all over England.

Then, in March, came the glory of a whole bundle of letters.

'From Mother, from Margaret,' said George, shuffling through them. 'And one from Edward! Edward has written!' The seal shattered under his impatient fingers. As he unfolded the paper we leaned close to read over his shoulders.

Edward wrote briefly of the battle at Mortimer's Cross, assured us all his family were well. Then followed:

*And now I must tell you of something else. With our cousin Warwick I returned to London with our army, and London received us right joyously, for no one there now supports Lancaster. And in token of my victory, and of my right as our father's heir, the Lords and Commons offered me the crown of England. Lancaster's Queen is held to have forfeited her husband's rights by making war on our father in breach of the oath she swore last year.*

*But I cannot yet sign this letter Edwardus Rex, for the will of the people and of the Lords is one thing, but to secure peace I must defeat Lancaster once and for all in battle. With our cousin Warwick I am mustering a great army, near twenty thousand men, and tomorrow we set out in pursuit of the Lancastrian force, which has withdrawn from London and is moving swiftly. Soon it will come to battle, and,* Deo volonte, *one way or the other the troubles that began when Margaret of Anjou married Henry of Lancaster will be at an end. Whatever happens, my dear boys, remember I have loved you. You must stay in Burgundy until England is secure, but with God's help it will not be long before I embrace you again. Pray for*

*Your loving brother and cousin, Edward York.'*


Glorious news indeed; but it was followed by silence from England, for weeks. Then one day in early April our schoolroom door burst open and a sweating messenger in Edward's livery dropped to his knees in front of us.

'Prince George, Prince Richard – there has been the most glorious victory! Your brother Edward is King of England! *Vivat Rex!*'

# Two

## 1464

You might suppose that we greeted this news with cheers, or wept or sent up prayers of thanksgiving. What we did was stare at each other, and nod: of course Edward had won the battle, of course he was king. George said, 'We can go home now. I hope it is soon.' It meant little more than that, at first; we had no understanding of how things had changed. We soon learnt.

The messenger had called George and Richard 'Prince', but it seemed merely a formal way of breaking the news. Hardly had the messenger left than other men came, and they all bowed, all said 'prince' or 'my lord'. Even I was addressed as 'sir' or 'Master Robsart'. People who that morning had been merely civil were now obsequious. Nothing was too much trouble. Instead of taking supper in our room we were conducted downstairs to a dining chamber we had not known existed – a long, high room decked with elaborate tapestries, the table laden with gold and silver plate that made us stretch our eyes. At bedtime we were undressed with ceremony, and we laid our heads on fresh linen scented with lavender and rosewater. In the morning new clothes were brought, and a selection of jewels. Richard and I got the giggles under this treatment, but George grew thoughtful, and by the time we set out for Bruges he had acquired quite an air, and I noticed him using some of his mother's gestures.

We travelled to Bruges in great style, and the day we arrived Duke Philip of Burgundy and his son Charles, Count of Charolais received us. Duke Philip treated us most kindly, but what I remember best is that he had the biggest nose I'd ever seen – I hadn't yet seen Louis of France. The high style of the Burgundian court was beyond our imagination, we felt ignorant and provincial, even George was quite subdued. But quickly we realised that whatever we did was accepted as right or merely the English way, and we were treated with a formal gravity befitting ambassadors.

It was that which finally brought home to us how things had changed. In our own eyes we were insignificant children; to the rest of the world we were the King of England's brothers and cousin. We were important. We had status. And with that knowledge came our first understanding of what it meant to be a king. King of England. Duke Philip was immensely rich, he wielded great power – but when all's said and done he was the ruler of a small dukedom which some would say – Louis of France did say – had no real independent existence. England was different. England was one of the great powers, and its King was to be courted; and feared. His brothers were to be flattered and pleased.

All this went to George's head like wine. In fact, he became a pain in the arse. Richard and I suffered his airs and graces, for we dimly understood that he was reacting in his own way to the turmoils of the last two years. Also, we were fond of him. But often we longed to kick his lordly rump, especially when he began to speculate on what title Edward would grant him: Duke of York? Of Clarence? Some new creation? And if he said, 'After all, I am the King's Heir,' once, he said it a hundred times. Richard's patience ended when, just before we embarked for home, George decreed that I should bow to them and call them 'my lord'. 'For,' he said pompously, 'you are neither royal nor of equal rank with us. People who hear you calling us by our names will think you presumptuous.'

There are some moments that stick in your mind for their hurt and humiliation. All these years later I've not forgiven that remark. I have no idea what I would have said or done, but Richard launched himself on his brother with such force George went flailing to the floor.

'Don't say that! He's our friend! He's our cousin! Don't treat him like that! Take it back!'

George wasn't much bigger than Richard, if he was heavier it was childish puppyfat, and Richard had the strength of pure rage. He got in a few shrewd punches and kicks before Master Skelton ran in and pulled them roughly apart. Well, of course children don't tell tales; we mumbled that it was only in fun, only playing, and Master Skelton had the sense not to push it. That evening George apologised to me, and nothing more was said of the matter.

I don't suppose there is any interest in the tale of our return to England, and should anyone reading these papers wish to know about Edward's coronation, well, I daresay there are histories enough. To be honest, I can't remember much of the coronation, except that I wept when the Archbishop put the crown on Edward's head. Nor do I have many memories of the next few years. Suffice it to say that Edward was crowned on the twenty-sixth day of June AD 1461, and that he duly created George Duke of Clarence and Richard Duke of Gloucester and Earl of Cambridge, and made them both Knights of the Bath and of the Garter. He made me legally his ward, and gave me a position as one of Richard's pages, and we lived in George's household at Greenwich. But while George peacocked about full of his own importance as the King's Heir, Richard and I were kept to our books, venturing into the wider world only for Richard's occasional official duties or when Edward was in London.

Not that he was often in London in those first years.

Never think that Edward ascended the throne to universal hosannas and England at once laid down its collective arms. That wouldn't be the English way at all, now would it? So frequent were the uprisings, so persistent and strong was the Lancastrian opposition, so sharp an eye to the main chance did our international enemies have, that for a long time no one would have put money on Edward still being King six months from then. Six *weeks*, often. The Lancastrian threat lingered on, with the Duke of Somerset first coming to terms with Edward then betraying him for the older allegiance. Margaret of Anjou had no trouble whipping up rebellions in the north, for that area was Lancastrian by inclination and the

Percies and the Nevilles had been struggling for control for more than a century. Warwick and his brother John of Montagu besieged the northern fortresses of Bamburgh and Dunstanburgh which Somerset had handed over to her, and she fled to our dear friends the Scots who, always eager to make trouble for England, gave her enough men to invade again. (That woman never learned.) Again Warwick and his brother defeated her, and this time she and her son sailed away to France to take refuge with her cousin King Louis. Yet still it wasn't over, by early '64 it looked like civil war all over again. For once Richard and I stepped forth into the greater world – he had commissions of array for the southwest, and led the troops north to join the King's army at Pontefract. However, John Neville routed the Lancastrians in two short but fierce battles, at Hedgeley Moor and Hexham. The King rewarded him with the Percy Earldom of Northumberland, which gave him not only one of the oldest titles in England but one of the greatest fortunes. King Henry was found wandering about Lancashire with only a handful of attendants. Edward sent him to London and lodged him in the Tower. Being Edward, he treated the poor old fellow with great kindness, and if you ask me Henry was far happier tucked snugly away with nothing to keep him from his books and prayers.

So I take up my story in the late summer of 1464, when I was twelve and Richard a month short of that age. It seemed the Lancastrian threat was over and England could enjoy peace for the first time in nearly twenty years.

There was plague in London that summer. This is nothing unusual, but with nearly two thousand deaths a day, anyone who could do so cleared out to the purer air of the countryside. Pursuing his policy of keeping Richard and me away from Court (thus giving it the allure of the Cities of the Plain) Edward packed us off to stay with his mother at Berkhamsted, her dower manor some thirty miles northwest of London. Also making holiday there were Lady Warwick and her daughters, and Warwick's brother John Northumberland;

Warwick, himself, was constantly going back and forth to the Continent on government business.

It was a pleasant, idle summer. The Duchess was lenient about our lessons, and in fact our tutor spent most of his time helping her establish her garden. We boys had to look lively not to be conscripted to help. Most mornings we took our bows or fishing rods and made ourselves scarce the moment we'd bolted our breakfast. Usually we took Anne Warwick with us, for at eight she'd become quite sensible, for a girl; she could climb trees with the best, and she liked our boys' games. Her mother was content to trust her to us and never minded her coming home wet and grubby. At first Isabel used to come with us, but she was thirteen that September and became very grown-up all of a sudden, much too grand to play with little boys. It was her loss, we thought, leaving her to the thrill of her embroidery and new ways of doing her hair.

The first crackle of autumn was in the air when Warwick returned in triumph from France. He came laden with gifts for his family, and he brought George with him. And to Richard's and my hooting delight Isabel promptly fell in love with him. He didn't seem to mind – what boy of fifteen minds a ravishingly pretty girl thinking the sun shines out of him? Nor did Warwick mind, for a match between his daughter and the King's brother was his dearest dream. And something more than a dream, for Warwick was the great man, the power behind the throne, and he was currently brokering the King's marriage to the French Princess Bona of Savoy. That marriage would write Warwick down in history as the man who secured peace between England and France, he could expect a dukedom at least for his reward; French honours too. If he wanted George to marry Isabel, the King would dance at the wedding.

And so, in the second week of September, Warwick and George rode away to Reading for the Great Council meeting at which the French marriage was to be ratified.

The night after they left, Lady Warwick, playing primero with the Duchess and John Neville, suddenly said, 'Cecily, what do you think of this French marriage?'

The Duchess laid out her hand, called the score, then looked up, her blue eyes guileless. 'Why, Nan, surely that sort of thing is not for us women to concern ourselves with?'

John Neville choked on his wine. Patting his back Lady Warwick said, 'Yes, Cecily, we all know your retiring nature. Come, what's your true opinion? Because I have my doubts. King Louis of France is pushing for it, and my husband is all for it – but it is not a popular idea. England has had enough of Frenchwomen marrying our kings. People don't want another Margaret of Anjou or Edward the Second's Isabella.'

'Can't see Edward letting her be,' Northumberland objected.

'Hmm yes, but that's hardly the point, is it?'

'No.' The Duchess picked up her cards, stared at them, then threw them down again. 'No, Nan, it is not popular. As to its wisdom … I'm not sure. Of course it would be a wonderful thing to have France tied up in a good binding peace agreement secured by a marriage – and certainly England could do with the dowry the Princess would bring. But, since we are speaking frankly, I don't entirely share Dick's confidence.' (It took me a moment to remember that 'Dick' was Warwick. Hard to think of him as a grubby small boy being chivvied by his aunts.) 'King Louis would make war on us whenever it suited him, marriage or no marriage. I cannot trust that man.'

'Dick believes,' his brother put in, 'that once we are allied to France the Lancastrians can whistle for any more help from Louis. That'll put a spoke in Margaret of Anjou's wheel.'

'Or the other way round – no marriage, and therefore no alliance, and King Louis whips up trouble for us.'

'Possibly.' Absently Lady Warwick swept up the cards and began to shuffle them. 'But I know Edward is not keen on this marriage, he's been dragging his feet. He knows it is not a popular idea, but it has gone too far now to turn back, it's all but settled, it needs only the Council to ratify it. Dick hopes the Princess will be here and married by Christmas. And of course,' she sighed, 'it means another journey to France; Dick and I are to escort Princess Bona to England.'

'Arriving in the dead of winter won't give her the best impression of her new country,' Northumberland remarked.

'She'll have the envy of every lady in Christendom to keep her warm; it is not every girl who marries a king *and* a young, handsome man.'

'Is Princess Bona pretty?' Isabel piped up.

'All princesses are pretty by definition,' Richard said.

'But is she?' Isabel persisted. 'The King likes pretty ladies.' Lady Warwick coughed and seemed to grow larger; we children weren't supposed to know about Edward's reputation with women. At Greenwich I had heard a new version of the old joke: What's the definition of a virgin? A girl who can run faster than the King.

'I am sure she is charming, Isabel. And it is past your bedtime.'

That made the Duchess chase us boys off to bed too. On my way upstairs I remembered I had left my bow outside, and stumped crossly off to fetch it. I took a few moments to find it, for one of the gardeners had tidied it onto a bench. As I came back past the rose garden I heard voices. One was Margaret's, and I stopped to listen – not because I was the sly sort of child who enjoys eavesdropping but because in the last few days I, like Isabel, had fallen in love. Laugh if you will, but the object of my affections was Richard's sister. Margaret was eighteen then and still unmarried, because a King's sister, be she never so ugly, is still too great a prize to be given to just anyone. Not that Margaret was ugly; on the contrary, she was the beauty of that handsome family – tall, slender, with lucent grey eyes and hair of the beautiful shade that is called strawberry blonde. She was my *princesse lointaine*, beyond my wildest dreams; although of course I *did* dream, innocent boyish dreams of winning her heart and hand by some feat worthy of one of Arthur's knights. So, because her every word was music to my ears, I stopped and listened.

She was talking to John Neville, and they were discussing the King's marriage.

'The thing is, Cousin Nan is right: Edward is not keen, but it has gone too far for him to draw back.'

'Yes,' John Neville agreed rather glumly, 'he has never been more than lukewarm about it, but my brother went ahead and arranged it. He still thinks of Edward as a child to be told what to do.'

'*Not* the way to handle Edward. John, between ourselves – and I would not offend you for the world – I have wondered if Cousin Warwick isn't riding for a fall?'

'You could never offend me, Meg. I don't disagree with you. My brother has not the faintest notion of how to handle Edward. I say, dear, look out, that bench is damp, let me ...'

I heard the silken rustle of her skirts as they sat down. 'Meg, since we are being frank, Louis of France has got my brother running tame. Louis says *jump*; Dick says *how high?* Between them they have presented Edward with a *fait accompli*. He's cornered.'

'Yet Edward could have been persuaded. But you know what he's like, bully him and he digs his toes in. Stubborn as a mule.' They laughed together. 'But Cousin Nan is right, England has had enough of Frenchwomen marrying our kings. And that's something else, John – Warwick doesn't realise how much Edward loathes Margaret of Anjou. It is real hatred and it's personal. Edward told me once that when he rode into York in '61 our father's head was still rotting over Mickel Gate. Poor Edmund's too. Margaret of Anjou did that.'

'I know.' John's mild voice had turned harsh. 'I too saw those heads. My father's and my brother's too. And I was held prisoner by the Queen after the St Albans battle, and she threatened me with the same treatment. If Edward had not won at Towton and come when he did ...'

There was a silence, then Margaret went on, 'Yes, Margaret of Anjou is responsible, and she brought England close to ruin. Edward hates her, and he is suspicious of France.'

'So he is definitely for Burgundy?' Because that was the thing. In the '60s England was pretty much forced into choosing between France and Burgundy. Much of England's vital trade, especially in wool, was with Burgundy, and our two countries had always been friends, or at least united in ancient hatred of France. Louis XI of

France could not abide Burgundy's independence, and was determined to bring it back under French rule. But for any move, either country needed England's help. Edward was too canny to commit himself outright to either side; he was a clever diplomatist, and for every French kiss there was a Burgundian cuddle. Short truces with both, was the rule.

'On the whole I think he is for Burgundy,' Margaret said. 'Though he would be more so if the Duke of Burgundy's son weren't harbouring Somerset and Exeter – and almost every other Lancastrian under the sun.'

'The moment Louis of France makes another move against Burgundy – as he is bound to – all those Lancastrian exiles will be booted out.'

'Yes, and they'll go to France,' Margaret said tartly. 'Between us, John, Edward has talked of a marriage to unite us to Burgundy. Count Charles has a little daughter, she would do for George or Richard. Or, who knows, I could marry Count Charles.' (At this, I almost gave myself away by crying out.) 'No, Edward doesn't want England tied to France; as we would be, with this marriage to Princess Bona, unless we were prepared to make outright war again. And he hates feeling he is forced into this decision. There are plenty of other ladies he could marry, it doesn't have to be a Frenchwoman. Princess Isabella of Castile has been suggested. He wants to keep his options open, and Warwick has put a spoke in his wheel. Too late now, though.'

'Yes,' John Neville agreed, and they rose and began to wander back to the house. 'Too late now, I'm afraid.'


She died in 1492, Edward's wife, and because in the end we were on pleasant terms I sorrowed for her death. She must have been close on sixty, for she was a good few years older than Edward. I wonder if she ever thought of writing down her life, to pass the time in her nunnery? What a romance that would make! Born a commoner – made a Queen – betrayed by her husband – forgiven by her brother-in-law – imprisoned by her son-in-law. (For it *was* imprisonment, though a polite word was put on it.) Poor woman. Well, I can say 'poor woman' now, but Jesu, the trouble she caused!

That day in mid-September we were in the Duchess's solar after dinner, loafing and daydreaming. Richard was reading to us from Chaucer's Book of the Duchesse. The ladies sewed, and Margaret, who was clever at languages, was translating to and fro between French and Italian versions of Chrétien de Troyes. I played a lazy game of chess with Anne, and I think we were all half asleep from good food and the warmth of the day.

The sound of galloping hooves roused us. Several men were approaching, and at speed. Richard leapt to the window. 'It's Cousin Warwick – and George.' It was scarcely three days since Warwick had left. Of course our first thought was for the King ... Plague ... Rebellion ...We ran to the hall just as Warwick burst in, nearly flattening the steward who held open the door.

'What has happened?' the Duchess demanded. 'Is it Edward?'

George pushed past Warwick to take his mother's hands. 'Edward is safe. Don't look like that, Mother!'

'Yes, I hear you. But what has happened?'

Warwick threw down his hat and gloves. Planting his fists on the table, he snarled, 'I'll tell you what has happened! Your son, Aunt, your son our glorious king has undone all my work, shattered any chance of agreement with France, brought this country to ruin, slighted me and insulted King Louis of France. Insulted all of us! Christ help us! The French marriage all agreed, everything arranged ...'

'Richard!' the Duchess said with such fury he was brought up sharp. 'If you cannot tell us the plain tale, take your tantrum outside. What has happened?'

'He is married.'

Well, Jesu, after that build-up we had expected war at the very least. The Duchess laughed with relief. 'Married! Is that ...' Then, responding to her own reaction: '*Married?* Whatever do you mean?'

'Oddly enough, Aunt, I mean that he is married.' The Duchess took cheek from no one; she gave him a look that had him shuffling his feet and tugging at his collar-band. 'Madam, your pardon. But when you hear –'

'I am waiting to –'

With a deep breath Warwick said, 'He has married Elizabeth Woodville.'

It meant nothing to me, and Richard and the girls looked blank. The Duchess and Lady Warwick stared at each other, then spoke in unison. '*Elizabeth Woodville?*'

'Yes. So you see.'

'Indeed I do.' Slowly the Duchess sat down. At her nod I poured wine.

'Who is Elizabeth Woodville?' Richard asked.

Warwick drained his cup in one swallow and held it out for more. 'She is the daughter of that jumped-up squire Richard Woodville – Baron Rivers – and Jacquetta, the old Duchess of Bedford. Jacquetta was Henry the Fifth's sister-in-law and Bedford was hardly cold in his grave before she eloped with this penniless nobody. They have twelve children. Elizabeth is the eldest daughter. A widow; she was married to Sir John Grey, he died in battle at St Albans. The whole family is a nest of Lancastrians; her father and brother and husband all fought for Margaret of Anjou – God's bones, it's probably all a Lancastrian plot to bring Edward down. She is years older than Edward, she has two great sons, she is nobody. A commoner. And Edward has married her.'

'I believe she is very beautiful,' George said innocently.

'Oh yes, she is beautiful,' the Duchess said. She too was on her second cup of wine. 'All that family are. Edward has actually married her? You are quite sure? It's not simply some promise?'

'No. Married. Aunt Cecily, madam, he married her four months ago. Nearly five. Slunk off while I was busy managing his kingdom and married the bitch at her home, Grafton Regis, isn't it? Married her in secret.'

'Clandestine marriages are illegal,' Lady Warwick objected.

'Did it with witnesses, though, and a proper priest. And he sat there in Council and let me go right through the marriage treaty, every detail right down to the bows on his wedding-night bed-gown, then smirked like the cat that got the cream and said he could not marry Princess Bona because he was married already.'

'Actually,' George said, 'I don't think he smirked, cousin. He was damn nervous about telling us – which makes me wonder if he hasn't already had second thoughts.'

Warwick cocked an eye at him. 'Think the marriage could be overset?'

'Much as I'd like to think so: no. And knowing Edward, the marriage has been well and truly consummated. That was the whole point, of course: she is the one woman he couldn't bed unless he married her.'

'The oldest trick in the book,' snarled Warwick. 'And that idiot fell for it! Unforgivable in anyone of breeding and alleged sense; the humblest apprentice wouldn't fall for that one – and Edward is *the King.*'

'Woodville,' said Richard, 'Lord Rivers – isn't he the one you and Edward took prisoner back in '60, Cousin, when you sailed across from Calais?'

'Yes. And his mincing son, Anthony. And, as if the marriage itself is not bad enough, the woman has this great family, two sons and eleven brothers and sisters, Edward will have to provide for them all, heaven knows how, and I bet they'll be trying to make themselves a power in the land. Oh, Jesu, why did he do it!' He was almost crying. Rather pathetically he asked the Duchess, 'Couldn't you speak to him, Aunt Cecily?'

'I most certainly will. But if the marriage is legal, and consummated, there is nothing to be done.'

'There must be something!'

'What?'

But Warwick didn't know. Or not then.

'Of course it's obvious why he did it,' George said to Richard and me that night in our bedchamber. 'The bitch is incredibly beautiful – Edward wanted her – she held out for a wedding ring.' He glanced around to be sure we were not overheard. 'They say her mother dabbles in witchcraft.' Instinctively we crossed ourselves. 'There was talk of it years ago when she was married to Bedford. Nothing easier than to cast a little spell to bewitch the king. Though I doubt it was necessary; the woman's famously beautiful, and no one has ever said no to Edward before. How could he be so stupid? Warwick's right, it's such an insult to France we will be at war soon. And it has insulted and humiliated Warwick.'

'Perhaps,' Richard said, 'he should have been a little less sure he could rule the King.'

George stared at him. 'But he *made* Edward king!'

'Did he?' This was heresy; George and I gaped. 'Look, of course Warwick is Edward's most loyal supporter; he is family; he controls more men than anyone else in the country. But he doesn't win battles, does he? He made a pig's breakfast of St Albans. He didn't fight at Mortimer's Cross; Edward alone won that battle, and then he won Towton. Warwick did none of that. And all the recent fighting, Hedgeley Moor, Hexham, all of that – those victories were John's.'

Yes, I thought, that's fact; Edward could not have done it without the Neville connection, but perhaps Warwick was more talk than substance.

George was gaping like a carp again. 'I know you think Edward's perfect …'

'No,' Richard said placidly, 'but I think he is a brilliant soldier and does his best to be a good king, and Warwick played a much smaller part than he cares to have people remember.'

'A good king – with *this* marriage?'

'No, there he was absolutely wrong. But he is king, and Warwick has to accept it.'

'He will not.'

'He must.'

And there, I later realised, you had the whole thing, in those two sentences between those two brothers. George was for Warwick, Richard for Edward. To Richard a subject must accept the King's decisions; to George, no. Nor to Warwick.

At Michaelmas we went to Reading to see Elizabeth Woodville presented as Queen. This was not her coronation, of course, but now the cat was out of the bag Edward had to put a formal gloss on things. Or, as George put it, to force the woman down the country's throat.

So you see us there in Reading Abbey, your humble servant squashed in between half the nobility of England and, in an impressive show of family solidarity, just about every Neville and Plantagenet above ground. In view of what happened over the next few years it might sound incredible that it was George and Warwick who escorted the new Queen into the chapel, but that is what happened. Edward had been at pains to make peace by giving them this honour, and I must say they carried it off well, even if they did look as if someone had clipped them over the back of the head with a brick.

I had expected Elizabeth Woodville to be boldly handsome, a bosomy, sensual woman, so the ice-maiden perfection of her beauty astounded me. She was small and slender, the top of her head barely reaching Edward's shoulder, and she had the unusual combination of brown eyes and very pale, almost silvery, hair. And she was truly, truly beautiful. No wonder Edward had been so thoroughly ensnared.

For ensnared he certainly was. Throughout the ceremony he couldn't take his eyes off the woman, and afterwards, when she was privately presented to his family, it went to my heart to see him frisking and simpering, hanging on her every word. Not that she uttered many words. Far from the simple, good-hearted country girl I had half expected, she was cold, haughty and arrogant, and clearly thought ordinary politeness beneath her. When I was presented to her she did not so much as look at me. Well, I was only an insignificant boy, yet she could have been civil. I was her husband's cousin, after all, and although I had no title or great fortune, the Sieur de Robessarte who came over with the Conqueror had been of high family when the Woodvilles were still serfs. Foolish woman, she made enemies that day, and by doing so she wrenched England's history out of true.

Elizabeth's many enemies, such as Warwick, called her haughty rudeness the mark of ill-breeding, but in fact she was quite well-born, for her mother was the niece of the Count of St Pol, and her father was of no worse than modest stock. As I was to learn, the trouble was that Elizabeth Woodville simply wasn't very bright. None of that family ever had any brains, even her brother Anthony was more learned than intelligent, and her two sons from her first marriage, Thomas and Richard Grey, were frankly thick. Also, the Woodvilles were not a rich family, and they had the touchy pride of poverty.

The other thing that struck me about Elizabeth was that she had no sense of humour whatsoever; she had the clear ha-ha-ha laugh of the utterly humourless. Well, she was lovely, chaste, devout and fertile, and I don't suppose Edward married her for witty conversation. Can't have everything.

What took place among the adults that night I don't know, though I can imagine. Sent off to bed, Richard and I exchanged a glance, then resolutely refused to talk about it at all. Even more resolutely did we refuse to admit, even to ourselves, that some of our adoring admiration of Edward had been chipped away.

# Three

## 1464-1468

In the following May, Elizabeth was duly crowned Queen. By then, however, Richard and I were up in Yorkshire, at Warwick's castle, Middleham, in the first year of our knight's training. It may seem odd that after the Reading fiasco, and the no doubt frank exchange of views between Warwick and the King, we should go to Warwick's household. But it was what had been planned, and to make a change would have caused an open breach, which no one was yet prepared to allow. Certainly Edward, saying farewell to us, spoke of nothing but his complete confidence in Warwick and the training we would receive, and he and the Earl embraced with genuine affection.

It took us two weeks to reach Middleham. I have since ridden the distance in three days, but on that first journey we were held down to the lumbering pace of the baggage wagons and Lady Warwick's litter. With Edward and Richard, I had travelled in royal style, but I was astounded when I first realised the size of Warwick's entourage. I had vaguely pictured a dozen of us on horseback and a couple of carts, and I could hardly comprehend this mile-long train. There were some five hundred men-at-arms in their scarlet livery, and ten of the wagons held their equipment as well as their arms. Two wagons carried Warwick's upper servants – his secretaries, his cooks, his butler and panterer, his *valets de chambre*, his grooms and pages, the minstrels, Lady Warwick's and Isabel's maids; Anne's nurse and the chaplains. (The rest of the servants piled hugger-mugger into a cart towards the rear of the train.) Three more wagons held linen, carpets, tapestries, chests of books and papers, Warwick's travelling bed and his beloved carved chairs, as well as such small items as cushions, stools and tables. Another was entirely given over to clothing; yet another, heavily guarded, to coffers of jewels, glass, and gold and silver plate. One wagon bore the wine Warwick had purchased in London and another was stuffed with food.

To my amusement I discovered that Warwick believed himself to be travelling light.

Add to all this the men surrounding Lady Warwick's litter, and the girls on their ponies; add too, Warwick himself with friends and kinsmen taking advantage of a safe journey north and, lost in the middle, Richard and me, and you have some idea of what a right royal progress it was: the progress of England's richest man. The first time we stopped overnight at an Abbey you would have thought it was the king indeed.

We came to Middleham at the close of day. Tired out, we looked at the high rectangular bulk of the castle with relief, sighing at the pleasant thought of baths and wine and comfortable beds. The steward came out to greet his lord and lady, and we were conducted straight up the outside staircase into the great hall. Here a fire was burning briskly, a welcome sight, for although it was spring, the North was still very cold. I had seen snow lingering on the highest peaks. The hall held a degree of luxury I had rarely seen even at Court or Baynard's Castle – arrases on every wall, carpets as well as rushes underfoot, splendid silver on even the lowest tables. Warwick would tolerate nothing but the best wax candles, so the room was lit with uncommon brilliance.

Supper was served at once, and an excellent meal it was. Ah, we thought, this is the life, and we could hardly bear to leave the hall for the chapel.

The moment Mass was over, however, Warwick beckoned over a man in the plain clothing of an upper servant. 'This is my Master of Henchmen, who will be in charge of you now. Boys, I bid you goodnight.'

A little bemused, we said our goodnights to Lady Warwick and the girls, and followed this man to what he called the dormitory. I had only heard the word used for monks' quarters in monasteries, and as we climbed staircase after staircase, up into the very highest and farthest reaches of the castle, I began to wonder if we had been mistaken about the good life we had come to.

At last the man stopped outside a door. 'Your dormitory, gentlemen. Your baggage has been brought up. There is a bed set aside for you. The other gentlemen will show you what to do. I wish you goodnight.'

I have since read of that Greek trimmer Alcibiades betraying Athens and going over to Sparta. No doubt he found his consolations, as did we eventually, but I wonder if Sparta was as great a shock to him as Middleham's training school was to us?

We went into a large, bare, stonewalled room with not so much as a cushion to soften its bleakness. There were three beds (which at least had good thick curtains), three clothes chests, six cloak pegs, three candelabra, and a table down the middle of the room holding three washbasins. Beside each of these lay a pile of towels, a comb and brush. That was all. No fire burned in the hearth – we were to learn that bedroom fires stopped on Lady Day.

I suppose we looked around in horror, for a brown-haired lad sitting cross-legged on one of the beds said, 'Cheer up, you'll soon get used to it.' Then at a nudge from one of his fellows, a blond boy mending a bow, he scrambled to his feet and bowed to Richard. 'Your Grace,' he said formally. 'May I present myself? I am Robert Percy, head of this dormitory. This is John Milwater –' the blond boy bowed – 'and Thomas Parr.' He was dark and had freckles.

'Good evening. I am Richard Gloucester and this is my cousin Martin Robsart.' We all looked at one another with the witless smiles of shy goodwill. 'Er – the Master said one of you would tell us what to do?'

'Go to bed,' Robert said with a grin. 'It's the rule: washed and into bed by eight of the clock, with the candles out. You two are to have the bed near the door; it's warmer.' And that, we learned, was the sole recognition of Richard's rank, that and the fact that we were placed in what we learned was the smallest dormitory, with only these three other boys. Warwick had some fifteen boys in training at the time, and the rest pigged it in one large room. 'The garderobe is along to your right outside the door,' Robert went on, 'and that is about all there is to know.'

'Oh, well, thank you.' Not meeting each other's eye, Richard and I prepared for bed. The moment we were snuggled down Robert extinguished the candles. Almost at once the door opened and the Master said, 'Goodnight, gentlemen.' Silence reigned. Richard slid his icy feet against mine. Shivering, we didn't quite like to huddle together as we usually did, in case the others heard us and thought us soft.

'Your Grace?' came Robert's voice out of the darkness.

'Yes?'

'We wondered – I hope it is not an impertinence, but here in private must we address you as Your Grace?'

'Oh no,' Richard said at once, leaning up on his elbow to pull the bed curtains a little aside. 'Not unless it's expected. I would rather you didn't. I'm Richard, he is Martin.'

'And I'm Rob to everyone.' I could tell by Robert's voice that Richard had passed a test. 'Tom is Tom and John is …'

'John, by any chance?'

They all laughed. 'Yes, never Jack. The Master calls us 'gentlemen', usually with sarcasm, and by our Christian names. He's good, though – tough but fair. If you have any difficulties at first you can go to him. Well, goodnight.'

'Yes, goodnight,' we all said. 'Sleep well.'

I thought I had barely fallen asleep when a bell rang. I jerked upright and tugged back the curtains to see the other boys climbing out of bed and the Master standing in the doorway swinging a large brass bell. 'Downstairs at once, gentlemen,' he said with what I thought an evil smile. Quickly I shook Richard awake and we joined the frantic bustle to dress and wash, then panted after the others downstairs into the courtyard.

'What about breakfast?' Richard asked Rob, who said only,

'Later. Exercises first.'

Exercises? It was barely light! But exercise it indeed was, by the light of the torch the Master held. Jumping and running on the spot, knee bends, push-ups, then just when I was sure I would die, it was light enough for the morning run – two miles, around the castle, down to the river, back again, all at breakneck speed. In warmer weather, we learnt, we would also play tennis or shoot, or start the day with a swim.

'Welcome to Middleham,' Rob said wryly as, red-faced and gasping, we staggered after him into a bare, scrubbed room downstairs. It held two long tables, so at least we were now to be fed. The food was good and plentiful – a mess of oatmeal which to my surprise I came to like; all the fresh milk and ale we could drink, bacon and beef, eggs, fish, cheese and day-old bread (pancakes on high days) and fruit, always fruit, for Warwick believed it kept one from becoming costive. Over breakfast we had a chance to meet the other boys who were to become our 'marrers', as the Yorkshire expression goes: friends, comrades.

After breakfast it was down to lessons: Latin, French, logic, rhetoric and grammar, penmanship, mathematics, law, until dinner at eleven o'clock. At meals we took turns to serve at table, for we had to learn the ritual of service, all the duties of laverer, butler, panterer and sewerer. After dinner we had an hour for quiet recreation, for Warwick believed exercise too soon after eating was bad for you. Afternoons were devoted to the knightly arts: learning to fight with sword and dagger, with the battle-axe, the mace, and every other weapon our instructors could think of; to fight on foot, on horseback, and unarmed, and to ride bareback and without reins, or on war-horses fully armed and accoutred. We learned to arm a knight for battle, and every other detail of a squire's duties, and to load and fire cannon and the new handguns Warwick was so keen on, to use a crossbow and longbow with deadly accuracy. An hour a day was given over to tilting at the quintain and learning the ritual of the joust. By late afternoon it was back to the schoolroom to study strategy and tactics and the great commanders' campaigns. Then, after a swim when it was fine weather, we had to wash and change for supper and for an evening spent making music, dancing, and practising elegant conversation with Lady Warwick and her daughters. We were expected to master at least three instruments, and to know something of the theory of music. The day closed with reading from the classical works, then after Compline, bed – except on Saturdays, when we had our baths. Warwick believed one should keep one's body as clean as one's weapons.

As I write this, using the elegant Italian hand we learnt at Middleham, I flex the finger broken at sword practice and feel again the twinges and aches of the first months of training, and remember the bliss of falling into bed each night, wondering in the few moments before sleep claimed me if I could survive another day. Survive I did, of course, and soon I began to like it. I discovered I had a knack for soldiering. I had to work hard, however, not to be quite out-stripped by Richard. By the end of the first summer we'd grown, we were brown and fit and hard. Our particular friends were Rob Percy, Tom Parr, John Milwater. Later Francis, Lord Lovell joined us – he was married to Warwick's niece, Anna Fitzhugh – and although he was a few years our junior we took to him and made him part of our group.

It was not all work, of course. We always made holiday on saints' days and festivals, or whenever there was a fair within a half-day's ride. In summer Warwick was fond of taking the entire household to some pleasant spot in the dales, there to eat our dinner in the sun and pass the lazy time with songs and stories or what games we chose. As well, there were outings to the great abbeys of Yorkshire, where Warwick bought his splendid horses, or to visit neighbouring landowners. We were always at York for Corpus Christi, and I still think the Miracle Plays by the York Guilds the best in England. Twice Warwick took us boys to Scarborough to teach us something of sea-faring. After the first experiment he left me at home, for I am living proof that those old sailors' cures – drinking a mug of seawater, or swallowing a lump of salt pork on a string and pulling it back up – do nothing for seasickness. There were also Richard's official duties to give us time away from learning, so really, after the first few months, once we became used to it, it was a good life.

Time passed, and soon we forgot we had ever known another life. Letters from London, although gladly received, could have come from a foreign country.

Quite often it was George who brought us the letters, along with scraps of news. If Warwick was at Middleham we could be sure that soon enough George would join him. Much as Richard and I enjoyed his visits – for George was good company when he dropped his airs, and, after all, we loved him – we soon realised that he came more for Isabel's sake than his brother's. What we had thought a girlish infatuation on Isabel's part had become a real love between them.

I saw them together once, in Lady Warwick's knot-garden. I had been sent with a message, so it wasn't that I intruded on their privacy; in any event, they were doing nothing the whole world could not have seen. But just the same my breath caught in my throat at the way they looked at each other. George had just given Isabel a sprig of rosemary he had plucked from a bush, and their fingers twined together. 'For remembrance,' George said, and all Isabel's gentle, simple heart was in her face as he brushed his lips on hers.

I had reached an age where I longed to know what it was like to kiss a girl. To do more than simply kiss. The sight of a laundry maid with her bodice loose and her skirts kirtled up for work could cost me hours of penance when I confessed my lustful feelings. Warwick saw to it that we were all instructed in the bodily facts when we turned thirteen, but the Middleham emphasis was on resisting unclean thoughts as much as deeds. Nothing had prepared me for the sad, lonely longing I felt as I witnessed that innocent kiss.

They saw me standing there, abashed, and they parted without embarrassment. I croaked out my message – dinner, I think it was – and George gave me a mischievous grin and they linked their arms with mine to go inside. They had nothing to be shy about, theirs was no slinking, difficult love. It was in the open, and Isabel's parents approved.

Not so the King, I came to learn. Not long after that little scene – I speak now of 1467 – Warwick went to France on an embassy. He came home delighted and proud at King Louis' favour, and he rushed to tell Edward of the promising trade agreements he had won. But Edward inclined more and more to Burgundy and was determined to tread warily with France, and Warwick found London full of Burgundian courtiers and ambassadors. Worse, some of them were the Queen's St Pol connections. Charles, Count of Charolais, was among the visitors, I believe, and there was a great ceremonial joust or some such thing between the Queen's brother Anthony and one of the Burgundian gentlemen. All well and good; that is the usual way of treating foreign guests. In the middle of it all, news came that Duke Philip of Burgundy was dead, and Charles, now Duke in his turn, had to hurry home. Warwick never liked him, so I daresay he shed no tears at seeing the back of him. But the thing was, Warwick had brought a train of French officials, ambassadors in fact, and Edward gave them short shrift, housing them meanly in quarters prepared for the Burgundians and barely sparing time to see them. Warwick and Edward quarrelled over the matter, and Edward said, among other things, that if Warwick thought he could marry his daughter to the King's brother he was much mistaken. It was about that time, too, that Edward stripped Warwick's brother George Neville of the Chancellorship. I daresay he had good cause, but it was the last straw for Warwick.

I know all this because Warwick came home to Middleham in a rage and took it out on Richard. I remember sitting there at the supper table, hoping I would do nothing to draw attention to myself, while Warwick lambasted Richard. Pale, and angry in his turn, Richard said only that he understood Warwick's concern but he could not discuss his brother. It ended with Lady Warwick and her daughters in tears, and Warwick stiffly dismissing us from table. Nothing more was said of it, or not in public.

And from then on we could never dismiss the creeping, back-of-the-mind knowledge that Warwick was turning gradually against the king. To a certain extent we could ignore the knowledge, for in fairness to Warwick, for a long time he never discussed such matters or spoke to us of the King without affection and respect. But as time went on we knew, and could ignore it no longer.

Why did Warwick rebel? With George it was largely cupidity and spite – he wanted to marry Isabel, and he wanted to be King. But why did Warwick take it so far? Was it, as many people thought, sheer hubris? He was what had come to be called an overmighty subject, but so were others, who stayed loyal. He genuinely believed he had made Edward King, and he genuinely believed Edward had a duty to be guided by him. And let's not forget that Edward was only in his early twenties and not born to be king. Probably to his seniors he seemed a callow boy; and he made dreadful mistakes. But I think that in Warwick's eyes Edward had debased his royalty by bestowing it on Elizabeth Woodville, and therefore had forfeited the right to it.

Of course all this was meat and drink to Louis of France, nothing pleased him more than the chance to drive a wedge between the King and his mightiest subject. No one realised for a long time how deftly Louis worked on Warwick, sending him loving messages, soothing his pride, flattering him; treating him, in fact, as if he were the true ruler of England.

And Edward did little to soothe Warwick. He could have, had he willed, but I think he was sick of Warwick's vaunting king-maker airs, and aware of the danger of concentrating power in any one small group, his own family or not. He had ended the civil wars, united the kingdom, established England again as a steady international power, he had seen that trade prospered. He was personally very popular, the people loved their young, handsome, soldier king, and they would take a good deal for the sake of peace. Yet the marriage was not popular. It was the stuff of romance – the king marrying a beautiful, penniless widow – and between the covers of a romance was where it belonged. The king's marriage was the country's greatest political asset, and Edward had thrown it away on a blonde beauty. Still, a Queen's duty was to bear heirs, and with two strapping sons and that horde of siblings Elizabeth Woodville should be fertile if nothing else, and she was probably better than some French virago. So people accepted what could not be changed, came to terms with the Woodville faction, and waited confidently for the birth of a Prince of Wales. Unfortunately, when the queen's first child arrived, in

February 1466, it was a girl. Called Elizabeth, of course.

No doubt Edward saw his marriage as a chance to build up a new group, a faction who would be entirely dependent on him – and had Warwick and George stayed solidly loyal, the Woodvilles might have gained much less power. By the time Warwick became truly disaffected, the Queen's siblings had been married into all the great, ancient families. For instance, the Queen's sister Margaret married the Earl of Arundel's heir; Anne married Essex's son; Elinor married Kent's; Mary married Lord Herbert's. Most shocking of all, at least for a time, Catherine married the King's cousin Harry Stafford, the young Duke of Buckingham. All the Woodville brothers did well – they were made knights, promised bishoprics, given military commands. Eldest brother Anthony was even made a Knight of the Garter, and I'll spare you George's comments on that. And John Woodville was married to the Dowager Duchess of Norfolk, the king's aunt. She was in her sixties; he not twenty. That marriage shocked even the most cynical, it was called 'the diabolical marriage', and what the Duchess of York said to her son on the matter I'd give my back teeth to know. The Queen's father was made an Earl and soon Constable of England and Treasurer.

And, as if deliberately to alienate Warwick, Edward allowed the Queen to buy the marriage of his niece Anne Holland, daughter of his sister the Duchess of Exeter, for the Queen's son Sir Thomas Grey. (They had all been knighted, at least.) And the point about that marriage is that little Anne Holland, an immensely rich and high-born heiress with a good claim to the throne in her own right, had been promised to the son of Warwick's brother, the faithful John, Earl of Northumberland.

None of this happened all at once, of course, but it was not long before people were pointing to a complete Woodville domination. Whatever Edward intended, there is such a thing as subtlety, there is such a thing as going slowly. So perhaps it is not so hard to understand Warwick.

And so, I suppose, Warwick's great scheme began, although no doubt it originated with Louis of France. He would overthrow

Edward, put George on the throne and see his daughter Queen; and I wonder if he saw that he would thus create a puppet state controlled by France? Make no mistake, George honestly loved Isabel, he would have married her whoever she was – so when the king flatly refused to permit the marriage, that was the end of George's frayed loyalty to his brother. He and Warwick sulked and plotted. And, with one of the King's brothers in his pocket, Warwick set out to secure the other.

One day I said thoughtfully to Richard, 'Next Warwick will be wanting you to marry Anne.'

'Yes. He does.'

'He has *said* so?'

'Hinted. Of course he would love to see both daughters married to the king's two brothers. Edward still has no male heir.' (The second child, recently born at the time of this conversation, late in '67, was also a girl – Mary.) 'If anything happened to Edward, I can't see the country accepting a baby girl as monarch. And who would be Regent? Warwick? George? No, George would be king, God help us. George and I are the heir and the spare until Edward has sons, and Warwick likes the prospect of one of his daughters being Queen.'

'Do you want to marry Anne?' I said curiously.

'Well, I like her, and I hate the idea of having to live abroad, which I would have to if I married some European princess. But it is not going to happen. And nor is George marrying Isabel, and the sooner he accepts the idea the better. And I wish he'd stop coming here, he drives me mad, whining and whinging.'

We left it there and got on with our lives, politics in the background. But after that conversation I noticed how Warwick was working on Richard. He treated him more and more as a son, as an equal. He began to talk as if it could be assumed they agreed on everything. And, dangerously, he began to drop hints about the King: really quite unwise of Edward to raise the Woodvilles up so high and so fast (now he always called him by his name, never said 'the King') … Richard was lucky Edward hadn't married him to a Woodville, ha ha! … Lucky we were not at war with France … Edward would be running into real money troubles soon … Thank goodness Edward still had his family …

Early in 1468 Edward concluded treaties with Burgundy and Brittany against France. You can imagine how the rabidly Francophile Warwick took that. Part of the deal with Burgundy was that Margaret was to marry Duke Charles. More sulks from Warwick, but Margaret was happy; Edward would never have married her against her will, and Duke Charles was handsome, learned, and an accomplished fighter with the nickname 'Charles the Bold'. Well, he was if you choose to translate *téméraire* thus; many people called him Charles the Rash. Later, Edward called him other things.

Trying to be tactful and show he still honoured Warwick as his greatest subject, Edward gave him prime position at the celebrations, and it was on his horse that Margaret rode, with her brothers alongside on their mounts, to Margate, from where she was to embark for Burgundy. As her cousin I had a small part in the proceedings. Although I had out-grown my crush on Margaret, I loved her deeply, and out of fondness I wrote her a letter wishing her well. It was a boy's foolish effort, packed with high-flown attempts at elegance, but she replied, and she kept my letter. She showed it to me a few years ago, crumpled and yellowed but put fondly away with the letters from her brothers. Thirty years she had kept it. My darling duchess.

The day after Margaret sailed I happened to see the King go into the garden. He was alone. I had been looking for just such a chance, and quick as a flash I ran after him. Hearing me, he looked up with a smile. He saw me, and the smile faded.

'Oh, it's you.'

'Please may I speak with you, Your Grace? It is important.'

He frowned, but seeing my anxiety said, 'Oh, very well, but make it quick.'

I had meant to ease into the matter, but in the face of his resigned impatience I said bluntly, 'I think you should take Richard away from Middleham.'

No doubt Edward had been expecting some private boy's trouble. Astonished, he said, 'Do you just! Why?'

'Because Warwick is – Sire, please understand that I make no accusation against him.' I waited for his nod. 'But he is – discontented.'

'I know. He's acting like a spoilt brat who cannot believe he is not getting his own way. Martin, I have Warwick's measure; don't worry.' His tone was dismissive, and he glanced past me.

'It's more than that. He's got Clarence won over to him and between them they are making Richard's life a misery. So I think you should take him away. He's sixteen soon and he has been at Middleham four years; no one would wonder at your making a change.'

'No? Well, Warwick would take it as an insult, and it might be the thing that tips him from discontent into real trouble. I admit I'm sick of their sulks and tantrums, and sick of Warwick thinking he is King of England, but while I don't believe they'd ever turn against me, they could cause me a lot of trouble. Therefore I am at pains to placate them. That way they will become reconciled.'

He said all this like an adult flattering a child with grown-up secrets. Thinking, here we go, I said, 'Have you Merlin's magic wand, sire, to turn back time? Because the only thing that would placate or reconcile Warwick and Clarence would be for you to divorce the Queen, pack her family off back to obscurity, marry some French princess and let Warwick and Louis of France rule your country. Or of course you could abdicate in favour of George.'

I had his attention now, and to spare. 'And Richard?'

'Sire, Warwick thinks Richard a gullible boy who can – must – be persuaded to his view. Persuaded or bullied.'

Giving me an odd look he snapped, 'Are you in trouble up there? You or Richard?'

'Trouble?' I wasn't used to a devious mind. When I understood, I was offended and hurt, and also annoyed at his refusal to see. 'No, we are not in trouble. We like Middleham and the other boys and could have no better training anywhere. We are fond of Lord Warwick and have had nothing but kindness from him. I thought I could talk to you about your brother without you thinking me the spiteful sort who would concoct a reprisal or try to blacken Warwick to get out of a mess. It's as I say. Please, Your Grace!' In my earnestness I seized his hand, a bit of boyish *lèse-majesté* that seemed to impress him more than my words.

'I believe you're overstating things, Martin, but I shall consider what you've said. Now run along, people are coming, and you are much too pretty for me to be seen holding hands with you in a garden. Off you go.'

'You won't tell Richard or Warwick what I have said?'

'No, no. Now go.'

Looking back I saw two ladies entering the garden. Pretty ladies, of course, and dressed to kill. I wondered which was Edward's choice – perhaps both. I was young enough for the idea to shock me. And I wondered if I had achieved anything besides that dubious compliment on my looks. The saying goes that cheats never prosper; well, nor do well-meaning meddlers.


I still think Edward might have ignored my warning, had it not been for the incident at that night's supper.

Richard was serving at the royal table. It was an everyday courtesy expected of a boy of fifteen, but it marked his position as youngest and least significant of his family, and because he resented it his mind was elsewhere. Serving with him I covered one or two small mistakes he made, but I could do nothing when he spilt Warwick's wine.

Warwick hit him.

It was little more than a casual clip over the ear, and at Middleham we would have thought nothing of it; we were there to learn perfect service and he often cuffed a clumsy boy. But this was in public, and Richard was the King's brother and greatly Warwick's superior in rank. It looked as if Warwick was demonstrating both his disdain for that rank and his assumption that he could treat the King's family as he chose.

Richard's only visible reaction was a tightening of the lips as he hastened to wipe up the spilt wine. Warwick had forgotten it already and was deep in talk with Clarence. Edward frowned, and I looked away before our eyes could meet; that was the sort of thing Warwick noticed.

The meal progressed. Bored, I fell to counting the jewels Clarence wore (I had long since perfected the servitor's out-of-focus gaze that lets you see what you want without being accusing of impertinently staring.) A ruby and two diamonds on his right hand, two of each on his left. In his doublet ...

Something close to an argument had sprung up as they talked of the uprising in the west, and I heard the name Jasper Tudor. 'Who is he?' I murmured to Richard.

With lipless skill he answered, 'Henry the Sixth's half-brother. Oldest of the bastards Queen Katherine bore her Welsh lover.'

'Oh yes, I remember.'

'Mmm. Hush.'

The King was saying, 'William Herbert will put Tudor down ...'

'Herbert!' Warwick sneered. 'That upstart!'

That should do it, I thought: first you hit the King's brother, now you insult one of his closest friends.

Very levelly Edward said, 'Herbert is a capable man and a loyal friend who has served me well and kept Wales for me these seven years. And I shall reward him with Tudor's old Earldom of Pembroke. But speaking of these bothers reminds me – Cousin, I think Richard's been long enough in your care.' Richard looked up sharply, and Edward saw the relief in his eyes before his lashes veiled them. 'He is sixteen in October and I was going to make that the time to bring him to Court, but why not do it now? Save him travelling all that way north merely to return.'

Looking stunned Warwick said, 'I am afraid I don't agree, Ned.'

'No? He's had four years with you. What he hasn't learnt in that time he never will. Time he gets some Court polish and sees the workings of government for himself. Should anything happen to George, which heaven forfend ...' a glint in his eye, he crossed himself '... Richard would be my Heir Male.'

'Yes but ...'

'You're not saying he has not learnt enough?'

'No,' said Warwick sadly. 'He is one of the best I have ever had.'

'Well, then! But it is time now for him to learn other things. He can return to London with me tomorrow. Martin too, of course, and any other particular friends, they can be his Squires of the Body, he'll need his own Household.'

Besides any covert ambitions, Warwick was genuinely fond of Richard. 'It is a sudden change, Ned. Give him another year. What's a boy his age to do with himself at Court?'

Edward smiled into Warwick's angry eyes. 'All the usual things, I daresay; all the usual things.'

# Four

## 1469

And so to London. From Margate, Edward had to gallop straight off to the west to deal with the troubles there. 'So your first official duty,' he told Richard, 'will be to escort the Queen to London. George will be with you.'

'*Enchanté*,' Richard said blandly, and Edward gave him a doubtful look.

The Queen preferred to travel in a litter rather than on horseback, so other than providing a gracious presence whenever we halted, our duties were not onerous. Soon we fell back and rode with George. He was very quiet, almost worryingly so, but after some miles' silent riding the reason came out. He missed Margaret.

They had always been very close. Margaret loved her brothers, but where Richard had had me, George was rather the odd man out in the family. He hadn't much knack for making friends, and Margaret had from an early age taken him under her wing. I think that because her marriage came so late – she was twenty-two – George had let himself believe it would never happen, that he would always have her.

'Do you think Duke Charles will treat her well?' he asked.

'Of course.' Richard leaned over to grip his brother's hand. 'I'll miss her too.'

'Yes, well, but you've been up in the north for so long, you've hardly seen her, it's different for you. You know what Mother's like, she refuses to listen to gossip, says what cannot be cured must be endured, loyalty to Edward comes first ... Meg always listened, she understood.'

Listened, perhaps, but didn't always agree: almost her last words to Richard had been, ruefully, 'Try to keep George out of trouble.'

'I'm glad you will be at Court now, Dickon,' George went on. 'I know we don't always see eye to eye, but you're my brother. It's awfully lonely, you see.'

'Lonely?'

'Yes. You'll see. Edward never has time for one.' I thought to myself: Edward might if *one* were a little more conciliatory.

'All he cares about is the Queen's family and their cronies. That woman has Edward right under her thumb, he's as hen-pecked as any simple-minded peasant.'

We were riding amidst George's own people, but just the same I said, 'Your Grace, have a care!'

'What? Oh, there's no danger, my people know what I think. Not that I would dare say anything like this where a Woodville could hear me. You'll see. It is all the Woodvilles and their cronies, all these new people, Edward never has time for anyone of the old blood.' He went on like this for some time, and I recognised many of the phrases Warwick used. Did George ever think for himself? 'And don't think, Richard, that if it comes to a choice between you and one of her crowd that you can rely on Edward. You'll see. Not that he is even faithful to her!'

There was real repugnance in his voice, and behind his back Richard and I exchanged a glance of mingled amusement and respect. George was fickle, gullible, selfish and as slippery as an eel, but he had his mother's devoutness and in sexual matters he was strait-laced. At fifteen he had given his heart to Isabel Neville and he was true to her. Edward's philandering honestly disgusted him, and I wondered if this was a card Warwick had skilfully played with George.

When we reached London – and crossing the bridge still gave me childish pleasure – George peeled off towards his own house, Coldharbour, just west of the bridge. He made a graceful farewell to the Queen, then gave Richard a kiss. 'Watch yourself at Court,' he murmured. 'Guard your tongue and trust no one. I'll come to see you soon.'

At Westminster the Queen's own servants and a horde of household officials came out to conduct her indoors. Dismounting, we gave our horses to a groom, then waited. And waited. At last Richard snaffled a passing page and asked to be shown to our rooms. But the page had to find someone more senior, who had to find the man who held the lists ... After nearly an hour we were taken upstairs to a suite of rooms in the western part of the palace, a long way from the King's quarters.

Fine, gracious rooms – a small outer chamber that would do for Richard's secretaries, another for our eventual attendants. Between them, a lavatorium and a stool-room with a modern double commode. Then, three chambers opening into one another. But all the rooms were completely empty. Bare. Disused for years, it seemed.

'I'm sure Edward gave orders,' Richard said. 'I'm sure it is just some mistake.' Quivering in the air were the words, 'I don't know what to do.' We had always lived under orders, taking it for granted that our creature comforts would be seen to. I felt responsible. If I had not talked to Edward as I did, Richard would have arrived at Court very differently. Also, I remembered George's warning.

'Richard,' I said, 'you are the king's brother. We're no longer insignificant boys at Middleham. You've been insulted. Don't lie down under it.'

He looked at me, his blue eyes taking on the cool slatey tinge that reminded me of his father. 'You're right.'

'Always am.'

He aimed a friendly buffet at me. I parried it neatly. It was a basic self-defence move we had learnt at Middleham, but it earned us a very odd look from the servant who came in, without knocking, to deposit our meagre baggage.

'In future,' Richard said, staring bleakly at the man, 'please remember that I expect anyone entering my apartments to knock. And take a message to the Comptroller of the Household. Say that the Duke of Gloucester presents his compliments and wishes to know why he has been shown to unacceptable accommodation. Tell him that while I wait for him I will be in the royal nurseries.'

When the man had grovelled away: 'Why the nurseries?' I asked.

'Why not? See my nieces. And I'm damned if I'm hanging about here till it suits some official to remember he has a job to do. Come on.'

An only child, my sole experience of a nursery was when Richard's younger sister Ursula was born. I was three, and almost my first clear memory is of standing with Richard, Margaret's arms around us, gazing down at the tiny swaddled creature in the ancient York cradle. I had taken a great interest in Ursula because she had been born on my own birthday, the twentieth day of July. Poor child, she didn't live long; her short life bracketed by my third birthday and Richard's. I know I wept when we were told she had gone to the Blessed Virgin, but I was too young to mourn for long. I had forgotten Ursula until now, when a senior nurse welcomed us into the Westminster nurseries.

The lime-wash of the walls had been mixed with red oxide to give it a fetching pink shade. A frieze of birds and flowers was painted along the top of the walls, the motif being repeated in the hangings. Fur rugs covered the floor. Two lovebirds twittered in a cage near the windows. There was a child-sized table and chairs, and piles of cushions. And toys. Every conceivable kind of game and toy: a miniature castle, the front of which opened to show several rooms all fitted out with furniture; wheeled wooden animals of a size to be ridden on; toys to pull along; cunningly sewn toys to be cuddled; dolls in sumptuous clothes and with real hair; painted wooden bricks.

At the far side of the room a small blonde girl was riding a rocking horse, flogging it on as if towards the end of a race. Reining in, she said, 'Who are you?'

'Madam, I am your Uncle Richard – Gloucester – your papa's brother. This is our cousin Martin Robsart.'

Royal children learn manners early. Not two and half, this moppet said, 'Good day to you, gentlemen. I am the Lady Eliv'bef of

York,' and held out an imperious hand. Bowing, Richard kissed it. I followed suit. She inspected us with eyes that blended her father's grey with her mother's brown. Apparently we passed muster, for she said, 'You may call me Bess. Lift me down.' Richard swung her neatly to the floor, and she seized our hands to tug us over to the table. 'You can see my animals. That's my sister Mary but she's just a baby.' Mary was much less like Edward, more Woodville in her silvery colouring, although she had the Neville blue eyes. She used my sleeve to haul herself to her feet. She didn't seem too steady on her pins, and shyly I put my arm around her. She seemed to like that, and clambered happily onto my lap. Teething, she dribbled too much for the good of my best jerkin, but I liked her confiding way and the feel of her warm little plump body; surprised, I discovered that I liked children.

Bess was piling toys onto the table, thrusting them into our arms. She introduced us to every last one of the things by name; I remember dolls, a rabbit, one of those cunningly jointed wooden monkeys that spin around a stick, about a dozen cats and dogs, and a rather engaging duck that flapped its wings when you pulled it along.

'I'd like a real puppy and a pussycat, but Papa says I'm too young. Do you have a dog?'

'Yes, two, but they haven't …'

'What's their names?'

'… come down from the north yet. Kenilworth and Corfe.'

'Why?'

'I named them after …'

'What's this called?'

'… after castles. It's an elephant.'

'Why?'

'Well, it just is. There was a real one in the Tower menagerie once.'

'Why?'

'Someone sent it to your papa as a present.'

'Did you bring me a present?'

'Now, Lady Elizabeth,' the nurse reproved, 'we do not ask for presents.' Bess obviously thought we did.

'I'm sorry, I didn't,' Richard said humbly. 'Next time.'

'Papa always brings me presents. He's gone away again. He fights bad people. When will he come back?'

'I'm not sure, Bess. Soon, I think.'

'Good. He has to go away a lot because he's a king. He's got a crown. So's Mama, 'cause she's a queen.'

'Excuse me, Your Grace,' one of the maids interrupted, 'but the Household Comptroller wishes a moment of your time, at your convenience.'

We stood up, and I handed Mary to the nurse. 'Lady Bess,' Richard said with a bow, 'will you excuse us?'

'Will you come and see me again?'

'Of course.'

'Tomorrow?'

'If you like.'

'Good.' She flung her arms around us and smacked a sticky kiss on our cheeks. Then, remembering her manners, she said gravely, 'You have good leave to go.'

'Madam, we thank you.'

We left her climbing back onto her rocking horse.

Outside in the corridor the Comptroller was giving a talented imitation of a blancmanger. 'Your Grace, I had your message – is there some difficulty with your apartments?'

'Well, we had expected a little more in the way of appointments. Nothing elaborate. The merest bed, perhaps.'

I thought the poor man would have an apoplexy. 'But Your Grace, I gave the strictest orders! Everything to be ready; all of the best! The king was most emphatic.'

'Then perhaps we were taken to the wrong suite.'

'If Your Grace and Master Robsart would be so kind as to come with me?'

Back we trailed through half the palace, back to those same rooms. The Comptroller stared around, anger making him quite human. 'Can no one obey the simplest order! Is everyone too busy delegating and jockeying for position ... Your Grace, I apologise most humbly, but with so many different departments, such a large staff ... But if you will give me a mere half hour?'

He was as good as his word. We found a pack of cards in our baggage and were still playing the first hand when the Comptroller returned. Behind him came a train of menservants shouldering rolls of carpet and tapestry, lugging furniture and feather beds, dragging hampers of linen and plate. Last came a giggle of maids with dusters and brooms.

Quickly the tenterhooks were nailed up around the tops of the walls and the arrases of our choice hung ('Achilles – I think not. An irritating fellow.') Dust vanished. Bedsteads were assembled, the featherbeds smoothed. Bed curtains and counterpanes (blue, with a floral pattern, for His Grace; green stripes for me) went up. Fine linen sheets and good woollen blankets were spread. Plate was rubbed up and arranged fetchingly on the dresser. The secretaries' room was fitted out with desks and tables, even paper, ink and wax placed just so. The room for our eventual attendants was made up with truckle beds and armour-coffers. More clothes chests were brought, and firedogs and book stands and chairs, a jet and mother-of-pearl chess table, a wine service of silver and Venetian crystal. The rooms smelt pleasantly of the pepper and herbs used to store the woollen goods against moths, and of the good wax candles.

At last the Comptroller looked about with the air of one wishing he dared mop his brow, and asked if there was anything else.

'I think not. Martin?'

'No, everything is very satisfactory. His Grace's other squires and his pages will be travelling down from the north as we speak, but meanwhile we will need the usual chamber servants – and I daresay the King has appointed secretaries, all that kind of thing?'

'Just so, sir. And chamber servants – I will send up a selection for you to choose from.' As if in a shop. Perhaps one purchased them by the ell. Or pound. 'And once again I beg Your Grace's pardon for the error.'

Richard gave him the reassurance he wanted. 'Mistakes happen, especially in a household this size. Consider it forgotten. The King will be glad to know how satisfied I am.'

'Thank you, Your Grace,' the man said with real gratitude, and bowed himself away.

'Instructive,' said Richard, sitting down and folding his arms behind his head.

'Very. An exercise in power.' Pouring wine I asked, 'Do you think it was simply a mistake, or a deliberate slight?'

'Remembering what George said? No, a mistake, I reckon.' But we looked speculatively at each other. 'No, you would be a fool to insult the king's brother on his first day. Still, it was fun throwing my weight around; though it would be a mistake to make a habit of it. Martin, my friend, I think we can enjoy ourselves here at Court. Good rooms, good wine ... Edward said he was sending for Rob and Tom and John Milwater, so we'll have good friends – yes, we can have good times here.'

'Girls?' Warwick had kept a tight rein on us in that respect.

'Why not? It's time we grew up. But let's start with some clothes, eh?'


We studied fashions and summoned tailors and mercers, hatters and furriers, shoemakers and shirtmakers. At sixteen I was close to my adult height of five feet and ten inches, whip-thin and strongly muscled from hard training. From both my parents I had inherited thick black hair, from my father green eyes and high cheekbones, and I was in fact damned handsome, as many girls and a few men (you'd be surprised) had let me know. So was Richard. (Later he had a couple of portraits painted, and neither did him justice, though in the better you can see the resemblance to Edward. The other, and unfortunately the official one, taken at a time of great grief, made him look like a Welsh nun with piles.)

With Edward meeting our bills we saw no reason not to have the richest materials: cramoisy velvet; scarlet, gold and silver tissue; silk; jewels; thigh boots of leather as soft as butter; shoes with the fashionable long pikes; embroidery; shirts of linen fine enough to read through. Fortunately, for the fashion then was for very short jerkins above skin-tight hose, we both had excellent legs; doubly fortunate in Richard's case, for on ceremonial occasions he wore the jewelled blue Garter of the Order, and it looks damn stupid clasped around a fat or bandy or spindle-shaped leg.

So there we were, handsome, likely, well dressed and randy.

Finding girls was no problem. I did none too badly for myself, but the brother of a king can have any woman he likes for the snapping of his fingers, especially at a Court like Edward's. Later it became licentious and went rotten, but in the '60s it was gay, luxurious, rich; and the pleasure was – mostly – innocent.

However, there were less pleasant aspects to our new life. For one thing, Edward seemed almost to regret bringing us to Court. I do not mean that he slighted or ignored us, but he gave Richard little private time, and that in a dutiful, off-hand way, as if his secretary had entered it in his day's list of appointments. Occasionally he would challenge us to a game of tennis, but there was no brotherly intimacy, no confidences asked or offered. Nor did he give Richard any new official duties, or any part in government.

Looking back, I think it was a deliberate policy of letting Richard find his feet in his own way. Because any overt favour, even brother to brother, would have made enemies for Richard.

George had not exaggerated. Court was riven with factions. There were the queen's family and their adherents, and the rest. Oh – perhaps that is putting it too strongly, for of course there were moderates, the people who managed to be on good terms with both parties; to put it another way, those who were loyal to the King and had the sense to keep their tongues behind their teeth about anything they disliked. But Warwick and George were far from the only ones who so despised the Woodvilles and their sycophants that they were prepared to do anything to unseat them.

And we quickly realised that Richard was regarded with suspicion by both sides. The Queen's party thought him Warwick's spy; the others thought him Edward's. That was the climate of suspicion at

Court – no one seemed willing to believe that Richard was simply a boy who admired and loved his brother, and never had a disloyal thought.

So life was not easy. One had to consider every remark, be friendly in all directions, avoid the faintest appearance of conspiracy or even favour.

We became used to it, however. We made friends. Behind closed doors the five of us – for Rob Percy, John Milwater and Tom Parr had soon come down from Middleham – could say what we liked. People like Lord Hastings – the William Hastings of my first encounter with Edward, and now his Chamberlain – and Lord Howard, known to everyone as Jock, and the new Earl of Pembroke and his son Will Herbert were strictly neutral and could be trusted; and, to be fair, the Queen's brother Anthony Woodville was another who treated us very kindly and had no truck with feuds. The Queen herself was civil to us in her remote way, unbending a little after she visited the nurseries and found Richard, Rob and me building a castle for Bess. In fact, the Woodvilles themselves were the least of the problem, unless, like Warwick, you counted their mere existence as a provocation. (Though of Thomas Grey, the Queen's elder son, I'll say nothing, for I hated his guts. The feeling was mutual.)

Thus 1468 came towards its end: no more Lancastrian trouble, Warwick sulking at Middleham, George about his own business, Richard and I and our friends giving the London taverns plenty of business and our respective mattresses a good thrashing.

Then after Christmas I met Innogen.

Red hair is said to be the sign of the devil, of the witch, of the harlot. So I should have been warned, should I not?

I was away from Court over Christmas, for Warwick had invited me to spend the season at Warwick Castle. He asked Richard too, but to no one's surprise Edward made a graceful excuse. Francis Lovell was there, however, so with him and the Warwick girls I had good company. It was a pleasant enough occasion, for no one mentioned politics or the Woodvilles, yet I missed Richard and my usual companions, and I was glad when Lord Hastings, similarly spending Christmas in the country, rode back to collect me. Never suspecting that my life was about to change forever.

Running up the stairs at Westminster I almost collided with a lady coming the other way. 'Madam, your pardon.'

'No, sir, yours.' She was carrying a dog, a plump spaniel, and trying to hold her skirts up.

'May I help you? Let me take the dog.'

'That's kind, sir; I would be grateful.' The dog snuffling limply across my arms, I followed her back down the stairs. Smoothing her skirts she bent to fasten a leash to the animal's collar. 'Belle is young and in need of training, she doesn't understand stairs yet. It was easier to carry her. Thank you, sir.'

In the light from the doorway I could see her properly. She smiled as she thanked me, and my senses jumped. If her voice hadn't already told me she was a lady, her dress and bearing would have done so. Also she was beautiful, and the most sensual girl I had ever seen. It was hard to know in what that impression lay, for her gown was modest and there was nothing bold in her manner – except that for the space of a heartbeat her eyes had travelled over me in a way there was no mistaking. Not blue eyes as I had thought at first, but that soft, changeable grey that alters to reflect the colour of the wearer's clothes. The fashion then was for high pure foreheads, and ladies shaved off their eyebrows and plucked back the first inch or two of hair to achieve the look. I thought it ugly, the little blunt caps then in mode seeming to be perched on bald skulls. But this girl was so new to Court that she had not yet learnt to copy the Queen, and I could see that her hair was red. Not auburn, or copper, or gold: bright, flaming, defiant red, and the little wisps around her face were curly and rather coarse. Her skin was nearly as pale as the Queen's, but the Queen would have dealt with the little golden freckles that lay like a band of pollen over her cheekbones and nose. With that colouring her lashes should have been sandy, but they were dark (or darkened). Also curly and thick.

I wanted to ask her name and in what capacity she had come to Court, but with a bow and a final smile she let the dog tow her outside.

Leaping up the stairs, I decided not to mention her to Richard.

It was three days before I saw her again. Instead of the usual disguising after supper the Queen had her maids of honour dance for us, some country floral dance with the women dressed in the pale clear colours of spring. It was a pretty conceit, but I had eyes for nothing but the girl in the lilac gown. My redhead.

Catching her eye, I bowed elegantly. The left corner of her mouth curved a little, and she turned away. One glance and I was lost. I would have her, or die trying.

Staring after her as they left the floor, I did not for a moment see the King's jester come in. He was a clever Fool, his jokes always witty, but this time puzzled silence followed him as he trudged the length of the hall up to the high table. He wore enormous boots and a flopping pilgrim's hat. His doublet would barely have fitted a five-year-old. He was soaking wet, and he helped his weary steps with a long marsh pike, the kind they use in the Fens to punt their boats along. He squelched to a halt, water sloshing from the tops of his boots, and stared sadly up at the King.

'Why, Jack,' said Edward, ready for a joke, 'whatever is the matter that you're so wet? A hard journey?'

'Aye, Your Grace, a hard and weary journey, for I have travelled the length and breadth of your kingdom to reach you and everywhere I went the *rivers* were risen so high there was no crossing them!'

Oh, Jesu. The Queen's father was Earl *Rivers*. But it was too good a joke, and too apt, for anyone to think of danger. A great, joyous, uncontrollable laugh rose to the ceiling. The King gave one startled crack of laughter, then sank his cheeks on his fists and giggled. Earl Rivers, butt of the jibe, was laughing in a jolly, good-sport way, and even his son Anthony looked mildly tickled. Only the Queen sat like Medusa, glaring at the Fool. The king's jester is by tradition sacrosanct, he can say or do what he likes and often he is the only person who dares tell the king the truth, but as the Queen looked at him I remembered her mother's reputation for witchcraft. George of Clarence showed no amusement, eyebrows raised as at a mild breach of protocol, but the glint in his eye told me he had been behind the joke.

Mopping his eyes, the King threw the jester a coin. In a parody of rustic suspicion the Fool bit it, mimed huge surprise at finding it good, threw it in the air, changed it into a bunch of flowers, and backflipped away. Tactfully the minstrels at once struck up a tune for dancing, and the King led the Queen onto the floor.

Of course I tried to dance with my lovely redhead. No luck. At my first attempt she was dancing with Lord Hastings – and him a married man, the old goat. (Come to think of it, his wife was Warwick's sister.) Next she was claimed by Harry Buckingham, not a day over fourteen. Then she danced with the most high and mighty Prince Richard, Duke of Gloucester and Earl of Cambridge, KG, KB, and see how famously they are getting along, all smiles and promising looks. For revenge I danced with a little brunette who had been making eyes at me for weeks. Then the Queen, who was nearly seven months pregnant, retired, taking her women with her.

You can imagine how closely the good squire Martin Robsart dogged his master's steps over the next few days, anticipating his every wish until he said it was like being haunted and had I nothing else to do? No, I had not, and the following week I was at his elbow when he went to see his nieces.

It was one of those clear, sunny days that come so suddenly in winter, and the Queen was in the garden with the children. Also with her were the nursery maids and some of her own ladies. Including my redhead, who with a pinafore over her gown was training the dog she had carried on the stairs.

'Uncle Richard!' Lady Bess ran to him, holding up her arms. Like most pampered, adored children she loved everyone in her world, but Richard was a prime favourite. So was I, I am happy to recall. 'Uncle Richard, Cousin Martin, I have got a pussycat now! Mistress Innogen gave him to me.' The darling, clever child flung out her arm toward the red-haired girl.

'How kind of the lady. Where did she get him?'

'I don't know. Mistress Jenny, where from you got Bess's pussycat?'

Her hand firmly on the dog's collar, the girl came over to us. She curtsied prettily, her grey eyes flickering from Richard to me. 'Princess, the kitten came from my house here in London, the mother had a litter of five.'

'Do you breed cats, Mistress ?'

'Your Grace, I am Innogen Shaxper.' (Oh, see them bowing and smiling at each other.) 'And I breed cats only by mistake. When I mentioned the matter, Her Grace was kind enough to allow me to give one of the kittens to Lady Bess.'

'It made a pleasant gift for the child,' the Queen said benignly. I had never known her so easy and gracious – I guessed the king had been at pains to compensate her for the Fool's jibe at her father. She looked very beautiful in her cloak of tawny velvet lined with fox furs, but then she would have looked beautiful in jute sacks stitched together. And she *was* in a good mood – not only that freely offered remark, but now a gesture inviting us to sit beside her.

'You are new-come to Court, Mistress Shaxper?' I asked, admiring Mary toddling about in her baby-walker.

'Yes, Master Robsart.'

'And glad we are that we invited her to serve us,' said the Queen, 'for she has a gift for handling dogs, and Belle has never been so well-behaved. A firm hand makes all the difference when creatures grow wilful, do you not agree?'

There was the tiniest pause, then Richard said, 'Indeed I do, madam.'

A wiser women would have left it at that. The Queen, however, went on, 'The King is glad of your loyalty, Gloucester. Perhaps you should discuss with him your views on firm control of – wilful elements.'

'Madam, I shall; although His Grace pays little attention to my views.'

Mary's baby-walker ran out of control and she fell over. The head nurse whisked her up and took her inside bawling, and with a murmur about the cold wind, the Queen followed. She did not give permission for Innogen to stay behind.

The next week the Queen went into the customary retirement before her confinement. As one of her most junior maids of honour, Innogen was seldom required to wait upon her, and so had more freedom. In the Queen's absence Court life grew freer, still decorous enough but with an edge of licence. Men openly paraded their mistresses, women took lovers. And I took Innogen, my Innogen, and the first time was in the gallery overlooking the Great Hall, after supper.

Not even at sixteen was I so crass as to plan it that way. Half in love with her, I wanted more than a quick fuck up against the wall in a public place. But that is the way it happened.

We danced together, and the touch of our hands was enough. My question and her answer were dealt with in a glance. No one saw us slide discreetly from the hall and up the stairs. The gallery was dark, empty, and although I had meant to wait until we were in my room I pulled her into my arms and kissed her. Her mouth opened under mine, and passion leapt between us. I had known nothing like this with other women. Her hands were in my hair, our bodies moving pliantly together. I slid my hand inside her gown, and her nipple sprang hard against my palm. Still kissing her, I tugged up the skirts of her gown. She touched me intimately, her fingers nimble on the fastening of my codpiece. I cupped her bottom in my hands and lifted her against me, and she flung her legs around me. Moaning, I entered her, knowing I couldn't last. I felt her response, stopped her gasp with my mouth, and was lost forever. Mindful, I withdrew at the last moment, and completed her pleasure with my hand.

Trembling, I set her on her feet again. She leaned against me, holding me, and I felt her heart hammering.

'My dear, Innogen, Jenny, never before … Nothing like this.'

'No. *Martin.*'

I began to say something else, but we heard men approaching, a group of them laughing as they came up the stair. At once Innogen straightened her gown and hair, and became a respectable woman who had merely paused to speak to a friend.

'Come to my room,' I begged.

'No. But you may come to my house the day after tomorrow. It's in East Chepe.'


I had not realised she was rich. I had assumed that like me she was well-born but of small fortune, the orphaned ward of some courtier. Chastened, I looked up at the handsome house with its glazed windows and painted front, but had she been the Queen of Sheba desire would have taken me inside. A maid showed me into a parlour, and here again were all the signs of wealth, and of a taste new to me. Above the panelling the walls were painted with a frieze of twining flowers. Carpets the colour of jewels covered the floor. A livery cupboard held gold and silver plate of a quality the King might have envied, and there was a shelf of exquisite glassware. Two carved chairs flanked the fire – and of course chairs are common now, quite ordinary people have them these days, but back then few but the richest or grandest people sat on anything but stools or benches. A lute lay on the table beside a stand of books in Latin and French as well as English; nearly a dozen books. Most extraordinary of all, on the walls hung two paintings. They were quite unlike any I had ever seen; foreign, I could tell. In one, two gentleman played chess, the squares of the board echoing the black and white tiles of the floor, and I swear you could see every detail of the chess-men, and every hair of the fur of the dog at their feet. Behind them a lady sat sewing in the light from the window, and again I could have sworn the lady's clothes and jewels were real, so cleverly were they worked. The other painting showed a hunting scene: courtiers and their ladies in beautiful, foreign clothes, and you looked over hills and valleys in which every leaf and blade of grass seemed to tremble in the spring breeze.

'Flemish,' said Innogen behind me, and for a moment I was too absorbed to turn to her. But only for a moment. I took her hand. 'My father traded much with the Low Countries and France. Do you like the pictures?'

'They're beautiful. All your house is. Was it your father's?'

'Yes. He died three years ago. Would you care for wine?'

'Thank you.' And that too was of a quality I'd rarely known. 'Did your father buy his wine in France?'

'Often. So did my husband.' She wore no wedding ring – that had been the first thing I'd looked for.

'You're a widow?'

'Yes. For two years. More wine?'

'No. But thank you.' She reached for my empty glass, and our hands touched. Let me make it plain that from the first I *liked* Innogen, I wanted to know everything about her and be her friend; but I was so far gone in desire I had no mind to sit making polite conversation.

Nor, as it happened, had she. She leaned forward and kissed me, and then we were hurrying to her bedchamber. Here, I reached for her at once. She said, 'No. Wait.'

'I cannot.'

'Oh yes you can. You'll see.' Smiling that curving little smile again, she stood back away from me and lifted her hands to her headdress. Those butterfly headdresses were all the rage then – a veil of transparent, stiffened gauze, intricately pleated over fine wire to stand up like a butterfly's wings from the front of the head. It was a pretty style that I wish would come back – but I had never realised how many pins it took to hold them. And Innogen took her time about pulling out those pins and setting the veil aside. Then more pins, before her jewelled hennin cap was put on the table. She took off her shoes, then her belt, then her over-sleeves, and turned her back for me to unlace her gown. My hands were shaking so much I could hardly find the hook under the collar, and I nearly pulled the lacings into an impenetrable knot. I managed, however, and loosened the lacings until the gown's own weight pulled it down off her shoulders and to the floor. She stepped out of the pool of velvet and stood there in her lace-trimmed petticoats. I said, 'Please ...' but she shook her head, smiling. Slowly, slowly, off came the two outer petticoats, and her smock was of lawn so fine she might as well have been naked. Then that too was off, and she stood there in nothing but her fine clocked stockings and black garters. God but she was beautiful – slender and finely made, rounded where it matters, her skin taut with the sheen of youth. Again I reached for her, and again she shook her head, smiling. Then one by one out came the pins that held her hair braided up on her head, until the whole glorious rippling red mass fell around her.

'And now,' she said, 'now it is your turn.' Of course I began to wrench at my clothes, but she put my hands aside and did it herself. And there were twenty tiny silk buttons fastening my jerkin, and six more on my doublet, and Innogen undid them one by one, slowly, her eyes never leaving mine, smiling. She unlaced my shirt, sliding her hands over my chest, then carefully untied the points fastening my hose to my doublet. And then everything came off, and there we were.

'I knew you'd be beautiful,' she said, running her hands from my shoulders to my thighs. 'I knew from the moment I first saw you.'

'And I you.' I kissed her, then swung her up in my arms and carried her over to the bed. And if there had been pleasure before, in that quick fumbling in the gallery, now I truly understood what delight and passion are, and the picture that will forever be in my mind is of Jenny on top of me, the slender length of her, her hair falling down around us both as she kissed me, moving to work her passion out.

Hours, we spent that time, and it was very late when at last we lay quietly together, her head on my shoulder, talking as lovers always do of nothing and everything. I think I told her my entire life story in that drowsy time. Of hers, I learnt that she had grown up in Kent, the daughter of a wealthy merchant, a knight who, like my own father, had fought for the Duke of York and then for Edward at Mortimer's Cross and Towton. She had been married at fifteen to a friend of her father's, who had died after six months of marriage. (No wonder, I thought, if she dealt with him as she did with me.)

'Have you children?'

'No.'

'Did you love your husband?'

'No.'

'Lovers?'

'Not while I was married.'

'Since you came to Court?'

She gave me a look I couldn't understand, then said shortly, 'None of your business.'

'Isn't it? Now?'

'No.'

'But I thought ... wanted ... I love you.'

'Don't say that.' I didn't know what I had done to spoil things, but she moved away and began to climb out of bed.

'Why not?'

'Oh, because, because, because.' Her back to me she swiftly plaited up her hair then went to her 'tiring-table to wash. I lay there, watching her put on her clothes. From the depths of my eight months' experience I wondered if I would ever understand women. With words and with her body Innogen had told me what pleasure I had given her, yet now she was treating me like just another man. One of many. Perhaps I was. The idea thrust me furiously out of bed. Clumsy with anger, I started to dress, determined to storm out of the house without another word. But I was used to a servant helping me, and I got into an undignified tangle trying to fasten the points at the back of my doublet. Innogen's fingers closed over mine.

'Let me do it.'

'You need not bother.'

'Don't sulk.'

'I am not sulking.'

'Good, because I need you to lace my gown for me.'

I wanted to refuse, but when, neatly fastened, I turned to her she was smiling anxiously up at me. I melted. 'Turn around, then.'

Knotting the laces, hooking the gown, I kissed the back of her neck and let my hands slide down to clasp her shoulders. She leaned back against me, her hands covering mine. 'Tell me,' I whispered against her ear, 'tell me what I did wrong. Because I want this to happen again. And not only out of lust.'

'So do I. Martin, look, you pleasured me beautifully. And it was more than lust. But don't talk of love.' She turned to face me, lifting my hands to her lips. 'How old are you?'

'Nearly seventeen.'

'Well, then. I am eighteen and I have been married; I enjoy my freedom. Leave it at that, for now.'

'But I may come here again? Will there be other times?'

'Of course. But now it's growing late; time for you to go.'

I felt as bereft as if we had parted forever. I didn't like the feeling; no one should have such a hold over me. Lying awake that night I decided: never again. She could go to her other lovers, I would have no more of her.


Like most decisions taken in the small hours, this one failed the test of day. Innogen and I met at dinner, she smiled at me, and that night I was at her house again, in her bed, learning more of the exquisite pleasure. And so it went on, all that spring. She obsessed me. I knew – well, suspected – she had other lovers, but then so did I, thinking jealousy might bind her to me. It didn't. She was loving, sweet, entertaining, clever, generous with her body, she was fond of me; but with that I had to be content. She taught me more than the refinements of sexual pleasure – it had never occurred to me before that a woman could be someone to talk to and discuss matters other than bed. But Innogen had been well educated, she read widely, spoke several languages, and she did not believe politics and war were entirely men's business.

'Why should they be? Women cannot fight, but doesn't war affect us too? We send our men off to battle, and look after them when they return – if they return. In war we lose our homes, we suffer rape

– what would you have us do, leave it all to you men while we get on with our sewing? Shouldn't we want to understand why we suffer these things? For instance, tell me about these disturbances in the north, all these Robin Hoods, whoever they are.'

I had not, yet, learnt. 'Oh, don't worry, it will come to nothing. Give me a kiss.'

Sweetly obedient she rolled over and put her mouth on mine, but instead of kissing me she said, thus against my mouth, 'Robin of Redesdale – Robin of Holderness – Robin Amend-All ... Yorkshire and Lancashire – insurrection and rebellion – horrible portents throughout the country. Armies riding through the air, a pregnant woman hearing the child weeping in her womb – the skies raining blood – talk of doom ... To the ignorant, sure signs that the Antichrist is abroad. *Think*, Martin. Who is behind it? Warwick? Clarence?'

'Probably.'

'Certainly!'

'You know?'

Leaning on her elbows to look down into my face she said, 'I hear things. Though it is not hard to work out, is it? Do they want to tempt the King into battle?'

'They wouldn't dare.' Though in truth I was none so sure.

'Not in their own names, perhaps. But should one of these Robins not, for once, be so efficiently put down by Lord Northumberland ... I mean should a rebel army *happen* to spring up and engage the King in battle ... Wouldn't it suit Warwick if the King were killed? Or defeated? Somehow compromised?'

'Well, yes. And I know the King is concerned.'

'Concerned!' She rolled over and sat up, bundling her hair out of the way. 'I should hope so! Preparing for action, I hope even more.'

'He is. He has ordered troops and equipment. Richard has asked the King if we can go on campaign with him, but he refuses.'

'Well, whether or not he takes you, the King should go into action soon. And tell your handsome friend Gloucester that his brother Clarence is negotiating with the Papal Legate for a dispensation to marry Isabel Warwick.'

'Do you think he's handsome? – a *dispensation*!' I sat bolt upright, staring at her. 'But the King has forbidden the marriage!'

'Exactly. What are they, second cousins? The papal court is finding that is not too close a consanguinity.'

'How do you know this?'

'I hear things from friends. And friends of friends. My husband had trade dealings in Europe, my father too. I inherited that business and I hear things that way. And I have land here and there. Warwick's brother, the Archbishop, helped with bribing the papal agent, of course.'

'Of course.' I knew the King didn't trust his cousin George Neville, Archbishop of York, although the distrust was partly dislike.

'Tell the King.'

'Is that why I'm here? For you to tell me things for the King's ear?'

'You should tell the King what I've said, but you're here for quite other things.' She demonstrated some of them, and we ended, as usual, in a tangle of red hair, sweat-stuck flesh, and kisses so tender I could have sworn she loved me.


That was in early June, and the next day the King sent for Richard and me. Thinking it meant he had decided to take us with him on campaign, we frisked delightedly into his private audience chamber.

'Afternoon, Ned!' Richard began to sit down.

'We did not give you permission to be seated.'

Warily Richard unfolded himself. 'I ask Your Grace's pardon.'

'Though of course,' Edward went on with oily sympathy, 'you must both *long* to sit down – you must be so tired.'

We glanced at each other – 'Sire?'

'Swiving everything with a heartbeat as you've been doing – exhausting. Is there a woman at Court, nay, in all London, who hasn't been covered by one or other, or both, of you? Far be it from me to expect two young, healthy boys to be chaste, but there are such things as discretion and moderation.' Folding his hands piously he added, 'And fornication is a sin.'

'You'd know,' Richard said under his breath. Not quietly enough, however.

'Which of you made that most impertinent remark?'

'I did, Sire,' we both said.

'Shut up, Martin, I know it was my clever-dick brother.' He smiled at the pun. Briefly. Picking up a sheet of paper from the table he said, 'My lord duke, Master Ogleby of London comes to me complaining that you have seduced his daughter and made her pregnant. What have you to say to that?'

'That I thought I had dealt with the matter.'

Whatever Edward had expected, this crisp response caught him off-guard. 'Your meaning?'

Reluctantly, because he was too fastidious to enjoy speaking of private matters, Richard said, 'Sire, Linnet Ogleby told me she is pregnant and that the child is mine. She said she was to go to an aunt near Windsor. I gave her money for her expenses, and promised to acknowledge the child and provide for its maintenance. I thought the matter dealt with.'

'You fascinate me. Go on. Why then is the outraged father coming to me?'

'Sire – Master Ogleby invited me to dine at his London house. He is a member of the Grocer's Guild and has ambitions to be an alderman. Also he wants some import licence to expand his business. I told him that whether he becomes an alderman is a matter for the City. The licence, I said I would speak to you about; and I did so, if you remember.' Edward frowned, then shrugged. 'The night I dined with him was foul, wet and cold; he invited me to stay at his house that night. I did so. And I found his daughter in my bed.'

'And thought it impolite to refuse the hospitable thought for your comfort?'

Risking a smile, Richard said, 'It was more that she is very pretty, and was stark naked; and eager. Thought played little part in it.'

'Yes, but the man's a pander, using his own daughter ...'

'I've never taken advantage of an unwilling girl. She was not coerced. Or innocent. Whether her father knew of it, or planned it, I don't know. But it seems he's trying to take advantage of the situation.'

'As so many people do. Hmm. Sure the child's yours?'

'Who can ever be? But it's likely. The dates fit.'

'I see.' Dipping his pen in the inkwell, Edward made a note on the paper. 'I think Master Ogleby can whistle for his import licence. I'm sorry, Richard; I should have trusted you to deal with the matter.

'Now, you, Master Robsart.' I jumped; I had thought I was only there to take a general warning. 'Her Grace the Queen tells me she has had cause to dismiss one of her maids of honour for unchastity and loose living. I refer, of course, to Mistress Shaxper.'

'No!' I cried. 'That is unfair!'

'Am I to tell the Queen she is wrong?'

'I – no – that is …'

'Oh, Martin,' the King said, not unkindly. 'The entire Court knows of your affair with the young lady. And I'm afraid you're not the only one. She has made herself notorious.'

'Edward, he's in love with her,' Richard cut in.

'I see. Martin, I'm sorry, but there it is. The girl must go. Let's be blunt: people say many things against the Queen, but no one can say she is anything but chaste and virtuous. And she expects the same of the women who serve her.'

'I know, sire. And no one has ever said otherwise of the Queen in my hearing, nor would I permit them to. But Innogen is – is – I love her and I want to marry her.'

Edward sighed. 'Oh, Martin. You're sixteen. It would be a grim world if we all married the first person we fell in love with.' I was watching him intently, and I saw something extraordinary: for a second his face changed, and a very young, confused, desperate man looked at me as if for help. Then in a heart's beat he was himself again. 'Sixteen is too young. An arranged marriage is one thing, but love? Wait until you're older. And I would not let you marry Mistress Shaxper.'

'Why not?' I cried, regardless of protocol.

'Because you can do much better.'

'I could not. *She* could. She is rich, educated, of birth, she has land; I've got nothing, I'm no one.'

Grimly hanging on to his patience the King said, 'Martin, dear boy, listen. I have known you since you were eight, and when I made you my ward and put you into Richard's household I said I would always take care of you. So listen to a little worldly wisdom. You are nobly born, you are my kinsman, you are Richard's dearest friend, and my mother's and my friend and protégé. Your father gave his life trying to save my father and brother. We are in your debt. Keep on serving Richard as you have, and serve me, and you will rise high. When you're older I will knight you, and I have had it in mind for some time to restore your old family barony. An earldom will not be out of your reach. You will have lands, money, and above all, influence. You will be able to look as high as you like for a wife.'

'I'll still want Innogen Shaxper.'

The kindly friend turned back into the King. 'Master Robsart, you will marry *whom* I tell you, *when* I tell you. I am sure you are aware it is illegal for a ward to marry without his guardian's consent, so do not think to defy me. You and the girl have been indiscreet and she has been dismissed from Court. Let the matter end there.'

'Has she already gone?'

'Yes. To her home – Kent, isn't it?'

'And I have your word she's safe?' Well, that was pushing my luck, and Edward frowned, but he said quite gently,

'Of course she is! She hasn't been banished from the kingdom, merely sent away from Court. And no, you may not see her. And don't go making it into a tragic romance, you're not Pyramus and Thisbe. Don't do anything stupid.' He was running out of patience and, probably, of time, but he went on, 'I know you're longing to throw it in my teeth that I've been licentious and an unfaithful husband. But there is a fine line between hypocrisy and giving younger men the benefit of one's experience. Be a little more discreet, both of you, and find something else to do.'

'You don't *give* us anything to do!' Richard burst out. 'A few ceremonial duties, dancing attendance at banquets and receptions. And once we've done our arms practice and played tennis, what is there to do? Edward, I've begged you to let us come on campaign with you –'

'No.'

For a moment they stared at each other, exactly alike in their stubborn anger. Richard went on more quietly, 'Give us the experience to make our loyalty useful. I'm nearly seventeen, and at that age you and Edmund were soldiers, you had served with our father and –'

'– and Edmund died. At seventeen. And I loved him more dearly than anyone in the world – except you. And I will not lose you too, Dickon, at seventeen.' His use of the old family nickname was both plea and warning. Richard bowed stiffly. 'You may go,' Edward said, sounding exhausted.

'Your Grace,' I said, 'one moment, please – I have some information for you.' I repeated what Innogen had told me about Clarence seeking to marry Isabel.

'I've forbidden the marriage. George wouldn't dare. Where had you this news?' I told him, and his face cleared. 'Women's gossip!'

'It is more than that, sire. She receives information from Europe …'

'Merchants' gossip, repeated by a woman. I'm sure you mean honestly by telling me, but I cannot believe it.'

'I think you should,' Richard said.

'Why?'

'Because George is hell-bent on marrying Isabel. He loves her and –'

It was like setting flame to kindling. 'Love!' Edward roared. 'Why is that all I hear these days? Love, love, love – what's that to do with anything? George wants to marry Isabel because she's an heiress and because he likes making mischief and Warwick helps him do it. I'll deal with George. Now, good-day to you both; I'm busy.'

Richard had the Plantagenet temper, brief but awesome. He

threw the pages and other squires out of his rooms and prowled, swearing vividly. If he'd had a tail he would have lashed it. 'Treats me like a child!' he finished, flinging himself into a chair.

'He loved Edmund and ...'

'Oh yes, yes, I know. God knows I'd feel the same, in his place. But when, *when*, is he going to give me something useful to do! Raising the county levies, oh yes, dear little boy riding at the head of his troops, so sweet, takes it all so seriously, bless him, the king's baby brother, splendid little chap, our little mascot, now run along back to the school-room. Poncing about waiting on every stray Burgundian who decides to honour us with a visit, waiting on the Queen ... He won't declare me of age, though he did it for George at sixteen – and he won't take Warwick seriously, or George. And he should. Christ!' He drank off the cup of wine I'd poured, and held it out for more. 'Sorry about Innogen, Martin.'

'So am I. What does it feel like to know you're going to be a father?'

'Strange. Be different, I suppose, if I loved her.' Someone knocked on the door. At the top of his voice and in the coarsest terms Richard told the visitor to go away.

'Charming,' said the King, striding in. 'Mother would be so proud.'

Not rising, Richard said, 'Had I known it was Your Grace ...'

'Come off your high horse. All right, you two, I've changed my mind. You can come with me on campaign.'

'You mean it?' Richard leapt up.

'Yes. Bring your fellow-fornicator here, and young Percy and your other squires, anyone you can find to ride with you. Armed, mounted, equipped. Got any money?'

'Not much.'

'Nor have I at present. Do your best. We ride out after Mass and fast-break tomorrow morning, nine of the clock. We'll head northeast to begin with, I have to see what this nonsense between the Pastons and Norfolk and Suffolk is about, I don't need feuds over inheritances. Then to Fotheringhay, Mother is there and the

Queen will join us. After that, we'll see. I hope it will be enough simply to show myself in strength around the country, stamp out all these uprisings and these Robins. Nothing will come of it, of course, but it's a hole through which every malcontent and Lancastrian can scurry into the country to make trouble. If Warwick's behind it, it's time he gets a lesson. So – nine o'clock tomorrow. Be ready, or you stay at home.'

At the door he turned back. 'Richard – don't expect it to be exciting. This is not war, and if it were, like it or not I would go on protecting you, my dear, and you'd have no part to play. I'm taking you only to give you experience of something other than dipping your wick. It won't even be very interesting.'

Edward had many gifts, but not the gift of prophecy. Nor was his judgement always very good.

Two months later Warwick took him prisoner.

# *Five*

'I'm a tyrant,' Edward read. 'A despot.' Robin of Redesdale's proclamation, torn from a village church door, was tattered and grubby. The King held it as if it were arse-wipes. 'A tyrant like unto Edward II – Richard II – oh and Henry VI. Never thought of the poor old boy as despotic; rather the contrary one would have said ... All deposed kings, you'll notice ... Hmm, avaricious favourites sucking the country's blood – *favourites*! Makes me sound like a damned sodomite. Refusing the rule to those with the right – Warwick, of course. And my darling brother George. So.' He screwed the paper into a ball and threw it into the fire. 'And this "Robin of Redesdale" is Warwick's man, Conyers. I apologise to all of you who tried to make me believe Warwick meant real trouble.'

'It's to your credit, sire, that you were loath to believe it.' That was his father-in-law, Earl Rivers, toadying busily.

'To my credit as a man, perhaps; not as a king or soldier. So. What's to do?' When no one spoke he said, 'Richard?' A few weeks ago his brother would have been the last man he would have called upon. I suppose he had expected us to be little better than a nuisance, a formless group of boys needing guidance and care. (If so, he had under-rated both Richard and Warwick.) He had blinked when he came down prompt at nine that first morning to see a neat, well-equipped little troop standing briskly under Richard's White Boar banner – blinked, then nodded in indulgent approval. Gradually he had forgotten about being indulgent, and by the time we heard that 'Robin of Redesdale' was advancing on us and we had had to bolt for the safety of Nottingham Castle, he treated Richard like any of his other captains. And now, surrounded by his in-laws, the King turned to his brother.

Richard said, 'Your Grace, if I may speak bluntly?' Edward nodded, and for a heartbeat their eyes met. 'Of course these "favourites" in Warwick's proclamation are the Queen's family, and they may be at risk. We have scarcely two hundred men with us; this "Robin" has perhaps five times that and is advancing on us rapidly. I think my lords and Sir John Woodville should get away to safety, now.' To his credit Anthony Woodville protested, but his father and brother couldn't agree fast enough. 'Then send for more men; Lord Hastings is closest, and Lords Devon and Pembroke can join us quickly.'

'Yes. Yes.' Edward clapped Lord Rivers on the shoulder. 'Gloucester's right. Head for wherever you can be safe, and lie low for a while. Go now.' They almost got jammed in the doorway, so quickly did they depart. 'Where's my secretary? Right, you heard the Duke. Prepare letters to Hastings and the Earls of Devon and Pembroke – the usual thing. And I think I'll call Warwick and Clarence's bluff.' Richard raised one eyebrow. 'Tempt them out into the open, dear cousin Archbishop Neville also. Martin, pen and paper, please. Right, now. Three loving letters in my own hand; that should impress them.'

'Depends what you say.'

'Why, that I'm distressed at the rumours that they are against me and long for the reassuring sight of their beloved faces.'


Whether Edward's letters ever reached the conspirators I don't know. They were in Calais, marrying Warwick's daughter Isabel to George of Clarence.

But they were soon back, and by late July three armies were about to collide – on our side, ours with the Earls of Devon and Pembroke; on the side of the Prince of Darkness, Warwick moving quickly up from the south and 'Robin of Redesdale' from the north. Once Lord Hastings arrived with reinforcements, we moved gingerly south from Nottingham.

The first we knew of the disaster was at Olney. There is no

mistaking refugees from a battle, and these scurrying men wore the badges of Devon and Pembroke. Quickly we had the story – the two earls' forces somehow became separated, and 'Robin' and Warwick fell on Pembroke's army and wiped them out. Pembroke and his brother had been executed at the Nevilles' headquarters, and Warwick and Clarence were even now leading a great force down upon us.

Caught out, under-manned, neither ready nor equipped for a battle, Edward dismissed those of his men who hadn't already taken to their heels. So there we were – the King, Lord Hastings, Richard, and me. They tried to make me go too, and called me brave when I refused, but I remembered a boy of eighteen holding me as I wept for my parents, I remembered Richard's friendship, and their mother's loving care for me. If they were to die, I would die with them. It was friendship, or love, and if that's courage, well, perhaps they are often not so different.

So we waited together, eating the last of our food and cracking bad jokes to pass the time, and soon we saw the cloud of dust on the horizon. Out of it appeared George Neville, Archbishop of York, ecclesiastically clad in full armour, the prick.

'Ah, cousin!' beamed Edward. 'Well met!'

'Er …'

'You come most timely to escort me to …?'

'Warwick …'

'Our dear cousin, the town, or the castle?'

'All three …'

'Excellent! Ex-cell-ent! He has had my letter, I trust? You too? Now tell me, is it true my scamp of a brother has married that pretty little niece of yours?'

Looking like seven bells struck, the Archbishop said, 'Quite true.'

'Charming! I must think of an appropriate wedding gift for them.' Edward smiled, or at least bared his teeth. 'Well, there's no point in stewing here in the sun. Richard, Will, Martin, thank you for bearing me company while I waited. God keep you.' He rode forward with such aplomb that the Archbishop could only turn his horse and follow.


We headed for Fotheringhay, where the Queen was still enjoying her mother-in-law's hospitality. Richard had sent his other squires ahead, so the castle was a-bustle when we rode in. The Duchess had mounted a guard – of course, she was an old hand at this sort of thing, and her fear showed only in the intensity with which she embraced Richard. By contrast the Queen was in a panic, near hysterics.

'Where is the King! What has happened?' Lord Hastings explained. The Queen fell back, blenching. 'Warwick has taken him prisoner?'

'In effect, Madam, yes.'

The Duchess said a French word that frankly I wouldn't have thought she'd know. Travel broadens the mind, of course.

So tired his eyes were crossing Richard said, 'Madam, they won't dare harm him.'

'They'll kill him!' the Queen shrieked, and began to scream and sob. I knew the Duchess itched to smack her.

'My dear, take heart of grace. All shall be well.'

'Well! Well! Oh! Oh! What will become of us?'

'Madam,' said Richard, 'you are safe here. Lord Hastings' men will guard you and your daughters. You will come to no harm, and nor will the king, I promise you.'

'*You* promise.' The pretty Woodville eyes moved over him in contempt. 'What can *you* do!' Again the Duchess made a tiny movement as of a slap aborted.

'Madam, I can raise an army.' As if ordering dinner. 'Between us Lord Hastings and I will rouse the country. London is always staunch for Edward, and Charles of Burgundy will help.' We hoped. 'Warwick has a lot of support, yes, but the King has more. We will write to and visit every man who can raise troops. England won't lie down under this – its king being taken prisoner by a couple of over-mighty subjects. And Warwick certainly won't harm the King, that's not the idea at all. No doubt Edward will agree to a few concessions to make them think they have their own way, but they are in for a surprise.'


And so it proved. I must have ridden more than a thousand miles in the next few weeks as we quartered the country calling on every nobleman whose loyalty we could trust, explaining, giving the formal letters signed by the King's brother and Lord Chamberlain. England was in uproar. The Duke of Burgundy threatened war; London rioted; John Neville refused to have any truck with his brothers' schemes.

Hastings' men found friends in the Warwick garrison, who reported that the King was in good health and heart and about to be moved north to Middleham. Off I galloped again, and at Middleham I was able to smuggle a message in to Francis Lovell, still reluctantly at his books in the household there. He would get news in to the King, and out to us.

I have to say that everyone thought the whole business would fizzle out. We trusted in Edward to contrive something. But Warwick and Clarence had executed the Earls of Pembroke and Devon, and some of their kin and supporters. And they caught and executed the Queen's father and her brother John.

At this, even the most rabidly anti-Woodville people rose up. No one wanted to see rebels assuming the royal power for private vengeance. Warwick tried to call a Parliament in the King's name. He could not. He tried to raise troops to put down a Lancastrian rising in the north. He could not. Not while he held the King prisoner. His *coup d'état* was a fiasco.

And in September Warwick and Clarence looked out from Pontefract Castle to see a force thousands strong, under the banners of Gloucester, Hastings, Buckingham, Howard, Suffolk, Northumberland, Norfolk, Essex, Arundel, Dacre, Mountjoy; I can't remember them all.

'My escort to London,' said the King (so he told us) and,

thanking his brother and cousin for their hospitality, he strolled out of Pontefract to freedom.

I remember that little scene vividly – the King strolling casually through the gate, pulling on his gloves and swinging his cloak over his shoulder; Warwick and Clarence behind him, their faces holding no expression at all. A squire unfurled the Royal Banner, and under its flapping shade Edward fell into Richard's arms. 'Oh Dickon, thank God for you,' he whispered, 'thank God.' He was shaking with tension released, and as they hugged you would have been hard put to say which was the elder of the two.

'It turned out quite exciting after all,' Richard murmured, and gave the King a hand up into the saddle. Edward laughed, and leaned down to kiss him again. And I saw Warwick's and Clarence's faces, and almost crossed myself at such open, vengeful malice.

The Archbishop had the gall to join Edward's triumphal procession to London. Edward sent him home.


Now Edward had to set about mending the damage. His grip on the Crown had been loosened; time, now, to show he was secure. Of course he should have sent Warwick and Clarence to the block for treason, and many people begged him to do just that, but he held off, and in fact was at pains to placate them. It was no time to goad them into civil war. But to the Welsh the time seemed ripe to rise against the English king, and with rebellion boiling they seized Carmarthen and Cardigan castles. Time for every last Lancastrian to emerge squeaking from the woodwork.

There was no more talk of protecting the inexperienced little brother. Edward made Richard Constable of England for life, and President of the Court of Chivalry and of Courts Martial, enlarging the Constable's traditional powers so he had the power to execute traitors. He also granted him lands, and appointed him Chief Justice of North Wales and Chief Steward of Wales for the Earldom of March. Then he sent him west to stamp out the troubles.

Military skill evidently runs in families. Under Richard we raised those Welsh sieges in no time flat, and soon the bards who had sung of glorious war against the Saxons were slinking back into the mountains. At first men who had fought under Edward looked dubiously at his younger, smaller, inexperienced brother, but those who had served with the Duke of York said *Chip off the old block*. In the field efficiency is more valuable, and rarer, than you might think, and Richard had the knack of handling men. Soldiers will always follow a brave leader; they will love one who cares about them as individuals. Edward was famous for remembering people, I've seen him greet by name a man met only once, ten years before. Richard had the same knack; perhaps it is part of the royal heritage. If the interest is genuine, men like a commander who remembers that a baby is due, or asks after Tom's ailing mother. On the other hand, anyone trying to take advantage of Richard never tried it a second time, especially once he realised that under his command they were well-fed, well-housed, well-equipped, and that he always put them first. It was the same in the towns – although the Welsh were never more than courteous, the English saw Richard taking pains to consider their civic pride. He always called on the Mayor and Council, asked permission to billet troops, noted down every problem they wanted referred to the King. In Gloucester, particularly, town of his dukedom, they thought the sun shone out of him – and eighteen months later that saved our lives.

So quickly did Richard fulfil his commission that we were back in London by Christmas. I would as soon have stayed away, for now I had had a taste of real soldiering life at Court was a hollow thing; especially without Innogen. But the King had asked Richard to come, to help him choke down the snarling jollities of a Christmas not only seething with outraged Woodvilles but honoured by the presence of Warwick and Clarence. All was sweetness and light, you see, forgiveness all round, everyone friends again.

We arrived in London late in the day, tired, wet and irritable, longing for hot water, hot wine, and bed, and in no mood to find our way blocked. (London's the very devil for that, or was in my time. Much as I love that city I'm the first to admit her streets are too narrow, straggling without form or plan and always filthy with mud and rubbish. If you ask me they should ban all wheeled traffic within the walls. There has been many a hand-to-hand fight when the retinue of one nobleman has found its way blocked by that of some other. Still, Londoners like a free show.)

We were about to turn off Watling Street when a group of men-at-arms filled the way, coming from our right. We pulled up, and peering through the drizzle I made out Clarence's Black Bull insignia on the men – and, behind them, Warwick's. Richard could have asserted his rank to make Warwick give way to him, but his lifted hand stayed us and we watched them pass. They didn't see us waiting there, the King's loyal brother and his men shivering in sopping cloaks over battered leathers and scratched armour.

Sleek with confidence, bouncing with hubris, the Earl waved to the street crowds. Behind him rode a little group of ladies. Warwick liked his womenfolk to ride sidesaddle in London, he thought it elegant. It always looks unsafe to me, but I admit it gives a pretty effect with the ladies' gowns draping gracefully down their steeds' flanks. In fact even in that murky light the whole cavalcade had the vivid elegance of an illustration in a Book of Hours – the bright flowing colours, the glint of gold and flash of jewels, the proud horses, the banners. No – it reminded me of the story that terrified me in childhood, that on a certain night the King and Queen of Elfland come out into the mortal world, riding in glory with their court, seeking humans to kill.

As they passed, one of the ladies glanced idly around. Her cloak's furry hood framed an enchantingly pretty face. I had recognised the Countess of Warwick, and from the way Clarence rode close to it that litter must hold his new Duchess; but this girl was unknown to me. I said as much to Richard when at last we rode on.

Yawning with cold he said, 'No, it was Anne.'

'*Anne*? Little Anne? She doesn't look like that!'

'I wish I knew everything like you. It was Anne. It seems she's grown up.' He sounded thoughtful. I knew that tone. Oh no. Not Anne. Anyone but Warwick's daughter.

Not that I was convinced that lovely girl was Anne, or not until the banquet the following night. This was the great kiss-and-make-up feast with most of the nobility, and on the King's left at high table we saw his dear brother George looking like the cat that swallowed the cream, and his loyal cousin the Earl of Warwick, late murderers of the Queen's relations.

It pleases me to report that that street glimpse of the treacherous pair riding so prideful and sleek had stung Richard into asserting both his royal rank and his position as the King's highest lieutenant. He took pains to arrive last, and had himself announced with the full formality of trumpet fanfare and the seneschal bellowing every title he possessed. And of course we had dressed for the occasion; we were fresh from our third bath in two days, our hair gleamed with washing, we were shaved, groomed and polished to perfection. I rather fancied myself in green velvet with cloth of silver and a tasteful diamond or two (I had also profited from the King's gratitude) but Richard was magnificent, and it was the first time the Court had seen him in his adult splendour. He wore dark blue that night, blue velvet cloth of gold, patterned with York white roses fashioned of pearls and diamonds, the huge sleeves of his doublet caught in by jewelled wristbands. His belt was of gold links clasped with sapphires and diamonds, his hose were of paler blue silk and his shoes scarlet leather (the devil to walk in, those piked shoes with the long stuffed toes; I was glad when that little fashion took itself into the past). He wore the Garter, and around his neck a gold and sapphire chain held a White Boar pendant of enamel. When he strode into the Great Hall there was a moment when few recognised him – he had grown physically as well as mentally in the last six months, irrevocably changed from boy to man; he had authority. Ignore or patronise him at your peril, now.

Among those with no mind to ignore him was Anne Neville. I saw her stare as he came across the hall, shyness battling delight in her face. She couldn't take her eyes off him. She sat open-mouthed, touching the place where his hair had brushed her cheek when he kissed her.

Let me try to describe Anne as she was that night, for she changed little in her short life. Her face was shield-shaped, pure curving lines sweeping from high square forehead to pointed chin. She had her mother's high-bridged nose, and her eyes were a speckly blue-grey. Her hair was the colour of good honey in the sun; as an unmarried girl she wore it loose under a jewelled band, a silky mass long enough to sit on. For this, her first adult party, she wore blue and gold brocade trimmed with fur, and a gold necklace drew discreet attention to the new roundness of her bosom. She was lovely, and happy, and innocent – and she might as well have worn a sign around her neck saying 'Richard of Gloucester: this is your prize if you support me, signed, Warwick.'

Edward knew, and he looked as if he'd sucked a lemon every time Richard spoke to Anne.

And all I could do was hope that Richard's sudden interest in Anne was only pleasure that his little cousin had become a pretty girl. But the King was taking no chances, and he had us back in the west a week after Twelfth Night.

But before that Richard was given something else to think about. So was I.


I was evidently in high favour with the Woodvilles, for the Queen's son Richard challenged me to tennis. I wouldn't go so far as to say I liked him, although I infinitely preferred him to his brother Thomas, but I found him quite pleasant now he had out-grown some of his prickly airs. But he was no athlete, and I had to work rather hard not to beat him too easily. It turned out, as we talked after the game and shared a cup of ale, that he was wistfully envious of Richard and me for our share in releasing the King and the campaign in Wales. He wanted to be a soldier too, he confided, but his mother worried about him and wouldn't let him. Jousting, in imitation of his uncle Anthony, was all he was allowed. 'Not that I suppose it is at all like the real thing?'

'No,' I said, 'not in the least.' I didn't care for the pretty ritual of the lists. It has its uses, of course, as an entertainment, but because Anthony Woodville – now Earl Rivers, on his father's death – was a prime exponent of the art I was tactful.

'Do you think Warwick will cause more trouble?' he asked over our second cup. 'The Queen is worried, you see. The Duchess of Clarence is with child. If it is a son …' Edward had three daughters, the last, Cecily, born more than a year ago, and there was no sign of another pregnancy. A would-be king with a healthy male heir has a strong advantage.

'Are you sure about the Duchess?'

'Yes. My mother thought she, er, had the look, whatever that is, and asked Lady Warwick. It is to be born in May, I think. So you see, I think Warwick will … do something. I think the King should be prepared.'

So did I. I thanked him for the game, and went thoughtfully up to my room. I found my lord and master sitting by the fire, his booted feet propped high on the hearth, smirking over a letter held in his lap.

'We look pleased with ourself?'

'We've every right to. Look.'

I looked first at the signature on the letter – Linnet Ogleby. Oh yes, the pregnant grocer's daughter. Or the grocer's pregnant daughter. I skimmed through the large unpractised writing. 'Richard, you have a daughter! Wonderful! Shall you agree to calling her Katherine?'

'Yes, I like the name.' He took the letter back, gazing at it fondly. 'I hope she's healthy. Do you think it's true girls are stronger than boys?'

'Yes,' I said with the confidence of total ignorance.

'But so many babies die. My mother bore twelve, and five died young. Remember my little sister Ursula? She lived such a short time.'

'Perhaps,' I hazarded a guess, 'when a woman has had many children, the later ones are more delicate? Though there's nothing wrong with you, and look at the Queen's children, great strapping healthy things all of them. Richard, that reminds me.' I told him of my tennis game, and Richard Grey's news.

'So Isabel's pregnant, eh? That's been kept quiet! She must be four months gone. I don't think the King knows; no, if the Queen has told her son she has told Edward. Hmm. I'll have a word with the King, of course, though he is taking Warwick and George more seriously than he wants people to realise. Now – I'm going down to Windsor to see my daughter, want to come?'

'Would you excuse me? I would be glad of the free time, with your permission?'

'Well, certainly.' He looked surprised at my formality, and I knew he thought I had a woman. Well, so I did, but not in the way he supposed. It was time to see if I was over Innogen once and for all.

I bought an ivory rattle as a present for the baby, then waved Richard off to Windsor. Then I put on my best clothes, brushed my hair till it gleamed, purchased a box of sweetmeats (anything more would look too eager), and trotted around to the house in the Chepe.

I didn't know the maid who answered the door. When I asked for Innogen she said she would have to see, the mistress wasn't having visitors much, and her sharp black eyes travelled over me in a way I did not quite like. I cooled my heels in the hall for quite a time before the maid returned and said Mistress Shaxper would see me. 'Top o' the stairs and turn right – though I daresay as you knows the way, Sir.'

Innogen was standing by the fire. She had been reading; her book lay open on the table, and the cushioned chair and footstool showed where she had been sitting. She looked different: paler, tired, her face fuller. Well, very different.

She was pregnant.

'Martin,' she said with neither pleasure nor displeasure. 'How good to see you. You have changed a great deal.'

'So have you.' I gestured at her swollen belly. 'Why didn't you tell me?' She looked at me gently, with pity, and I understood. I swear I felt my heart contract with pain. 'You mean it is not my child.'

'I don't know.'

'*Don't know!* Christ, how many …'

'*Martin.*'

'Sorry. But – I can't help – I thought you knew ways to prevent …' Of course I had never confessed my share of the sin of trying to prevent conception; I had begged the question by telling myself it was too private a matter. And, like many of the Church's teachings, it seemed curiously unrealistic, almost as though the Church designed hurdles in the way of human nature and called them sins. When Innogen let me into the female secret of the vinegar-soaked sponge she put inside herself, my surprise was not at the sin but at her practicality.

'I thought so too,' she said wearily. 'I was wrong.'

'You could have told me, though?'

'Men value their friendships.'

Very well, it was slow of me, but this obscure answer puzzled me. Then again I understood. 'It's Richard's child?'

'I don't know. Oh, sit down, Martin, don't loom over me like this.' She sat down, with that pregnant-woman's hand in the small of her back. I realised, with a shock, that I found her condition sexually arousing. The high gathered skirt of her gown did little to conceal the triumphant swell, and her breasts would no longer fit into my cupped palm, nor could I now span her ankles with my thumb and finger, but I wanted her more, in this state, than ever before.

'When will it be born?'

'February.'

I calculated. May. Hmm. Angry, I cried, 'But how could you!'

'How could I, or how could he? Or both of us?'

'I – you – he – I don't know! But you knew I loved you. So did he.' With more pain at the thought, I asked, 'Were you two lovers, all the time, when I thought …'

'No.' I had made her angry. Leaning forward, or as far forward as she could, she said with cold intensity, 'You men, you think it is all up to you, don't you. Well, it's not. I chose Richard, then I chose you. When he realised I was the lady you'd been babbling about …'

'*Babbling* …'

'... about, he oh so kindly, so generously, so honourably, so *malely*, stood aside. Because he knew you thought you were in love with me and ...'

'Thought – I was!'

'... and he valued your friendship, your love, more than me. Well, all very fine, very noble. Not that I was in love with him, and anyway he had other fish to fry, but what of me? Why could it not be my choice? What if I had wanted him more than you? No, it's always up to the man to decide, isn't it? Or so you think. You dispose of us women as if it's your right.'

I was only seventeen. 'I don't know what you're talking about. I suppose you think it's a clever way to justify the fact that you're a whore. I bet if I was richer and titled that would be my child, you'd have hustled me to the altar as fast as you could. Pity you can't marry Richard, eh? How many lovers have you had? I bet you've enjoyed yourself laughing at me, you must have split your sides every time I said I loved you. No wonder the Queen dismissed you, you're enough to choke even a Woodville!'

I had one quick impression of her ashen face, her eyes silver with hurt, then I was racing down the stairs. The maid gave me my cloak, avoiding my eye in a way that carried more contempt than if she'd spat in my face. I wanted to damn her for an insolent slut and her mistress for a hell-bent whore. Looking down my nose, I waited for her to open the door.

But, my hand on the door latch, I stopped. Some sound on the edge of my hearing, or perhaps the memory of things said or unsaid, made me go back up the stairs.

Her head down on her crook'd arm, Innogen was weeping as if her heart would break.

I had the sense to say nothing. I put my arm over her back, curling my hand around her head. She gave no sign of knowing I was there. She merely wept on, her tears soaking the tablecloth and my sleeve, sobs shaking her body. I had never seen her cry, and I noted absently that she was not one of those rare women, Isabel Neville for instance, who can cry without looking ugly. Yet her sticky lashes, red nose and curranty eyes moved me more deeply than her most triumphant moments of beauty. I loved her, and I finally knew it. Still I said nothing, for all I had to give her was my undemanding silence.

The maid had followed me upstairs. She stood in the doorway, arms akimbo and her mouth squaring with female reproaches. I silenced her with a gesture, mouthed 'Bring wine,' and shoo'd her away.

Innogen was still crying. I feared she would harm herself or the child. I put my handkerchief into her hand, and she began to calm, the sobs giving way to little snuffling whimpers. I lifted her in my arms, no easy task with a heavily pregnant woman who neither resists nor co-operates, and carried her through to her bedchamber. The bed was neatly made. Holding Innogen with one arm I tugged the counterpane back and laid her down. She was in housewife's undress, a loose gown and slippers, and her hair netted under a velvet cap. I took the slippers off, managed the cap and hairpins. Innogen lay unmoving, her eyes shut. I went back to the parlour for the wine, and made her drink a few mouthfuls, her head propped on my arm. Tears were still trickling from under her lashes. I closed the shutters, took off my boots, and lay down beside her. After a while she sighed and closed her hand over my wrist. Unlearned in the ways of pregnancy, I was astonished that then she simply fell asleep. I watched her for a while, but I too was short on sleep and soon I let my eyes drift shut.

It was almost dark when I woke. Innogen's head was on my shoulder, her arm around me. I squinted down at her. 'Are you awake?'

'Yes.'

I wriggled my arm under her, holding her closer against me. 'I'm sorry for what I said.'

'I deserved it. Martin, I'm sorry, I'm so sorry. I have made such a mess of things.'

'You have, rather.' I felt as if I had grown up in those few hours' sleep. 'But I don't think you're a whore, that was hurt pride talking. Forgive me. You said you are not sure who fathered this child. Tell me.'

'Remember that night, back in May, we argued …'

'You threw me out.'

'Yes. You were being childish, and possessive, and you made me so angry that I determined to have no more of you.'

'And I of you.'

'Exactly. And a day or two later, there was Richard. Don't ask, for I won't tell you. It was revenge, of course, on both of you. I didn't know something had gone wrong and there would be a child. And next night I forgave you, I'd missed you. So this baby could be yours or Richard's.'

'So I see. Well. Richard's gone to see the girl who has just given birth to his daughter.'

I'm ashamed to say I thought this might hurt her. But she raised her eyebrows, no more than interested, and said, 'Well, well, what a *busy* young man he's been. As bad as his brother. The King has two bastards that I know of and probably more. And more mistresses than you could poke a stick at – or anything more personal.'

I laughed, and when she fell silent I let the pause go on. It was curiously peaceful. Out of sudden new knowledge I said, 'Jenny, Innogen, I do love you. Before, it was little more than lust and delight in having you. But now I know. I love you. I hope that baby is mine.'

She looked at me. 'So do I.'

Goddam it, I'd been slow. 'Innogen, you do love me!'

'Yes. Yes, Martin, I do. I love you very much.'

There was more power in those sober words than in a hundred love songs. Tenderly I turned her face up and kissed her. Her lips clung to mine, then we sighed and settled into one another's arms. 'If the child were definitely mine I would marry you.'

'The King would not let you.'

'Oh yes he would. His bark's worse than his bite. He loves me. Besides, I'd only have to go to his mother and she'd have us married before you could turn around. But my love, I'm afraid that as it is …'

'I know. You're still under-age.'

'Not for much longer. The King's drawing up the documents to declare both me and Richard of age. Can't give us the sort of responsibilities we've had, and will go on having, yet keep us children. Actually, Jenny, I'll be quite rich.'

In making me his ward the King had taken his guardian's duties seriously. He had put good people in to manage my family manor, and although the house was beyond repair the lands were in good heart. I had inherited more than I had expected; my family had not been rich since we had had to ransom some ancestor from one of the Crusades, losing the title when we no longer had the money to keep it up, but the estate had been quite sizeable. After all, my father had been able to wage a dozen men in the Duke of York's service. Carefully invested all these nine years, the income had swelled, and Edward's people had bought more land, built up good herds. As well, Edward had rewarded my exertions on his behalf, and I now had a second estate, and some London property. I had been delighted when the King's Treasurer presented me with the proofs of all this husbandry. I knew I could always count on Edward and his family, but it was a pleasant thing to be independent.

'Well, I'm glad about that,' Innogen said when I told her. 'But you still cannot marry without the King's permission, and he'll not give it. Not as things are.'

'No. But later ... If the child is mine we'll marry and the child can be legitimated. Edward will do that – or if we have to get Papal approval he will do whatever's necessary. I'm sure there's no bar to legitimation.'

'I should think not. Richard the Second legitimated his cousins the Beauforts when their parents married, even though the Duke of Lancaster was married when they were conceived. I think their mother was too. A double adultery.'

'And that was one bit of legitimation that should never have been done. The Beauforts have been nothing but trouble ever since they helped bump off King Richard and make their half-brother King.'

'But if they hadn't been legitimated, don't forget, Joan Beaufort could not have married the Earl of Westmorland, and then the Duchess of York would never have been born.'

'No,' I said, rather struck: I had forgotten the Duchess was part Beaufort. 'And think on, I'd not exist either. Well, as to marriage – later, perhaps?'

'Perhaps. I think we'd better make no promises yet. If this child is yours, then we shall consider ourselves bound to marry and have the child legitimated. Otherwise … things may change, Martin.'

'Love doesn't change.' But for some reason I found myself remembering the King saying it would be a sorry world if we all married our first loves. Dimly, for at seventeen it is hard to overestimate your maturity, I understood that I had more growing up to do. Nothing is certain; once I would have scoffed at the idea that Warwick could turn against the King. In a year's time I might find myself bound to a woman I disliked and whose chastity I mistrusted. Or no, I would not. The thought had been enough to make that clear to me. I had found my heart's companion, and my life's. 'I love you, Innogen, and that will never change. But any number of other things might. So let's make no promises yet.'

For a while longer we lay there, the talk drifting. I told her about rescuing the King, about Wales.

'No wonder you've changed so much,' she said soberly.

'Have I?'

'Yes, greatly. You were a boy last year, but now you are a man. Responsibility suits you.'

'Thank you. I've turned out quite a good soldier – all that training wasn't wasted.'

'And you'll be needed more. These troubles aren't over. What will happen, do you think?'

'I've no idea. Warwick has gone too far. At present he is lying low … Jenny, you were lucky to miss Yule at Court, everyone was walking on eggs, George making his little barbed comments, the Queen seething … I don't know what will happen.'

By tacit consent we rose up then, and went and had supper. We talked of indifferent things through the meal – books, music; nothing personal, nothing political. Innogen ate like a horse, I noted. Eating for two. The thought made me uneasy. If I had been certain it was my child, how different things would have been.

Innogen noticed, of course, and as soon as the meal was cleared she said, 'This is difficult for both of us. Go now, Martin.'

Half relieved, half resentful, I said, 'I should. You don't mind?'

'No, I think it is better if you do. Besides, I'll be asleep again soon.' Her wry little smile lit her face. 'That's about all I do: sleep. Twelve hours of a night, then again in the day. Will you come again?'

'I cannot. Welsh delights for Richard and me. Windsor first – Garter meeting – then west. Jenny, are you well? Healthy? Do you have good people? Midwives, nurses?'

'I'm very well, just tired. Yes, good people. It would be healthier, I daresay, in the country, but my Kent lands were my father's and the northern ones my husband's, and I don't care to dishonour them by going there unwed and pregnant. Later it will be different – if I choose to foster a child, well, who's to make gossip of that? People will, of course, but it's different. I think I might go abroad, perhaps to France or Burgundy, it's time I cast an eye over the wool business there.'

'And if you're in need, if I can be of help, you will tell me? And tell me when the child's born, even if it looks like another little Plantagenet?'

'Of course. And if it does, I suppose I should tell Richard.'

'He doesn't know?'

'No of course not.'

'Oh. I see. Shall I tell him? Because he'll be anxious to do the proper things, acknowledge it, provide for it and you. He will want to know.'

'Tell him, yes. Thank you.' She came gladly into my embrace. I felt the child moving, something I had of course heard of but hadn't quite believed in, and quite savagely, desolately, hoped it was mine.


On the way to Windsor I planned the sensible, adult talk Richard and I would have about Innogen; friends could discuss anything, and of course nobody was actually at fault. But when I went into his rooms he was singing to himself as he studied a map of Wales. *Singing.* And looking like a dog with two tails. Pleased to see me, of course.

'Martin, what fettle?' Yorkshire idiom always meant he was on top of the world.

'I've been to see Innogen Shaxper. You remember her.'

'Oh, yes.' Was that a faint blush under the remnants of the summer tan?

'Yes, I just bet you do. She's pregnant.'

His lashes flickered. Surprise, shame, guilt, wonder, all crossed his face, but the expression that came back and set up camp with banners flying was wary guilt.

'Yes,' I said, 'I love her and you knew it – yet you fucked her.'

Probably it's treason to hit the King's brother, but I would have gone to the block for the pleasure of that first blow. He reeled back, blood trickling from his mouth, then launched himself on me. He was smaller than me, but just as strong and well-trained, and I'd got his temper up. I only got in that one blow before we were grappling together, punching, gouging, kicking. We rolled, fighting, neither winning, until suddenly my anger fled and I was clutching at him more for comfort than to overcome him. At once he rolled off me, and we struggled up to sit panting against the wall. To my shame I was crying. He put his arm around me.

'Oh Martin, I'm sorry.' He gave me his handkerchief, and I honked and spluttered for a while.

'Sorry,' I said at last, one word for many offences, his and mine.

'So am I. I didn't know you loved her.'

'She said, Jenny said, that men value their friendships.'

'She's right. I do. I value yours. I love you. If I've lost you over this I can't bear it.'

He stood up and held out his hand. I took it and let myself be hauled to my feet. 'I truly didn't know you loved her. I know it's no excuse, but …'

'You did know.'

'No,' he said gently. 'Martin, you've had so many girls, and although you talked a lot about being in love … Anyway, I thought you always knew that Innogen and I …'

'You were first, weren't you? While I was away with Lord Hastings.' He nodded. 'And later?'

'Not once I realised you and she … Except once.'

'She told me. We'd quarrelled.' He looked hopelessly at me. 'Oh, never mind. She told me how it happened. She was angry with me – and with you – angry that we decided the matter. I'm not sure I quite understand it. *She* wanted to choose between us.'

'She would have chosen you. She did. She loved you, I think.'

'Not enough, at the time.'

He had the habit of fiddling with the rings on his right hand when he was worried or unhappy. 'I did think it was over between you; that's all I can say. Martin, if this makes such a difference that you no longer want to stay in my service, then it is your choice. You could go into the King's service, or Hastings', or Norfolk's – anyone like that would be honoured to have you. Or you could be independent, you've your lands, a good income, you can be an independent gentleman with your own squires. But I hope you will stay with me, for you are my best and dearest friend; always have been, since we were born.'

When it comes to it, Innogen was right, men do value their friendships. And why not, friendship is a rare and precious thing. So I said, 'No. I'll stay with you. After all, I've just got you trained to my way of doing things.' It wasn't much of a joke, but he took the will for the deed.

'I'm glad, Martin.'

'So am I. Well, how was little Katherine?'

'Pretty, healthy, looks exactly like my father.'

'Jenny said her child could be yours or mine. Not knowing, she refused to marry me.'

'Then she is an honourable lady.' His highest compliment, for he always valued honour.

'And you're a randy devil,' I said without animosity.

'*Mea culpa.* Are we friends?'

'Always.'

# Six

## 1470-1471

So much happened in the following year or so that it is hard now for me to put each incident in its place. Suffice it to say that in the early months of 1470 there seemed to be unrest and actual uprisings all over England. Warwick and Clarence busily protested their loyalty to the King, but there was no doubt they were behind the trouble. We were rather out of it over in the west, but without our military presence Wales and the western counties would have risen too. By March there was trouble in the Midlands, in Lincolnshire and in Yorkshire. Gathering an army at Grantham, the King routed the rebel forces so fast and thoroughly that the battlefield became known as Lose-Coat Field – and the badges on the jettisoned coats were those of Warwick and Clarence. It was out in the open now, even before the rebel leaders confessed. Time to settle the issue. The King sent an ultimatum to his cousin and brother: join him, or take the consequences. Choosing the latter, they fled west, and the King sent for Richard, both to bring in more men and in his capacity as Constable.

And so you see us late in March, heading north through Cheshire, hoping we won't collide with the rebel armies. It was one of those miserable nights that make you wonder if you've died without noticing it. I say 'night' but it was really no more than dusk. All day snow had threatened; now it was raining in a spiteful sort of way, and cold as a witch's tit. We were seasoned campaigners by then, and knew the soldier's tricks of husbanding our strength, but we were a wretched, wet, tired troop, without the spirit to grumble.

We were still some distance from Manchester when Rob Percy

lifted his head and said, 'There's a large force on the road ahead.' No one else could hear anything, but Rob had the keenest ears of any man I knew. A few moments later we could all hear the sounds. A large force indeed. Richard gave the order to halt. Warwick and Clarence were in this area, each with a big army. If we had run into one of them ... Battle? Flight? Death or imprisonment ... Richard taken, and used as a bargaining counter against the King ...

The other force rounded a bend in the road, saw us, and stopped. Rob Percy and I rode forward. Two men from the other troop did the same. We halted a wary four paces apart, and began the who-goes-there routine. They were cagey, but so were we, and peer though I might I could make out no badges or banners. I kept my hand on my sword's hilt (sometimes it's useful being left-handed; people watch your right hand, giving you a tiny, vital advantage). Whoever this was, moving troops so late in the day, he had more men than us. And, heading south, they certainly weren't going to the King.

'Whose men are you?' Rob called. 'Please clear the way.'

I heard a sword being drawn, and the nock of a crossbow. Oh, marvellous. I was going to die in a roadside scuffle over right-of-way. A third man rode forward from the other troop. I recognised him, and my heart sank. Lord Stanley was Warwick's brother-in-law. Famous turncoats, the Stanleys; it would be a fool who trusted them.

'I demand to know who you are,' he called.

'We are the Duke of Gloucester's men, on the King's business.'

'Gloucester – that young pup! Clear the way.'

But Richard too had ridden forward. 'Lord Stanley!' Thick with cold, his voice came out rasping with menace. 'Young pup I may be, but it's an old dog who can't be taught new tricks. Which new trick are you having trouble learning, my lord, treachery or loyalty? Because I ride to the King, on the King's business, and I doubt you can say the same. Be wise, Tom Stanley, and go home. Now move your men by the time I count ten, because I don't care if I ride through you or over you, but pass down this road I will.' He held up his hand, folding down the fingers one by one. Stanley stood his ground for five counts, then shouted an order and his troop gave way. Richard led us straight on as if they didn't exist.

He made an enemy of Stanley, doing that, and fifteen years later he paid for it.

Stanley had in fact, we learnt, been taking that army to Warwick, but he heeded Richard's warning and slunk off home. (And he had the brass neck to complain to the King that, peacefully going about his innocent business, he had been rudely set upon and abused by the Duke of Gloucester.)

Warwick and Clarence had been counting on Stanley. Without him they hadn't enough men to come to battle with the King, and they fled southward.

Time, now, to pursue them.

It was in Gloucester, waiting to join with the King's army, that I had Innogen's letter. It came with a bundle of others, personal and official, that were handed around during a staff officers' conference. Recognising Innogen's arms on the seal, I took it over to the window to read it.

Briefly she wrote that she had borne a son on the sixteenth day of February. The child was baptised John after her father, had red hair, was healthy and strong. She too was well. Then followed: 'While I cannot yet be certain about the particular matter we discussed, I believe you are not after all concerned.' Then on a separate line came, 'Please give my good greetings to His Grace of Gloucester.' She had signed it, baldly, with her name; no greetings to me, no word of fondness.

Richard was droning through a report on troop numbers and supplies. I crossed the room and threw the letter into his lap. This was familiarity beyond the line in public, and I got some odd looks. But Richard had learnt in his first week at Court to school his expression; he read through the letter and handed it casually back. 'Yes, thank you, Martin, I was waiting to hear. If you are writing, please say I am grateful for the information and send my good wishes.' Only if you knew him very well could you see the muscle pulling in his cheek.

Finished with the report, he took up another letter. Glancing at the seal he said, 'From John Neville.' A moment later he yelled 'Fucking hellfire!' so violently his startled secretary spilt the ink.

'Richard, what is it?'

'The King has taken the Northumberland earldom from John Neville and restored it to Henry Percy.'

'What!' cried Rob Percy, whose opinion of his cousin was unrepeatable. 'That backstabbing swine? Why, he was in prison for years for supporting the Lancastrians! The King must be off his – er, I forgot what I was going to say.'

'Off his head,' said Richard. 'Harry Percy's my cousin too, remember, and among us, gentlemen, I agree. But the thing is, while John Neville's loyalty is not in doubt, Harry Percy's has to be bought. Christ, think of the men Percy can raise – if he turned against us … It's blackmail, of course – give me back my earldom or else.'

'But what an insult to John Neville,' Rob persisted. 'He has been the King's most loyal supporter, his best general – he's just put down that Yorkshire rising, yet this is the thanks he gets. And it's not only that – think of the lands and money that go with the Northumberland title; the rent roll alone is worth thousands. I'm sorry, Richard, but with respect I think the King has made a bad mistake. Apart from hurting a loyal man he has told others he can be bought.'

Bought by a Percy, too, I thought – for generations the Nevilles and the Percies had been rivals for power in the north; ancient enemies. And, never forget, John Neville was Warwick's brother. Another insult. Back at Christmas the King had made John's son Duke of Bedford and betrothed him to Lady Bess; a suitable reward, we had all thought, for a loyal man. Now I wondered if the King had always intended to do this – first the honey, then the medicine. Do you know, I felt a twinge of sympathy for Warwick? Of course I saw the difficulty for the King trying to balance all the conflicting claims and demands, but if this was a sample of his judgement – and think of his foolish marriage! – then perhaps Warwick had rebelled less from hurt pride than from real care for his country in this King's heedless hands.

Richard said defensively, 'Of course John Neville's loyalty can never be doubted; the King is trying to show he knows that. People like Harry Percy have to be bought – a Neville does not. And he has made John Marquis of Montagu. But,' he added miserably, 'I'm afraid John is furious and hurt, in fact his letter was to beg me to make the King reverse the decision. I can't, of course. And you're right about the Northumberland income, Rob, because poor John says that he has been given forty pounds a year – a 'pie's nest, he calls it. Well, I'm sure it's more than that, but still …'

And, as John Milwater said later, as we polished our armour together, the King seemed neither to know nor care what strain he put on people's loyalty. 'Richard wouldn't turn against the King even if he found him eating children's flesh – but they are brothers. It's different for other people. And John Neville is already torn between his brother and the King. It's all very well saying he doesn't have to be bought, but people expect loyalty to be rewarded, it's the way of the world. If the King goes on like this he'll find himself with no one *but* Richard. Bad judgement is the same as bad luck, and people will start to wonder if Edward is any better than King Henry.'

Curiously, because he too had grown up at Middleham, I asked, 'Would you ever turn against the King?'

Milwater brushed the blond fringe out of his eyes, thinking. Of course we were friends, but this was the most intimate conversation we had ever had. At last he said, 'I'm loyal to Richard of Gloucester.'

'Begging the question.'

'Is it? Look, Martin, I used to admire Warwick beyond all other men, I loved him in fact. But I believe one must be loyal to one's king, so I hate Warwick's treachery. I would never go over to him or that fool Clarence, and I would certainly never turn Lancastrian; like yours, my father died with the old Duke of York. But my personal loyalty to Edward is wearing rather thin, and if the worst happened I suppose I would settle down quietly under King George. So I've decided that my loyalty goes with my friendship. After all the campaigning of the last six months I see that frigging White Boar banner in my sleep, but I shall go on following it while I or its owner live. Does that answer your question?'

'Yes. And you've got metal polish on your face.' I wiped it for him. 'I feel the same way.'

'Let's hope the new Marquis does too,' said John.


If only. If only we'd been in time to stop Warwick and Clarence escaping. If only Edward had stopped the ports so they couldn't get away to France. If only.

But they were a half-day ahead of us, and at sea by the time our army pelted into Exeter. Warwick tried to land at Southampton, but was beaten off by Anthony Woodville's fleet. He tried Calais, but the garrison under Lord Wenlock shelled him back out to sea. Finally, late in April, he landed at Honfleur, where King Louis' messengers were waiting to conduct them as honoured guests to the King.

Later we learnt that poor Isabel went into labour off Calais. Her child, a son, was born dead.

In no hurry now, Edward moved his army north. We were at York the day the King's squire burst into our room crying for us to go to the King. Rob and I were lolling half asleep by the window, our feet up, cold ale to hand; it took us a moment to understand what the man was saying. 'Please – there's trouble – it's a matter for friends, it's Gloucester …' That had us on our feet. Running after us the squire said, 'A messenger came with letters from London, and the King read one then sent for Gloucester, and when he came the King kicked everyone else out and you can hear him shouting like he's run mad. No one dares go in, but it is bad.'

Upstairs we had heard nothing, but down here it sounded as if the King was taking an axe to his audience chamber. He was bellowing at the top of his voice, and the few discernible words were obscenities. Rob and I shouldered through the crowd of servants and men-at-arms and knocked on the door. The King gave a yell of rage, and we heard a splintering crash. If Richard was in there, he was silent. I knocked again and this time lifted the latch. The door wasn't bolted, and we slipped inside.

I had heard of Edward's temper but never seen it. I hoped I never would again. The table was overturned, its contents trampled. A window was broken. A lute was smashed to firewood. A lovely old book of French songs had been ripped apart. All the plate from the sideboard was strewn on the floor, dented or broken. The hangings were in ribbons. The room stank of wine from the priceless carafe lying splintered in the hearth. At the end of the room the King rampaged, purple in the face, weeping, shouting. In his hand was a length of wood – the leg of his fine carved chair, and that chair was two-inch oak.

Richard was standing against the far wall, hands pressed flat back against the stone. His face was ashen, his eyes dilated black. Neither he nor Edward seemed aware of us, then Edward turned like a baited bear and said, 'Get – out,' with such menace that I nearly obeyed.

I hand it to Rob. Saying, 'Your Grace, you can be heard. It will not do, Sire,' he stepped up to the King and took the chair-leg from his hand. Edward took two great shuddering breaths, and the red madness faded.

I edged past him to Richard. When I spoke his name he stared through me. I had once seen Lady Warwick slap a girl who had had bad news and gone blank with shock like this; I made do with gripping Richard's arms and shaking him. Slowly his eyes fixed on me, and he slumped forward to lean his head on my shoulder.

'Martin. Christ, my dear, Martin.'

We righted the one bench the King had left intact, and made them sit down. They perched there like two whipped schoolboys, and after a moment Edward slid his arm around his brother. Rob opened the door a crack and asked for wine, and we made them drink.

'Can we help?' Rob asked. 'Is it something you can tell your friends?'

Richard downed his wine in a gulp. As if continuing a previous conversation he said, 'It is Warwick, you see.'

In relief, for I had been afraid it was the Duchess of York or Margaret, I asked, 'Dead?'

'No. Would that he were! God forgive me, would that he were!'

'What has he done?'

'Made alliance with Margaret of Anjou. With Lancaster.'

Rob cried 'No!' and clapped his hand childlike over his mouth. I simply gaped, beyond speech.

'He has,' the King said. 'His father's head rotted with my father's on a traitor's spike at that bitch's order. His father and brother died, with mine, fighting that bitch. He was driven into exile by her. Yet now in his hubris he has made alliance with her.'

'George too,' Richard said. 'Martin, George was at Ludlow, he stood with us and waited for that army to take us, he listened to Queen Margaret rating our mother like a whore, he was bundled onto that ship with us when Queen Margaret's army was attacking London. Warwick, yes, because he never really understood, he sorrowed for his father and mine but it meant glory for him, he couldn't be king but he could control one, then found he could not. But he never understood, and I knew it. It's George I cannot bear, that he's done this. He's none too bright, and he's greedy and proud and untrustworthy, but he's my brother and I never thought he could betray our parents.'

'Warwick and Louis dangled a crown in front of him,' Edward grunted.

'So?'

'Are you so sure you could resist?'

Richard looked at him as if he were barking. 'At this cost, yes. Anyway, do you think I haven't been offered it?'

'What?'

I thought: if Edward was genuinely surprised, no wonder his judgement was often so poor. He and Richard stared at each other in mutual disbelief, and Richard said slowly, for the dullards down the front of the class, 'Edward, I have lost count of the clever schemes to put George or me on the thrones of England, Burgundy, Zeeland even … Nor was it always Warwick making the suggestions, either – or he was only the conduit for them. Warwick wouldn't have cared much whether he used George or me, so long as he overthrew you and made one of his daughters Queen …' He flinched at the words. Gripping my hand he said, 'Martin, they are marrying Anne Neville to Queen Margaret's son.'

I felt as if he had hit me in the gut. 'Can't be …'

'They are. You see, Warwick has promised to restore Henry VI. Anne is the guarantee and the price for both sides.'

'*Restore Henry VI*!' It was high summer, but I shivered as if in snow. I had, suddenly, an abominably clear memory of my mother trying to fight the men who had raped and killed her.

Head in hands Edward said, 'Well, I'm sorry about Anne, she's a dear little lass, but it's not as if she'll come to any harm. But don't you see, this makes George superfluous? Irrelevant? No one is interested now in making him King. From Warwick's point of view, Anne will be Princess of Wales and Queen one day. George is to succeed if Anne bears the Prince no heir. From Louis' and Queen Margaret's point of view, old Henry will be king again, then his son. No place in that for George, don't you see?'

'Of course I see!' Richard snapped, and slammed out of the room.

'What's the matter?' Edward asked, bewildered. Well, I thought, where do you start? Then his brows drew down in a glower and he said, 'Back at that Christmas feast Richard looked far too interested in Anne Neville for my liking. Is he?'

'Sire,' said Rob with more courtesy than I could have mustered just then, 'he has said nothing about Lady Anne. But she's his cousin, he grew up with her, as did Martin and I. We are all very fond of her and hate to think of her being used like this.'

'Hmm. Well, I hope that's all it is. Because you can tell him from me that Anne Neville is the last person I will ever let him marry.' He stood up, casting a glance around the room: 'My mother then my tutor tried very hard to train me to control my temper. On the whole they did well. But it's as Richard said: *this treachery.*'

In the middle of September the ships carrying Warwick and Clarence and their army broke the English blockade and landed at Plymouth and Dartmouth. We were still in the north when the news came, for John Neville had sent word that he was unable to put down the latest Yorkshire rising. Whoever took London first would have an inestimable advantage, and with the rebels moving rapidly eastward Edward wheeled his army about and raced south, leaving John Neville to catch him up.

I dreamt I was at Middleham – no, on board ship and – I woke to find Richard shaking me. 'Martin, wake up! Get up!' His sinewy hands closed on my arms, dragging me to my feet. 'Wake up!'

'Wh… where are we?'

'Still at Doncaster, you idiot. Come on!'

Exhausted from the day's march I had fallen asleep in hose and shirt, a cloak huddled around me. Richard was forcing my arms into my doublet, Rob thrusting boots onto my feet. A single candle flared in the draught from the open door. Men were running full-pelt down the corridor. 'What's going on?'

'John Neville has turned against the King.' Richard pushed my coat of brigandines into my arms. 'He couldn't betray his brother after all, poor sod. One of his men broke away, he's loyal, he has just come in with the news. John Neville is coming down on us fast and he has twice our numbers. We have to get out of here, there's nothing else for it. So hurry up, Martin. Five minutes, in the courtyard.' He latched a buckle on my brigandines, kissed me, and strode out, a baggage roll over his shoulder.

I plunged my face into the icy water in the basin, shook myself like a dog and started to pack. My two books; my cloak, spare shirt and hose; soap, razor, comb. Hell, what else? Candles. Tinderbox. Money – I had three marks in my belt-purse and my emerald ring. The stale taste of sleep was in my mouth, and because I wasn't really awake it seemed important to clean my teeth. I had barely dipped my finger in the saltbox when Richard raced back in.

'What are you going to do, smile at them? Come on.' He bundled me out and down the stairs.

The courtyard was seething with men. Panicky shouts and the neighs of frightened horses rose on all sides. The flickering torches lit the King's golden head, and Anthony Woodville's paler one beside him. They were already mounted, the King holding the reins of Richard's horse. The gates crashed open, we threw ourselves into the saddles and were off.

'Where are we going?' I shouted to Richard.

'Don't know. East. Warwick is to the south with his army.'

We had done this a year ago. But this time there was no question of letting the King be taken, things had gone far beyond that. We galloped on eastward, because Anthony Woodville owned land around Lynn. We took boats across the Wash, but at Lynn there was no safety, merely a breathing space in which to take stock. The rebel armies were closing on us fast. Norfolk was hostile. There were only about a dozen of us: Hastings, Rivers, Richard, a handful of us squires. We had no arms but our personal weapons, no money, no supplies.

'Burgundy,' said Edward. 'There's nothing else for it. We have to buy time. Duke Charles won't dare not support me.' No one had any better suggestion, and he went away to arrange our passage. The best he could find were fishing boats whose masters would take us, at a cost. We pooled our money (I kept quiet about my emerald ring, for it was all I had of my father) and Edward gave his fur cloak to one of the masters to make up the fee.

As the boats cast off Edward halloo'd from his boat to Richard.

'What?' Richard bellowed back. In the morning mist we could just make out the King's figure. He waved solemnly then cupped his hands around his mouth again.

'Happy birthday!' he called.

He was right. It was the second of October. It was Richard's eighteenth birthday.

And so we went into exile to the sound of those two royal lunatics laughing.

They told me afterwards that it was an exciting voyage. Our boats had been chased by ships of the Hanseatic League, whether on general principles or because they somehow knew the English king was aboard, I don't know. For my part, I would have begged the Germans to take us and put me out of my misery – I hadn't grown out of my childhood seasickness, and Richard dragged me ashore at Alkmaan more dead than alive.

To assume it was Duke Charles who rushed to our aid, would be wrong: it was the Seigneur Louis de la Gruythuuse whose ships chased away the Germans, and he saved us, housed us, succoured us. Governor of Holland, he was immensely rich, a cultured man who, fortunately for us, was firmly Anglophile. While Duke Charles temporised, waiting to see which way the political cat would jump, Gruythuuse opened his heart and his house to us. And what a house it was: the finest in Bruges, a palace crammed with beautiful and extraordinary things from all over the world. Not in any English castle have I known such comfort and such luxury. Gruythuuse liked novelties and jokes – toys, automata, books that puffed dust in your face when you opened them – and, a learned man with an interest in all things modern, he supported Master William Caxton's printing press. (Although I didn't remember it, I had met Master Caxton in '61.) Gruythuuse gave us clothes, we had only to ask his treasurer for cash, he opened credit for us to wage soldiers and buy arms, horses and ships.

Meanwhile, back in England, Warwick and Clarence had entered London on October the sixth, promptly whisking King Henry out of the Tower and parading him through the city in what came to be called his 'Re-Adeption'. Warwick's brother Archbishop George was restored to the Chancellorship, Parliament reversed all the attainders on Lancastrians. And, to popular disapproval, Warwick made an alliance of peace with France and promised King Louis to join him in attacking Burgundy.

At this, Duke Charles saw the light. His only hope of keeping his beloved country from the munching jaws of France was to restore Edward to the English throne. He coughed up fifty thousand crowns, and we set about provisioning ships and recruiting an army.

Our chances were given another fillip when news came that the Queen had borne a son. When Edward fled England she had scurried into Westminster Sanctuary and there, in November, she at last produced a Prince of Wales. The child, called Edward, of course, was reported to be healthy, and Edward gave thanks upon his knees.

In February I went with Richard to visit his sister Margaret at Lille. I think Edward did not go because Duke Charles was still hesitant about giving him too open recognition as rightful King of England, and wished to avoid anything that smacked of a state visit, but there could be no objection to Richard paying a private visit to his sister.

Margaret had a pretty little palace, and we were taken to a room that for rich and elaborate furnishings made Westminster look like a cottage. It was also, unlike Westminster, beautifully warm. We were inspecting the closed stove that heated the room when the doors were flung open and a steward announced the Duchess of Burgundy.

She came towards us with her arms held out, saying, 'Dickon, my dear! And Martin!' but I could hardly credit that I had once called this awesome woman Meg. She was dressed in the high Burgundian style – a gown of blue velvet and silver tissue, with ermine lining its full hanging oversleeves and bedecking its hem and neck. The under-sleeves were silver tissue embroidered with pearls and diamonds, and the buckle of her silver belt was solid sapphire. She wore that curious 'steeple' headdress, a slender cone near two feet long, with an embroidered gauze veil falling to the ground. Her earrings and the rings on her fingers were diamonds, pearls and sapphires. Round her neck she wore a necklace of marguerites, her namesake flower, fashioned of white enamel and pearls. Her scent was intoxicating, and her lovely face, more beautiful even than I remembered, was subtly painted.

We bowed, of course, but she laughed at us and swept us into her arms to kiss us. 'So good to see you!' she said, and had to dab away some tears. 'But whoever would have thought we would meet like this! Come, sit down, we'll have wine.' She gave an order in her new language to the servants, then dismissed them. 'Now we can talk,' she said as cosily as any ordinary good-wife. 'Tell me everything.'

By 'everything' she meant not politics or war but home gossip: news of her mother, whom she clearly missed; was it true their sister Elizabeth was having another baby? She'd had a letter from the other sister, Anne, who sounded none too happy with her Sir Thomas St Leger; what was this she heard about Richard peopling the world with bastard children? Oh, all sorts of things. We did our best for her, but I think she knew more than we did of recent events in England.

'And you, Meg?' Richard asked at last. 'Are you happy here?'

'Oh yes, never doubt it.' But her eyes shadowed a little. She and Duke Charles seemed to live apart more often than not, and I had heard all sorts of scurrilous gossip: that he preferred the love of men; that she had other lovers; that on their marriage he had declared her experienced and complained he'd been wed to the greatest whore in Europe. I knew Richard had heard the same tales, although of course we never discussed them, and when Margaret spoke of her longing for a baby his glance crossed mine. 'Still, it's early days yet,' Margaret said valiantly, 'although I can't help remembering that Anne only ever had the one child. Though who can blame her, married to Exeter!' Richard laughed, but Margaret had been married more than two years, and I knew we were both thinking of his mother's twelve children and his sister Elizabeth's growing brood. It was clear Margaret was deeply fond of her stepdaughter Mary, and it seemed they shared an interest in learning and in Christian provision for the poor and sick. Poor Meg, I thought, having to make do with another woman's child.

By supper – which we took in another deliciously warm private room – we had exhausted our small talk, and with a sigh Margaret spoke of George. 'I've had letters from him. He is unhappy.' Richard raised a sardonic eyebrow. 'And don't look at me like that, Dickon – he is.' Richard said, more or less, that it served George right and he could go to hell in a handbasket for all he, Richard, cared, then they both appealed to me for support and we squabbled for a few moments as we had done at Fotheringhay, as children. Very refreshing it was, too. Then Margaret said, 'Handle him carefully and he will desert Warwick and his coterie. Write to him, Dickon. I tell you, I know our George. Forgive him, Dickon, and tell him so.'

'Yet you were with us at Ludlow, Meg. If it hadn't been for Somerset keeping some sort of rein on that Anjou woman we could have been killed. You and Mother could have been raped. And George has allied himself with them.'

'Yes. I know.' She shivered, remembering. 'Warwick's been leading him by the nose. '

'With promises to make George king; and it is only because that has not come to pass that George is having second thoughts!'

'You used not to be so hard, Dickon.'

'No, well, I've changed. I have had to.'

Margaret sighed again. 'And so I see. I hardly recognised you two when I came in – I had expected the two boys I said goodbye to, and here are two hard, experienced men. But I tell you this, Richard – you speak of Ludlow and what could have happened to us there … but I remember our mother stepping forward to meet who- or what-ever came into that courtyard, and I remember George, a boy of ten, and terrified, going with her and holding his head high as he took her arm.' Richard nodded, his mouth tightening. 'Write to him,' Margaret gently urged. 'He is our brother. He loves you. You won't say you no longer love him?'

'No,' Richard admitted.

'Then write. Do it now.' She rang a bell and when servants came she asked for ink and paper, and made Richard write the letter there and then.

Despite the private nature of the visit we were allowed only two days. It was a little island of luxury in our existence as exiles, and a taste of home for all that Margaret was so emphatically Duchess of Burgundy now. We would have stayed if we could. Kissing her goodbye I wondered if we would ever see her again – if we would live to see her again – or if our exile here would be forever.

A few days after our return Edward called a conference. 'It is nearly time to go,' he said, looking soberly around at us. 'We have all the men I can raise here, and while fifteen hundred isn't marvellous more will come to us in England. The thing is to go, and soon, before Warwick can get a real grip on the government. Anjou is holding off, she won't risk her darling son till Warwick has secured the country, but Louis is pressing her to go. Can we be ready to go within a month?'

Considering it, we looked at one another. Ships, arms, provisions... We nodded a joint agreement.

'What about Clarence, though?' Rivers asked, without enthusiasm.

'He's ready to turn. He will come back to me.' Rivers looked as if he had stepped in dog shit. 'Anthony, I respect your feelings, but I hate being at odds with my brother. And he can put five thousand men into the field, perhaps more. We need him. Also we need him for the look of the thing. To the people, if the King's brother turns against him, he must have had good cause. (They don't know George, of course.) If he returns to the King, well, that looks as if his *is* the good cause.'

'Do you trust him?' Hastings asked bluntly.

'About as far as I can throw him. No, with George it's self-interest. And I have a good deal of information about George and his self-interest, I have had a spy with him for months.' He grinned around at us, almost giggling. 'Let's hear my spy's latest report.' He went to the door and in the next room spoke to someone for a moment, then returned to announce, 'Gentlemen – the cleverest spy in English service!'

Astounded, we scrambled to our feet, for the spy was a lady.

It was Innogen.

Edward said, 'Your Grace, my lords, gentlemen: Mistress Shaxper. I believe she is known to some of you.' Oddly, for she smiled pleasantly and said nothing, it was in that moment that I realised Innogen disliked Edward.

I had heard nothing of or from her since her letter about John's birth. I had told myself she was dead to me; I had had a thousand other women; I had put her from my mind. Now, I took one look at her and knew I truly loved her.

'Yes,' I said, bowing, 'I am acquainted with Mistress Shaxper. How do you do, madam? How does it happen that you are spying for the King?'

She gave me a little glance under her lashes, and winked. And no wonder, for she proceeded to play on that gathering of hardheaded men like a skilled lutanist on her instrument.

Sinking gracefully into the chair she said, 'I am in the wool trade, and last year business was taking me up and down England. My path crossed the King's. You see, I was briefly at Court a year or two ago, so his Grace remembered me when we met.'

'And I learned she was about to go to Burgundy on business, then on to France – what could be better?'

'What indeed?' Richard murmured.

'But using a *woman* …' Hastings said, and Innogen's eyes turned silver. Richard and I hastily crossed our legs.

'I had, shall we say, special qualifications for the task, my lord. Not only my legitimate business interests that allow me to travel without question, and the several languages I speak. You see, I was in Her Grace the Queen's service – until she dismissed me. She had cause, but you see, I was able to present myself to Clarence as yet another malcontent, victim of Woodville spite.' She gave Anthony Rivers a smile that nearly set his hose on fire. 'Forgive me, my lord; the subterfuge was necessary.'

'Of course, dear lady, of course. The tale would have appealed to Clarence.'

'Well, it did. I let him think the Queen dismissed me because I was the King's mistress. That is not the case, gentlemen –'

'No no.'

'Of course not!'

'Who would believe it?'

'Perish the thought.'

Lying sods, they had all thought precisely that.

'But it made it credible that I should be both loyal to the King and sympathetic to the Warwick-Clarence grievances. I went first to the Duke and Duchess of Clarence; they were kept well away from the French court. The poor Duchess still mourns the baby she lost, and she was lonely, homesick, bewildered. She was glad of another English lady for company. I became quite friendly with the Duke, too.'

'Wonders will never cease,' said Edward.

'Well, all you have to do is agree with him all the time. Simple. He's not the clearest thinker in the world, is he? But the alliance with Lancaster shocked him; sickened him.'

'Glad he has that much feeling,' Richard grunted.

'Yes he has. It's not only that he is now out in the cold. He despises being allied with the Lancastrians, he loathes Exeter and Somerset and Tudor. Also he's lonely and miserable and hates being at odds with his family. In short, if you handle him deftly he will return.'

His chin on his hand, Edward asked, 'And the situation in England?'

'Things are in a wretched state there, Sire. It would break your heart to see poor King Henry loving and trusting everyone, saying all will be well, longing to get back to his prayers, not a clue what's going on. London's seething with every Lancastrian under the sun. Of course the Tudor connections are riding high. Lady Margaret Beaufort is parading her weedy son Harry Tudor as if he were Prince of Wales; he's calling himself Earl of Richmond again.' Edward snorted. 'His uncle Jasper Tudor has gone into Wales, they say, and he was boasting he can raise five thousand men.'

'And the rest?'

'Every faction is turning on the next. Warwick cannot control it, and he knows it. And Clarence wants to return to you, Your Grace. It will have to be a matter of everything forgiven and forgotten, you'll have to honour him and restore him to all his old positions.'

'The prodigal son, in short.'

'Yes.'

'Edward, you cannot!' cried Rivers.

'I must. That or have his head.' Rivers looked as if he thought that a small price to pay. 'And I cannot bring myself to that. Warwick, yes. Not my brother, once he's returned to me.'

'*If* he does,' Hastings said wryly. 'It could be a trap. I don't doubt this lady's honesty, but what if Clarence and Warwick spun this story to gull you into thinking you can count on Clarence?'

'I shall return anyway. I don't count on him – or not as you mean, Will.'

'And it is not just Mistress Shaxper's say-so,' said Richard. 'Our mother and sisters believe the same. So do I, because I know George. He never could stand being in disgrace.'

'And he loves you and the King,' Innogen said gently. 'It's not entirely self-interest.' She turned to Edward. 'Your Grace, write to him. Write again. Assure him of your love and good intentions, promise him whatever's necessary. Because he is in too deep to stand aside now, he must be for you or against you.'

'I know it. Who else is for me? Would John Neville …'

'I think not. He made the hard choice, and can't turn back now. As for who else is for you –' She listed the people we'd thought of, and a few who had previously been waverers. 'The people want peace and good government, they don't much care for rights or feuds – but they know you'll return, Your Grace, and they want you back, and they know Warwick can't go on like this in King Henry's name.'

'Would George,' Richard asked, 'still think of making a bid for the throne in his own right?'

'Quite possibly, if things go on as they are.'

'Well, I'll write to him,' Edward said, 'a mixture of threats and promises, laced with my fraternal love. Will you carry the letter back, Mistress Shaxper?'

Innogen agreed, and the meeting broke up. I found myself standing with Innogen and Richard. 'Would you care to come back to my house?' she said. She seemed to mean both of us, and exile had taught us to accept any invitation.

Her house was near Gruythuuse's. It was one I'd passed many

times and had admired. Now, entering it with Innogen, I couldn't have told you one thing about it, except that she led us to an upstairs room. I tripped twice on the stairs.

And in the door of that upper room Innogen stopped and said confusedly, 'Oh – I'd forgotten – I meant –' Then with a resigned little gesture she moved aside. Of course, in my jealousy, I thought that she had a man there.

No.

A woman in nursemaid's clothing sat sewing by the window. On the carpet at her feet a small red-haired child crooned happily to a toy wooden horse. His hair was Innogen's. His slatey blue eyes and everything about his face were Richard's.

Seeing Innogen he said 'Ma-ma' and displayed a couple of splendid teeth. He started to crawl toward her, then remembered a better way. With frowning effort he rocked back onto his bottom. His hands came down, his arms took the strain, then he was balanced and with the bandy high-stepping gait of the new pedestrian he came giggling towards us. After four steps he lost his balance, windmilled briskly, and sat down with a thud. This was evidently hilarious. 'Mama,' he commanded, and Innogen picked him up.

'You will have gathered this is John. Look, John, these are friends of mine.' The blue eyes inspected us, and, Christ, I had seen the Duke of York look over troops like that. I hadn't known until then how much I had still hoped that he was mine.

Richard said, 'May I hold him?' and took him from Innogen with an uncle's casual expertise. They smiled at each other, and John began to eat his hair.

I knew little of children, but something was expected of me. 'He seems very healthy,' I offered. 'Er – is he forward, or do they all walk and talk at this age?'

'Rather forward. I think he's clever. Though saying Mama is about his limit so far. Will you take wine?' She signed to the nurse. We sat down at the table. John went back to his horse.

'You look tired, Jenny.'

'I am. I've been travelling so much. Frankly, if I never see the

Channel again it will be too soon.'

'Do you get seasick?'

'No, why?'

'Martin gets seasick on damp grass. Innogen, you're sure about George?'

'As sure as one can be. He's like a child who's stolen the jam or damaged a book; he knows he has done wrong, feels he's suffered enough and longs for his mother to forgive him and make it better with a kiss.'

'That's about George's level of understanding, yes. *He's* suffered! And I suppose by 'make it better with a kiss' you mean Edward will have to butter him up, honour him, make it seem he has never strayed?'

'Yes.'

'Mmm, that's George. When you were in France, did you see Anne Neville?' His voice was casual, but Innogen shot me an intrigued look. I nodded.

'Not to speak to. She's in Queen Margaret's household. The Queen wanted only a betrothal between her son and Lady Anne, so it could be repudiated later and the prince married to someone more suitable. Warwick and King Louis of course held out for a full marriage. You know they married last December? They don't live together. She's not pregnant, it would have been trumpeted from the rooftops if she were.' The muscles of Richard's face tightened. Jealous. Serves you right, I thought, pays you back for all the times I've had to think of you with Innogen.

'Does he treat her well?'

'He wouldn't dare not to. Well, he ignores her. Thinks, like his mother, that she is not good enough. Poor Anne, poor little pawn. Did you hear that when Warwick first met Queen Margaret she kept him on his knees before her for a full hour, grovelling and publicly repenting all the 'wrongs' he'd done her? They say she made him kiss her feet.'

'Only her feet? What's the prince like? I saw him once, at Ludlow. Fat brat.'

'Plump. Spoilt brat. Arrogant, bloodthirsty, hasn't the brains of a flea. He believes he has only to set foot in England and the roads will be lined with adoring crowds cheering him home. Believes too that once he takes the field you and the King will either run away, or be thrashed in five minutes.' With an edge of malice she said, 'He is very handsome.'

'Oh.'

'But only a mother could love him. And of course mother-love is the thing – Margaret of Anjou is desperate to keep him in France, and if Warwick and Louis insist he goes to England she will do anything to keep him from actually fighting. To her, that is what Warwick is for; he's expendable. Richard, tell the King he must go very soon. It's as if – well – as if there's a tide in these affairs, and you take it at the flood or not at all. Tell him to go back, honour George, defeat Warwick. Then Margaret of Anjou and her son will rot in France the rest of their days and it will be the end of Lancaster forever.'

'I agree, and the King knows it too. We go within a month. Well, speaking of armed invasions of England, I must go, there's a fleet awaiting my all-seeing eye. No need to come, Martin. Innogen, my dear, we shall meet again soon. Goodbye, John.'

'Bye – bye,' said John, and waved a solemn hand. He even had Richard's hands: long, slim, shapely; deceptively delicate.

'That's new,' Innogen said. 'Saying goodbye. Now, John, my precious, it is time for bed.' John didn't seem to agree, but Innogen handed him firmly to the nursemaid. He gave me a nasty look over the woman's shoulder, clearly believing it was all my fault.

Pouring wine, Innogen asked, 'Does Richard like children?'

'He seems very fond of his nieces and nephews. Well, he's going to like his own child, isn't he? Oh Lord, Jenny, you bitch, my darling love, I wanted that baby to be mine. I love you, Innogen, I always have loved you. Very well, before it was a boy's love, infatuation – and as you told me, I had to grow up. But the love was real. I thought I was over it, over you, till you walked into the King's room just now. I'm jealous of Richard, jealous of any other man you love,

147

even jealous of John, and if that's a sin, *mea culpa*. I love you. I want to marry you.'

'Despite John?'

I had already decided. 'Yes.'

'Then ask me to!'

'... Innogen?'

'I loved you much more than I ever told you; you were quite conceited enough at sixteen. Martin, I know you read Chaucer – think of the Merchant's Tale. The girl, married to the old man. That was my first marriage. I had an old man for a husband – kind to me, proud of me, jealous of me. He was fond of me in the way a doting father loves a pretty little daughter so long as the daughter remains pretty, and little, and adoring. He was proud of me as proof of his wealth and virility. He wanted me pregnant as soon as we were wed, and when I didn't conceive he stopped being so proud of me, he beat me. That's common, he had the right, many men do that – but no man can know what it is like for a woman. Do you see what I mean?'

'Yes, my dear, I do. Jenny, I was so angry with the Queen for dismissing you, but it was my fault, I boasted of having you, every time I heard a man admire you I was there, hackles up, snarling like a dog over its bone. So damnably sure of myself. Jenny, can I ask you one thing, then never speak of it again?'

'Yes,' she said warily.

'When the King told me you'd been dismissed the Court, he called you notorious, said you had many lovers. No names, but was it true?'

'No. One other, when I first went to Court. It turned out he preferred boys.' Startled, I laughed and mentioned a name. She nodded. Same chap had made me an offer. 'Then I saw Richard, or he saw me – Martin, that smile of his should be made illegal. Well, then I saw you. You are the most beautiful man I've ever seen, my darling, and I have to admit that I was indiscreet too, every time I heard ladies sighing over you and wondering what you'd be like in bed.'

'Did you ever tell them?' I asked, laughing and pulling her close.

'No, but I bristled a lot. Mind you, many of those ladies seemed to know.'

'Some, yes. And I'm afraid that some of them were while I was with you. Oh, Jenny my darling. Do you really love me?'

'Yes, sweetheart. I made a mess of things, and even if it had been possible I was too proud to marry you before. It wouldn't have worked. But pride is cold comfort and I've missed you so much, I love you so much.'

'So you will marry me?'

'What about John?'

'He shall be like my own son. I promise to treat him well. Jenny, Innogen, love me, let me love you ... No, wait.' Carefully I placed my father's emerald ring on her finger. 'There.'

She stared down at the ring, saying nothing, for so long that I feared she'd had second thoughts. Then, at last, she looked up at me again. Tears were pouring down her face.

'Innogen, my heart, what is it?'

'Happiness. If you only knew how lonely I've been all this while and how much I've missed you – knowing it was all my fault that I'd hurt us both so much ... And now ...' She pressed the emerald ring to her lips. 'Now I have my heart's desire. I have you.'

I took her in my arms, wiping the tears away with my finger. Then I bent my head and kissed her. Our lips met lightly and sweetly but with a power that shook us both. For a long time it was enough just to be holding each other, united at last. Then the other kind of need began to matter badly. I kissed the side of her throat, her shoulder, took her face between my hands to kiss her savagely. She answered me with the same passion, then seemingly without moving we were in her bedchamber and tearing off our clothes, and the long starvation was over. It was like the first time – better – as if we'd been born to fit together; as if, apart, we'd been trying to live without our souls. It was love, and forever.


We had that one half-day and night of love, then Innogen had to leave for England, bearing the letter of fraternal love to everyone's favourite duke. To say I missed her is an understatement; it was like trying to exist without food, or breath, or drink. Richard noted the absence of my emerald ring, but he asked no questions – for which forbearance I took him to a tavern and, swearing him to secrecy, told him everything; almost everything. He was as delighted as if it were for himself. We got very drunk; I remember staggering home, arms about each other, enchanting Bruges with a rendition of 'I sing of a maiden which is matchless'. But we opened our hearts to each other that night. I had not known quite how deep my hurt and jealousy of him had gone, or that he had been jealous of me, and tearing himself apart with guilt. That night, though, these rifts that could have damaged our friendship were repaired.

We had little more time for indulgence, for we had charge of outfitting our ships and victualling our army. The days sped by in a jabber of four languages, of checking endless lists. At night we fell into bed too exhausted for thought. Then, suddenly, everything was done. We were ready – except for news from George.

It came after a week. Exhausted from the double journey, Innogen came to another meeting with the King. 'It is done, it's assured. He wept, Your Grace, when I gave him your letter.'

'Tears cost nothing.'

'I think it was genuine. He asks – well, it's in his letter – he asks you to forget the past and restore the estates and titles he held before. He says that when you land he'll stay with Warwick until the last moment – that moment being up to you – then come over to you.'

'Mmm-hmm.' Richard finished with his brother's letter and passed it on to me. It was about what I'd expected, and typical of George – incoherent, passionate, self-justifying. Warwick had wronged him – he had been beguiled from his true allegiance – Mother would be pleased now – he had some five thousand men – he longed to embrace his brothers once more and enjoy their love and favour – don't land in the south-east – whatever happened, Isabel must be protected – perhaps Warwick had even used witchcraft on him – all forgiven now and he was the King's liege man forever.

'Forever meaning as long as it benefits him,' snorted Edward. 'But he is in good earnest now? You are sure, Mistress Shaxper?'

'As sure as one can be.' She looked at Richard. 'Your Grace, I was to tell you this particularly. He said, "Tell Dickon I too remember Ludlow".'

A swift flush mantled Richard's cheekbones. He nodded slowly, and in answer to Edward's raised brows said, 'Yes, I think we can trust that.'

'Yes,' Innogen agreed. 'But move quickly, Your Grace, before he gives the game away to Warwick or gets a better offer.'

'I agree. Yes. Very well, gentlemen, let's say the second day of March.'

I waited until all but Richard had gone then, taking Jenny's hand, I said to Edward, 'Your Grace, I ask your permission to marry Mistress Shaxper.'

Re-reading George's letter, Edward swung about, startled. 'Marry the lady?'

'Yes, Sire. Please.'

'Let them, Ned,' Richard urged. 'Reward their loyalty.'

Edward frowned, but he said, 'Well, Martin, you are of age now and I daresay you know your own mind. Very well. You have our leave.'

'We want to marry now. Here. We've just time before Lent.'

'Do you! *Now* – in between provisioning ships, training an army … There's no time to call the banns more than once before Lent. Still, there are ways around that, if you're determined.' But it appealed to Edward's romantic streak, and I suppose he thought a wedding would put everyone in good heart. A good omen, even. 'Well, why not? Yes. I will speak to Gruythuuse, we must do something decent for you, Martin's my ward and cousin. And Margaret will want to help. Yes.'

And he turned the mind that could organise an armed invasion to planning the best wedding possible in the circumstances. It amused him, and he meant well by us. And so, three days hence, in the Church of Our Lady, Innogen and I stood up before the English Court in exile, some merchant friends of Innogen's, the Seigneur de la Gruythuuse and, unexpectedly, Duke Charles and Duchess Margaret. The King of England gave Innogen away. Richard was my groom's-man, a role which by tradition, he pointed out, entitled, or obliged, him to marry the bride if I didn't show up. Innogen wore green velvet and cloth of silver, and her gorgeous hair loose.

Seigneur Gruythuuse gave us a splendid wedding feast, and I still have his gift of silver plate. Duke Charles' gift, an ivory figure of St Martin, was one of the things lost when I fled England an attainted traitor.

Towards the end of the celebration, after Richard had made a witty and mercifully brief speech, Edward rose and called for our attention. 'It is a humbling and disconcerting experience,' he began, 'to be a King yet unable to provide a suitable wedding present for friends. The very clothes I wear I owe to the gracious kindness of my dear brother-in-law Duke Charles' (applause) 'and to our generous friend in need the Seigneur de la Gruythuuse.' (Warmer applause.) 'Even the coins in my purse are come to me by charity.' (Consoling murmurs.) 'Now, I have known Mistress Robsart only a brief time, but she has served me and England faithfully and with skill. In short, she is as clever and loyal as she is beautiful.' (Wild applause, and the groom and best man both kiss the bride.) 'Martin, now, is my kinsman and I have known him from a child. He has been a loyal friend to my dear brother of Gloucester' (cheers) 'and a friend to me and all my family.' (More cheers, and Duchess Margaret kisses the blushing groom.) 'He has twice gone into exile on our behalf – though if one must be exiled, what better place than Burgundy?' (Laughter and many cheers, and Duke Charles unbends into a smile.) 'He has been loyal when perhaps the easier part would have been to forget his first allegiance.' (Applause while people begin to look longingly at their drinks.) 'Therefore,' said Edward, taking the hint, 'it behoves me to give this charming young couple some suitable wedding gift, but what, I asked myself, could I in these circumstances give them of my own? Come here, Martin.'

Bewildered, I went to him. He lifted his sword, and I thought in confusion, He cannot be giving me his sword! And no, he wasn't.

'Kneel, Master Robsart.' The sword touched me twice. 'Arise, Sir Martin.'

Astounded, delighted, I nearly wept as I stammered some clumsy thanks.

Edward never missed a chance. 'If thanks are due,' he said, 'I shall take them in the form of a kiss from Dame Robsart.'

Our honeymoon was a week in a house lent by Margaret. The seven days passed like so many hours. Neither of us slept on the last night. We made love, then lay holding each other until the dawn. Innogen squired me, dressing me and buckling on my sword; I was her lady's maid. Sentimentally I cut a lock of her hair and folded it away in my purse. We had agreed on a quick farewell, or we'd break our hearts. We parted halfway between Bruges and Flushing, leaning from our horses to kiss.

'I love you, Innogen. No woman was ever so loved.'

'Nor any man. *Au revoir*, my darling. God keep you safe.'

'And you.'

I left without a backward look.

# *Seven*

It was an unpropitious start. The wind was against us, and for nine days our ships rode at anchor, unable to leave Flushing harbour. To those who don't suffer from it, seasickness is either hilarious or contemptible, but those nine days nearly killed me. I wasn't the only one; our own men grimly endured, as did I, but some of our Flemish and German hirelings began to mutter about bad omens and would have deserted if they could. Richard nursed me devotedly, and obtained some dose that helped a little, but I hardly noticed when at last the wind changed, and on the eleventh day of March we set sail for home.

Once at sea the voyage went well enough, but you can imagine how we cheered when at last we sighted the English coast. But George had been right – the southeast of England was hostile. The scouts sent ashore at Norfolk scurried back to report that the county was against us and to land there would be our death warrant. So on we sailed up the east coast to Yorkshire.

I revived enough to vomit all over the beach when at last we landed. Then, being ashore worked its usual cure and although I was weak as a kitten I was in better trim than many of the men. The weather was vile, high seas, a wind straight from Russia cutting through our wet, salt-stiff clothes. The first hours were a cacophony of the neighing of frightened horses, the shouting of orders and obscene complaints in three languages, but we managed to make our landing. But we were alone.

'Where are the King's ships?' Richard croaked; he looked as deathly as I had felt for the past two weeks. 'And Rivers'?' I volunteered to investigate, and set off munching noisy cheese and a lump of that garlicky German sausage. All I could discover was that we'd come ashore north of our target, Ravenspur, and there was no sign of the rest of our fleet. I picked up vague word of other ships having landed to our south, so we got our men formed up, and in the early dark we set out hopefully southward. A few miles on someone hailed us, and sure enough it was the King. He and Rivers were safe.

Next morning we began our march through England. We moved inland and south, and for every town that welcomed us with joy, another shut us out. York closed its gates to us, but with Richard interpreting in the broad Yorkshire dialect we had learnt at Middleham, Edward used Bolingbroke's trick and vowed he had only come to reclaim his York dukedom – throne? What throne? The burghers of York enjoyed the joke, and let us in.

And then we broke out our banners in good earnest: the Royal Arms, Edward's Sun in Splendour, Richard's Blanc Sanglier. Men flocked to us, and by the Midlands we had an army of nearly five thousand. Percy of Northumberland neither aided nor molested us, which was better than we had hoped. John Neville did the same. At Coventry Edward proclaimed himself King, and sent a formal offer to Warwick: battle, or a life pardon. No reply came. And just outside Coventry we met Clarence.

Looking over his army of some six thousand in their warlike array I understood why the King was at such pains to placate him. Even as our two forces closed up I wondered if it was a trap. Surreptitiously we all readied our weapons. Clarence rode forward with his personal bodyguard. The King and Richard did the same. Clarence waved, and Richard spurred his horse forward, full-pelt towards his brother. I thought, God, no, you're riding to your death – then their right hands clasped and they were embracing, clumsy figures in their half-armour. George took his brother's face between his hands and kissed him, and from both sides a great cheer went up.

As they rode back to us I was struck by the difference between them. George had gained weight, and the fullness of his face made him look boyish. His hair crackled with recent washing, he was shaved smooth, he was clean and glossy. No dent or scratch marred his beautiful Italian armour gleaming silver in the sun. Richard, by contrast, showed all the strain of exile and work. Like all of us he had lost weight: helping to arm him that morning I could count his ribs. From boots to helmet his leathers and armour were scratched, stained and scuffed. Tanned and weathered, with the sharp lines of authority and tension in his face, he looked ten years his brother's elder. As indeed he was, in character and mind, for George was forever caught at the age of eleven, the pampered golden boy.

George knelt before the King. Holding out his sword across his palms he raised his voice to carry to every man in the two armies. 'I am your Highness's loyal subject and true liege-man.' Cheers went up. Edward said, 'George –' very quietly, then swung off his horse and took his brother in his arms. For a moment they clung together, then George lifted their clasped hands in the air and yelled, 'God for England! Edward and Saint George!' The battle cry rang out valiantly, echoing as every last man took it up. But I thought Clarence had only just remembered to insert the word 'Saint'. Sodding hypocrite.

Another offer of pardon was sent to Warwick, this time by George, a nice irony. Again no response, and we learnt that his brother Montagu and the Earl of Oxford had joined Warwick. And again the race for London was on. Both sides ordered the City to hold. In a last-ditch attempt Archbishop Neville paraded King Henry through the city, then read the runes and popped Henry back into the Tower and galloped off to submit himself to Edward.

Any doubts about the feelings in England fled at the reception London gave us. The city went mad for us. Every citizen who could walk was out in the streets. The air was thick with flowers, we were garlanded with laurels and white roses, every hand seemed to hold a wine cup, every throat was hoarse with cheering. I've never kissed so many girls in so brief a time. Edward was back.

We went first to St Paul's to make offering, then Edward pelted off to Westminster Sanctuary to the Queen. Dog-tired and with no wish to intrude on their reunion, I went straight to Baynard's Castle. The Duchess of York welcomed me like a son, kissing me and patting me gently when from joy I wept all over her. She was in her mid-fifties, and looked it, but she was still one of the loveliest women I ever saw, and she was the nearest thing I had to a mother. I loved her, and I was home.

'And married now!' she said. 'Margaret wrote to me about your wedding and your knighthood. You deserve the honour, Martin dear. And Margaret says your wife is as beautiful and charming as we would want for you.'

'She is, and near as beautiful as you, madam.' It was cheek, but she liked it, although she disclaimed it as arrant flattery.

'Not that I *mind* compliments from handsome men ... My dear, if you are as tired as you look, no doubt you would like to go straight to your room. And would a bath appeal?'

'It sounds the most wonderful offer in months.'

'Good. The steward has orders – and here is someone you'll remember?'

I looked at the tall, slim boy with dark-blond hair flopping in his eyes. 'Francis Lovell! How good to see you!'

He was shy. He said later that we seemed so much older, so entirely changed from the boys he had known at Middleham, that he hardly dared speak to us.

'I didn't think you would remember me, Sir Martin. How do you do? How good to have you home.' The Duchess was glancing toward the door, her hands clenching and unclenching. Tactfully Francis said, 'You will want to go to your room – you'll allow me to squire you?'

'Gladly.'

And gladly I trod up the narrow, worn stairs to the room I remembered. The beds had new red and yellow hangings, the walls were fresh-plastered and hung with a tapestry showing Dido greeting Aeneas. Fur rugs on the floor. A table with a shelf of books. Candelabra blazing from the mantel, the table, beside the bed. A cushioned clothes chest. Spring flowers in a silver bowl. A tray of wine.

In a daze I watched the servants set up the bath-tent of red silk. The sheet they draped over the wooden tub was of finest linen, the water scented with rosemary. Since leaving Burgundy there had been no chance for more than a quick once-over at the basin, so this was bliss indeed.

Kneeling to pull off my boots, Francis said shyly, 'One thing about growing up in Warwick's household, you learn to squire a knight.'

'Yes. You do. Lord, it's only three years – feels like thirty. Who could have imagined what has happened! But how come you are here, Francis? I thought you were still at Middleham?'

'I was, but it became – difficult.' His fingers nimble on my buckles and laces he gave me a quick, bitter smile. 'So a short time ago I simply left. I was with my wife's people, but once I heard you were coming I threw myself on the Duchess's mercy. Martin, sorry, Sir Martin, would – do you think – I'm fifteen and well-trained, so – do you think the King would let me fight?'

Naked for the first time in a month I stood up, stretching luxuriously. My clothes lay in a filthy, malodorous pile. Burn them, I thought to myself. 'You can ask, Francis, but the King has a rule, no one under sixteen.'

'Richard might …'

'You can ask,' I repeated, and sank into the benison of hot water. Despite his baron's rank Francis dismissed the servants and did for me himself, washing my hair, scrubbing my back and feet. Half asleep I idled, luxuriating, drinking wine and telling Francis about Burgundy, my wife, the journey home.

'Warwick won't accept any offers of pardon,' he said when the talk came round to present matters. 'You know his pride. He has gambled and lost. There's no choice now but battle.'

'No.'

'After Easter?' Tomorrow was Good Friday.

'Sooner, I think. Francis, we could still lose.'

'No,' he said with enviable confidence. 'Martin, about fighting – should I ask Richard?'

'Ask me what?' The man himself entered as we spoke. He was in tearing high spirits. 'Christ, I'd give an arm and a leg for a bath!'

'We'll send for a narrow tub.'

'Out. My turn. Why, it's Francis Lovell! How are you?'

'Well, thank you, Your Grace. I hope you are well?'

Richard was flinging off his clothes, he never had any patience with servants undressing him. 'I'd be better if Martin would shift, I want a bath. And you used to call me Richard, why so formal?' To the boy's delight he kissed him fondly. 'What did you want to ask me?'

'If I could fight for you. Would you take me?'

Reluctantly quitting the bath I said, 'I told him the King's rule about being sixteen. But we know he's well-trained, so why not?'

'Hmm. He is certainly a good squire.' Francis had laid towels over the wooden bath mat and had more warming by the fire. The servants emptied the tub, cleaned it, and re-filled it. Francis wrapped me in my bed-gown and I settled back on the bed with another cup of wine. Watching critically Richard said, 'So far as I'm concerned you can. If the King asks, you're near seventeen. You can be one of my squires. And you can start by washing my hair, but watch out, I'm sure I'm lousy.'

'Thank you!' Francis plied the soap as if charging the enemy colours.

'I trust the Queen is well?' I didn't like her, but I felt sympathy for that haughty woman crammed helpless into Sanctuary for six months, stripped of her dignities, terrified no doubt, bearing a baby who might have no future except as a political football.

'She is.' Richard laughed. 'Martin, she kissed me! Threw her arms around me and kissed me and called me Richard!'

'My word.'

'Indeed. And, among ourselves,' (the servants had gone) 'for the first time I believed she married Edward for more than ambition. She came running out of the inner room, and saw him, and her face lit up, and she flung herself into his arms and kissed him and called him Ned, which I've never heard her do. She was crying with delight, and her headdress came off and her hair fell down and she never minded, she laughed. And then the little girls came out, and Edward knelt down and hugged them, all three of them at once, and he was crying.'

'And the Prince of Wales?'

'Skinny, pale, going to be tall. Pale hair, brown eyes – pure Woodville. Healthy, though. You'll see him when we go down, everyone is here, downstairs – well, I daresay Edward is *up*stairs; the way he and the Queen looked at each other there'll be another baby nine months from now. Mother's arranged a great feast. Martin, there will be a conference tomorrow then we march out on Friday.'

'Where to?'

'Northwards. Warwick is to the north of London, none too far away. Word is he has about the same numbers as we have.'

'His chief captains?'

'Montagu of course, and Oxford and Exeter.' He grimaced on this last name, for the Duke of Exeter had been married to his eldest sister Anne. After a stormy marriage Anne had obtained a divorce, and it is an understatement to say there was no love lost between the two sides. 'Martin, the King has given me command of the vanguard.'

Well, leading the vanguard is an honour, but with a chill I remembered that Richard's great-uncle the Duke of York had led the van at Agincourt, and died. It was the most dangerous position.


We marched out on Saturday the thirteenth of April, along the northern road. Just through Barnet, at dusk, the scouts ran back to say Warwick had halted a mile ahead, forming his army up across the road. At once we halted and pitched our camp. I'm always surprised by soldiers' speedy genius at looking after their comfort; I had barely dismounted when campfires were crackling and the cooking pots were out. Some made do with roasting a rabbit or pigeon, others fried ham or eggs while some stewed meat and vegetables into quite elaborate meals. I was well fed, therefore, of their kindness as I went around my troops. They were in good heart, their faith in the King complete. Well, so was mine, but I was afraid, with that gut-churning terror only battle brings. Leaving the latrine for the third time in an hour I ran into old Lord Say, whom Edward had placed with Richard because of his experience.

'Sir Martin, all secure?'

'I think so. Fed and bedded down. They know we'll move up early.'

'Good. I wish that damn' cannon fire would stop, it shreds the nerves. Warwick likes artillery.' It shredded my nerves too, which was probably the idea, or else the enemy didn't know we were out of range. 'Frightened?' the old gentleman suddenly asked.

'Yes.'

'Everyone is before a battle. In and out the latrines, shitting blue lights. Some throw up. The ones who don't are the ones with no imagination, and they're often not the best fighters.'

'Good.' He was looking at me so kindly I told the truth. 'My Lord, it's not death so much as …'

'The thought of being maimed? Living out your life crippled, blinded, gelded even? Bless you, that's every man's great fear. We put our trust in the Lord and know our souls are safe, we go into battle shriven – but we all fear living on as half-men.' He lowered his voice. 'I speak of what the Church would call a sin – but in my experience many men make a compact with a friend, so that if they are so gravely wounded life would be unbearable – well, you take my meaning?' I did, even without his graphic little gesture. 'But don't dwell on it, son. Trust the Lord and our cause, trust your good armour and weapons. You fight with the sword? The axe? The mace is best left to big men like the king or when you're fighting mounted.'

'Sword, mostly; the axe too.'

'The young Duke uses the axe. If you're handy with it it's useful, providing you have room for a good swing. Sword and dagger are my preference. If you're in close, remember the two best places, groin and throat, in through the gaps in the armour. Keep your visor down.' I didn't want to hear him explain why – I knew. He patted my shoulder, blessed me, and moved on.

Despite the cool night, Richard's tent-flap was pinned open. Stripped to shirt and hose he and the squires sprawled on the floor, scoffing chicken.

'Martin, good. Where have you been? I looked for you.'

'I was having a cheering talk with Lord Say.' This wasn't sarcasm, for that little conversation, ghoulish though it may sound, had left me in better heart. I did not repeat what he had said about arranging with a friend to get myself finished off in extremity. The Bible says 'Thou shalt do no murder', but the rule doesn't hold in battle, where killing is no murder. And afterwards? Richard was devout; how far would love go in conflict with Holy Church? I had often suspected Edward paid no more than lip-service to religious teachings; perhaps I could ask him. Or no, better do it myself. But if one ended handless – blind – I had heard of a man whose neck broke, leaving him paralysed –

'Martin, what's wrong? Are you ill?'

Clammy with gooseflesh, retching, I could barely manage the one word: 'Imagination.'

'God, yes.' Richard took my hand. His was as cold as mine. 'Imagining the worst. Not death; or not a quick death.'

'Yes.'

'Well, in God's name,' said Francis Lovell, with a sigh that near burst his lungs, 'I thought I was the only one. You've had experience, so I thought it was only me.'

'No. All of us. I think,' Richard gave me an odd slippy glance, 'one can only trust in one's friends, and in Providence. And not talk of it, or I for one will go into screaming hysterics. Have a drink, Martin.'

We were interrupted by the flare of a torch and the King's voice. He had Lord Hastings and Clarence with him. Hastings would lead the rearguard tomorrow, with Clarence safely stowed behind the King in the centre, in charge of the reserve.

It looked like a commanders' conference, but the King stayed us when we rose to leave. 'It is nothing you can't all hear. In fact I wanted to ask you, you trained with Warwick – does he have any tricks up his sleeve? Other than driving me raving mad with his artillery?'

We thought. John Milwater said. 'He's keen on those new-fangled handguns. They'll never be of use in battle, of course. And he always said that being caught flat-footed in battle at St Albans taught him the use of flank attacks.'

'He'll have no chance of that tomorrow,' Clarence said. If that was the extent of his understanding it was a good thing he wasn't leading his own wing.

Edward made due note. 'He's spread out east-west across the road ahead. The land drops away to our right, we're on a plateau of level ground. Warwick is tucked away snug behind a lot of hedgerows. We shall take up the same formation, three wings abreast. Oxford has their right wing, Exeter the left. Richard, the van takes the right so you are facing our dear brother-in-law. He's a good fighter, he'll press you hard.' Richard nodded. 'The thing is,' Edward went on, 'Warwick will press on our centre, and therefore I will need you, Richard and Will, to hold as long as you can, and longer, without calling on the reserve. It's a matter of fine judgement, but you can always last that bit longer than you think. So the word is, hold, and spare the reserve for the last push. Be alert for flank attacks – well, you know. We'll move up closer near to dawn, right in close so their guns overshoot us. Move up silently so he doesn't know our range, allow us the element of surprise.' He broke off, rubbing his hand over his face and through his hair. Those big hands were trembling. 'Sorry,' he muttered. 'Nerves. It's these last few hours ...'

'You're not afraid!' Clarence burst out.

'Of course I am. Every sensible man is.' Clarence was almost green, but at this he managed a smile. He was genuinely terrified. Serve him right. What could it be like to know he was as responsible as Warwick for bringing us to this? Twenty thousand men, twenty thousand possible deaths, through his hubris. And did he understand that he had been given the reserve because no man would follow him in battle? I wondered too if Edward was tempted to put George in the forefront of the battle, for a convenient and blameless death.

Sometimes I wish he had – I would have.

'In battle,' Edward said, 'in the thick of it, you've no time to think or be afraid. Which is as well. It is now, the night before, that I think of my responsibility. A king is married to his country, to his people. Or, say, he is like a father – responsible – one does one's best, as a father or husband would with his family – one tries to govern well – to keep the peace – to provide – and always the responsibility is one's own – alone – and the knowledge … If it comes to war, you ask men to fight for you – if your cause is just it is no sin, but if sin there be, it falls upon the king – your subjects are masters of their own souls yet the sin is on your head …' He spoke as if to himself, or perhaps to George. Suddenly he broke off as if waking. 'Sorry. Maundering. I'm tired. Have we covered everything? Then I'll say goodnight. Get some sleep. Eat what you can in the morning, even if you feel no hunger. Don't drink wine or thirst will torture you. Don't drink much water or you'll piss yourselves; most unpleasant, and I speak from experience. Be ready by three at the latest, we'll move up then. Well, goodnight. God keep you safe tomorrow, my loyal friends.'

Richard followed them out, and in the doorway Edward enfolded him in a hug, kissed his mouth and his brow, and made the sign of the Cross.

We managed some sleep, although we had thought we could not. By three we had heard Mass and were armed, and although last night's fear had gone we were all nervy. Time seemed out of joint, slowing or speeding up. I watched Richard, and hoped I looked as tranquil. We ate without appetite, forcing down bread and cold bacon, and took one cup of watered wine each, for spirit. Then it was time. We made no gestures of affection, spoke no hopes. It wasn't necessary. We went with God's blessing, and each other's.

Fog had fallen in the night, reducing visibility to a few feet. Probably it would lift soon after dawn, but that would be too late. We had to fight now. So, carefully, we moved up as close as we could to the enemy lines. It is no easy task moving an army in silence, and the fog made everything worse. We could hear the enemy soldiers talking as they made their own preparations. I stood beside Richard,

Francis behind us, Rob Percy to my left, Parr and Milwater on the right. We crossed ourselves and kissed the earth.

Our trumpets sounded. Warwick's answered. Cannon fired, but the shot passed harmlessly over us. So did their arrows. They didn't know we were so close. Our guns boomed. Our archers fired, and we had the range.

We were moving steadily forward, but something was wrong. The ground was falling away before us, we were running down into emptiness. Somehow we had overshot Exeter's left wing. In the dark we must have formed up too far to our right. No enemy ahead, no visibility, the slope leading us ever downwards. I remembered that the hollow was called Dead Man's Bottom. Richard's trumpets yelped the order to wheel left. Up the slope we climbed, hard going in armour. I heard some incredible thumping din and thought it cannon, then realised it was my own breath echoing inside my helmet.

Up and up, then level ground underfoot. We wheeled further left. And now the enemy was in front, I saw Exeter's badge on the men facing me. Then for hours I ceased to think. In battle your training takes over and you only act and react, you keep your commander's flag in sight, strain your ears for orders. I saw a man go down with an arrow in the face – the idiot had put his visor up. Christ, was mine down – yes. Noise, it's so noisy. There's Rob. Where's Richard? We're moving left still. A blow sends me reeling – someone using a mace. Blood coating my arm, blood all down my armour. Being left-handed is useful, they always cut to my right; it leaves my heart side dangerously exposed, though. My sword's too bloody to grip. Wipe it. Press on. Cut, thrust, parry. A man in front of me looks up, the fool, and I see the gap at his throat and in goes my dagger. Parr beside me – and an axe nearly has his arm off. Move forward, no longer to the left. I've lost Richard's banner, and risk lifting my visor. There it is, I was straying right. Visor down just in time. Cut a man's throat and my sword sticks in bone. Pull it free. Thirsty, so thirsty. And Edward was right, I've pissed myself. A blow across my back sends me staggering forward. Rob rights me. We're moving faster.

That's Richard, using the axe and he's red from head to foot. He's taken a man's head off with one blow.

They rush us, dozens together, they've been waiting. We are falling back. The King's runner tugs at Richard's arm and I hear: 'Can you hold?' No, I think, but Richard says yes. Spare the reserve. Hold. Oh Lord help us, the White Boar banner's down, Richard, Richard, Richard, he's down, he's not moving. Run, Francis with me and unbidden he guards my back while I lift the visor. Pure relief. Not Richard. Then sadness. John Milwater has followed the White Boar to the end of his life.

There's the banner again and Richard by it, using his sword now. Francis falls, rises, stabs short-armed and runs on. Good fighter, that boy.

We're advancing. Faster. Our pike-men are doing stalwart service. The enemy ranks are thinning before us. Another runner comes from the King and now I'm so close to Richard I hear the plea and his reply, 'We can hold. Tell the King I need no reserves.' There's blood coming from under his gauntlet. No time to ask. Advance. Press on. Back to back with Rob as Exeter's men close in, and we fight like that for a while, each protecting the other's back. They're down. I'm winded, I can't go on. I have to. Snatch a breathing space, hands on my knees. Take another blow, a bad one.

More of Exeter's men. So noisy. Hot. Thirsty. How long has it been? The sun is up – five? Six? Noon? A blow across my back and I hear my armour crumple. Where's Richard? Tom Parr is down. Richard bends over him and shakes his head. Press forward. And we're running, I'm using my axe now, the enemy is turning, turning, running away, and the ground's clear ahead. No, the enemy reserve's come up – no, it's the King, see his Sun in Splendour banner, they're the King's men and that great figure is the King himself, blood all over him. We've cut through to join up with our own centre. Exeter's gone. Press forward, but now there's no one to resist us. It is over.

I'm sitting on the ground, my sword stuck upright between my knees, my helmet off. The bliss of cool air on my face. My hair's sopping and sweat has rucked my arming doublet under my mail;

agony. I pull off my gauntlets. Am I intact? Seem to be. A tall man, all red, hauls me to my feet and hugs me, kisses me. The King. What's he saying? Yes – 'It is over.' Someone shouts that it's seven of the clock, the battle took a scant three hours. We've won. Glory be to God, we won! Exhilaration floods me so that I could run all the way back to London like Pheidippides taking the news of Marathon. Or no I couldn't, I'm battered and sore and bruised and tired, so very tired. Where's Richard? Why was he not my first thought? Oh Lord, Holy Mother Mary, *where is Richard?* Where's his banner? It's there. Richard's sitting on the ground and George of all people holds him as he bares his arm. He's hurt, a dagger must have penetrated under the wrist join, for a great cut runs from wrist to elbow. George is talking to him, worrying, calling him 'Dickon' and 'my dear'. It's not for George the traitor to do that.

'Richard.'

'Martin. You're wounded?'

'No. Bashed about; it's nothing. Richard, thank God you are safe. Let me see that arm.' The cut was deep, gaping. There was no jetting blood, however, and he could move his hand; the blade had missed the great blood vessels and sinews.

Hearing me, the King loomed over us. He swore, and told me to take Richard to the surgeon's tent. 'Dickon, you were beyond praise, I knew I was right to give you the van. Thank you. George, my thanks to you too. Will, you were magnificent.' I doubt if Richard heard. Hastings nodded, too exhausted for talk. I bent to help Richard to his feet but the King said, 'Martin, you've a whacking bruise on your brow. Go with Richard, be sure the doctors tend you.'

Outside the surgeon's tent I recognised Lord Say lying on a litter. His squire wept beside him, and the question did not have to be asked. Richard looked down, his face full of sorrow. 'He was a good man. A good fighter.'

'Do you know John Milwater is dead?'

'Yes. I saw him go down. And Tom Parr, God assoil them both.'

The King's own doctor, Doctor Hobbes, came to help Richard. He had the unusual qualification of being both a surgeon and a physician; after years as surgeon with the army he had managed to get himself accepted for what the profession considered the higher trade of physician. He inspected me, moved my head gently, asked about double vision and nausea, and passed me fit. I could not watch some of the sights in that tent, my worst nightmares. Nor could I look too closely as Doctor Hobbes tweezed shreds of cloth from Richard's wound. When he reached for a great curved needle George turned green and bolted, but I managed to stay, and stay on my feet. Richard couldn't watch it either, so I held his hand and we stared resolutely into each other's eyes till it was over. Doctor Hobbes poured wine over the wound to cleanse it, and I thought Richard would pass out. I drew his head against my shoulder until the bandaging was done, then we were out of there as fast as we could go.

Outside Francis said, 'There's sad news. I'm sorry. Lord Warwick is dead, his brother John too.'

For two years I had schooled myself to think of Warwick impersonally as an enemy, but this news hurt. After all, Warwick had been kind to me, educated me. And I had liked John Neville for his kindness and modesty, his steadfastness.

Richard said dully, 'How'd they die, in the battle?'

Francis's hazel eyes slid sideways. His voice shaking he said, 'After. Warwick was unhurt. He saw the day was lost and he tried to get to the horses back behind their reserve. Impossible to run in full armour. Our men caught him. John tried, I think, to save him. They were both killed. Richard, I used your name, I put men to guard their bodies. Our men were – taking vengeance. Rob is there.'

'Thank you, Francis. I – will you two come with me?' It was a request, not an order, but of course we went to where the two bodies lay. The King was there, looking down expressionless. Clarence knelt nearby, vomiting. No wonder, for I won't write down details of how best to kill a man in armour once you have got him on the ground and lift his visor. I saw Richard's lips move in prayer, and I tried to pray too, but all I could think of was, 'Lord have mercy.' I suppose it was as good as anything.

Edward stirred. *'Seulement Un'* – his motto. 'Ah well, the wheel turns. George, arrange a wagon, have them taken with all good care to London, to St Paul's Church. Come, my friends.'

When they stripped John Neville's body of his armour, they found he had fought for his brother wearing Edward's badge, concealed.

And that was the battle of Barnet, as it came to be called, fought on Easter Sunday the fourteenth day of April in the year 1471.


London gave us a reception that made Thursday's seem like a polite murmur, though in truth I was too tired and aching to enjoy it. That day and evening I swung between the euphoria of victory, and a bleak sorrow that came close to sickness. Battle-deaths might be no murder, but only a brute could be unmoved. My friends felt the same; there was relief, but none of the high spirits I had expected. None of us could talk of anything else, however, and over supper we pieced together the day's action, the shape of the battle.

The fact is that, as I had thought, at the start in the darkness we had formed up too far to our right. Warwick's army wasn't evenly across the road; only part of Exeter's wing had been to our right. So we had formed up more or less with Edward's centre facing Warwick's left, and our right was way off to the side, on the lip of Dead Man's Bottom. Thus, when Richard's wing fought its way back up out of the hollow we made an inadvertent flank attack on Exeter's extreme left. Over on our left, Hastings had been attacking not the enemy right as he thought but the right part of their centre. Oxford, driving forward, had found, like Richard, no enemy before him and had wheeled left and fallen on Hastings' unprotected left flank. And routed it. Hastings' men broke and fled, running frantically back through Barnet Town – some got as far as London with the news that the King had been defeated. Then Oxford's men gave up chasing the deserters and charged back into the battle. However, the two flank attacks had swung the whole battle-line about so that it ran north-south instead of east-west. Thus Oxford's men fell not on the

King's but on their own – in the poor light Oxford's Star-with-Streamers banner was confused with the King's Sun in Splendour. It seemed like treachery when half of Oxford's force saw the other half attacking it, and they did much damage to themselves before any order could be brought. Then Hastings' men rallied, the precious reserve was used, and Edward fought like a lion in the centre. Over on our right Richard's wing savaged Exeter's. And so through valiant fight and confusion, the battle went to our side.

The next day we heard that the Lancastrians had landed at Weymouth on the very day of the battle. Hearing of Warwick's death, Margaret of Anjou had been all for going back to France, but her son and advisers over-ruled her. There was no sure news of their numbers, but over the next day or two we heard they were apparently marching on London, gathering a sizeable army as they came. Jasper Tudor was in Wales, and he would be able to raise thousands of men there. We had to stop the two forces joining up.

Lady Warwick had fled into sanctuary at Beaulieu when she heard of her husband's death. No one knew what had become of Anne Neville.

We celebrated St George's Day at Windsor, then began the march to meet the Lancastrians. Once started, we set a cracking pace, for word came in that men of the West Country were flocking in their thousands to the enemy banners. Any venture towards London had been but a feint, Margaret of Anjou was said to be heading for Wales where she would join up with Jasper Tudor and his force. She had gone to Bristol, I don't know why, but when she heard of our advance she headed in our direction. Or so we were told. On May the second they were said to be nearly at Sodbury Hill and ready to meet us in the field. Margaret's chief captains were the Duke of Somerset, Lord Wenlock who two years before had kept Warwick out of Calais, the Earl of Devon, and, of course, her martial son.

The weather was more like high summer than spring, clear and hot: bad weather for moving an army at speed. Gratefully we pitched camp on Sodbury Hill, and the moment we had eaten the entire army fell into an exhausted sleep. Not for long. At three in the morning our scouts pelted back to tell us we had been duped and the Lancastrians were racing through the night for Gloucester. They were heading for Wales, as probably they had meant to do all along.

'And we are not going to let them,' said the King. 'We must stop them crossing the Severn. Jasper Tudor has thousands of men, we'll be outnumbered two to one if he joins that mad bitch. Richard, send Gloucester Herald with mine, tell the Governor of Gloucester he is to keep the enemy out, I don't care what it takes. She won't have time to set a siege so tell the Governor to bar the gates, fire on her, whatever is necessary. If they let her through I'll burn that city to the ground and dance in the ashes. Tell the Governor I am not a day away and he is to hold to the last man. Get going!'

The heralds raced for their horses, and we set about waking our men and getting the army moving. Grumbling, hot, foot-sore, the men fell in, and by four we were on the move. It was a race – the next Severn crossing after Gloucester was Tewkesbury, and we had to reach it first.

I still dream about that day's march. Jesu, it was hot. We began in full armour, but by ten in the morning it was strip or be boiled alive; more literally, die of heat stroke. Even brigandines were torture enough with their chain-mail sleeves and metal plates between two layers of leather. By midday we were a motley crew, sleeves rolled up, men marching bare to the waist with their shirts bound around their heads, here and there some stalwart, red as a lobster in remnants of mail. One group marched blithely in nothing but boots and braes, and I wished dignity would let me join them. The Lancastrians travelled along the low ground, and foul country it was, all lanes and ditches and woods. But I think they had the best of it, for we took the higher ground with nary an inch of shade or whisper of breeze. There was no water, no fodder for the horses. Once we came to a brook and our horses smelt the water and damn' near bolted. So did our poor men, but the baggage wagons churned up the shallow stream so much that by the time the vanguard had crossed, the water was little more than mud, so fouled it was undrinkable. Men drank it just the same; it was that or die. I would have sold my soul for a mug of cold ale – a safe offer for there was no drink but the dirty half pint in my flask. I should have kept my gloves on, for my hands were so sunburnt I could hardly grip the reins. We were all burnt red except where sweat mingled with dust.

Gloucester held against the Lancastrians. The scouts galloped back to tell us the Governor had barred the gates and primed his cannon, and from his walls defied Queen Margaret. She couldn't believe it. They say she was near demented, raving in French (a tactful touch that had the townspeople jeering). She was all for besieging the city for daring to defy her, but her captains bundled her onto her horse and dragged her away raving. On to Tewkesbury.

Pushed, an army can do thirty miles in a day. We did more than that, in weather more like Spain or France than England in May. Men were shambling with exhaustion, horses dropped in their tracks – but we kept going, for we had the enemy in sight and they were a bare five miles away and clearly in a worse state than us. The scent of victory kept us going – and the King. I saw that day why men would always follow York's sons, for Edward and Richard (and even, credit where it's due, Clarence), led their men as if it was the greatest game on earth. The darker Richard suffered less from the sun, but Edward and George were badly burnt, and we all sweated off several pounds that day. But they kept their spirits up, they laughed and made jokes as they rode, they cantered back and forth along the lines cheering the men on with that inspired mixture of praise and wittily foul abuse that'll keep soldiers going. It worked, not least because the men saw their commanders sharing every hardship. (The King of England with a wet handkerchief knotted round his head is a picture I'll treasure to my dying day.)

But for all the royal men and we company leaders could do, the army was on its last legs. We would be lucky to get five more miles.

But we did not have to. At Cheltenham our scouts reported that the enemy army had closed on Tewkesbury and there had given up. Queen Margaret could throw all the tantrums she liked, her army could go no further. Battle, if battle there would be, now would be fought outside Tewkesbury.

At this our men took heart. Edward had held back food and drink for precisely this, and once we had refreshed ourselves we moved on, quite briskly now the end was in sight, and pitched our camp for the night three miles from the enemy. Edward stood high in the stirrups so every man could see him, and shouted, 'Well done!' at the top of his voice. I daresay Henry V was more eloquent, but no more effective. Then our sunburnt, tired, filthy King went into his tent and was asleep straight away. It was the same with all of us.

Again Richard led the vanguard, but this time we were on the left. Again the King commanded the centre with George behind with the reserve, and Hastings had the rearguard over on our right. It was foul land for a battle. Perhaps I should draw a little map, but I'm no artist, so I shall describe it and let you picture it in your mind.

See a ridge of high ground running east-west. Place on it the Lancastrian army facing south. On their left is a stream attractively named Swillbrook. On their right, a woody hill. At their backs, the town of Tewkesbury and its abbey. Further back on their right, a slope down to the Avon. In front of them, and in front of us, is a patch of uneven land cut by lanes and ditches, hedges and little hills. Filthy territory for a battle, but that was where the Lancastrian army had collapsed the night before, and we were giving them no chance to move.

We attacked at first light. The vanguard had the fun of discovering just how impossible the terrain was. We couldn't get near the enemy, so we held back and left it to our archers and cannon. We were facing Somerset on their right, and he made a flank attack, sneaking round under cover of the little hill on our left wing. Damn near took us by surprise, too, but we rallied, re-formed our lines to face them, and fought. Barnet all over again: press forward, slashing, hacking, making what ground is possible. Time passes – hours? Can't tell.

I go down and this time I'm dead, I see the axe come down. Then it is gone. Richard is there, standing over me and up goes his sword and my killer is gone too, he's down, bleeding, his head half off his shoulders. I hear, 'Are you safe?' and I shout 'Yes,' because after all I am, and Richard hauls me up and I'm back into it.

Fight on: Somerset is falling back. Then the group of spearsmen Edward had hidden on that hill rush down on Somerset, making enough din for an army. It works, Somerset's lines break, they're running. We chase them across the meadow down towards the Avon, and it's a massacre. The King crashes forward with the centre and Richard's trumpets order us right, onto the naked right flank of the enemy centre. I see the Lancaster prince, he must think it's a tourney, see his pretty gilded harness and his decorated armour. And what is happening, that's Somerset riding up to him, up to Lord Wenlock, he's screaming in fury that Wenlock should have supported his attack on our left. And, Jesu, he lifts his axe and hits Wenlock, cleaves his skull with one blow, I see the two halves of Wenlock's head flop apart. And that's it, the Lancastrians see their leaders butchering each other and they have had enough, they're retreating, running, and now we are after them full pelt, our whole army, and the enemy is no longer an army but a fleeing rabble. The Swillbrook ran red, and now they call that slope down to the Avon 'Bloody Meadow'.

Many of the rebels took shelter in the Abbey. Still lit with the fury of battle, the King charged after them and pounded on the closed doors. The abbot came out and looked up at his King. Brave man, he said, 'You will not defile the Lord's house with slaughter. My son, be merciful. These men within have sought sanctuary here. They are under my protection.'

'This church has no Papal Bull giving sanctuary rights, Father. But I offer pardon to the men within. They need have no fear. Look.' He cast aside his weapons, signing to the rest of us to do the same. 'Father, I seek only to list the men within. There will be no killing in God's house. Step aside, I pray you.'

With a resigned little gesture the Abbot obeyed. The church held that metallic smell of blood, and in the dim light we saw some hundreds of men slumped in the posture of defeat.

'Who's that?' the King said, and strode forward. 'Somerset?'

'Yes.'

'And have the rest of your captains scurried here? Ah yes, I see them. Traitors. What of your prince?'

Somerset's face twisted. 'Surely you know? He is dead.' Edward's face didn't change. 'Clarence's men overtook him as we fled. Cut him down.'

'That's the way of battle. Where is he?' Somerset waved a limp hand and we went to where a priest crouched beside a tomb, cradling a dead body. Margaret's Edouard wasn't pretty any more.

'Is it he?' Edward asked Richard.

'Yes.'

'So, the end of Lancaster. My lord Abbot, I pray you see he is given proper burial.' He raised his voice to fill the church. 'For the common soldiers, my offer of pardon stands, you need have no fear. But you, Somerset, and the other leaders, have rebelled against my lawful rule and you will pay the penalty. Traitors die, Somerset.' With that he turned about and left the abbey.

On Monday, the sixth day of May, Richard put on his Constable's robes and with the Duke of Norfolk, Marshal of England, proclaimed the death sentence on Somerset and a dozen others. They were beheaded in Tewkesbury marketplace.


But that wasn't quite the end. At Coventry news came that the Bastard of Fauconberg was attacking London. (This gentleman, as his name suggests, was the illegitimate son of Lord Fauconberg, one of Warwick's kinsmen.) London held valiantly, Anthony Rivers and Lord Essex drove Fauconberg back, and when the King sent a small detachment of his army, Fauconberg scuttled off to Sandwich.

On our third day at Coventry, Sir William Stanley sent word that he had found Margaret of Anjou and some of her ladies in a nunnery across the Severn.

'I must see her,' Edward said without enthusiasm. 'I hope her son's death has convinced her that her cause is dead, but she has to understand. Women have no place in war ... What is she like?' He had never seen her.

Remembering Ludlow, Richard said, 'A virago. Proud as the devil. Very French. Adored her son.'

'Hmm. Well, Stanley's bringing her in tomorrow.' Miserably he repeated, 'I must see her.'

The back window of Richard's bedroom overlooked the courtyard. The following morning, dressing, we gathered there, curiosity overcoming good taste, to see Margaret of Anjou brought in.

Stanley had put her in a common baggage cart. She was a haggard, greying wreck in a filthy gown, her eyes staring sightlessly, dribble running from a slack mouth. Did I pity her? No. Oh – honour her belief in her husband's rights, understand her grief for her son, yes. But for the rest, fuck the bitch. She was pathetic now, even pitiable, but she had shown England no pity.

The cart rattled to a halt out of our sight. Behind it came a group of mounted men guarding a pale girl. It was Anne Neville. *Guarding* her – what need, what could she do? No, those men were to blazon her new status as prisoner, one of the defeated rebels. Little Anne.

The horse they had given her was far too big for her, a war-horse, and the brute was fighting her every inch of the way. Her hair was bundled in a coarse linen snood of the kind servants wear, and her horrible black gown, mourning for her father and uncle, had been borrowed from some much bigger woman. She was dusty and travel-stained, she was trying to keep her place on a man's saddle – and she rode with her head high and her face resolute. The Lady Anne Neville. I think that's when Richard fell finally and forever in love with her.

Stanley called the halt. One of his men told Anne to get down. She looked around.

'Is no one to help me dismount?'

'Rebels don't get waited on, so no, there is no one to help you dismount.' Viciously accurate, Stanley imitated Anne's aristocratic voice with its sweet underlying hint of Yorkshire. 'Get down or fall down, it's all one to me.'

I doubt Anne had ever in her life dismounted unassisted. There was no mounting block, and that horse would have been too high for the average man. As she swung her leg over the horse's rump her skirts got caught up, and for a moment she was revealed bare to the hip. Stanley's men laughed, and one shouted a filthy remark and pumped his hips obscenely.

Richard vaulted the windowsill down into the yard and flattened that man with the sweetest right hook I have ever seen. Another took an elbow to the groin, and waddled away. I think Stanley's men had not recognised Richard; he had reached only the shirt and boots stage of dressing, he hadn't been shaved or brushed his hair, and he looked scruffy and insignificant. I arrived just in time to stop Stanley drawing his sword.

Anne was still struggling off that horse. Gently Richard clasped her waist and set her on her feet.

'Anne ...'

'Richard!'

'Your Grace ...' stammered Stanley. It was pretty to see him writhe.

'The King sent you to bring this lady *with courtesy* to him. Watch yourself, Sir William.'

Anne was staring transfixed at Richard. 'Lady Anne, the King has sent for you to – to see you're safe and – and cared for. I regret the treatment you have had, and so will the King.' Fury made his eyes blaze like sapphires. 'Please, won't you come inside? Look, here's Martin, and Rob, and Francis.' He held out his arm as if they were at Court.

Inside, Anne's composure crumbled and she burst into tears. Out came four handkerchiefs and we clustered round her, patting and petting her like children. Well, three of us did – Richard held back looking noble, glowering; I think he dared not let himself touch her.

'Lovey, hinny,' crooned Rob, and I suppose they were the first loving words Anne had heard in days – months – for she sank her head on his shoulder and frankly bawled. 'Don't cry, pet, it's all right, you're safe. There now, there hinny.'

'Yes – sorry – stupid of me –' Anne gave her nose a good honking blow and mopped her eyes. 'I'm better now. Thank you.' She offered Rob his kerchief back; he declined it. 'M-must I see the King?' Anne asked.

'Blossom, yes, but he only wants to greet you and know you are safe, nothing to be afraid of. Er – you'll want to wash and tidy up … There are few women here but I can find a maid.'

'Take her to our room,' I said. 'With all of us there it'll be quite proper. Besides,' I remembered, 'I'm married, I can chaperone her.'

'Married?' Anne blinked. 'Martin, when? I didn't know.'

'Recently.' To say: 'In Burgundy,' would have been too sharp a reminder. 'Come along, lovey, let's get you tidied up.'

Fairly incompetent lady's maids, we beat the dust from her gown and offered combs. More practically, Richard got pages to bring fresh water and towels. I don't know how women do it, but with a quick wash and her hair pinned up, the pathetic, grubby girl had gone and Anne looked fit to meet every monarch in Europe. She shot me a glance, and with married propriety I got rid of the others and showed her to the garderobe, discreetly asking if she had any other needs (she still looked so pale it might have been her female time). No she hadn't, but, emerging and rinsing her hands she said, 'Is the King – will he be – I know everything is different now. I am a traitor's daughter and a traitor's wife. So the King – Martin, I've always been afraid of him.'

'Don't be. He bears you no ill will. None of this is your fault. Edward only wants to look after you.'

'Oh. Good. How kind of him.' But she didn't look convinced.

Richard had brushed his hair and finished dressing. Again he offered Anne his arm, and we conducted her to the King's room.

I don't know what had passed between him and Margaret of Anjou, but Edward looked both haunted and as if he had been through another battle. Clad in one of his elaborate long gowns he sat with his hands on his knees, staring at Anne – his mind elsewhere, I think he hardly recognised her.

'Lady Anne.'

'Your Grace.' Knees trembling she swept him a perfect Court curtsy. His face softened.

'Cheer up, cousin, I know you're tired and heart-sore, but it is over now. Here, sit down. I'm sure one of your escort here can find some wine; hop to it, Francis. Lady Anne, do you know Martin is *Sir* Martin now? And a married man?'

'I didn't know he was knighted, Sire. Martin, I'm glad, my congratulations.'

The wine came. We all drank. 'Do you know your mother is still in Beaulieu, Lady Anne?'

The cup in her hand began to shake. 'No. That is, I supposed so. Is she safe?'

'Quite safe, and well so far as I know. You did not think of staying with her?'

'Your Grace, I had no choice. I was in Margaret's household, I had to go where she did.'

'You don't mean,' Edward said incredulously, 'that that demented bitch dragged you across England with her army? Through that ghastly day's march?'

'Yes, Sire.'

'Well of all the … Were you close to the battle?' Anne nodded. 'I'm sorry, sweeting; no sight for ladies. Er – you know your – the prince is dead?'

'Yes.' One cold little word.

'I see. And what happened after the battle? To you, I mean.'

'Sire, Margaret saw what happened. She knew her son was dead and I think her mind broke. She would have run to him … Doctor Morton, I think it was, got her and found a boat to take us across the river, he got us – Margaret and me and some of her ladies – to that nunnery. Then,' she spread her hands, 'we didn't know what to do. So we waited.'

'Edward,' said Richard, 'Sir William Stanley and his men treated Anne badly, they insulted her and spoke foully. See to it, will you?' Anne shot him a wondering look; it was new to her that he had the right to order the King so casually.

'I will – though that's the Stanleys for you, coarse brutes the lot of them. I'm sorry, cousin. Now – we leave for London in a day or two, I thought you'd like to go to your sister.'

'I suppose so.' Anne stared down into her wine. 'I mean, yes of course I want to be with Isabel, I haven't seen her for so long. Yes please, if it suits Your Grace.'

'Good. Good. And I hope your lady mother will soon join you. George is somewhere about, I'll put you in his charge. If ever you – er – need anything, I am at your command.'

It was a dismissal. Anne curtsied again, and we rose to take her away. 'Richard,' the King said pleasantly, 'stay behind if you will. There's business to discuss, more news from London. I'll see you later, Lady Anne.'

By no coincidence, the King's business kept Richard busy most of the day. Late in the afternoon, when she had had time to rest, I went to ask Anne if she would care for a walk. 'Or a ride? Whatever you'd like?' She hesitated, but George, coming in behind me, seconded me.

'Do, dear, it will do you good. And I know! – Richard's finished his important business with the King, I think he's looking for you, I saw him go into that end room just now. Rout him out and take him with you, that's the thing!'

I should have known. Clarence never had an altruistic impulse in his life.

In that end room Richard was embracing a pretty red-haired lady who wept on his shoulder. On his knee sat a bright-eyed little boy whose paternity was all too obvious. When they saw us, it would be a brave man who said they didn't look guilty.

'Martin!' cried Jenny.

'Anne!' cried Richard.

'Jenny!' I cried.

'Lady Anne!' cried Jenny.

'Ang!' cried little John, eager to help.

I caught up with Anne in the corridor. She absolutely, definitely was not crying, no not she. 'Anne, hinny, don't! It's nothing, it's not …'

'Quite right. His Grace of Gloucester's *private affairs*' (she made it sound like necromancy) 'are nothing to me. I was merely embarrassed at intruding upon him with his *whore*.'

'Oh, Anne. She's no whore. Innogen is my wife.'

Furious colour surged up her face. 'Martin, forgive me. But – that baby is …'

'Ah yes, now *he is* Richard's. His name's John.'

'But – Oh. Ah. Um …'

'Say it.'

'If she'd been his mistress and borne his child, how could you marry her?'

I leaned against the window embrasure. 'I love Jenny; she loves me. About a hundred years ago when we were all young, yes she was briefly Richard's lover. The child – well, these things happen. And where's the difference from marrying a widow? After all, I came to her with many women in my past.'

I could see the question, 'How many?' trembling on Anne's lips, but she was an adult now, she had learnt discretion. Warwick had reared his daughters strictly, protecting them from the dirt and muddle of ordinary people doing their best; perhaps it was time she faced some new realities.

'My dear, you can torture yourself with jealousy, or you can tell yourself the past is the past and you are the one in possession. I think Richard loves you, and I think you love him.' She looked away, her eyes veiled. 'Well, that's between the two of you – but did you think he's inexperienced? Would you want him to be? He was jealous of Prince Edward.' She blushed again, this time with that deprecating little female smirk. 'I don't know what you and Richard plan, or want, but I do know you would be the last woman in his life, and that's better than the first. But there have been others; accept that. And there is John, and there's a daughter too, about the same age.'

'*Two* children!'

'There was not much to do in the spring of '69.'

'So it seems.' Suddenly we were giggling together, good friends again. I said, 'If I were you, lovey, I'd go back in there and *talk* to him.'

I daresay Innogen and Richard had been flapping their ears behind the door, for Innogen came out at that moment. 'Lady Anne, have you finished with my husband?' she asked cheerfully.

'Yes,' Anne said in the same tone, 'and now I shall go and talk with Richard.'

Shutting the door behind her Innogen said, 'I like that girl.'

'So do I, but I like you better. I love you so much. Come here and kiss me, and tell me what you do here.'

Her arms around my neck Innogen said, 'Sweeting, they told me you were wounded, that's why I was sobbing all over Richard, he was the first person I met and he told me you were safe, and the *relief* ...'

'And you disobeyed me, I told you to stay in Burgundy until I sent for you.'

'Well,' she said, 'I was an obedient wife and waited there, in fact Duchess Margaret had me stay with her, and together we read the letters, we heard of the battle of Barnet, and then, well, I could wait no longer, I couldn't bear to be on the other side of the Channel from you.' Looking as if butter wouldn't melt in her mouth she said, 'Duchess Margaret bade me come, and you would not have me disobey a royal command?' Not for the first time I thought what a clever woman I had married. And a beautiful one. Why were we standing here in this corridor when there was a bed not far away? 'Oh dear, I left John's nursemaid somewhere back on the road, some inn, I don't even know where, she couldn't stand the pace I set. Perhaps it sounds silly but I brought John because if you were – if there was bad news, it would be some comfort to have him ... But darling, are you hurt?' For I'd flinched when she ran her hands through my hair.

'Only bruises. Perfectly fit to take you to bed, my darling.'

'Yes?'

And we were locked in a knee-trembling, head-spinning embrace when the King's voice behind us said, 'Whatever's – oh, it's you, Martin. Dame Robsart, how came you here?' We explained, and because no detail escaped him, Edward said, 'There was a Martin *Roberts* much wounded; someone muddled the lists. I'm sorry for your worry, my dear. And you are welcome. Well, I won't keep you when – what's that sound? A baby?'

Before we could stop him he pushed open the door and strode into that room. We followed, awash with apprehension. But whatever Richard and Anne had been up to – and her hair was ruffled, his shirt band awry – now they were placidly chatting from far sides of the room, Anne in the chair, Richard by the window. With what even to my inexperienced ears was temper, John grizzled at Richard's feet.

'Ah,' said the King. 'Richard, Anne. Who is this little boy?'

'My son.' Innogen picked him up.

So rarely at a loss, Edward put his big foot right in it. 'Yours, madam? But he looks like Richard!'

'There's a reason for that.'

'Then I have completely misread this situation. Richard, I thought it was a daughter you had?'

'I have. As well.'

Demurely inspecting her fingernails Anne said, 'There was little to do in the spring of '69,' and I had the satisfaction of seeing Edward look as if he'd missed the last stair. Then he roared with laughter.

'That would explain much. Well, come here, youngster.' Confidently he swung John up in the air. 'You're a fine little fellow, aren't you! Hello, pet, I'm your uncle.' John grinned. 'Well, well. Is your daughter as pretty, Richard?'

'Of course!' Innogen glared. '– not.'

'Well, he's a fine boy. How old is he? Fifteen months, excellent! Name? John. Very good. And very wet. Go to your mother, pet. Well, Richard, I had hoped we could get on with that business, if Lady Anne will excuse you now?'

Anne rose and curtsied, but Richard said, 'Edward, I want your permission to marry Anne.'

'Then want must be your master.'

'Edward!'

'Now look, Richard. It is not Anne herself, of course not, it's *who* she is. Warwick's daughter, the prince's widow. It won't do. No, Richard.'

'You married for love and it was no more suitable.' A flush of temper mantled Edward's face. 'Or is it "do as I say, not do as I do"?'

Scarlet now, the King said, 'I take that talk from no one, Richard.'

'Well, you're taking it from me.' Richard might have been telling him the time. 'Your Grace, I have followed you and served you for love. You have given me much and I have never asked you for anything. Now I am asking you for this. Let me marry Anne, and give me Middleham.'

Narrow-eyed Edward said, 'Middleham was Warwick's. His estates revert to the crown under attainder. Who gets what, if any, of his lands is up to me.'

'I know. Unlike George.'

'Your meaning?'

'He expects to receive all Warwick's estate. He says it's his by right.'

'Does he just.' Cold anger vibrated in Edward's voice. Innogen had her arm around Anne, frowning. 'Well, if you want that godforsaken patch of Yorkshire I daresay you can have it. But you can forget Anne.'

Possibly I was the only one who realised quite how angry Richard was. Edward still didn't know his brother; and I wondered if he really knew how much he owed him. Icily Richard said, 'And if I don't?'

'You will.' Silence. Almost pleadingly Edward said, 'Richard, see it. Not her. Anyone but her. I need your marriage for international alliance.'

'You have children for that.'

Incredulously Edward stared. He swung around on Anne. 'You were the prince's true wife?'

'Y-yes, Sire.'

'When did you last lie with him?'

Poor Anne had never been asked so intrusive, so personal, a question in her life. She was lucky Edward hadn't been a good deal blunter. Almost soundlessly she answered, 'The – the night before the battle of Tewkesbury.'

Richard made a sound in his throat as if she had hit him, and gloatingly Edward said, 'How can you want to marry her if you're squeamish as a girl about the facts? Perhaps you should ask Martin to instruct you!'

Innogen, Anne and I did nothing more useful than gasp with outrage. In a voice that would have etched glass, Richard said, 'That, Edward, is going very much too far. Apologise to my friends.'

Edward had the decency to look ashamed, and he said very gracefully, 'Martin, Dame Robsart, yes, that was unforgivable. I apologise. But Richard, see it – what if Anne is pregnant?'

There was no answer to that. Sheet-white, Anne looked piteously at Richard. Innogen said, 'Then best marry them at once, Your Grace, and pass the child off as Richard's.' Which was hard, political good sense.

Anne said, 'No!' in a whisper.

'No!' said Edward. He was no longer the man who had laughed at Anne's joke and played with the baby. This was the King, a cold, hardheaded, calculating monarch to whom no personal loyalty mattered. 'I will have no more Lancastrian uprisings. Lancaster is dead.'

'I will marry Anne on those terms,' Richard said.

'Very noble. I forbid it. Any child born to Lady Anne within the next nine months will be said to be Lancaster's and used as a focus for rebellion. Or murdered. I would prefer not to see my brother's child treated so.'

Throwing up her hands Innogen cried, 'Then wait! Sire, let me take Lady Anne down to Kent with me. Or abroad. She can live in seclusion until we know. If there is a child it can be fostered out, the whole thing can be kept a secret.'

'No.'

'Edward,' said Richard, more placatingly now, 'if there is no child, will you think again?'

I saw the King's lips framing the word no, and said, because someone had to, 'Your Grace, you knighted me and let me marry Innogen for much less than Richard has done for you. And he has never once wavered. Very well, he's your brother – but while you dole out titles and lands and rewards to others, will you refuse him the one thing he has ever asked for?'

I could see myself begging my bread around Europe, a death warrant on my head. Or writing poetry in the Tower of London. Very long poetry. But Edward let out a gusty sigh and said, 'I will go thus far: I won't forbid the marriage yet. Wait until we know whether there is a child. If not, we'll see. I promise nothing, and you are to do nothing. Is that understood? All of you?'

'Yes, Your Grace.'

'Good. Anyway, Richard, you will be too busy for a while to think of marriage. The Scots are boiling up on the border, I want you up there as soon as that arse Fauconberg's dealt with. Anne can go to her sister. The Warwick estates are in my gift and no one has a right to one inch of them or a single groat except at my will.'

'Tell George, not me.'

'Oh, I will. And be advised, say nothing to him about marrying Anne. And now good-day to you all.'

I once stood too close to a cannon being fired. It was much the same feeling. Anne was in tears, sobbing that it was hopeless, that she'd take the veil …

Richard strolled over and kissed the top of her head. 'Cheer up. That was more or less a yes.'

'It was?'
'You'll see.'

# *Eight*

I have nearly finished this part of my story. But for Clarence, it would be finished, I could deal in two lines with Richard and Anne marrying, and then a happy ending.

Before I go on, I must speak of the death of Henry VI. The night after we returned to London poor old Henry died in the Tower. Of course everyone believed Edward had had him murdered, for it was such a convenient death, the end of Lancaster indeed. I remembered Edward saying at Coventry, 'Lancaster is dead,' and I wondered if it was only in hindsight the words had had a sinister emphasis. And make no mistake, Edward was quite ruthless enough to bump the poor old boy off. Although it was given out that he had died of melancholy, people who saw his body whispered of a fractured skull. It occurs to me that one person who would have done the murder and whistled while he worked was the Queen's son Tom Grey – but there, that is only a comment on Thomas, not an accusation, and I can't remember if he was even at that night's council meeting at the Tower.

In fairness to Edward, however, I must say that although convenient, it was perhaps not such a surprising death. Henry was fifty, and frail; and he had that night learnt that his throne was lost, his wife was a witless prisoner, his son dead. Could he not therefore have taken a heart seizure or stroke and, falling, hit his head? But there, I don't know. It all appeared very pat – and if Edward was ruthless, he was also subtler than that. And, too, he would have had to face his mother and Richard, neither of whom would have condoned murder. So let's leave it at the plain statement that Henry died. He was buried at Chertsey, and a curious belief grew up among the simple people that illness could be cured by making an offering at his grave, as if he were a saint. And I believe that wretched charity school he founded near Slough struggles on.

We were only briefly in Kent, for by the time the King joined us Fauconberg had given himself up. Riding back to London I felt a weariness and lassitude I'd never before experienced. All the strain of the last two months – really, of almost two years – caught up with me and, like a bow too long strung, my mind and body were demanding release. The wars were over, but there was no exhilaration now, only weariness. It was the same for Richard, and more so because his responsibility had been greater. For the past few days we had been snapping at each other like fretful children, and as we rode onto London Bridge he could hardly raise a smile for the people who came out to hail him. London is at her best in summer, but for once her beauty had no power to charm me. Only our training kept us straight in the saddle; when I briefly shut my eyes against the dazzle of the sun on the Thames I very nearly fell asleep. I daresay the King was in the same case, for I saw his head nod once or twice, and he kept shifting in his saddle. We rode down Thames Street, and by Baynard's Castle Edward halted.

'Your Grace,' he said to Richard, formal in front of our men, 'we will confer at Westminster tomorrow. For now, good-day to you.'

'What?'

Edward lowered his voice. 'Richard – we are at Baynard's. Go to Mother, give her my good greetings, then go to bed. Martin, see that he does. I'll see you tomorrow.' He lifted his hand and rode on. Richard stared after him, too tired to understand. I took his bridle and turned his horse's head about.

'The King's order. Sleep.'

Comprehension dawning, he laughed. 'I'll gladly obey. You'll come in with me?' Innogen would be at her house in the Chepe. I longed for her, but I knew I could manage not even that short distance more without respite and a drink. Too tired to speak, I nodded and followed him into the castle's courtyard.

I seemed to have been coming home to Baynard's Castle all my life, but this was the first time we had arrived unannounced, and the hall was empty. Handing his cloak and gauntlets to the servant Richard asked for his mother. Her Grace was in her solar, we were told. The stairs seemed endless. Only the thought of a seat and a drink kept my leaden legs climbing.

'Mother, I'm – oh.'

We had walked in on a charming domestic scene. Little John on her knee, the Duchess sat under the window, Innogen beside her. Around them, George, Isabel, Anne. Wine cups stood about, a plate of honey cakes lay on the table. Flowers and dried rose petals sent out their dainty smell. Staggering amazedly about the floor, a ginger and white kitten fluffed its tail and hissed miniature defiance at us, then scampered for the safety of Innogen's lap. I could have done the same – I wanted to fold my arms around her, lay my head on her bosom and sleep forever.

'How come you here?' I asked her when we had greeted everyone. I had planned to present her formally to the Duchess when we returned; Richard and I had discussed how best to explain John to that formidable lady.

But, over-hearing, the Duchess said, 'The King told me Innogen was returned from Burgundy, so I called on her. I was anxious to meet your wife, my dear. And we have been very pleasant together, haven't we, Innogen?'

'Indeed we have, madam.' She smiled at me, sliding her hand into mine.

'You look very tired, Richard,' said Anne.

'That's probably because I am.' He meant no more than he said, but Anne took it as a snub and bit her lip in dismay. Drinking wine, Richard didn't notice.

'Dealt with dear cousin Fauconberg?' asked George, grinning.

'Yes. Took little doing. Mother, what's this kitten?' It had bounced back to the floor and was stropping its claws on his boots.

'Innogen gave it to me. You can help me think of a name for it.' Richard picked up the kitten, and for a while we all discussed names.

I saw Anne watching Richard under her lashes. He hadn't spoken to her bar that one remark, nor even looked her way. I wondered if she understood that it was only weariness that made him so uncommunicative. She looked tired too, and not very well. Black did not suit her, although her gown was stylish and flatteringly cut. Nor did Isabel look too sprightly. I hadn't seen her since the Christmas of 1469, and you would not have known her for that giggly, happy girl. Of course she had always been her father's pet, and no doubt she missed her mother, still in sanctuary at Beaulieu. It was over a year since she had lost her child on that flight to France, but she had the pinched, listless pallor of a woman who has recently miscarried, and sadly, greedily she watched John bouncing in the Duchess's arms.

She flinched when George said, 'This is a fine boy of yours, Richard. Proud of your stepson, Martin?'

The Duchess would dislike it if I punched him in the face. 'Immensely, Your Grace.'

'He seems very healthy. Bastards often are, of course. How's that daughter of yours, Richard?' I caught him looking covertly at Anne for her reaction, but even if she had not already known about Richard's children she was too well-bred to show anything but bland interest. 'Shall you have her to live with you? – I understand you've acknowledged her.'

Forcing his eyes open Richard said, 'She's with her mother's family. So, George, what have you been up to since we returned to London?' He meant, of course, *While I've been helping the King subdue his enemies.*

George flushed, but he put on a jovial face as he said, 'Oh, this and that. Looking after my two poor girls, my little blackbirds.' He patted the sisters' hands. 'Of course we don't visit much at present, but Mother was eager to see them.' Sudden doubt crossed his face: had his mother after all known Richard would return today, and planned to throw him and Anne together? He rose, bowing politely around. 'And charming though this visit has been, I think it is time for us to take our leave. Going north soon, Richard? Good luck. Mother, Dame Robsart, good-day to you.' He began to shoo Anne and Isabel toward the door. This seemed to wake Richard up. As Anne passed him he took her hand. I think she would have drawn it away but, smiling intimately up at her, he kissed her fingers and then her palm. Colour flamed in her cheeks, and the sweetest, most tender smile I have ever seen curved her lips. George made a noise like a goose and almost swept her off her feet in his haste to take her away.

'What was he doing here?' Richard demanded. Lifting her brows at his tone his mother said tartly that she was not yet accountable to him for her visitors.

'I worry about those two girls; they have had a very bad time. They're my great-nieces, after all, and while Nan persists in staying in sanctuary ... And Innogen said she had met Anne at Coventry and I thought it would do the poor child good to meet friends.' Frowning, she added, 'I didn't consider it might be tactless to have John here while Isabel visited. Poor girl, to lose her first child like that.' I remembered that the Duchess's first son had died young. Richard remembered too, for he rose and put his arms around her.

'I was ungracious. Forgive me. And Isabel has seen other children. Are you pleased with your grandson?'

'He's a beautiful child, and so like your father! And Innogen has been plain with me about him, so we shall say no more. Richard, when must you go north?'

'In a day or two.' But his mother looked at him with painful intensity, and before Innogen bent to give John his toy horse I saw the same emotion in her face.

The Duchess took Innogen's hand. 'You have married a soldier, my dear. Your life will be a succession of partings.' Sadly she went on, 'And when your sons grow up, you will spend your life saying goodbye to them too.'

'Oh, come now, Mother,' Richard unwisely expostulated, 'the wars are over now!'

The Duchess gave him a bleak blue glance. *'Tu dis?'*

Two days later we rode north to read the Scots their fortune. What applied to the Welsh and the Lancastrians went also for the Scots, and by August King Jamie was suing for a truce. In September, therefore, we were back in London, and at Baynard's Castle, where Innogen was now living with the Duchess of York. You see, back in June Innogen had written to me that she was to bear a child in December – our honeymoon, although brief, had been productive. Richard had written this news to his mother, and of her kindness the Duchess went to visit Innogen. And, apparently, took one look and whisked my wife off to her own household.

'Please don't think I am not perfectly well,' Innogen wrote, 'for I am, but the Duchess doesn't care to think of a pregnant woman alone with no female kin around her and only hired women. I don't remember my own mother, but it is very pleasant to be cosseted. So here I am, my darling, until the child is born.'

When on my arrival I tried to thank the Duchess she laughed at me and said Innogen was good company for her – 'So it is quite selfish of me, Martin. And the little boy is a delight. Wilful, though. Takes after Richard.'

'And after Jenny. You're sure she is well, madam? The baby? You didn't bring her here because you're worried?'

'Never think it! She'll give you a dozen children; good strong stock. She shall have the best midwife when the time comes, and I shall attend her childbed.' So nothing would dare go wrong. I longed to ask the Duchess if making love would do harm, but the Church teaches that it is a sin during pregnancy. Well, it would, wouldn't it? Sex is for the procreation of children, not pleasure. And the Duchess was a devout lady and might be shocked at the idea.

Innogen had no such qualms. 'Of course there's no danger. But I thought you might not want to, many men find pregnant women repellent.' Stripping me, she discovered the proof I was not among them.

'After four months on the Scottish border, my love … Oh Innogen, Jenny, darling sweet, oh Innogen …'

Afterward she held me against her breast, stroking my hair and playing with my fingers. In battle and the skirmishes on the border I had acquired a number of scars and bruises, and her clever fingers found them all out, and soothed them. She was six months' gone, and I could feel the baby moving. Looking at that splendid swelling, stroking it, I felt primitive male pride: I had done this, created this child. I was nineteen, married to my heart's love, a knight, an honoured soldier, about to be a father. Life was good.

Less good for Richard. The following day he went to visit Anne at George's house, and came home in a filthy mood, lashing the tail again. 'They said she doesn't want to see me!'

'Tell us, darling,' said the Duchess. 'And sit down, no prowling, please!' I saw Innogen hiding a grin by sorting through the sewing silks. Peering magisterially over her spectacles the Duchess asked, 'Is Anne ill?'

'Don't know. Probably not. George looked like the cat that swallowed the canary – you know, Mother.'

'Only too well. And stop kicking your chair, Richard, I trained you out of that when you were five.' The Constable and Admiral of England stopped kicking his chair. 'Perhaps Anne really doesn't want to see you.'

'Why not? Back in May she – we – I thought we had agreed to marry when we could. Has she changed her mind?' Motherless myself, I was interested to see that a man can command armies and rule vast territories yet still need his mother's reassurance.

'Well, darling – Innogen, the blue silk please – maybe she is of the same mind but needs a little time. After all, think what she's been through: her father turned traitor, and betrayed everything she was brought up to believe in – she was wrenched from her home and everything she knows then sold into marriage to ensure that betrayal – her father and uncle died, her mother bolted into Sanctuary – then Anne was dragged back with that Anjou creature, forced to watch a battle in which everyone she knows and cared for could have died – dragged a prisoner before the King. Might she not need a respite from men, and war, and politics?' She watched Richard fiddling with his rings. 'And don't fidget.' He stopped fidgeting. 'Think about it, my dear.'

'But Anne and I always have been friends; we're cousins. Surely she can be honest with me?'

'But you've changed,' Innogen said gently. 'You have no idea how different you are now. And perhaps to Anne you represent things she doesn't care to think of.'

I said, 'What did you mean about George's cat-and-canary look?'

'He's up to something. Isabel looked nervous. I can't help remembering what Edward said at Coventry. If Anne is pregnant, sorry Mother but I wouldn't put it past George to have another go at rebellion, using the child to win Lancastrian support.'

The Duchess dropped her sewing in her lap. 'Surely he wouldn't!'

'Do you really put any trust in George's commonsense? Or loyalty?' Very sadly the poor Duchess said no. 'And,' Richard went on, 'think how much support there still is for Lancaster. Louis of France would adore helping to overthrow Edward in Lancaster's name. Even a feigned child – all George has to do is keep Anne out of sight, then in a few months trumpet the birth of Prince Edward's child. And that makes Anne very dispensable.'

Aghast, the Duchess crossed herself. 'But what possible benefit would it be to George?'

'Oh, a nice long regency – he'd be Protector, sixteen years of feathering his nest – or the Lancaster heir would fail and it's King George again. Of course he'd be finished off within a month, but George never thinks that far. No one is going to rebel for his benefit.'

Innogen took the embroidery hoop and set a few swift stitches. 'When I was here last year I saw how strong the Lancaster support is; you're right, Richard. They would use poor silly George. But not for some suspect child *said* to have been born to Lady Anne, oh no. They'd focus on quite another candidate – for instance, that brat of Lady Margaret Beaufort's.'

'What, Harry Tudor?' I scoffed. 'Never!'

'Oh yes.'

'But his father was a bastard – some say Queen Katherine married her Welsh harpist, but no one believes it – and his mother's descended from a bastard. England would never see him on the throne!'

'He would do as a focus for rebellion, though.'

'Yes,' the Duchess agreed, 'and Margaret Beaufort is fanatically devoted to her son – the more so because she has lived apart from him most of his life. How old is he? Let's see … Margaret was fourteen when she bore him, so he's nearly fifteen.'

'I thought her older!' Innogen said. 'Horrible little cockroach of a woman with her airs and graces.' Then she put her hand over her mouth, blushing. 'Madam, forgive me: I forgot she is your cousin.'

'It's something I try hard to forget myself. Margaret Beaufort cuts no ice with me. But you are right, Innogen, any meddling with Lancastrian heirs makes a chance for those people. Therefore,' she began to fold away her sewing, 'I will go to the Erber tomorrow to visit George, and I will insist on seeing both Isabel and Anne. Now bring out the rest of that peculiar Scots drink you brought back, Richard, I will give it a second try.' And with that Richard had to be content.

But his mother returned the next day looking grave. Anne had sent a loving message but begged to be excused; Isabel had looked ill with misery; George smug. 'Though I doubt he is plotting rebellion. He was very bitter about you trying to get the Warwick lands, Richard. He's furious that Edward has given you so much.'

'Should have thought of that before.'

'But as you yourself say, when did George ever think? No, he is holding out for all those lands, or at least the greater share – he says it is Isabel's right as the elder sister. Oh, I know, I know – I told him it is entirely a matter for the King. In law, I think I'm right in saying, neither girl has any legal *right* to any part of their father's inheritance?' Richard nodded. 'The thing is, darling, George's nose is well and truly out of joint. He's jealous. You are the King's loyal brother, you are the clever soldier who led the vanguard in battle, you are the King's favourite and the darling of the people – and you will reap the harvest.'

'Well, yes,' said Richard coldly, 'but then, I didn't rebel, did I?'

A few days later he paid another call on Anne, taking me to show this was merely a pleasant social visit from concerned friends. Again he got only a message that she was too ill to see him.

'What's wrong with her?'

'Oh, little enough,' said George with an airy laugh. 'You know what women are.'

''Have you had a doctor to her?'

'Naturally.'

'Who? What did he say?'

'A man who has attended Isabel. And really it's none of your concern, little brother. Anne is my ward; her well-being is up to me. And perhaps you might stop to think she doesn't want to see you.'

'Then she can tell me so. In person or in writing.'

'She's too ill to be bothered. And she is no business of yours, or are you too conceited to understand that? She said you pestered her at Coventry when she was tired and low and hadn't the spirit to say she wasn't interested – so if you are counting on anything she said then, you'd better think again!'

'Indeed,' said Richard, eyeing his brother. 'But perhaps I know her better than you do, for I find that hard to believe.'

'You know,' said George, steepling his fingers, 'you're becoming as bad as Edward – can't believe any woman can resist you.'

Riding home I said, 'None of that's true – I was at Coventry, remember. And I too know Anne. She's honest and straight-forward.'

'Yes … she said she loved me, you know. I told her I loved her and I asked her to marry me, and she agreed. If she has changed her mind she'd tell me. So what is George up to?'

'Telling Anne that you have lost interest? Not telling her you've tried to see her?'

'Yes, that sounds like George. I think the time has come to see the King.'

But he got cold comfort. Perhaps Anne had changed her mind – perhaps she really wasn't well – take the advice of an older man and let the matter drop for the time being.

'By which he means he's falling over himself to keep George sweet,' snarled Richard. 'George is after that entire Warwick inheritance. Anne can't fight for what is hers, not without me – or any husband – so by keeping her and me apart George thinks to scoop the lot. He'll say it is Isabel's in right, then even if I do marry Anne it will be too late, George would never part with any of it.'

'Why not let him have it all?' Innogen suggested. 'You don't need it.'

'I want Middleham.'

'Very well, but the King's already said you can have it – make that your sole demand and tell George and the King so.'

Richard thought about it. 'But the King wants me to keep the North for him, and it's what I want too. I want to live there. Imagine what it would be like if George owned most of it? I'd always be looking over my shoulder, he'd be complaining about everything I did, if I set foot on his lands.'

'Point that out to the King.'

'I have. Anyway, why should Anne lose? I'm not asking this for myself. But I admit I don't want George to have it all. Any claim he makes for himself, in his own right or Isabel's, I'm making too. If he'll give up all claim, forever, so will I. Whether Anne would agree to that is up to her; but I will not see her cheated. What Isabel gets, she gets. What George gets, I get. But yes, Innogen, I'll repeat my offer to withdraw my claim, providing George does the same.'

The King took this well. George did not. I believe he had genuinely convinced himself he had a right to the entire Warwick inheritance, and he wasn't going to part with any of it. Morally it was Isabel and Anne and their mother who had sole right; legally, no one had but at the King's discretion. But the more George asserted his non-existent claim, the more Richard dug his toes in, and the angrier the King became. The three of them were as stubborn as each other.

'This has gone far enough,' the Duchess finally said. 'I am not interested in claims to the lands, but I am interested in Anne's welfare – and yours, darling. So I will go again to the Erber and I won't leave until I have seen Anne.'

'Tell her ...'

With a look that sent Richard right back to the nursery she said, 'I will tell her that you love her and wish to marry her and want only half her father's lands in her right. And I will ask her what her wishes are in the matter.'

She came back from the Erber in a rare old temper. I'd not have liked to be in George's shoes, for it seemed he had given her a mouthful of cheek and told her to mind her own business.

'But did you see Anne?'

'No. And he was very odd about it, and Isabel looked like her own ghost. I will speak to the King. And you will not accompany me, Richard.'

But a lady cannot go unescorted about London – I went with her, and somehow I insinuated myself into the King's audience chamber. I felt quite sorry for Edward – he could fight both his brothers, but not his mother. In the end he commanded George to bring Anne forthwith to him, for the whole matter to be settled there and then.

And George looked the King coolly in the eye and said he could not fetch Anne because she had left his house. 'You have said I have no guardian's rights over her; I have washed my hands of her. She chose to leave my house and my care. I have no idea where she is. If Richard wants her so badly, let him find her.'

And from that there was no budging him. Nothing the King threatened produced any different answer. George neither knew nor cared where Anne was. She had chosen to leave his house – that was the end of the matter.

But where had Anne gone? She could not have had much money. She would have no idea where to hire a horse. Nevertheless we asked at every livery stable, we asked every Thames boatman. Richard sent to Lady Warwick down at Beaulieu, to Warwick Castle, to Middleham, to Calais where Anne had lived as a small child, even to Margaret in Burgundy. He sent to the Duke and Duchess of Suffolk, less because Elizabeth of Suffolk was his sister than because the Duke had recently bought Francis Lovell's wardship from the King, and Francis was living, reluctantly, with the Suffolks at Wingfield. He sent to every port. But for the need for discretion we could have had Anne cried in every town in England and at every Cross in London; as it was we could only speak carefully to the Mayor and Watch. And speaking of care, Rob Percy and I went secretly to every inn and brothel, where many a girl has ended up through her innocence. George had been made Lieutenant of Ireland, so enquiries were sent even there.

October became November. November passed. No trace of Anne.

There was plague in the city.

Then except as Anne's friend I lost all but a remote interest in the matter, for on the second day of December Innogen went into labour. Of course men have no part in child-birth, nor did I want to have, for I suspected battle was one thing but seeing one's wife going through the torture of labour quite another. I had no idea how long a birth took; Innogen had said of John's that it was the usual thing, and when I dared ask if it hurt she'd said only, Yes. I had heard ghastly stories of women labouring for days only to produce a dead child or to die themselves.

'Nonsense!' said the Duchess when she came downstairs after the first few hours. 'We have all heard these stories, but Innogen is doing very well.' She kissed me as if I were her own child. 'I had twelve, my dear, and I've helped at many births, including yours, so believe me when I say there is nothing to fear. Richard, make yourself useful and give Martin a drink – several; your father always did.'

Richard gave me a drink. It didn't help much. It was ten hours since Innogen had been sure she was starting. Eleven hours. Then I heard a baby's cry, and the Duchess swept into the hall, beaming all over her face.

'All is well. It's a girl, the loveliest big healthy girl you ever saw! You may come in, very briefly, to see them.'

The room had the metallic smell of blood. It was stifling hot, for cold air is dangerous to a labouring woman or a newborn. I had expected Innogen to be unconscious, but she was sitting back against her pillows, grinning from ear to ear as she gazed down at the baby in her arms. They say men always want sons, but I wouldn't have swapped a million sons for that little daughter of mine. She had thick black hair, and she looked like me, and she clutched my finger when I touched her. She was beautiful. I loved her.

'Shall we call her what we planned?'

'Yes,' said Innogen, 'Cecily. If you will permit it, Madam? For my own mother could not have been kinder. And would you honour us by being her godmother?'

'My dear children, of course! The honour is mine. Now you must go away, Martin. Leave them to me.'

I was allowed to kiss my wife and daughter, then out I was firmly put.


I was in such a daze of happiness that when Francis Lovell was announced next day I thought he had come to congratulate me. Well, he did congratulate me, and he listened sweetly to a recital of my daughter's charms, but as soon as he could change the subject he turned to Richard and said, 'I've heard something rather odd. Don't get your hopes up, but …'

'About Anne?'

'Well, that I don't know. Look, I'm on my way to spend Christmas with my wife's family. Anna charged me with various errands and visits, so I called yesterday on a cousin of her father's; a Lancastrian family, you understand.' Richard made a get-on-with-it gesture. 'Please don't put too much importance on it, but this fellow said something about the Duke of Clarence sending a girl to his household a few months ago. He, well, he assumed the girl had been Clarence's mistress, an embarrassment now to be got rid of; it was the sort of winking men-together talk you hear in taverns. But this cousin of Anna's fought for Warwick, and he is one of Clarence's tenants. He talked as if this girl was a maidservant, but I couldn't help wondering?'

'About two months ago? And a young girl?'

'Yes.'

'It sounds likely,' Richard frowned. 'A Lancastrian household …
Let's go and see.'

We took a couple dozen men at arms, and silently surrounded the
house. It was a decent place, the house of a man of some money and
standing. The Fitzhugh cousin was a respectable sort, and he
blenched when Francis introduced the Duke of Gloucester –
thinking, no doubt, that old sins had caught him up and Richard
came from the King.

'I have had a report,' Richard said, 'that a young lady was sent
here recently by the Duke of Clarence?'

'What? Oh no, sir.' There was something wrong with the staunch
response. Slowly Richard said,

'Perhaps you would not think of her as a lady. Has any female
been sent here recently?'

'Well, there was the kitchen maid. From His Grace of Clarence's
household, yes; she couldn't stay there any more, if you see what I
mean?' His voice leered.

'Bring her here. Now.' Richard's tone was more effective than
any threat. 'No, wait – we'll come with you.' He dropped his hand to
his sword-hilt as he spoke.

The man led us through the house, and at the kitchen door said,
'You'll see, Your Grace, she's not the sort you would be interested in,
she's just a cook-maid.'

But Richard was walking dazedly towards the girl chopping
onions at the far side of the room. She was a pallid, grubby little
thing, bone thin in a too-big apron, her face smeared. And she was
Anne.

A kitchen is a noisy place with supper preparations underway.
She hadn't heard us. She looked up as Richard stood beside her, and
her eyes widened in desperate relief.

'Richard! Oh, Richard!'

'Anne. O God be thanked, you're safe. My darling, I've found
you.'

The master of the house was slumped against the doorjamb, his face ashen. My dagger at his throat, I said, 'Did this lady never try to tell you who she was?'

'No! What – I don't understand – I swear – I have never even spoken to her!'

'But you said the Duke of Clarence sent her to you?'

'And so he did but I don't talk to the kitchen maids! The Duke's men brought her, she went straight to the kitchen – I don't talk to the slaveys!'

Well, he had a point. Except as a child on our small manor, I had never spoken to a kitchen maid in my life. It was an effective way of hiding someone: servants would never in a thousand years credit that someone brought to slave in a kitchen could be anything but a servant. None of them would have passed on to the master or mistress any wild claims a kitchen maid might make, they would think her crazy and forget it. Or worse.

Every servant in that steamy, busy kitchen had stopped work, staring horrified at the little maid being passionately embraced by a man of Richard's clothes, jewels and bearing. The cook looked about to faint.

'Wh-who is she?' stammered my victim.

'Did Clarence never say?'

'No! His men said, a cook-maid, her name's Nan ... Who is she, sir?'

'She is the Lady Anne Neville. The King's cousin. The Duke of Gloucester's betrothed wife.'

Shock made him slump so that my blade nearly took his head off. 'Never! No! I didn't know! Please believe me, sir! I did not know!'

'Anne?' Richard asked. 'Did he?'

Through her tears she said, 'I daresay not. I was brought here and put straight to work – kitchen maids don't wait on the people of the house – I've never been out of the kitchen and the attic bedrooms, no one would listen to me, I've never seen that man or the mistress of the house.'

'Did anyone here mistreat you?'

'N-no.'

'Sure?'

'Yes.' I saw looks of relief and wild gratitude, and surmised that there had been the odd slap or curse. Probably she hadn't been a very good servant.

'Very well. Come along now, my love.'

'Wh-where to?'

'Sanctuary, I think. I doubt even my mother's house is safe for you. Saint Martin-le-Grand is closest. Will that suit you?'

'Yes! Oh Richard, yes!'

Richard wrapped his cloak around her. To the householder he said, 'Say nothing of this to anyone. Do not report to the Duke of Clarence. The same goes for everyone in this house. This lady was never here. Or you will answer to the King.'

Richard put Anne up on his own horse for the short journey to St Martin-le-Grand. She rode in silence, seeming dazed; occasionally she looked down at Richard, and touched his hand on the bridle. Once he said, 'You smell very oniony,' and she laughed in the way that is very close to tears. Another time he said, 'George has told a lot of lies; he tried to keep us apart. I've been searching for you for weeks now.' She smiled vaguely, and touched his hand again.

At St Martin's the Sanctuary brothers scurried about, showing Anne to the best guestrooms, ordering food and a bath. Anne simply sat there, smiling into space, I think hardly daring believe it was true. Looking at the bathtub she said, 'But I've no clean clothes,' as if it was a conundrum she'd never solve.

'Anne,' Richard knelt and took her hands, 'listen, my darling. You're safe now. Worry about nothing. I'll deal with George. Soon we'll be married and I'll take you to Middleham.'

'Yes ... Middleham. With you.'

'Yes. But for now, I'll stay if you want me to, but I think I can be more use fetching you some clothes and whatever you need. Yes?'

'Mmm-hmm.' Then with visible effort she roused herself. 'But you will come back? Soon?'

'Before nightfall. I promise. Anne, have a bath, eat the food these good brothers are bringing, perhaps sleep for a while. Tonight I will see you again.'

'Mmm-hmm. Tonight. I love you.' Dreamily she touched his hair, then pulled him towards her and kissed his mouth. 'I love you.'

'And I love you, with all my heart.' He put a kiss on the inside of her wrist. 'Till tonight.'

But although we returned at evening with all the things the Duchess and Innogen thought Anne would need, it was the following day before Richard could talk to her. Simply, she fell asleep, the brothers told us, the moment she'd bathed and eaten, and from exhaustion she slept for eighteen hours. When she finally awoke and could see Richard, he shut the door in my well-meaning face, so I've no idea what passed between them. However, from the way Richard came home singing to himself and saying 'Mmm-hmm,' in answer to everything, I can guess.


Well, now the great to-do over those lands began. Taking a high hand, denying he had ever meant Anne any harm (and somehow getting away with it), George held out for the entire Warwick inheritance. Held out – he simply demanded. In fact he held the King to ransom. And Richard dug his heels in and demanded a fair division right down the middle, half for Isabel, half for Anne. George refused. The King temporised. The dispute dragged on. Playing with my new daughter, planning her glittering future, I cared less than nothing.

In the end George went from swearing he would 'part no livelihood' with Richard, to some understanding of reality. He held out for Warwick Castle, the earldoms of Warwick and Salisbury and the Great Chamberlainship – this last was Richard's, by royal grant as a reward for loyalty. And he gave his gracious consent as Anne's guardian – or so he claimed – for Richard to marry Anne, on the condition that no grants of lands made to him were ever to be cancelled by parliamentary act or other authority. Richard was given Middleham and some other Yorkshire estates that had belonged to

Warwick. And then the King seized all the lands Lady Warwick held in her own right, and divided them up between his brothers. This was illegal – Warwick had died under attainder, so naturally his estates were forfeit, but a woman cannot be held guilty of her husband's treason, and her own inheritance is in law inviolate. But that is what Edward did, and why Richard condoned the illegality I don't know. Perhaps the King said take it or leave it. Perhaps he knew it was the only way to keep George in check.

That is the end of this part of my story. After Easter Richard and Anne were married, and they went to Middleham to live. Innogen and I went with them, as did Rob Percy and Francis Lovell and our other friends.

# Nine

## 1475

It is little exaggeration to say that England is two countries, north and south, and that in many ways they are more alien to, or at least suspicious of, each other than, say, of France. The south has the gentle, fertile land yielding corn and wheat and barley, fruit and grass-fattened meat; it has the major ports and big cities, the trade, the money. The north has the grandeur, the sheep and the best horses, the wool, the coal, the hard men. Northerners consider the south populated by whores and effeminates, soft-living do-nothings who'll cheat you as soon as look at you. Southerners consider the northerners wild, dangerous, close-fisted barbarians little better than the Scots. Neither can understand the speech of the other. Well, pretend they can't. Unless it suits them.

So I suppose the men of the north were not very impressed to have the King's little brother foisted on them as their overlord. True, his mother was a Neville. True, he had been trained at Middleham. True, he had married Warwick's daughter. True, he was a bonny fighter and he'd dealt with the Scots. Still, a southerner by birth and upbringing ... Well, give the lad a chance, eh?

By the time I take up my story in 1475, you wouldn't have found anyone north of the Trent with a bad word to say for him. Except perhaps for the Stanleys over in the northwest and Harry Percy of Northumberland. Rivalry between the Percies and the Nevilles went back generations. Richard's Wardenship of the West Marches had authority over Percy's of the East and Middle Marches, but Richard was tactful with the prickly Earl, and if they were never close friends they soon achieved a modus operandi for the common weal. Percy was smart enough to see that it was a matter of coming to terms, or else see the North overrun by Scots. Despite the truce there were constant border raids, and to Richard fell the duties of seeing that the border castles were kept repaired and victualled, prisoners exchanged, envoys buttered up. He formed a council, a provincial seat of government and a court to which anyone could bring a dispute or complaint.

On the domestic side, Richard's household was the greatest in the north. Although we roved between Sheriff Hutton, Pontefract, York and the border fortresses, Middleham was always our main residence. I still recall the day we arrived there. It was May, and spring had decked Wensleydale in lilac and green, blue and gold. The sky was an azure bowl, flecked with lamb's-tails of cloud. Beside the road primroses and windflowers stretched gaily to the sun. All around us reared the high hills, and ahead lay the stern bulk of the castle. I had been concerned about bringing Innogen here, for she had never been north of York, and what if she hated it? To me it was home, and I had planned for it to be so again. Of course we had our lands and houses in the south – Innogen's in Kent and towards York, my patrimony in the Midlands and the new estates of Edward's granting – but I was one of Richard's household knights and commanders, and our brief was to keep the North. I could no more command Innogen to live unhappily than I could fly, yet I wanted her with me. But to my relief as we entered Middleham town I saw she was looking around in pleasure. Catching my eye, she nodded. For the last few miles John had been perched on my saddle bow, prattling questions about everything we passed on the way; now he too looked about brightly and said, 'Pretty!'

I had wondered too about Anne. She had always loved Middleham, but might not returning here bring too sharp reminders of her father and a different form of happiness? She was gazing ahead, half-frowning at the banner flying from the castle's topmost tower; no longer Warwick's Bear and Ragged Staff in its scarlet and gold, but the Blanc Sanglier of Gloucester. Then, as I watched her, a smile lit her face. Her lips framed the word 'Home,' and she reached for Richard's hand. Above us the castle gates opened, and Anne's people formed up to welcome her back.

The townsfolk too gave us hearty welcome, running out to cheer us. Some of the women had little gifts for their new lady – a pot of honey, the cheesecakes they make so well in Yorkshire, a bunch of flowers, until she could hardly hold them all. Running backwards beside her horse to look at her, a grubby urchin stumbled and fell almost under her palfrey's hooves. Terror flashed through Richard's face and he grabbed for her bridle, but even with her lap full of presents Anne was a good horsewoman. She reined in, saying sternly, 'Be careful there. You're one of the Postlethwaites, aren't you? Jacky – aye. Well, you should know better. Give my good wishes to your mother.' It was no great feat of memory, for there was no mistaking one of the Postlethwaite brood, but the lad scampered away shouting that Lady Anne remembered me, aye she did, she knew me for Jacky Postlethwaite right off! And that was it – to all the Middleham people she was Lady Anne, who had come home. When they tried they remembered to call her 'Your Grace', but ask anyone who Lady Anne was and they'd look puzzled that you shouldn't know.

Those towns-people remembered most of us, and kindly gave us a cheer as we rode through. Look, it's Master Martin, eh, with the pretty new wife and the baby, and Lord Lovell, and that's Rob Percy for sure, and Sir William Parre and Lord Scrope, and ain't Duke Richard the fine man now, eh, and look at all the men-at-arms and the wagons. A few people noted John's likeness to Richard, and there were knowing grins and elbows nudging ribs, but country people take a robust view of sexual peccadilloes. Richard had married Anne and brought her home, he was their good lord now, and to the people of the north he could do no wrong.

Thus we came home, and soon the north became our life. Middleham was always full, I suppose it was a rare day when less then three hundred sat down to dinner. There were always visitors – the Scropes of Bolton, the Scropes of Masham, Lord Greystoke, Miles Metcalfe the Recorder of York, Richard's various Neville cousins, Lord Northumberland, the merchants and landowners of all around the North.

Also there was Lady Warwick, for in 1473 the King gave her permission to leave Beaulieu, and James Tyrell had conducted her north to Middleham. Whether George ever offered her a home with him and Isabel, I don't know.

And children. A year after our Cecily's birth Innogen gave me a son, Martin, and in 1474 twins, a boy and girl whom we called Richard and Alison. With Rob and Joyce Percy's children, John, and Richard's wards, quite a horde, especially once Richard's daughter Katherine joined the household on her mother's death.

So life was going along contentedly, when the King decided to invade France.


'Who does he think he is,' Innogen asked, 'Henry the Fifth?'

Anne could still be faintly shocked by Innogen's outspokenness, and she knew how Richard took any criticism of the King. But Richard and Innogen had settled into a relationship like that of brother and sister; they bickered and sparred, teased each other, united against outsiders, said the things no one else would dare to.

'I believe he thinks he is King of England.' Richard settled back with his feet outstretched and his arms behind his head. 'But pray give us the benefit of your thoughts, Dame Robsart.' He and Innogen regarded each other with a glint in their eyes.

'Well,' said Innogen, 'this idea that England has some claim to France ...'

'It has.'

'Oh yes, I've read the *Gesta Henrici Quintus*, I've studied the arguments; rather thin, some of them. But yes, an hereditary claim. But who in their right mind would take it up?' Innogen said thoughtfully. 'So I wonder what he's up to?'

'Pray continue.'

'Well, *consider* Henry the Fifth. He won a battle – all well and good. And spent the rest of his life, and half England's money, trying to keep the French kingdom he'd won. And it went soon enough, didn't it? Because it was impossible to maintain without committing all of England's resources to just that task.'

'It would have been different had Henry not died in 1421 leaving a baby as his heir. It was bad management and English faction-fighting during Henry the Sixth's minority that lost us France.'

'True – as I'm sure the King has considered. The same situation could arise again, his sons are only four and two. Now, the King being in full possession of his wits ...' Richard bowed ironic thanks '... he is not going to waste years and fortunes fighting to hold what he wins in France. So what is he up to?'

'England's honour?' suggested Anna Lovell. Innogen snorted, and I saw the corner of Richard's mouth twitch.

'Louis of France is a constant thorn in Edward's flesh,' he said. 'He's behind all our troubles with the Scots, and if he's not behind these uprisings the Earl of Oxford's always fomenting, I'll be very surprised.' No one wanted to remember, much less say, that Clarence was probably hand-in-glove with Oxford.

'No one wants war?' Anne said. 'Surely? Especially not after a decade of civil war?' She spoke calmly, for she was a rational woman, but I caught the glances that flew among the women. For the first time I wondered what it was like for them to send their men to fight. I even worried if Innogen went to London without me.

'No,' said my darling, 'no one wants war. The King surely doesn't. But it is a real threat to France. Burgundy and England together – perhaps others – France has many enemies. But war? Invading France. No, it's obvious.'

'Then explain, my dear Innogen, for us less witty mortals.'

'Oh dear, it's bad enough for sarcasm, is it? Well, my dear Richard, I believe that the King will take a vast army to France – invade, in fact – and will make peace the first chance he gets. For a price.'

'You think that, do you?'

'Yes.'

'Wager on it?'

'Whatever you like.' Both angrier than they would admit, they eyed each other.

'That jet and ivory chess set you love so much?'

'Done. And I, dear Richard, have a great fancy for a diamond necklace. Earrings to match, I think.'

'Done.' They shook hands on it.

With the sublime tactlessness of children John piped up, worried, 'Is Father angry with you, Mama?'

Innogen looked at Richard, eyebrows raised. Smoothing John's hair he said, 'No, John, I'm not. Your mother was merely speaking her mind. A short speech.'

Laughing, Jenny allowed the hit, and the matter rested. No one cared to make the point that there is nothing like a foreign war for keeping the peace at home; and George of Clarence had spent the last four years stirring the pot of domestic rebellion.

Well, then we were busy raising our army to take to France. Parliament had granted money to the King and, kicking and screaming, the people coughed up their 'benevolences', pretty word for a tax at sword-point. They say that one lady offered twenty pounds, whereupon Edward kissed her and she increased it to forty. All the great landowners were indentured to supply a certain number of men – in Richard's case a thousand archers and a hundred and twenty men-at-arms, although eventually he raised some hundreds more, so eagerly did the men of the north respond. From my own lands I was able to raise nearly a hundred. Oh, it was a popular cause, despite the hated benevolences.

Not popular among our women, of course. Loyally Anne received the gentlemen who flocked into Middleham with their troops, carefully she mended Richard's banners and saw to her side of the provisioning, but she went about heavy-eyed and silent. Innogen was sharp-tempered, Anna Lovell wept when she thought no one was watching. Joyce Percy was her brisk and practical self, but I knew she shared Innogen's view of the venture and she grew quiet as time went on.

Supper on our last day was a miserable affair of food toyed with, conversations broken off. Once, when the minstrels ended a song, I heard Richard say in an undertone to Anne, 'When it's a matter of chivvying the Scots you send me off cheerfully enough.'

'Cheerfully!' She'd spoken too loudly – everyone looked up. They smiled unconvincingly around, and changed the subject.

In bed that night I asked Innogen, 'Why is it different this time? Why does it seem so bad?'

She rolled over to face me. In the candlelight her eyes were wide, dark. 'Do you think we can ever take it as a matter of course? We get used to it, but we never cease to worry. But it is different this time, or it seems so. Patrolling the borders, or civil strife, is one thing. If England were invaded, that would be one thing. But seeking out war, making war, is different. You men, you like it, you want to go, it is more than duty or an exercise of power. And all we women can do is let you go, and wait, and hope that each letter isn't bringing word of your death, every wagon we see coming isn't bringing you home to die.' She put her hand on my face, her fingers playing in my hair. 'And if you did die ... I'm twenty-four, Anne is nineteen, and that's a long time widowed. Oh, I'd survive, I have money, I could be independent; but what of all the life we've made? Our children? And for Anne – her life has been shattered once, by her father, she lost everything. She adores Richard. If he dies, she loses not only her husband but her home, her life, her lands. What is there for her but being forced to marry again at the King's whim; that or a convent in the end. Me too.

'Martin, I love you. Those are simple words to say you are my life, my heart's desire, my companion in mirth, my friend. You complete me.'

We had our arms around each other now, she was crying, and if I'm honest I was near tears too. 'All I can say is that I love you too, in the same way. I hate to leave you; but yes, I want to go. It is more than duty.'

'And do you understand that this is *unnecessary* war?'

'I think so. Yes. Though remember, sweetheart, that this is a way of drawing Louis' sting, if we don't take action against him it may well come to defending England against a French invasion.'

'Perhaps. Yes.'

'But anyway, you don't believe it will mean battle.'

'No. But still I fear for you.'

'If you're right the worst you have to fear for me is sea-sickness.'

She laughed despairingly, understanding, I think, that I joked because of my own fears. I licked the tears from her eyes, caressed her, and when I looked down at her during our lovemaking I saw her watching me with the hurt intensity of a child. No, not of a child – of a woman.

And so to the vasty fields of France, Harry V's 'Normandy Song' in our ears and an army of some twelve thousand at our backs.

At Canterbury, where we mustered for the crossing, the first person we met was George.

Richard greeted him warily, but George was full of high spirits and kissed him with what looked like real affection. Well, probably it was, let's not be too hard on him. I had forgotten how charming he could be, and my defences fell around me when he embraced me and greeted me by name. 'Going to be sea-sick again?' he teased. For a moment I wondered how he knew. It was odd to remember that within the changing, fleeting traitor lay the boy who had done his best to look after me and Richard on that first voyage to Burgundy.

'Unless I've grown out of it, Your Grace, probably I am. What about you, do you still feed the fishes?' For he had joined me at the rail many a time in 1461.

'Hmm, not sure.'

'Well, I hope not,' said Richard, 'for two of you might be beyond me. How many men did you bring, George?'

'Around twelve hundred. You?'

'About the same.'

'Good,' George said absently then – like Innogen – 'Do you think this is all that it seems? Invading France seems rather rash. We'll win, of course, but after that?'

'No idea. I hope it doesn't dwindle to a long-drawn-out campaign. Edward thinks one brisk battle will do it, then we can treat with Louis as victors.'

'And I hope he's right. What about dear brother-in-law Charles?'

'It's in his interest to support us.'

'Meaning you think he won't?'

'With Charles, who knows?'

'True. Well, at least we'll have the chance to see Margaret. Well – how is Anne?'

'Well, thank you. Isabel? Your children?' George had two now, a daughter Margaret, aged almost two, and a son Edward born earlier that year. His face lit up as he talked of them; he loved Isabel, but his children meant everything to him. Little Margaret, it seemed, was not only the most beautiful but the most intelligent child ever, and the boy full of promise. And through all that happened, that is how I remember George, prattling like any proud father about his children.

They were right to doubt Charles of Burgundy. For some reason known only to himself he had darted off to besiege Neuss, a place of no strategic importance, and Edward cooled his heels at Calais for ten days until in mid-July the Duke appeared. And where, pray, was the army he had promised? – if it had ever existed outside his head, which I doubt, for he arrived with no more than a bodyguard. But never fear, he assured Edward, with an army such as this English one we could sweep through Europe even unto the very gates of Rome. With, of course, a detour to help Charles bring Lorraine to heel. All for the greater glory of Charles of Burgundy. One could almost hear the fanfares, the triumphal marches being sung.

Edward kindly declining these weird suggestions, Charles came to the point. The Count of St Pol was on our side and would turn St Quentin over to us – why not begin there, take the city and make it our base? Why not indeed, so off we set. Without Charles, of course, who went to visit Margaret at St Omer. We passed the site of the battle of Agincourt, wondering if we were bound for the same glory.

But at St Quentin we found that either Charles had been deceived – or deluded – or St Pol had turned his coat again, for the town was heavily defended, and opened fire on us.

Louis was marching upon us with a great army, laying waste to the countryside so there was no provisioning for us. Edward had nearly exhausted his money. Charles was nowhere.

So what to do?

I must say that in Edward's shoes I probably would have done what he did; perhaps it was what he had intended all along. A captured nobleman was allowed to overhear certain conversations, then to escape back to King Louis – and promptly then came the French offer to meet for parley. Alluring hints were dropped about peace terms.

Edward called his commanders to conference. It was three years since I had seen him. He had put on flesh, yet his face was more lined than I remembered. His eyes were bloodshot, and he looked older than his thirty-three years; older and, despite the paddy flesh, harder. He had come to this meeting in a long gown of royal purple lined with crimson – the King in Council, not the royal warrior. By contrast his brothers wore short jackets over riding breeches and boots, and they looked more alike than I ever remembered, both sitting with one booted foot on the other knee.

In the warmth of the night the tent sides had to be looped up for air – and, no doubt, for the convenience of French spies – as some thirty of us heard the case for accepting a truce. Not that Edward himself put his case – except for brief introductory words, he left it to Doctor Morton. This Morton was Doctor of Laws, firmly Lancastrian, and last seen dragging Margaret of Anjou across the Severn to safety. Since then he had come to terms with Edward and was now highly placed in his service. He was Master of the Rolls and often used for diplomatic dealings with our foreign neighbours. And a slimy, shifty-eyed turd I always thought him. As Chaucer more elegantly put it, he was the smiler with the knife beneath the cloak.

Morton rose, smoothing his legal gown. Frankly, I didn't listen with too much attention. Or not until he said, with a bow towards

Richard, 'Of course it is in the interests of martial young men to speak for war. Such men must be conscious that their fame rests on their prowess in the field.' Princes of the blood royal, brothers of the King, Richard and George raised their eyebrows. Several men stirred angrily, and I heard the Duke of Suffolk mutter 'Cheeky devil'. His face expressionless, Edward signed for Morton to go on. And on he went, and on. He said once, 'Let us remember that Our Lord said "Blessed are the peacemakers."'

George cut in, 'And He also said, "I come bringing not peace but a sword."'

Edward grinned, for quoting scripture is a two-edged weapon. Nettled, Morton bowed and went on. He broke into Latin, a long peroration that had men shuffling. 'But I see some of our northern contingent looking at a loss,' he said with an oily smile. 'I shall therefore construe.'

Well, it's not for a Lancastrian lawyer to call the King's brother an illiterate yokel. Lord Howard growled, 'It's not your Latin we need translating, Doctor Morton, it's some point to your argument we want. Get on, man, get on.'

Morton looked down his nose then turned to Edward with a bow. 'Then hear me, gracious sovereign. In short I feel we would be wise to accept any French offer of peace that carries advantageous terms. We do not want a long campaign here in France, and we needs must think of the cost of maintaining lands won here, and of the cost in terms of human life. Doubtless we would win in battle, but need we pamper our pride at such a cost, when we can achieve the same by peaceful means?' I think he would have continued but Edward's look discouraged him.

'Thank you, Doctor Morton,' said the King. 'You put the case well. But there is another side to the issue. Gloucester?'

'Thank you, your Grace. While I cannot hope to emulate Doctor Morton's eloquence, I will do my best in plain speech.' I saw Morton smirk as Richard rose. I think the doctor expected a stumbling speech full of martial allusions and wild promises of victory. Why Morton disliked Richard so much I don't know, unless it was on general principles, the Yorkist yoke sitting uneasily on the Lancastrian neck, and he thought Richard a safe target for jibes he dared not make against the King. Or perhaps, urban to the core, proud of his erudition, he thought Richard a petty provincial lordling who had gained his position by nepotism, barbarous as the men he ruled. How did he imagine Richard carried out his Constable's and Admiral's duties? His judicial duties? But no doubt to Morton such things did not exist outside London.

'Your Grace, gentlemen, Doctor Morton has put the case for peace well. The cost of following a contrary course must be borne in mind – as indeed it is by any man who has seen battle at first hand. Yet I feel that other, less concrete, things must be considered. I feel that England's honour is in the balance here. I admit the worth of the pragmatic solution, but would it not be best to treat with the French as victors? Because otherwise, Your Grace, King Louis will not hesitate to break any truce agreement when it suits him.' With a swift smile he said, 'You would be lucky, in fact, to see more than one instalment of any financial settlement. As for any agreement to support us against rebellion' – no one looked at George – 'or invasion, well, I think we all know Louis would hold such transgressors' hats and egg them on. Also I think you should consider that Parliament granted money, and your subjects gave yet more money, for war, in expectation of a victory and glory for England, for Edward IV to live alongside Henry V in English memory. A purchased peace may be sensible, but it is neither honourable nor any guarantee of permanence. Will you have it all to do again in three years time? And find your people unwilling to finance another venture? Besides, what of Burgundy?'

'Your Grace is very sure,' Morton interrupted, 'that his Majesty King Louis would break faith. Need we be so cynical?'

'I bow to your greater knowledge of the French King.' This shrewd hit brought mottled colour surging up Morton's face, and I wasn't alone in wondering if there was more in this for him than his King's gratitude. In fact, just which King did Morton truly serve?

Louis de Bretaylle's accented voice broke in, 'I share his Grace of

Gloucester's view of King Louis. He is not to be trusted. He will bind us to support him against his enemies – by which we may understand, Burgundy.' This brought a murmur of worried agreement.

Nodding acknowledgement to de Bretaylle Richard said, softly but very intensely, 'Yes – Burgundy is Louis's enemy and his *bête noire*. The ink will hardly be dry on any treaty before Louis turns on Burgundy. Will it be with England's help?' Edward's eyes flickered. 'If you bind us to such a treaty as we are discussing, then yes, we will have to help dismember Burgundy – or be at war with France for breach of treaty. I believe this is what Louis wants.' By now the murmurs of agreement or indecision had turned to a swell of conviction. Edward's face showed no expression, but I could tell he was angry. 'By all means set aside personal considerations – our sister Margaret will understand the hard facts of political necessity – but pray consider that England's trade depends on Burgundy. Pray consider the possibility of all the Channel ports being in French hands. England held them all once; now we hold only Calais. We need the Low Countries if we are not to be entirely isolated and helpless in the face of French aggression.

'I do most earnestly beg Your Grace,' Richard finished, 'to consider the advantage of proving England's strength. Frighten Louis, in short, into realising he cannot deal lightly with us. Do not let it be said that England's honour can be so easily bought.' He bowed and sat down.

Morton stared, lips pursed. George caught Richard's eye and grinned.

Edward let a little time go by before he said, 'Both cases are well argued. However, I incline toward accepting any proper offer of peace. My agreement depends, of course, on an advantageous offer with firm safeguards. But a good settlement would not only avoid all the costs of war but allow me to live with England's finances steady for the first time in decades. Let us therefore take a provisional vote upon the matter. All those in favour of letting the French know we incline toward peace?' Most hands went up. 'Those against?' –

Richard, of course, myself, de Bretaylle, a handful of others. 'Does anyone wish to abstain?' To general surprise George raised his hand. 'You, Clarence?'

'Yes.' Flushing, he said, 'Your Grace, I hope you are right, yet I fear Richard is. After all, I have had dealings with King Louis. And any vote of mine will be suspect. I therefore abstain.' He looked appealingly at Richard, who after a moment smiled back, his genuine, sweet smile of affection.

'Carried, then. Thank you, gentlemen. Let us await King Louis's offer.'

The King swept out, Morton scurrying alongside.

'I do not love thee, Doctor Morton,' George said. 'Nasty piece of work, isn't he? You made an enemy there, Dickon. Why does Edward tolerate him?'

'He's clever. Experienced.'

'And Lancastrian to the bone.'

'Oh, of course. A time-server. And thick as thieves with old Louis.'

'D'you think Edward trusts him?'

'Not at all, would be my guess. Probably he thinks the man's better right under his eye.'

'Something in that, I daresay. That was a pithy little speech.'

'Full of pith and vinegar,' Richard agreed. 'You do realise Edward knows exactly what the French are going to offer? And that it was a foregone conclusion from the start?'

'Oh, yes. In fact, I wonder if Edward didn't know before he left England that it would come to this. He's nearly as devious as Louis. Well, let's wait and see what Louis comes up with.'


We did not have to wait for long. Mid-August the French and English ambassadors met near Amiens, and the French offer was indeed attractive. Seventy-five thousand crowns to begin with and fifty thousand per annum – the Dauphin to marry Edward's daughter Bess – seven years' truce with lucrative trade agreements – each King bound to support the other against domestic rebellion. Not a bad day's work in the marketplace. Of course the offer was immediately accepted.

Richard's only comment was, 'Wait until Charles hears.'

He heard at once, and the news brought him straight to Edward for a right royal tantrum. Edward said, All very well, but where was Charles when Edward led his army into France, where was all the promised support? To which Charles had no answer – which didn't sweeten his temper. With a few barbed references to Henry V he flounced away.

And now all was amity and goodwill. Celebrations. Louis threw Amiens open to our army and laid on food and drink for all. A bridge was built across the Somme at Pecquigny, on which the agreement would be signed. And behold the King of England striding forth, glorious in cloth of gold lined with red satin, a diamond fleur-de-lis in his velvet cap. And behold the King of France shuffling forth, clad in a ragbag of garments he could have filched from his kennel-man. Beside him was his poor secretary Philippe de Commynes, identically dressed so as to confuse assassins. On a piece of the True Cross these two ill-matched monarchs signed the treaty.

Louis was generous, it was pensions all round for the English who had supported the peace. I remember Lord Hastings got two thousand crowns a year. De Bretaylle, who had been heard to say in disgust that Edward had won nine victories only to face this disgraceful defeat, was given dinner and invited to join Louis' service. The offer was refused, but he was given a placatory present of a thousand crowns and Louis' promise of favour for his brother – oh and by the way, would he work to see that the peace held?

What Doctor Morton got out of the deal, I have no idea.

Richard attended none of these junketings, and we were packing for home when an invitation came from Louis. Would His Grace of Gloucester delight His Majesty of France by coming to dinner? Impossible to refuse, and Richard came back well fed, thoughtful, and the proud possessor of some excellent horses and silver plate.

Louis had sent the kindest compliments to Anne, remembering *la pauvre petite* from five years before, and they had discussed music and ordnance, a choice of subjects which tells you a good deal about both men.

And so, home again. I wonder if Edward had realised how unpopular his lovely truce would be in England? For make no mistake, it was unpopular. People had given money for victory, not this sneaking peace with the detested French – and the men of Edward's army, returning home with none of the usual booty of war and with no outlet for war-fervour, turned to robbery and murder.

Edward dealt with it. He travelled about his kingdom, punishing anyone who committed breaches of the peace, and soon people came to think it wasn't so bad: no war, and a French pension to relieve them of taxes. Edward, in fact, even traded Margaret of Anjou back to France for a fifty thousand crown ransom.

But it was Richard who had come home with the honour. People knew he had been against the peace, and they were proud of him. No welcher, he gave Innogen her diamond necklace. As he clasped it around her neck she said, 'Coals of fire?'

'Never. I was wrong.'

She took his face between her hands and kissed him. 'But although I am grateful for peace, I think you were in the right of the matter.'

In bed that night she said, 'And if the whole thing nibbles away at Richard's hero-worship of Edward, all the better, don't you think?'

'Might not Richard need that? Always to admire and trust Edward? And don't forget he has good cause.'

'Mmm, but Edward knows that, and he relies upon it far too much. He knows Richard would always serve him loyally, but he likes having that loyalty well mortared by adoration. I think it is time Richard grows out of it and sees the King with clear eyes. Or one day when it's too late he'll suffer a disillusion he won't recover from.'

'As might I?'

'Perhaps – or do you now see the canny, unscrupulous King instead of the glorious golden boy who won your heart when you were eight?' I found I didn't know. 'What's your opinion of this peace agreement?'

'All the pragmatic arguments are on Edward's side. But the heart says Richard was right.'

'Mmm … So George of Clarence had the courage to abstain. I wonder why? After all his trouble-making you'd think he would be at pains to butter the King up.'

'Perhaps,' I said, neither convinced nor interested, and we made homecoming love with her clad only in the necklace of black pearls that was my present to her.


If ever I had repeated that conversation Innogen would have been hanged as a witch, for two years later Richard was pleading with one brother for the other's life.

# Ten

## 1476-78

It was a year of births and deaths, the year after the French expedition. We were returned a week or two from France when in the middle of breakfast Anne turned a peculiar colour and unceremoniously bolted from the hall. Concerned, Richard rose to follow her, but Lady Warwick gestured him back to his chair and went after her daughter. I recall that Northumberland was there, for he caught my eye in a glance combining speculation and amusement. Oblivious, Richard began wondering aloud if Anne had eaten tainted food, and drifted into talk of the French rations. Not daring raise false hopes, the rest of us at table let him maunder on.

But later that day I found him wandering through the courtyard with a disbelieving smile of pure joy on his face.

'Martin,' he said, clutching at my sleeve, 'Anne thinks – she is sure – she is to have a baby! *Deo gratias* – a baby! After three years, when we had almost given up hope!' Then, remembering all the listening ears, he lowered his voice. 'There have been false hopes before, but now Anne is as sure as she can be. She wondered, before we went to France, but … well, you know how it is.' Anxiously he wound his hand tighter in my sleeve. 'Martin, you do know. Will she be – be safe? Is it wrong to hope, or wrong to doubt? But what if I were to lose Anne?'

I soothed him as best I could, though I knew those male fears all too well. But as it happened Anne was well throughout her pregnancy, although Richard kept a stream of doctors and midwives pouring into Middleham until Lady Warwick asked him in exasperation if he wanted to drive Anne mad with worry.

The birth was expected in the middle of March. All the usual preparations were made, and as the days went on the whole household, nay, the village and half Yorkshire, was walking on eggs. The night came, not long after the anniversary of Innogen's and my wedding, when one of Anne's waiting-women woke Innogen, who dressed and went away saying, 'Look to Richard.' I had no need to look *for* him: Lady Warwick marched him downstairs like a felon under guard and gave him into my keeping. He was new to all this, poor devil; he had kept me and our other friends company and given us drinks when our wives were in childbed, but his complete exclusion from the process was something he had never thought of. We sat around, sharing a jug of wine and later breakfast, Rob Percy and Francis Lovell helping me keep his spirits up. But a very long time passed without word, and it was after dinner when Innogen snatched a moment to warn me privily it would be longer yet.

'For it is a first birth and they often take longer. and Anne is – is small. But don't let Richard worry; after all, I was much longer delivering the twins.' She hurried away before I could give voice to my frightened questions.

Richard said, 'Twenty hours! Anne began not long after midnight. Of course one hears of long labours …'

Naturally I said nothing to him of it possibly being longer, but longer it was. Twenty hours; a full day. A night, a day, another night. None of the women now came down to give us word. Once Richard could not prevent himself going upstairs and although I was quickly after him I was too late to stop him hearing the worst sound a man can hear: his wife screaming in the agony of child-birth. He went to the chapel then, his friends with him, and we waited on our knees in prayer. We had all seen mares birthing foals, or bitches their puppies, and I think we all wondered as we prayed why easy births should belong to the animal kingdom while our women have to suffer. The sin of Eve? – aye, tell that to a man who has never waited in that agony for his child to be born.

But born that child was. It was after dinner on the second day that Lady Warwick came downstairs, weak, haggard, exhausted yet triumphant, to tell Richard he had a son.

'Alive?' he said sharply, then, 'And – and Anne?'

'Both alive. A fine son, my dear. You may come to see him.'

Richard went away upstairs, and came down soon with that look I daresay I had worn when I looked at my firstborn.

'A boy!' he kept saying. 'We shall call him Edward, of course. A boy! With pale hair like Anne's, and blue eyes. Small, but well. A boy!'

We rejoiced with him, we had the bells rung, word sent to the village, Richard's secretary John Kendal wrote a letter telling the King. But none of us told Richard how ominous it was he had not been allowed to see Anne.

She nearly died in that childbed, Innogen told me later, or as much as I could bear to hear, for men are squeamish about such things. 'Three times we thought we had lost them both,' she said. 'I've never seen a woman bleed so much, yet live.' I flung up a protesting hand. 'Aye, you men, it's all pleasure for you.'

'No! We don't bear the bodily pain, but we have to wait, and fear. Every time you're in childbed … And I love Anne so dearly. Will she …' I couldn't say the word.

'I think she will live. But she will never bear another child. She suffered … damage … during the birth.' Innogen fell asleep then, and slept the day and night through. Leaving me and Lady Warwick to prepare Richard for the chance that Anne might still die.

But she lived. It was a full three months before she could leave her bed, but she lived, and so did her child.

By coincidence she had been up only a day or two when a letter came to say that her sister Isabel was expecting a child in December. By that time we knew that Innogen and I were to have another child, so wantonly had we celebrated our fifth wedding anniversary. By that time I had let myself forget the dreadful time Anne had had, I could afford to think only of Innogen's previous safe deliveries. It was summer, Richard had an heir at last, John and Katherine were puffed with pride in their little brother, Anne was well again, Innogen sailing serenely through her pregnancy. So the year passed, in happiness.

In November a letter came saying that Isabel of Clarence had been safely delivered of another son, to be named Richard for his uncle. I was only mildly interested, for Innogen was near her time. I sent my felicitations and a gift with Richard's messenger, then forgot the matter.

Our baby arrived in time for Christmas. For some reason we had both expected a son, and had no name for the large, healthy baby girl. I fancied calling her Margaret for Richard's sister, but Innogen didn't care for the name. Lying back on her pillows, crooning to the baby, she rejected all my other suggestions. In the end it was Lady Warwick who suggested Philippa, the name of Edward III's queen and Chaucer's wife. We liked it, and the baby looked like a Philippa, so it was decided.

The day after the christening I was going about some ordinary business when I ran into Francis, standing irresolute outside Richard's private rooms. Swiftly he took my arm. 'I wouldn't go in, Martin. There's bad news. Isabel of Clarence is dead. She died just before Christmas.'

The news hit me like a blow. 'Oh no. Isabel? Oh no, Francis.' We had known her so well from our boyhood here at Middleham. She was only twenty-five, and I had liked her. Then with a clutch of fear for Innogen I asked, 'What was it, child-bed fever?'

'I shouldn't think so – the baby was born more than two months ago. Martin, the baby is dead too.' Hearing my new daughter's lusty screams from above he quickly added, 'But he was very frail from birth. Don't worry about your Philippa.'

Silently I told myself our baby was strong, so big at birth that she had turned the kitchen scales at a little over eight pounds. Strong and thriving, for although Innogen never had any milk after the first two weeks we had a good wet-nurse, a clean, healthy country woman who Innogen insisted should eat good food and drink nothing stronger than home-brewed ale. The nurse's own six children had always thrived, and Innogen showed no signs of fever or illness; surely there was nothing to fear.

'Don't fear for her,' Francis absently repeated. 'Anna's with Anne and her mother, they are grieving badly, of course.' I had forgotten that Isabel was Anna Lovell's cousin. 'Richard is with them, and …'

As he spoke the door behind us opened and Richard came out. Grim and tired, he said to me, 'You've heard?'

'Francis told me. I'm so sorry. Poor little Isabel, may God have mercy on her soul.'

'Yes, she was a good woman. Poor little Isabel, yes. Silly, often, but sweet, wasn't she, and kind.' He glanced down at the crumpled letter in his hand. 'Martin, Francis, come to my business room. Where's Rob?'

Following him, and he strode quickly when angry or bothered, I said, 'Not sure, shall we send for him?'

'Later will do.' Richard dismissed his pages and himself poured wine. 'Shut the door, no one must hear this.' He downed his wine in a gulp and spread out the letter on the table. 'This is from George. It's barely coherent – no wonder – but I think he has gone mad. He writes that Isabel was poisoned.'

There was a fraught moment of silence. 'Poisoned!' Francis and I repeated.

'Yes.' Richard ran his hand through his hair. 'I know, I know, it sounds typical George, doesn't it, you needn't say it. And he loved Isabel, so it's no wonder if he … But he writes that although she had a hard time at the birth and the child was small and not strong, they seemed to be doing well enough – he took her back to Tewkesbury a month after the birth.' The baby had been born at Warwick. 'For all I know that was the trouble, that she wasn't well enough to travel. Especially in this weather. But George says there was nothing to worry about, then suddenly Isabel took ill, and died. And he says it was poison.'

'I hope,' Francis said bluntly, 'that he has had the sense to write this only to you.'

'So do I.' Richard filled his cup again. 'Because the implications are plain, aren't they? George has many enemies. And even here among us three we don't name the ones who hate him most.'

'No we don't. But how could … people in London, manage to

poison George's wife at Tewkesbury?' Though of course servants could be suborned. 'Does he accuse any person?'

'No, thank the Lord. But just the same I'll burn his letter.' Turning to the fire he did so, poking the flaming paper deep into the coals. 'A man who has just lost his wife and child is naturally distraught; nothing he says at such a time counts. And I hope I don't have to spend the next few months repeating that to everyone in England.' He stood for a moment, thinking, unconsciously fiddling with his rings. 'Anne wants to go to Tewkesbury for Isabel's funeral. I can't deny her, though I don't want her travelling right across the country in this weather. I have managed to convince my good-mother she mustn't think of going too.' Never robust, the Countess suffered dreadfully from rheumatics, in winter she was hardly fit to leave the warmth of her bedroom. 'We must go. I want to, to be with George. I would anyway, but I have to convince him to stop any talk of poisoning. I haven't told the women of that, and I want to keep it from them. So it is among us three only, and Rob.' We nodded. The less said, the better. 'Anne and I will leave tomorrow. Francis, Anna wants to go too, of course, so you'll accompany us? Martin, you and Rob must look after things here, Council business and so on – though it's only for a month, I hope.'

'When is Isabel's funeral to be?'

'As far as I can make out George's writing, there will be the usual three weeks lying in the Tewkesbury chapel, then the funeral on the twenty-fifth. Poor George. He asked me to be that baby's godfather, you know. Masses here, of course. In fact, if you'll excuse me, I'll speak to the chaplain now.'

More slowly finishing our wine, Francis and I looked at each other. 'Makes you glad to have no brothers, doesn't it? Would George do as much for Richard?'

'Who knows? But the thing is,' I said, remembering things in the past, 'George does love Richard. In his own peculiar way.'

'Oh, I daresay – but would you put a groat on George's discretion? Because I wouldn't. And if he has some bee in his bonnet and makes trouble with this poisoning story – which frankly I can't believe in for a moment – what's the wager he'll drag Richard into it too?'

'Then your duty's plain,' I said with a flippancy I later bitterly regretted, 'you must murder George before his big flapping mouth can get anyone into trouble.'

Richard and Anne were away a month, and they returned only a day before the royal courier galloped in with a letter. Charles Duke of Burgundy was dead. He had died while besieging the town of Nancy; frozen to death, his body eaten by wolves.

'And of course,' Richard said, 'Louis of France is already moving against Burgundy. He claims that Burgundy now reverts to France, and he is making a military strike against all the territories in that area. And he expects England's help.'

'So you were right.'

'Yes, and I wish I weren't. The King's called a Great Council meeting. Though what he intends to do is anyone's guess. Poor Margaret. And what about Duchess Mary?' For there was the nub: Charles's only heir was his young daughter Mary by his first marriage. 'She'll have to marry,' Richard said thoughtfully, 'and damn' quickly, and to someone damn' powerful, if she's to hold off Louis. Hellfire, we need Burgundy to keep France off us and our trade. Well, I bet that's the last of Edward's treaty.'

Of course he was right, and at an acrimonious meeting the Great Council, having ignored Richard's advice about France, chewed the bitter cud.

'Oh, nothing was actually *decided*, of course,' Richard said with commendable malice on his return. 'It's a case of all help for Burgundy short of actual aid. Edward has suggested to Louis that the truce be extended to last for their lifetimes. Louis must be pissing himself laughing. But now comes the interesting part. My sister Margaret suggested that her stepdaughter Mary should marry George.'

I nearly said 'George who?' – so wild did the obvious answer seem.

'George?'

'George. Of Clarence. My brother.'

'But …' The bleak glint in Richard's eye warned me not to go on.

However, Anne, who had been quietly sewing while she listened, said, 'George? Well, I'm sorry, Richard, if it truly was Margaret's idea, but I have never heard anything so indecent. Isabel died hardly two months ago. And, say what you will, George loved her, he wouldn't think of re-marrying for a long time!'

'Well …'

'You mean …?'

'Darling, I'm sorry. He was all for it.' Anne was a placid woman, but under her quietness she had her father's temper. Richard unwisely hurried on, 'It cannot be looked at as a personal matter, it would be a political alliance only, so …' He ducked as Anne threw her embroidery frame at him. She followed it with as neat a verbal picture of him and his entire family as I could ever wish to hear, then stormed out of the room with a slam that had people in two counties starting nervously.

'You handled that well,' said Francis, picking up the embroidery.

'I forgot she was here,' Richard sheepishly confessed. 'I wasn't going to tell her. I knew she would take it personally.'

'Who wouldn't? She's right, it's not decent, not so soon. It insults Isabel's memory. Would you think of remarrying so soon? Richard, you can't be *for* the idea?'

There was quite a long pause, in which we avoided one another's eye, before he answered, 'No I am not. Not on any grounds. I'm afraid it was Margaret's fondness for George overcoming her good sense. By the way, George is drinking like a fish … In any case, the King flatly refused to consider it. But what no one quite understands is that the brother or sister or child of the King does not have the luxury of personal choice. George and I married for love, and we were lucky, for the King disapproved in both our cases. I admit he was in a poor position to object, but not one of you, my closest friends, has ever known how hard the King made it for me to marry Anne. If he hadn't been so angry with George he might have forbidden it – and loyalty and need of me be buggered. Marriage, for people like us, is not a matter of love or choice; you all know that.' Francis flushed: his had been the usual arranged marriage, he had been Warwick's ward and married off willy-nilly to Warwick's niece, and no one could say they more than rubbed along together. And, thinking of all those Woodville marriages back in the 1460s, I recalled that I, the King's ward and cousin, had only married where I chose because I wasn't important, and the King owed Innogen and me a favour.

Watching us, Richard went on, 'But you don't know how much more it is the case for the King's own family. If Anne died ...' he crossed himself, '... and the King commanded me to marry some foreign princess for the sake of political alliance, do you think I would be allowed to refuse? Short of giving up everything here and hiring out my sword as a mercenary in Europe? In which case I would lose my son. That, my disapproving friends, is what it is like when you're the brother of the King.'

I had rarely heard him speak with such intensity. It was too easy for us to fall into the way of thinking that he of all men had earned the right to do as he chose; but just how far would affection and loyalty go with the King in such a case?

Then, lightening, he said, 'Well, it doesn't matter in this instance, because as I said the King forbade George even to think of marrying Duchess Mary – and the lady herself refused. Barely politely. George is the last husband she needs! Though I can't help wondering if George saw the idea as a way to the power he would need to rebel again.'

'Richard, surely he wouldn't? Hasn't he learnt his lesson?'

'Does George ever learn? I've had weeks of him – and London. And telling everyone that it's his grief over Isabel is wearing damn thin as an excuse; especially after this marriage idea. Perhaps he is mad.' He hesitated a moment, then went reluctantly on, 'Though I felt some sympathy for him. The King refused the mere idea of

George marrying Mary of Burgundy – then put forward Anthony Woodville as the ideal bridegroom.'

'Anthony Woodville! To marry Mary of Burgundy?'

No wonder Richard was tired and on edge. Keeping the peace between his brothers, with this sort of provocation ... Surely not even the Queen in all her ambition could have taken the idea seriously? Despite his mother's St Pol connections, Rivers was a petty English earl without wealth, power or martial prowess; and the King had put the idea to the premiere heiress of Europe! How far under the Queen's thumb was he these days?

Well, we learnt the answer to that soon enough.

'Mary refused, of course,' Richard said wearily. 'She was insulted. Word is she's going to marry the Emperor Maximilian. And of course someone let George get wind of the thing – about Rivers, I mean – and he was flouncing about insulting everyone, refusing to take meals at Court, talking of conspiracies ... Oh, and the King has a new mistress. Shore or Shaw. Her name's Elizabeth but he calls her Jane.' He stood up so sharply the table rocked, spilling papers everywhere. Normally meticulous, he ignored the mess. 'If you'll excuse me, I must go and make peace with my wife.'

Following at a safe distance, I saw him come face to face with the beady little confederacy of Innogen and his two elder children. 'What have you done to Anne?' my wife demanded.

'Nothing. Mind your own business, Innogen.' Behind him I signalled frantic endorsement of this advice.

His blue eyes full of tears little John said, 'But Lady Anne is crying! Is someone else dead too?'

'Darling, no.' Guilt-stricken, Richard knelt down and wiped the tears away. 'No, John, it's just that I had to tell Lady Anne something annoying that happened in London. She's cross, that's all. Ladies sometimes cry when they're angry. Don't they, Innogen?'

'Indeed they do, Your Grace. Particularly when men are tactless and unkind.'

As she intended, this tickled Richard's sense of humour, though it was a close-run thing. 'Famously brutal as I am to women … Where is she?'

'In her room.'

'She locked the door,' John said. 'And Lady Anne *never* cries. You'd better go and kiss her like Papa does to Mama when she's cross.'

Richard glanced at Innogen and me, but we were both studying the ceiling. 'I shall take your advice, my dear,' he said gravely, and went.


There was little else to amuse us the rest of that year, for now George's troubles really began. I never did quite understand what happened at first – I wonder if even George did – but as far as I know it, this is the story.

Mad, drunken, or even justified, George took it into his head that Ankarette Twynho, one of Isabel's serving-women, had poisoned her, working in concert with a fellow called Thursby whose task it had been to poison the baby. What evidence George had for this fantastic-sounding story I don't know; probably none. Though it was *so* fantastic that he must have had some reason for believing it. Had the matter stopped at mere accusations, there would have been little enough harm done, perhaps, but George sent a gang of his men-at-arms to break into Mistress Twynho's house and haul her off by main force to Warwick to be tried for murder. Warwick was the centre of George's influence, the jurymen were all his. The trial was hustled through in a day, and Thursby and Mistress Twynho were found guilty and hanged immediately.

The point is obvious, of course. George had subverted the course of justice by pushing through such a quick trial by a stacked jury. And he had taken the King's justice into his own hands as surely as if he had run the poor Twynho woman through with his sword. He had overthrown the rule of law that Englishmen hold dear.

Bad enough for lovers of justice, but worse – for George – was to follow. A month after the Twynho business, an Oxford clerk called Stacy was accused of sorcery. The alleged offences were grave: Stacy was charged with casting horoscopes to foretell the death of the King and his heir, and of disseminating treason. In his confession Stacy accused two other men. One of these, a fellow clerk, was of no great importance. The other, called Burdett, was a Justice of the Peace and Member of Parliament. He was also a member of George's household, his friend and associate.

Burdett and Stacy were hanged, the other fellow, small fry, was pardoned. Burdett protested his innocence to his last breath. But then, so had Mistress Twynho.

Was it a hint to George to behave? Or was it, as he was soon telling anyone who would listen, a conspiracy to bring him down? First his wife died of poison, then his associates were falsely accused of one of the gravest crimes in the Calendar ... Poor, foolish, pathetic George made things as bad as he could for himself. He rushed into a Council meeting with Doctor Goddard and ordered the latter to read aloud Burdett's dying claim of innocence – and this was the Doctor Goddard who had proclaimed Henry VI's title to the throne back in 1470.

Still the matter might have died down, but George was thorough. Soon he was arming his men as if for war, and sending out proclamations that the King himself was a necromancer. He even managed – shades of '69 and '70 – to raise a rebellion over in the east. And dear Louis of France added the final touch by informing Edward that his spies told him George's seeking to marry Mary of Burgundy had indeed been only the first step towards overthrowing Edward.

It was the end of the King's precarious patience. By the end of June 1477 George of Clarence was a prisoner in the Tower, awaiting trial for subversion of justice and high treason.

He would be tried before the January parliament, but by November his entire family was converging on London. Because by now we knew that George's life hung in the balance.

# *Eleven*

Westminster stank. I suppose the palace had had the usual quarterly sweetening not long before, but still it smelt. It stank of the Thames, of too many people in too small a place, of wine, of the piss of people too lazy or drunken to reach the garderobe, of sex. Call it my fancy, but it stank of corruption. Even my beloved London seemed changed – small, crowded, dirty, its people strident and greedy. I had been too long in the north, where the air is clean and people speak their minds without resorting to abuse.

And the King had changed. In France two years before I had noted he was heavier and seemed harder, but now there was no trace of the handsome, slim, lively Edward of my youth. In his place was a coarse, fat, red-faced, almost gross man, who only put down his wine-cup to seize one of the whores who surrounded him. The days of discretion were over; all was licence, every appetite indulged. I'm no prude, and I'd not care to have my every action made public, but Edward's court disgusted me. It was venal. It had gone rotten. And, again, the Woodvilles were riding high, as if Edward had ceased to care, or had lost the ability to strike a balance.

That said, I felt some sympathy for the Queen. Over forty now, at first glance she looked barely thirty, but a closer look showed the heavy face-paint over sagging skin, the crow's feet around her eyes and the discontented droop to her mouth. She had borne ten children, and it showed in her thickened figure and plump jaw. She was still better looking than the average, but now people said not, 'Isn't she beautiful!' but, 'She must have been pretty.' Perhaps she yet retained some of her earlier fascination for Edward, for she had borne a child that year – ironically named George – or perhaps now he used her merely as a brood-mare and took his real pleasure with other women. Openly.

For I give you my word that the first time he saw Richard privately – I should say 'privately' – Edward had one of his bawds sitting on his knee, and his hand burrowed inside her gown while he talked to his brother. Richard's nostrils pinched with distaste until he resembled a buzzard, and at last he said, 'Perhaps, Your Grace, the lady could be excused while we talk?'

'Excused? Why, what's she done?' Edward roared with laughter at the feeble joke. I thought it a toss-up whether Richard would lose his temper or vomit as the King wheezed and squeezed. (I was there, officially, to carry the gifts Richard had brought for the King and Queen; unofficially, as a witness).

To her credit the whore slid off Edward's lap and said, 'His Grace of Gloucester is right, Edward.' ('Edward', to the King, in public!) 'With your permission?'

'Oh, very well. Run along, Jane.' She curtsied smartly and ran along. Edward looked dotingly after her. 'That's Mistress Shore. Divorced her husband for impotence. Can you imagine, with a girl like that? Poor sod – or perhaps he really is. Prefers boys, I mean. Isn't she the most fetching little thing you ever saw?'

'Extremely fetching,' Richard upheld the truth against all odds. And it was true. Jane Shore wasn't beautiful, but her heart-shaped face with its snub nose held a charm that Helen of Troy might have envied. Blonde, slender, small, pale-skinned, she was not unlike the Queen in her youth (which, as my wife pointed out when I told her, was only a further insult to the Queen). To be honest, I rather liked the look of Jane Shore. Shore the Whore. But there was something sweet about her, a quality that, odd though it may sound of a tart, was close to innocence. And although she had quite openly sized Richard and me up, assessing the length of our purses and no doubt of our pricks, she had had the decency to make herself scarce.

'Now, Edward,' said Richard, 'I must speak to you about George.'

'No.'

'But, Edward –'

'But me no buts, Gloucester.' Hell-fire, the King had said 'Gloucester' – not Richard, not Dickon.

'Your Grace, I must insist.'

'"Must" and "insist" are not words to use to monarchs, my lord duke. Up in the north you might rule: here you do not.'

Richard looked as if the King had hit him. Never, ever, had Edward spoken to him like that, as if to an importunate, crawling, insignificant stranger who had taken a liberty. Stiffly he said, 'I do not believe I do, Your Grace.'

'Good. Because I can take away your powers, my lord duke, I can break your might with a word.'

Perhaps a simple cry of 'Ned!', an appeal to brotherhood, might have been better, but Richard was so furious, and so flabbergasted, that he said, 'Of course you can do that – if you want England overrun by Scots.'

'Other men can guard my kingdom.'

Name one, I thought.

With a change of tone Richard said, 'I am, as always, nothing but Your Grace's humble servant. And brother.'

Something flickered in Edward's eyes. In another man I would have called it sheer misery. 'Yes,' he said, and his own voice had changed. 'Yes, I believe you are. And as my servant, humble or otherwise, your duty is to rule the north for me.'

Richard was sheet-white. Keep your temper, I silently urged him. As if he had heard me he said, 'And so I do. Always. And I do it well for you, out of duty and love. I do not seek to advise or oust you or any of your other servants. I only wish to ask you as your brother what you intend with George.'

'I don't know,' Edward admitted, and the tension eased a little.

'He has been unwise – but that's George.'

'Unwise? He's a fucking traitor!'

'Ten years, eight years, ago, he was that. Now he's guilty of much but surely not of treason?'

'Breaking England's laws is not treason? You of all people say that? And how can you plead for him after what he did to Anne back in '71?'

Richard let it go. 'Edward, Your Grace, in fairness, Isabel's death sent him half out of his mind.'

'Not difficult.'

Caught unawares, Richard couldn't stop a laugh. Edward grinned too, and for a moment it was like the old days. Except that in the old days none of the preceding conversation would have taken place, and Richard would not have been kept standing like a supplicant before the King.

'Yes,' Richard went on, 'but he genuinely seems to believe in the poisoning story, and isn't it natural for a new widower to blame anyone, everyone, for his wife's death? Take that into account.'

'I do.'

'Well, then?'

'Is a mad traitor better than a sane one?'

'Surely he's not a traitor. Edward, he has had months in prison. Let that suffice. If you wouldn't act against him when he was neck-deep in treason years ago, surely you can be lenient now. Take Isabel's death into account. You know George, he does eventually see sense.'

'Perhaps.'

'If I talk to him, he'll –'

'No.'

'Sire?'

'No talking to him.'

'But surely I may see him?'

'No.'

'Edward! For God's sake, he's my brother!'

'No. And that's final. Push me no further, Richard.'

Richard opened his mouth. Shut it. Bowed. Edward lifted his hand in dismissal. I put the gifts on the table. Bowed. We left.


Outside, the Queen's son Thomas Grey – now the Marquis of

Dorset – was lounging about the anteroom with a bunch of his cronies. At the back of the room Jane Shore played chess with Lord Hastings. She was studying the board; he was studying her with open, yearning lechery. The room stank of wine.

'So. Gloucester,' said Dorset. Insolent bugger. Like his mother, whose pearly colouring he shared, Dorset looked less than his age. He was about a year or so our senior, but could have been eighteen to our twenty-five; that's the soft life of a Court favourite for you. I used to wonder if he put his hair in curling-rags at night, like a woman.

Richard stopped. Looking Dorset up and down he said, 'So. Dorset.'

'Enjoy your chat with the King?' Dorset smirked. His cronies giggled.

'Thank you, I did. My brother and I understand one another.' That wiped the smirk off Dorset's fat face.

In retaliation he glanced at me and said, 'Must you always take your bum-boy with you everywhere?'

'Dorset!' snapped Hastings, appalled.

Richard gave the Marquis the enchanting smile of pure rage. 'Jealous, darling? Don't I remember you applying for the position when you were younger and prettier?' Dorset went white. Tell you the truth, I had once or twice wondered about him when we were boys together. Perhaps others had too, for Hastings wasn't the only one laughing at the jibe.

On that wave of laughter a pleasant voice said from the doorway, 'Your Grace of Gloucester! I did not know you were here – Greetings, cousin, and to you, Sir Martin.'

'Harry! Good day to you.' Richard was relieved and pleased to see the Duke of Buckingham – and if a royal duke, cousin to the King and next in rank to his brothers, can observe protocol, how much more should an upstart like Dorset?

'Had I known you had arrived I would have called,' said Buckingham, walking with us down the corridor. 'Where are you, Crosby Place on Bishopsgate? You're hiring it still?'

'Yes, but my mother is at Baynard's Castle, I seem to spend most of my time there. Not that I've been in London more than a day or two.'

'I shall call on my lady aunt, I've not been here long myself. I wonder – would you two care for a drink with me? Sample London's inns as you used to?' Under his breath he added, 'And wash the taste of Westminster out of your mouths.'

At the Boar's Head, drinking excellent ale, Buckingham said, 'I used to envy you two back in the sixties, for being old enough to go out drinking and for being able to do whatever what you liked.' He didn't have to say, 'and for not being married to the Queen's sister and kept under the Woodville eye'.

Gently Richard said, 'Had we known, we would have smuggled you out with us. Though I suspect the King kept us on a tighter rein than we knew; a little roistering, all very well, but any sign of bad company or of getting a taste for drink and we would have felt the twitch of the tether.'

'Yes, he used to worry about you. About all of us youngsters. And I remember you used to take me riding.' Flicking back his bright fair hair Buckingham said bluntly, 'That scene in his rooms – that's typical now. He drinks too much. Too many whores. Too much of everything. He's thirty-five and looks fifty. I take it you met Jane Shore?'

'Yes.'

'Well, I wouldn't worry about her, she's the pick of the bunch.'

'She struck me,' said Richard without much disapproval, 'as the sort who'd fuck a snake if she could hold onto its ears.'

Buckingham laughed and said he wasn't far wrong. 'But she's not vicious, Richard. She likes sex, but that's not the worst sin in the world. And she loves the King. I'm at Court quite often, as you know, and I keep my eyes and ears open. My wife is much in the Queen's confidence.'

Ah, we had reached the nub of the matter. Richard murmured something polite about looking forward to seeing Buckingham's wife again, they must come to dinner.

'In between Council meetings and wedding preparations,' said Buckingham.

'Yes.' Slate-blue eyes gazed into sea-blue ones. 'So many people are in London for the business. The marriage of the King's son is a great event.' The King had secured the hand of Lady Anne Mowbray, heiress to the Dukes of Norfolk, for his second son Richard. The marriage was a great one, for the little girl – she was six; her bridegroom four – would inherit enormous wealth, and would bring the prince the Dukedom of Norfolk in addition to the York one he already held. 'I hear that the Prince of Wales is coming up from Ludlow for the wedding.'

'Yes, with his uncle Anthony and half-brother Richard Grey.'

'All the Woodvilles, in fact.'

'Precisely.' Even in the private room of a London inn it was wise to be discreet. 'My wife tells me that her family are much concerned for the – the safety of the realm. They fear the King may grow slack about guarding against such dangers. It is not long since we learned, painfully, how easily treason spreads. My wife's family would have the King be severe with anyone who spreads slanders and stirs up treachery. They fear the King is too easily swayed by – by those with an older and in its way closer claim upon him.'

'Perhaps they should reflect on the danger of creating new enemies.'

Buckingham slammed down his cup. 'Is there,' he said through his teeth, 'anyone left to become a *new* enemy of –'

'Harry,' Richard's tone warned him back to discretion. Buckingham sagged back on his bench. I refilled our cups.

Turning his between his fingers the duke said, 'The people you saw today – the way they behaved – take the hint, Richard. They're riding high, they think they can treat the royal blood as they like. The King is ... undecided.' His voice changed to reflect his smile. 'Now, Hastings is a good chap, isn't he? Of course you are old friends and comrades-in-arms; I needn't tell you. And the Howards. And it's always pleasant to see the Herberts at Court, young William's a splendid chap too. Plenty of ... of the old people about. Well! My wife will be looking for me, so if you'll excuse me ...'

'Of course. I trust she is well. Please give her my compliments and say I shall have Anne invite you soon.'

'I'll look forward to it. Perhaps we can do this again, it's good to have a quiet drink with friends. Good day, Sir Martin.'


We arrived back at Baynard's Castle to find that Richard's sister Elizabeth, Duchess of Suffolk, had arrived. With her were her ineffectual husband and her eldest son John, Earl of Lincoln, a lively, pleasant lad of about twenty.

'Richard!' Elizabeth descended on him like a ship in full sail ramming a smaller vessel. She was one of the tall ones of her family, and bearing several children amid the bucolic life of Suffolk had given her, at thirty-three, the sort of figure best described as Juno-esque. A handsome woman, fair and blue-eyed, unlike her namesake the Queen she used no face-paint and probably would have scoffed at the idea. She had no need of it, for her husband might have been dull but he plainly adored her.

'Liz, my dear.' Richard kissed her fondly. As a child he had hardly known her, but as adults they had become deeply fond of each other. I always liked her greatly; I would have liked her for my elder sister. 'How lovely to see you. You are all well?'

'I always am.' Elizabeth gave me an absent but very sweet kiss. 'Suffolk does not change.' The Duke stood by, smiling, rocking on his heels, unchanging. 'Jack, greet your uncle.' Lincoln, who had been trying to do just that, jumped and looked furtive. Richard almost burst out laughing. They embraced, grinning in shared affection for the overpowering Duchess. 'Now, Richard, what's to do? This business of George, I mean. Poor Mother is very worried. As am I.'

'We all are, Liz. I've just come from the King.'

'I know, Mother said. And?'

'Hmm. Difficult. On edge. Angry. Implacable.'

'That's bad,' Elizabeth said at once. Her Suffolk accent blurred her words – thass baad. 'Yes, that's bad. Ned has a temper, and an unforgiving streak. Heaven knows George is the biggest fool in shoe-leather, but why must Ned wait until now to punish him?'

'That's what I asked.' Richard sank into a chair, gratefully taking a cup of wine. Anne sat beside him, absently stroking his neck. 'Not that I got any answer. I think the King has simply run out of patience with him. And who can blame him? After all, Liz – subversion of justice … There is no excuse for what George did in the Twynho business.'

'But he has imprisoned George for treason!'

'Stirring up rebellions.'

'Which came to nothing!'

'Mother,' Lincoln put in, 'whether they come to anything isn't the point. Uncle George actively rebelled against the King. He thoroughly deserves a spell in prison; anyone else would have had it long ago.'

'I agree, and that was my point: why now?'

'I think,' Richard wearily repeated, 'that Edward has simply run out of patience. High time George learnt his lesson.'

'Well, yes,' Elizabeth admitted, 'but surely we, his family, have the right to know exactly what Ned intends? There must be a clear penalty – mustn't there? The King must announce how long he means to keep George in prison?'

Richard didn't answer. Suddenly losing her composure Elizabeth said, 'But if – if Edward wouldn't tell you … Dickon, I've heard he means to try George for high treason. Dickon, he cannot kill his own brother!'

'Of course not.' Richard managed to sound quite convincing, but his sister stared at him, biting her lip.

'Did Edward tell you he would not?'

'Oh, he was on his high horse – you know, Liz. Touchy. He has done what he should have done years ago and taught George a lesson by popping him into prison, and now he has to find a solution that pleases everyone.'

'If he's trying to please the Queen's bloodsucking family – and of course they have never forgiven George for executing her father and brother back in '69 – they'll see to it that George ...'

'Has a good long spell in prison,' interrupted Lincoln, 'and comes out a sadder but wiser man. Perhaps, Uncle Richard, you could offer to stand surety for him in some way, get the King to place him in your custody for a while, something like that.' Quicker than the rest of us, he had heard the Duchess of York in the corridor outside. 'Now, what of this new printing business of Master Caxton's? I think it's a marvel – printed books! Do you realise it means that everyone will be able to afford books? More and more people are learning to read, there are more schools and quite ordinary people read – and now they'll be able to buy anything they want. I think it's the marvel of our time. A new age is starting, and who knows what inventions we might see next?'

Clever boy: this was a subject after Richard's own heart – and his mother's – and everyone had an opinion. What of the copyists it would put out of work? Surely printing would be all very well for common works but not for books of religion? Just how cheap could printed books be? Who cares, I'm buying all I can. And Lincoln won the day by saying, 'Well, I hold it's a marvel – for now everyone can read my great-great-grandfather!' Who was, of course, Geoffrey Chaucer.

That night when I went up to bed I found all the women in my room, Innogen, Anne and the two duchesses. I was for it. 'Now, Martin,' said the Duchess of York, folding her hands on her knee, 'we want to know exactly what passed between Richard and the King today. All of it, please. Richard's putting a good face on it to soothe us, which is very dear and kind of him, but we know things are much worse than he is saying. So tell us.'

Cravenly I said, 'You won't tell Richard I told you?'

'Of course not!'

'But he'll know!' I whined. 'For instance, where does he think you all are at the moment?'

'Comparing gowns for that wretched Court wedding banquet,' Anne snapped. 'Tell us, Martin. I can't look after Richard unless I know.'

So I told them. I even told them of Jane Shore, and Dorset's insolence (I left out the bum-boy remark) and I gave them a tactful version of our talk with Buckingham.

'So it is the Woodville influence,' the Duchess of York said when I finished.

'Probably. Although, Madam, remember George has committed serious crimes.'

'Oh yes, but there's more to it. Ten years ago Edward would have seized him, tried him, and sentenced him to a clearly defined term of imprisonment. Cut and dried. There would have been none of this shilly-shallying. At its best it seems like revenge, not justice. For, Martin, Edward has refused to answer my letters. Margaret's too.'

I spread my hands in a helpless gesture. The silence held. At last Anne said the unspeakable. 'High treason means the death penalty. Would the King let it go so far?'

'I think he would have done it already. Therefore, he neither wants to nor will.'

'Then,' Anne said sadly, angrily, 'it will be up to my poor Richard to find a way out. As usual.'


Richard tried, but as November turned into December he gained no ground. In between Council meetings and the other official business of the realm the King gave him short shrift, either refusing to see him or granting him only the briefest audience. In the end he prepared what was in effect a legal brief, setting out every point of George's undoubted crimes, citing precedents of punishment, suggesting an acceptable penalty. Whether the King ever read it, I don't know. He would not let any of the family visit George, and although he eventually allowed them to write, George was not permitted to reply.

Speaking of writing, the first book to come from William Caxton's printing shop at the Sign of the Red Pale was Anthony Woodville's translation of a French manuscript, *The Dictes and Sayinges of the Philosophers*. Credit where it's due, it wasn't bad, though I doubt it will last.

And while the King's brother languished in prison, all was merriment at Court, the usual Christmas festivities plus the celebrations for the Prince's wedding. Parties, banquets, jousting, games, at which everyone was extremely cordial and polite. Let the Woodville faction make of it what they liked: unusually, the King's entire family was there. Even the Duchess of York attended every event, and although she wore her usual widow's black her gowns were exquisite brocade or velvet with sable trim. For the first time since her husband's death she wore her magnificent jewels, and made the Queen look like trash.

No one spoke of George. On the twentieth day of November the King had issued writs calling a Parliament. The implication was clear – George was to be tried by his peers. Already all his estates and possessions had been sequestered to the Crown.

On January the fifteenth came the wedding. I liked the little Duke of York, the dearest, merriest boy you could hope to meet – pure Plantagenet, nothing Woodville about him. I don't think he had a clue what the wedding was about; he looked on his bride as a new playmate, but confided to me at the banquet after the ceremony that she was too old and girls were boring. He had too many sisters, he said, and would like to live with his older brother at Ludlow. Overhearing, Richard told him he knew Ludlow, and talked of first meeting Edward there. At once the boy was on fire with interest, and nothing would do but for Richard to tell him the whole story. His sister Lady Bess came to listen too; near twelve now, she was a pretty girl, bar a bit of puppy fat. But no sooner were we deep in talk than the Queen rustled over and said the Prince must not bore his uncle and must talk to his bride. Sulking, the poor boy was led firmly away, Bess too. The Prince of Wales, a tall weedy boy who looked as if he had been grown under glass, watched everything with a bread-and-circuses air.

Next day George was tried before Parliament. The charge was high treason, the penalty death. Richard had asked to be excused from attending. The King refused.

Francis, Rob and I dressed Richard that morning, acting as the body squires we no longer officially were. He needed us, you see, he needed his friends, and not only because his hands shook so much he couldn't fasten a button. Trembling with tension, he was as deadly white as before a battle, and we had to stand over him like children's nurses to force him to eat something. He said not one word, not even when Anne kissed him goodbye or when his mother with tears in her eyes held his hand and blessed him as if for a journey. In its way it was a journey; to the end of his childhood, to the end of his adoring love for the big brother who had been his idol.

I had no business in Parliament, but I was not going to let Richard be alone that day. If you look confident people think you've a right to be where you are, so, clasping a book or two, I strode busily into the building and insinuated myself into some sort of ante-room to the main chamber. I could hear what passed and, if I was cautious, see much of it.

And so I heard and saw the House of York destroying itself. I saw that gross, concupiscent swine King Edward IV accuse his brother George of 'conduct derogatory to the laws of the realm and most dangerous to judges and juries throughout the kingdom'. I saw the so-called witnesses, all of whom added to the so-called evidence against George. I saw George, thin, haggard, hopeless, yet with a dignity and calm unusual in him, stand alone in the middle of the chamber and answer his brother's accusations. He did it well. His answers were cogent, sensible, deferential. Of course he was fighting for his life, but I thought, yes, he has learnt his lesson, he has in fact matured at long last; let that be enough punishment.

But of course it was a foregone conclusion. No one accused but the King. No one was allowed to speak in George's defence but himself. And soon the Duke of Buckingham, High Steward for the occasion, and nearly as ashen as the King's two brothers, pronounced the death penalty.

Richard had sat through the proceedings as still and pale as a marble effigy, looking at no one but George. The moment the sentence was pronounced he rose and strode out of the chamber. The unceremonious exit, the refusal to bow to the King, was the only protest he was allowed to make.

I found him outside. He was crouched in the street, his velvet Parliament robe spread around him, puking his heart up. A Royal Duke, vomiting into the public drain while passers-by watched curiously.

Careless of who might see, I crouched down and held him as I do my children. There was nothing to be said, so I kissed him and helped him up. He looked at me vaguely, then said, 'I'm glad it's you. Get me home.'

Everyone was gathered waiting in the hall at Baynard's Castle. We did not have to tell them. The Duchess of York cried, 'No!' and shoved her knuckles hard against her mouth. It was the only time I ever saw her cry.

Elizabeth said in disbelief, 'The death sentence?' Richard nodded, once. In the silence Anne came and took him in her arms and led him away upstairs.


But the death sentence was not immediately carried out. The King held off. I believed – I hoped – that when it came to it, he couldn't after all kill his brother. Nor could he, now, refuse to see his family. What passed between him and his mother I don't care to imagine. Elizabeth of Suffolk had an audience with him that left her weeping helplessly, with hope as much as anger. Lord Hastings did his best; so did Lord Howard. Harry Buckingham too, I believe. From Burgundy Duchess Margaret wrote imploring Edward to commute the sentence. Richard saw the King twice, briefly, and came away hopeful. A week passed, and still the King held off.

And in that week the wedding celebrations continued unabated. There was a great joust, for example, a Woodville affair from start to finish, Dorset and Rivers pretty as pictures in their velvet tents and decorative armour. Richard didn't bother to attend. Buckingham told me that the King watched it all expressionless, and never said a word.

Then the King sent for me. The written message said only, 'Pray heed the bearer of this,' with the meat in the oral message. Which was: come now, come alone, tell no one. If the messenger, some anonymous fellow in plain clothes, had not shown me the King's ring as proof, I'd have thought I was being lured to my death. Well, I don't say I really pictured myself being kidnapped or secretly murdered – why would I be? – but I made the excuse of fetching a cloak, and told my wife. 'Say nothing – but it looks so odd … Be discreet.'

The messenger led me not to any part of the Palace that I knew, but to a room high in a tower. Bidding me wait, he left me alone, and I heard him lock the door on the outside. The room was furnished as a bedchamber, the bed neatly made. A table held a lute, wine flask and cups, and a few books, the two I glanced at of such a filthily erotic nature that the purpose of this secret room was clear.

I waited almost an hour before a concealed door in the panelling opened and the King entered.

With no more greeting than a nod he told me to sit down. There was nowhere to sit but the bed, and from sheer terror I had the frivolous thought that the King's new depravities included sodomy and I was for it. But he remained standing, staring down at me from a distance. 'Martin. I know you for an honest man. Are you still?'

'Yes, Sire.'

'You are Richard's friend. Since you were children. You love him?'

'Yes. All our lives. Yes, I love him dearly.'

'If you had to choose between him and your wife, which would you choose?'

Thinking, Oh Christ, I said carefully, 'Circumstances alter cases, Your Grace, so how can I say?'

'Answer me.'

'Well then – my wife, because she *is* my wife, because we love each other, we are dear companions and she is the mother of my children.'

Without expression the King said, 'You would choose your wife. Yet you are loyal to Richard and you love him.'

'Yes.'

'Even though he fucked your wife?'

I don't know how I kept from showing my reaction. 'That was long ago, before she was my wife.'

'Are you sure?'

Probably it was beyond his brutish comprehension that two people who had been lovers could shake down into an almost fraternal relationship, that their spouses could trust them. 'Yes I am sure, because I know them both. They both love me. Richard loves Anne and would never hurt or dishonour her. He believes in the Commandments.' I thought, if he mocks or makes a joke I'll hit him. But he said, still without expression,

'Give me your opinion of my brother George.'

'Sire, I really knew him only as a child.'

'People don't change. You have observed him since. Tell me.'

'Well then, he strikes me as vain, ambitious, rather foolish though not unintelligent, a fickle sort of man, yet capable of kindness and love. Most people can reason from A to B. George can't reason from B to C.'

'Explain.'

'Well, take the events of 1469 and '70. 'A' is that George wants the Crown – 'B', so he rebels. Most people could see as far as 'C': that he would have to give in and return to you, or encompass either his death or yours and Richard's. But George couldn't see that. Nor could he reason ahead to 'D', which is exactly what did happen.'

'Well put. You would make a good schoolmaster, Sir Martin. You've been loyal, Richard could not have achieved all he has without you and the others like you. I'll make you a baron, I think; even a viscount. Or why not an earl?'

In for a penny, in for a pound, I said: 'That's crude, Edward.

Whatever you want, you can't bribe me.'

He nearly hit me, pulling the blow at the last moment. I remembered how back in '70, hearing of Warwick's pact with Lancaster, he had broken up the room in his rage. But he calmed himself and said, 'So you are the one man in England who can't be bought.'

Beyond caring what I said to this man I answered, 'No I am not. And what have you become if you can think that, even in mockery? Now tell me what it is you want of me.'

He raised his eyebrows. 'Tell me your opinion of Richard. And don't worry, he's not hidden on the other side of the door with his ears flapping. It's no test.'

'Then what is it?' But he only gestured impatiently for me to go on. 'Very well. Richard is loyal, clever, honest, diligent, kind. He'd never betray anyone to whom he's given his loyalty, his friendship or his good-lordship. He's a brilliant general and fighter, and no one can lead men like he can. In the north he is very much loved as well as admired and respected.'

'And his faults?'

'He can be stubborn, contrary, dogmatic, uncompromising, naïve, and often thinks too well of people.'

The King sat down. 'If I put George to death, will Richard still love me?'

Suddenly we were talking as equals, even friends as the kinsmen we in fact were. 'How should I know, I've no brothers, I've no idea how far fraternal love goes. He will despise you. And, if it matters to you, you'll have destroyed something in him. Will you put George to death? Must you?'

'God above, why can no one see it! List his crimes – rebellion, treason, subversion of justice, inciting others to those same crimes, executing an innocent woman, necromancy, spreading lies and slanders about me and my family, putting it about I was base-born, slandering the Queen, my children, her family, my marriage … And people expect me to spare him?'

'He is your brother. Take Isabel's death into account. Imprison him for a good long time. Be merciful. Please.'

The King took my chin in his hand, turning my face towards him. 'Why do you care? I thought you never liked George?'

'He's my cousin. I've few kin, so I care about that. And I care for Richard's sake and for your mother's; your sisters' sakes, too. And yours. I remember a little boy at Fotheringhay. I remember an eleven-year-old boy who was sea-sick with me going to Burgundy, and who looked after me and Richard there and told us not to fear because his wonderful big brother Edward always won battles and could do anything. I remember him kissing Richard when your armies met at Coventry.' My voice was trembling with emotion, I was nearly crying. 'I've often disliked him, true, yet I just as often liked him. I'm not sure I'd ever trust him far, and I don't love him, yet it's not entirely for others' sake that I don't want him dead.'

There was a long silence. 'Could George keep his mouth shut?'

Christ, about what? I have always regretted I didn't ask precisely that, for in this mood Edward just might have told me, and all our lives might have been different. 'No.'

'Could Richard?'

'Yes, unless you mean about some – I don't know – some vicious crime, some great wrong it was possible to right.'

For a moment Edward put his hands over his face. 'People don't know what it is like for the King. What I suffer. I spoke before of choosing between your wife and your friend – a metaphor – a King is married to his country.' He spread out his hand, the Coronation ring glinting in the candlelight. 'Married to his people, his country. Responsible. What would be a sin in a private person cannot be in a King if he does it for his country. I, as King, cannot say, "I love my brother, therefore let him go free". And anyone but George would have gone to the block years ago.'

'You said something like that the night before the battle of Barnet. And in that battle George fought for you, out of love. Edward, I admit his crimes, but must it be death?'

'What else?'

'Prison,' I repeated. 'Or ship him off abroad, strip him of his titles and lands, make him powerless, disgraced. Or put him into Richard's custody, he'll stand surety for him and I think George loves and respects him enough to behave. And Richard is the one person George could never corrupt or suborn.' Edward looked at me out of his bleared, bloodshot eyes. He really was suffering, and that knowledge gave me the courage to say, 'Don't do it, Edward. You'll never forgive yourself. Nor will Richard, or your mother, or your sisters. If it counts, nor will I. And if you do decide for mercy, don't they deserve to think it was because of them? Out of your love for them?'

'I don't know. I don't think I can.' He stood up. 'Very well, Martin. Go. Tell no one of this talk, especially not Richard. If necessary, say I offered you a title and you refused it. You might still get one.'

'Not now, please.'

'Fuck you,' he said without animosity. 'Go on, get out.'

The messenger conducted me down into a side court with a gate to the street. It was early evening, dark and foggy, and when a figure popped up at my elbow I nearly screamed.

'Shhh. It's me, Jane Shore. I knew you were with Edward; no one else knows. Please, Sir Martin, listen, I can't approach the Duke of Gloucester. But tell him I will do what I can to save his brother. You see, I love Edward, and killing his brother will ruin him. And it is *wrong*. I might not succeed, but I will try.'

'Why?'

'I told you, I love Edward. No one believes that but it's true. Not because he's King. I love *him*. Goodbye.' Saucy frippet, she kissed me.

I told Richard the moment I got home. I thought he should know the King's mind, and although he would never doubt me, it's impossible to keep a secret at Court and I didn't want rumours flying around about my interview with the King. Besides, I would not have put it past Edward to give me a title anyway; it would suit him, or at least the Woodvilles, to have people thinking Richard couldn't trust his closest friend.

Richard said, 'I don't know what is going on. Martin, would you say – did the King seem – is it yes or no? Death or mercy? Though, Lord Jesu … life in prison, poverty … I think George would prefer death. I think I would.'

'Me too. Richard, my dear, I honestly don't know. But I think you should be prepared for the worst.'

'I am. I think.' He was close to tears. I put my arms around him, and he clutched me like a frightened child. For a moment we embraced desperately, then he said with a shaky laugh, 'It's come to something when I have to rely on the King's whore to save my brother. Did she mean it?'

'Do you know, I think she did.'


Perhaps she did, and perhaps she did try. Perhaps many people did. But on the eighteenth day of February the Speaker of the Commons went formally to the Lords and requested that the death sentence be carried out with no more delay.

That night, George was executed in the Tower.

It was secretly done, by what means no one knows. Word went around that George had been drowned in a butt of Malmsey wine, but surely that is only ribald comment on his drinking habits? His family was told no more than the fact of his death. The King sent a herald with a formal letter addressed to Richard – leaving it up to him, of course, to tell their mother and sister.

I need not belabour the point. Despite everything I still had some fondness for George, and had he died a natural death I would have grieved and wished it otherwise. But like this … And almost the worst was losing all my lifetime's adoration of Edward. What had happened to the kind, glorious boy who seventeen years before had kissed away my fears?


The following day I went with Richard to see the King. Clad in the black of mourning Richard strode through the rooms of Westminster as if they were empty, and this time people damn' well fell back before him. No one but Hastings and Buckingham had had the decency to put on mourning; in the Woodvilles it would have been hypocrisy.

The King was alone in his rooms. He wore black, and he looked as if he had had word of his own approaching death.

'Richard, Sir Martin.'

'Highness.' We bowed. Richard looked at his brother.

'Dickon …'

'Your Grace asked to see me?'

'I had no choice. He was a traitor.'

'He was my brother.'

'And mine!'

'Yes.'

The King's shoulders slumped, then stiffened. 'Is our mother …'

For a moment Richard's control cracked. 'You *dare* to speak of her … She is on her knees in her chapel, Your Grace, praying for the repose of her son's soul. And, no doubt, for the Christian courage to forgive his murderers. She will return to Berkhamsted tomorrow, and now she will take her vows as a nun. She wants no more part of the secular world.'

'Richard …' For a moment the King held out his hand, then let it fall helplessly.

Ignoring the gesture, Richard said, speaking very fast, 'Our mother bore eight sons – Henry, you, Edmund, William, John, George, Thomas, me. Four she buried as infants. Edmund she lost in battle. Those deaths are what happens in our world, and our mother found the courage and the faith to bear those losses. Whether she can bear the loss of a son killed by another of her sons, I do not know. So don't dare speak to me of our mother. And take a word of advice, Highness: do not write to her or think to visit her.'

So quietly I could hardly hear him, Edward said, 'Has she disowned me?'

'She would never do that. I mean, merely, have some regard for her feelings.'

Still in that soft, faltering voice the King said, 'And have you disowned me, Richard?'

'You are my brother. I am Your Grace's loyal servant.'

'And with that I must be content?'

'What do you think? Now, as Your Grace's loyal servant – as your brother if that still has power to move you – I have two requests to make of you.'

'Of course.'

'Please put George's children into my care, make me their guardian; that request comes not only from my heart but from Anne's, their aunt. And, secondly, I wish licences to found colleges to pray for – for Their Graces the King and Queen, and for my dead brothers and sisters.'

'Of course. Where?'

'Barnard. Middleham. Your Grace, where is George to be buried?'

'Tewkesbury. In the Abbey. With Isabel.'

'Thank you. And the children may –'

'I have already granted their wardships to my stepson Dorset.'

'To Dorset! Edward, no!'

'It is done, Richard. But I have reserved the earldom of Warwick for George's son. The earldom of Salisbury I have granted to your own son.' Richard was staring at him incredulously. 'And I want you to be Great Chamberlain again.'

'No.' George had held the post since 1472.

'It is done. It is necessary.'

For a moment Richard stood frowning down at the carpet. 'Your Grace, please reconsider about the children.'

'No. It is done. Although,' dryly, 'Dorset will not be able to play ducks and drakes with their lands.' This was the sole concession; though we discovered later that the King had in fact kept most of George's sequestered estates for himself and his brother-in-law Anthony.

'I see.' Richard bowed. 'Have I your leave to depart?'

'Yes. You return at once to the north?'

'My mother wishes my escort to Berkhamsted. Then, yes, I go home.'

Edward sighed. 'Very well. Godspeed. And, Richard, keep the north for me.'

'As I always have, for the King. Goodbye.'

# Twelve

## 1480-1482

It was in the spring of 1480 that our friend Louis of France tickled up that Scots fool James III to start the border raids again. Louis of course wanted England kept busy in the north while he got on with his own games, and his Scottish puppet was only too happy to oblige.

Politics always bored me stiff. Suffice it to say that the kings of England, Scotland and France, and Emperor Maximilian and Duke Francis of Brittany were engaged in manoeuvrings as complex as a Scottish reel as they each tried to win alliances and exclude others. Thus, Maximilian was dickering with both England and Scotland for the help he needed against France; Duke Francis, the same. Louis XI was desperate to prevent a triple alliance of England, Brittany and Burgundy against him. Edward was desperate to hang onto his French pension and Bess's betrothal to the Dauphin, while at the same time negotiating with Burgundy for an alliance against France and a marriage between his daughter Anne and Philip, son of Maximilian and Mary. Is that clear? No, nor was it ever to me. Richard once claimed to understand it, but he was drunk at the time. But the upshot was that with England occupied with a war in the north, the way would be clear (so Louis hoped) for him to get on with his own plans to annihilate Burgundy and Brittany.

In the middle of 1480 Duchess Margaret came to England to negotiate with Edward on Burgundy's behalf, and although I of course went with Richard on his hasty visit south to see her, she had little time to spare for personal matters, and her grief for George so overwhelmed her still that she could bear no recollections of happier times. Still, it was good to see her, however briefly – although it was during her visit that spies revealed to Edward Maximilian's dealings with the Scots.

At first the raids were intermittent and none too serious, but they could come at any point along the border so that we had little chance of preparing for them. The Scots would mass silently on their side of the border, then in the night dart into England's part of the Debatable Lands. Sometimes it was no more than harassment, a few livestock taken, a peel tower burned, a man forced to watch his wife or daughter raped. Often, though, whole settlements were left in smoking ruins in which women searched hopelessly and abandoned children wailed in terror.

Even after the truces of the 1460s and '70s there had been raiding from both sides of the border, it was a local sport or natural hazard like the weather – but as 1480 went on it became clear this was an organised campaign. Edward appointed Richard Lieutenant-General, and he and the Earl of Northumberland prepared to move against the Scots.

And then the Earl of Angus led a war-band right into English territory and torched Bamburgh. Our enemies had teased the English lion once too often, and the lion roared and bared its claws. In September Richard led an army into Scotland, chasing Angus, but the Earl and his gang fled for cover, and by October we were riding home to Sheriff Hutton. The approach of winter saw the Scots as eager to lie-up as we were. The raids ceased, and Richard took the opportunity to put Carlisle into good repair. Also he and Northumberland carried out a census of the north to determine available numbers of men, for no one believed the Scots had given up.

And sure enough, as soon as the snows had melted they were at it again. Resignedly we packed our gear, tended our weapons and made ready. Then John asked if he could come with us.

'What do you mean, come with us? It's not a pleasure outing.'

'I know. Don't treat me like a child.'

'My dear boy, you are a child! You're only eleven. Anyway, what do you mean?' He was helping me polish and pack my armour, something I never left to anyone else. Of course we always took full armour, because you never know, but this inconclusive warfare of fast raid and counter-raid, skirmishes and chases more than battle, usually called for brigandines and sallets; at most, the half-armour of breast-plate and greaves. Each piece as it was polished was rolled up in felt and packed in exact order, and absently I noted that John was doing all this with casual expertise. I noted too that he lifted my brigandines nearly as easily as I did myself – and the boiled leather jacket with metal plates between the layers weighed some forty pounds. John had grown lately; on his birthdays I measured him, and the new mark was four inches higher than the last. What I had not noticed was how he had filled out. Already he was moving towards the changes of adolescence; he would be a well-built man, perhaps nearly as large as his uncle Edward. He would be handsome, too, as you would expect of a child of Innogen and Richard. We had sent him to Richard's household at Pontefract for training, but although he never complained he had pined so markedly that, softhearted, we brought him home to Middleham. He was clever at his books, and his masters spoke well of his intelligence, but he had always taken an absorbing interest in military matters.

So now when I asked him, he gave an answer he had clearly thought out with care. 'I'm eleven, and I've had three years' henchman training. I'm a good page, I know all the duties, and I've squired you and my father. I'm quite bright, but not bookish like Edward or your boys. I want to serve with my father and you and be a soldier. And so I want to come with you on this campaign. Not to fight, of course, or put myself in danger; just to see it and get experience. When my father was eleven he was leading out levies for the King.'

'An honorary position. Very, very different from campaign. John, it is not possible.'

'Please.' He had Innogen's pale skin, and intense emotion always drove the colour from his face so that freckles stood out on his nose. 'Please,' he repeated.

'John, this sort of rough-riding campaign isn't like a set battle where we could leave you safely behind the lines. Even our base camp could easily be taken by the Scots.'

'But you establish headquarters well on our side of the border. That's all I want – to come. You take boys as runners or flag-bearers, or camp servants or to mind the baggage.'

'Well, yes, but … It's too dangerous, dear. Think of your mother.' Innogen would take a dim view at the best of times, but a few months previously we had lost a child. Our son Peter was born in 1479 and died before his second birthday. We were lucky he was the only one we had lost, but that was cold comfort. We felt it more because our children had always been healthy. So this was the worst time to ask Innogen to part with her first-born. Nor, when it came to it, could I bear the thought. John and I had grown to love each other dearly; he called me Papa as my own children did – yet suddenly, with this request I understood that he was not my son, but Richard's.

Staring anxiously up at me he said, 'I understand about Mother and I know it is a bad time.'

'Yet you ask.'

'Yes.'

'Why?'

'Because it feels as if it's time. And because I'm a bastard. I can't explain more than that. But it is different for us – for bastards – for me and Katherine. I love you and Mother, and I love my lord father and Lady Anne, but the – the fact makes a difference. I can't explain.'

'You feel you have more to prove?'

'Something like that.'

'I see. Or rather I don't see, except that it is important to you. Important enough to distress your mother.'

'I don't want to but I can't let that count or there will always be some reason. So please let me come with you.'

'It's not up to me. As you've just reminded me, I'm not your father.' John flushed. Poor child, torn between his adoring devotion to Richard and ten years' loyalty to me. I put my hands on his shoulders to look directly at him. 'John, dear, that's a fact, not a matter of emotion. I made myself responsible for you when I married your mother, but in things like this the decision is not up to me. Therefore, if you can talk Richard into it, I'll agree; and I'll even try to reconcile your mother. Which won't be easy.'

'I know. Thank you.' He was too old for the ready kisses of childhood, but when I hugged him he returned the embrace fiercely.

Of course I had thought I could persuade Richard to issue a flat veto, but John forestalled me, showing a tactical skill that argued well for his military future. And Richard said yes. This enabled me to earn marital good-will by standing around shaking my head, but still neither Innogen nor Anne spoke to us for days. Anne loved her stepson as much as I did, and John's delighted preparations brought it home to her how soon her own Edward would be making the same request.

So, when in the spring we rode out again, John came with us, and when in March Richard went south to confer with the King he took John. I didn't go. The Clarence business had sickened me of the King. He and Richard had to work together, and somehow they had patched things up enough to meet civilly; but the King was not my brother. I couldn't forget that strange secret interview with him – and with trust had gone all liking. So I gladly seized the excuse of overlooking our stores of arms and gear, and let Francis and Rob accompany Richard.

Richard returned uncommunicative, except on military matters. He said the King was busily raising taxes, and in fact had resorted to the hated benevolences which in '75 he had sworn he would never need again, and would come north himself if real trouble threatened. As in the old days he would take the field at the head of his armies.

'Though I wouldn't hold your breath,' Francis told me. 'God's bones, Martin, it would break your heart to see the King now.'

'Ill?'

'We-ell … it's more that he's fat and out of condition; he has stomach trouble. Of course those big men often run to flesh, but … wine, women, Woodvilles. I think the '78 business killed his heart. And he has to rely on Richard now, and he knows it.'

'How does Richard …' I made one of those complex gestures which between friends say everything.

'I think he loves his brother and wishes he didn't, but cannot forgive him. Nor does the King forgive himself.'

'He kissed me!' Francis and I had forgotten John was in the room, so deftly quiet had he become about his page's duties. Still, he had enough sense to repeat nothing he heard in private. 'My father introduced me and the King said he had seen me when I was a baby and that I look like my father and he kissed me!' The eager tone told me that Edward hadn't quite lost the power to charm; but he damned well wasn't going to make an acolyte of John as he had of Richard and me. 'And I met my cousins,' John bubbled on. 'Lady Bess and Lady Cecily and the other girls, and Prince Richard – I like them. And I met Lord Hastings and the Duke of Buckingham and Mistress Shore.'

Francis and I came close to rupturing ourselves. As casually as possible I asked, 'You met Mistress Shore?'

'Yes,' John said innocently. 'Father doesn't like her but I quite did. She's pretty.' Now he understood our silence, and blushed. 'Father explained that she is the King's – I mean, Father told me about … about …'

'Men and women.'

'Yes. Well, I sort of knew anyway; you do when you live in the country and with soldiers. But he had to tell me so I would know not to say the wrong thing about Mistress Shore.'

'Ah. Yes. Of course.' Shocked though I was that the King should have let John meet his bawd, I would have given much to see Richard's reaction. Well, I could imagine: cool politeness, noticing nothing out of the way, then the private explosion.

Unaware of my thoughts, John was rushing eagerly on. 'And the King said he relies on my father to keep the Scots at bay, and he's buying lots of ships, and he has a cunning plan, and will lead the army north, he was all eager and he talked of Mortimer's Cross and Towton and Barnet and Tewkesbury, and I know they were great battles – but I think Lord Lovell's right and the King's too old to fight now.' Edward was just turned thirty-nine.

'Yes, thirty-nine,' said Richard later. 'And that's only middle-age, yet he looks an old man. And everything in London is as it was in '77 and '78, only more so. Hastings and Dorset encourage him in his boozing and whoring.' We shared a bitter look at that, for we had liked and trusted Hastings. 'I saw the Queen only briefly, a courtesy call with gifts: civil, cold.'

Suddenly I remembered the King's visit to York late in 1478, escaping plague in London. By chance I had been in York when they arrived and, paying my respects, I had been with the King and Queen when Richard rode into the city. Of course they had thought the cheering and the din was for them, until they had heard the shouts of 'Gloucester!' and 'Duke Richard!' and looked out on the usual scene of half the city out in the streets, mobbing him, merrily shouting hello, running alongside his horse, treating him as if he were one of them, throwing him flowers and presents. Thinking to please, the Mayor had grinned and said, 'Ah, always the same when our Duke rides in; he's our good lord, you see, and everyone knows it.' The King had looked rather taken aback, realising that here he was a curiosity – 'I've seen the King!' – but the people's real love was reserved for his brother. The Queen had looked icily, forebodingly furious.

'I think,' Richard went on, 'that she lives quite apart from the King now. There were the two more children, but I think she's reached that time of life ... They live separately. And you see how things are at Court when I tell you I took John for what I imagined was a private talk with the King, and Jane Shore was more or less acting as hostess. Though she conducted herself decently before the boy, I'll give her that. But if he'd been five years older ... I'm sorry for Edward's children. But now when it comes to England's defence, Martin, it is up to me. We're back thirty years to when Henry VI had to rely on my father.' A cry broke from him, 'And he's not yet forty!

He should be able, fit – remember Barnet … Well, it's up to me, now, and Northumberland, and people like Jock Howard and Lord Stanley. It is up to the North, Martin, for the south is in turmoil.'

'Real trouble?'

'Oh – the King's goddamn benevolences and taxes, it's near as bad as in the old days: riots, uprisings. I hope nothing too serious, but trouble enough.'

He was right. In the summer of that year, 1481, Lord Howard sailed the English fleet into the Firth of Forth and captured eight capital ships and scuttled many more. It was a brilliant raid – and the King sent word he was riding north to lead a land attack to consolidate the sea victory. He did not come. Nor did the promised army. Richard had the Border garrison, his loyal northerners, and the few thousand raised by the King's indentures. That was all, and it was not enough. The Scots outnumbered us, but throughout that summer we held them off. It was touch-and-go sometimes. Raid and counter-raid, skirmishes: towns and crops burned. No set battles. For months on end we were in the field patrolling the Marches, lucky if we got home one week in ten.

In September of 1481 the King got as far as Nottingham. This time I accompanied Richard. But for his height, I doubt I would have recognised Edward. The glorious grey eyes were small and piggy now, lost in folds of fat; he wheezed as he heaved his great body about. He could hardly sit a horse. Richard had always measured like a boy beside him, but now the contrast was ludicrous – and in Richard's favour as you looked from his whip-thin, tempered hardness to the King's grossness. No longer could one trace the family resemblance imprinted in their bones.

And now the King admitted he could go no further north. He spoke crisply enough, discussing the situation acutely – debauchery hadn't dulled his wits – but I saw the shamed misery in his eyes every time he had to say 'you' instead of 'we'.

Word came that the Scots were massing on the border for

invasion. It was outright war now. We still had no reliable report of their number, but it was clear they had at least twenty thousand. The harvest that year had been one of the worst on record, and I know farmers always claim that, but this time it was true: people were starving the length of the land. Of course such shortages are always worse in the north, and to provision his army Richard had to secure licences from the King to buy food wherever he could, as far afield as Wales or Ireland if necessary – and it did become necessary.

We raised some twenty thousand men, the largest army ever mustered in England, and not a man more could we raise. The King had taken about twelve thousand to invade France – and I can tell you we all thought bitterly back to that venture and wished we had thrashed France into submission while we had the chance. For the great fear was, of course, that while every English man-at-arms was busy on the Scottish border, France would launch against us in the south.

'Or,' said Richard, 'since invading England is easier said than done ...'

'Remember the Norman Conquest!'

'Even so. Now I've forgotten what I was saying. Oh yes. Well, Louis might try – but I think what he's up to is carving up Burgundy. He wants France to rule from the Spanish border to the North Sea. I doubt Maximilian has much chance, though heaven knows he is doing his best.' Mary of Burgundy had married the son of the German Emperor, and he was a clever statesman and general, but the problem was, as always, lack of men and money against the might of France. 'So what we have to do is whip the Scots and secure a good, tough, lasting peace so our northern border is safe and we've got men and money to help Burgundy.'

'Would the King ...' I didn't know how to say it: the King needed his French pension and he wanted his daughter Bess to be Queen of France. Would he, in fact, lift a finger to help Burgundy, or anyone else, against France? But Richard knew what I meant.

'I don't know. But just the same I'm going to sort out the Scots.' This conversation took place on our way home from Nottingham.

We rode for a while in silence, then I said, 'Where do we start?'

'I don't suppose.' Richard said elliptically, 'that in fifty or a hundred years anyone outside Yorkshire will remember me. But it would be nice if our grandchildren's generation could say, "Richard of Gloucester? Yes, he won the war against the Scots for Edward IV." So let's see if we can be a bit clever. Let's see if we can get Berwick back.'

It was more than twenty years since Margaret of Anjou had bartered away that northern fortress to the Scots. From time to time the King had made attempts to win it back, but the Scots were well entrenched and all efforts had come to nothing. It was shaming for England that the enemy held one of our citadels on our own land. Getting it back would be triumph indeed.

'You'd be famous and no mistake if you did.'

With his swift glancing smile Richard said, 'What, like that Greek fellow who burnt the temple so his name would live forever? Can you remember his name?'

'No.'

'Nor can I. But we'll have a go at Berwick just the same.'



We did. Sieges are dull work to talk about, and there is little I can say except that we disposed a wing of the army outside Berwick and set about starving and firing them out. It was very different from the swift business in Wales back in '70, when Richard had relieved Cardigan and Carmarthen castles in a few short weeks. This would be a long-drawn-out affair. And, meanwhile, Richard had other ideas for harrying the Scots.

I suppose that in the end almost every nobleman and landowner in England was in that army we turned against Scotland. Some half of them Richard disposed against Berwick, the rest he called to his headquarters at Carlisle; and I noted that this group was largely composed of the men who had worked with him the last two years and knew the Borders as well as he did.

I am going to write down something I have hesitated ever to tell anyone: I saw a ghost.

We were camped near Hadrian's Wall – 1482, this was. As usual I had done the evening round of my troops, and because it was a fine night, though chilly, and because I was tired, I walked off a little way by myself, gazing up at the early stars and wondering if we would ever see an end to this border warfare. To my right someone moved, and I swung about ready to give the alarm. At first I thought from his silhouette that the man was a Scot, then I saw the metal helmet with its horsehair crest and cheek-guards, his short sleeves, his thonged calf boots and the fringed leather tunic. I had seen drawings of Roman legionaries, and knew this was what I was looking at. I recognised the round shield and short, broad-bladed sword. Perhaps the odd thing is that I was not afraid. My grandmother used to boast that she had Roman blood – rather dilute after a millennium, one would think, but I had inherited the profile one sees on the old Roman coins that are still to be found. I had the fleeting fancy that perhaps I was seeing an ancestor of mine. Like me, this man was taking a moment's ease at the end of a busy day, listening to the sounds of his camp. Fellow soldiers a thousand years apart, we stood together, united in the duty of keeping the Scots out of England. He looked at me, that Roman, this I swear: he saw me. I had the impression he looked with curiosity, or amusement, at a soldier whose hair fell to his shoulders, who wore leather breeches and high boots, and whose sword was three feet long. Perhaps he thought, So you're still at it, still manning the border, still using the Wall. For a moment we looked at each other, then I murmured a Latin greeting (well, it seemed polite) and then I blinked and he was gone.

Very thoughtfully I went back to camp. They had been looking for me, John came running to say Richard wanted me in his tent. As the other leaders straggled in from their own evening duties, I casually asked Richard if he had ever heard of ghosts up here.

To my surprise it was Northumberland, who had the imagination of an onion, who said, 'Up here on the Wall everyone believes in ghosts. Plenty of men have seen Roman soldiers or the little people:

the Picts and the Celts. Go to Buttermere and they say you'll see the last of the Vikings who made their stand against the Normans four hundred years ago. Domesday Book doesn't run there, so well did the Cumberland men keep the Normans off.'

'Well,' said Richard, 'I believe most things are possible, but I'd be glad of anyone, mortal or ghost, who could interpret this map for me.' He had it spread out on his table, cursing mildly as his wolfhound's eager tail got in the way. Peering, I made out the northern part of Cumberland, the coast of Solway Firth and the southern parts of western Scotland. There was little detail, however.

'What's in your mind?'

'We're going to raid north-west into Scotland, to Dumfries.'

'Why Dumfries?' someone asked.

'Because it's an important town for the Scots. See, it's on the River Nith, just inland from Solway Firth. Close to Ireland. A supply town and garrison. Gentlemen, we are going to take and burn Dumfries and every town on our way. My intentions are to show the Scots we mean business, and to tempt their army out into the open so we can get some real idea of their numbers – also, if possible, to bring them to decisive battle. If we succeed, it should be enough to end this business once and for all.'

'What about Berwick?'

'The siege continues. Lord Stanley is in charge there. No one expected it to be a quick business.' He looked around. 'This raid will be the usual dirty business, but let it be understood I'll have no looting or rape. Any man who does so is to be hanged out of hand. And give the common people of the towns time to get clear. This is a warning raid and a reprisal for the Scots raids into our country, not a slaughter of innocents. Now find me among your troops any men who know the area well, we must learn the territory as best we can.'

'Large raid?'

'I think ten thousand, more if possible.'

War is war, and you can't be dainty about it. We hoped for battle as a cleaner and more decisive alternative to this rotten work of raiding and burning, but at the cost of people left homeless and destitute we taught the Scots what it is like to be on the receiving end of such raids. What the Scottish King was up to was anyone's guess, but we saw neither hide nor hair of his army that May, and we retired back across the border unmolested.

In June the King sent for Richard, and I shaved off my beard, trimmed my hair, dug my good clothes out of my campaign chest and went with him down to Fotheringhay Castle to learn the King's cunning plan.

Maddeningly, the King had given Richard only the vaguest hints in his letters, so you can imagine our surprise when he introduced us to his guest the Duke of Albany. This devious gentleman was the Scottish King's brother, and three years ago, after plotting to overthrow his brother, he had escaped by the skin of his teeth to France.

Edward's plan was simply this: to use Albany as a figurehead in our war, which would now have the aim of putting him on the Scottish throne. In return, Albany would, once King, do homage to Edward for his crown, give up Berwick and some other lands and, most important, sign a treaty of peace between our two countries.

'And if anyone so much as mentions George ...' Richard said that first night when we had retired to the privacy of our chambers. There was a fraught silence, then we all burst out laughing. Wiping his eyes Richard said, 'My God, it's a case of the biter bitten. It's perfect, it's 1469 all over again, with positions reversed. We're using the King's brother against him exactly as Louis and Warwick did. Wrap Clarence in a plaid and you've got the Duke of Albany. And Fotheringhay, of all places! The King's as subtle as a smack in the chops. Remember '69, Martin? Galloping in here with Hastings, the King a prisoner and his brother seeking to overthrow him?'

'Do you think it will work?'

Staring at me as if I had started barking, Richard said, 'Of course it won't work! The Scots may not think too highly of wee Jamie but they like his brother even less, they would never accept him as king!

But it makes a canny bargaining ploy. And I suppose stranger things have happened. So we all pretend the sun shines out of dear Cousin Alexander's arse.'

And so, genuflecting in the direction of the Albany posterior, we rode back north.

The city of York had word of our coming, and set out to show the Scottish King's brother just how Richard was regarded. The Mayor and the Alderman greeted us in full fig of scarlet and crimson, all the Guildsmen too, and behind them every citizen, all cheering their heads off. The Council put on a great dinner, and presented Richard with their best wine and fish and demain bread. Albany was visibly impressed, and quite welcome to think it was in his honour.

And now we settled down to reclaim Berwick. The King had sent money, arms, men, cannon; every sort of supply. We had nine surgeons under Doctor Hobbes, the King's own physician. To receive news quickly, the King had also instituted a mounted courier service with thirty men each riding a stage of ten miles, flat out, then handing messages and letters on to the next relay. This way, London could have news from the north in only twenty-four hours.

The town of Berwick quickly yielded under our dogged assault, but the fortress itself held out.

Now James III at last stirred himself to lead his army south. Scottish politics were a sealed book to me, but I knew that the Scots nobles were constantly at war with one another and their King. And James had been rather too free with his lowborn favourites – shades of Edward II and Richard II. At Lauder these nobles turned against their King, hanged his pretty-boys and clapped the King into Edinburgh Castle, a prisoner. Clearly they had studied English history. Albany danced with glee.

Richard left Lord Stanley to continue the siege of Berwick, and took the rest of the army north into Scotland again.

And we took Edinburgh.

We seized the enemy's greatest city. It was the greatest English victory since Agincourt. And we did it without losing a single man on our side.

If the Scots expected the customary usages of war, they were in for a pleasant surprise. Richard did not burn or sack Edinburgh, and he so rigorously enforced his rules against looting and rape that no citizen of the town could complain of being molested.

Then, leaving Edinburgh under military control, Richard led us east to Haddington, where the elusive Scots army was lying low – for all their reputation as fierce fighters, they had been remarkably slow to engage with our army. But now it was to be battle, once and for all ...

No, actually not. The Scots had had enough. The lords now in control sent envoys to Richard asking for a truce.

Years back our King had, as part of the old truce agreement, promised his third daughter, Cecily, to the King of Scotland's son. That had fallen by the wayside, of course, but now the Scots were all for signing up again. The problem was, Edward had made a half-promise to marry Cecily to the Duke of Albany.

'So?' said Richard, who knew Albany cut no ice in Scotland, and proposed his own terms for treaty. Cecily could still marry James's son if that in time suited everyone; if not, the Scots would repay the dowry Edward had already handed over. Berwick was to be left alone. Albany had to sign an oath to keep faith with England – and in the end Albany saw the light and struck a deal with Scotland's Chancellor, pledging that in return for his dukedom and lands he would be loyal to his brother the King.

On August the fourth, the magistrates of Edinburgh clinched things with an offer. If Richard would withdraw from the city without further harm, they would make themselves responsible for paying back that troublesome dowry if Cecily didn't marry James's son.

It was the best deal we could win. The Scots would not fight, and there was too much internal turmoil for any treaty of real meaning. Content that the Scots had been taught a lasting lesson, Richard led his army back to England.

He knighted or made knights banneret of the men who had particularly distinguished themselves, he paid off the common soldiers, and then he dismissed most of his army and with the rest turned his attention back to Berwick. A band of Scots made one raid on us, but they got nowhere, and on the twenty-fourth day of August Berwick was back in English hands.

When I tell you that all England rejoiced – that the King wrote to the Pope himself boasting of these successes and of Richard's prowess – when I tell you that Calais celebrated with bonfires, parades, firing of their guns – you will have some idea of what the news meant to England. When we rode south just before Christmas for the January Parliament every town we passed through gave us a reception like after the battles back in '71. We were conquering heroes indeed, and Richard the saviour of England.

And all this good news was just as well, for in December poor Maximilian could fight on alone no longer. His wife Mary of Burgundy had died in 1482, and now he made peace with Louis of France. Part of the treaty was that his daughter Marie would marry the Dauphin. Louis had had his revenge on Edward at last. No glorious French marriage for his daughter Bess, and never again would he see a sou of his French pension won in '75.

I have said I had grown sick of the King after the Clarence business. Yet it wrenched even my mean little heart to see Edward that Christmas. Broken, ill, old before his time, his European diplomacy turned to mockery, our alliance with Burgundy and Brittany gone for nothing, French ships raiding in the Channel – gone for good was the glorious soldier and wily diplomat of the '60s and '70s. The only hope for his kingdom's safety was his brother Richard.

The country knew it too. Parliament granted Richard hereditary possession of the Wardenship of the West Marches; the castle and constableship of Carlisle; all the King's lands and revenues of Cumberland; the more than thirty miles of border lands he'd brought under English control and any more he won from the Scots. In short, he was granted more lands, revenues, offices and honours than any

English subject had ever had before. It was virtually a principality.

There were other honours too, for other men. The thanks and praise of Parliament, grants of money – and titles. Francis Lovell was made a viscount to honour the work he'd done in the Scottish war.

And I was made an Earl.

We rode north in March of 1483. Going home gladly.

And none of us could know how soon, or in what circumstances, we would see London again.

# PART II

## *Thirteen*

### *April-May 1483*

That day in April I took the children out hunting. At first I had planned to take only my own children, but winter had clung long in the North and young ones take it hard being pent-up indoors. No one could resist the fine spring weather, and in the end every child of the household was in the party.

The children all rode well, having been put on ponies as soon as they were old enough to cling on, and when someone proposed a race home I laughed and allowed it. Anne feared that her Edward was too frail, but mothers worry about an only child. It was the pale, fair colouring that he had from Anne herself that gave Edward his air of delicacy, and as a child Richard too had been very thin. Edward was a pleasant boy – his parents tried not to spoil him, but it would have been easy for Richard's son to grow conceited and demanding.

As for Katherine, also thirteen, soon it would be time to think of a marriage for her; though I doubted Richard would think the Archangel Gabriel good enough for his girl. Oh, she was pretty! A dear girl with a good heart. Our Cecily too, eleven last December, and already so beautiful she would break your heart. No hairy great randy ruffian was going to win my treasure from me in a hurry. The rest of the children were too young for such plans – Martin, ten, was likewise in henchmen's training and currently Richard's page. The twins Richard and Alison, that terrifying pair who had walked at nine months, talked at thirteen, mastered Greek, Latin and French at six and mathematics at seven: university for Richard and I would see him Lord Chancellor one day, and I wished the same were possible for Alison. Perhaps I would send her to Duchess Margaret of Burgundy, another learned lady. Philippa and William were mere babies of six and one; ten placid years before we need plan for them.

Musing thus, and keeping an eye on the racing children, I scarcely noticed the courier on the road ahead. It was Katherine who reined in beside me and said indignantly, 'Look at that poor beast!' She meant the horse, not the messenger, though it was hard to say which was the more exhausted. The horse was plodding along at a stumbling walk, its head down and its skinny flanks heaving. The rider wore Lord Hastings' bull's head livery, and I wondered as I pulled up alongside what Hastings thought so urgent his courier need ride himself and his horse half to death.

'Here, man,' I said, 'your steed's near foundered. You're for the Duke at Middleham? Get up behind me and we'll lead the horse.' He stared dully at me, too tired to understand. 'You're almost there, but that horse will be dead before you're through the village. I am Lord Robsart, Duke Richard's friend.'

Comprehension penetrated his mind. Like a ninety-year-old he swung down, and stood blinking at me. 'Lord Robsart. Yes. Gloucester's lieutenant. All speed to the duke.'

'Yes. Come up, man. Or stop at the inn in the village, you can trust me with your letters. What is so urgent from Lord Hastings?'

'Trouble in London. The King is dead.'


Only Katherine had heard the messenger's words. She had never met her uncle the King, so her shock was impersonal and she made no demur when I asked her to say nothing for the present and to see the other children home. They were used to sudden messages, and took little notice when I stayed behind.

I heaved the messenger up onto my horse and led the two steeds back to the castle. The man revived enough to tell me a little more of what was happening in London. None of it was reassuring. The King had died a fortnight ago, it seemed, and although this servant wasn't in Hastings' confidence he knew the Queen's family were rushing to gain control of the government. My thumbs began to prick – you see, when we were last in London for Parliament Richard had told me that Edward had promised to make him Protector in his will in case he died while the Prince of Wales was still under-age. Unless he had changed his mind, Richard was now Protector, Regent of England and lawful head of government. He should have been the first to hear of the King's death. Hastings' man had done the journey from London in a little under four days: we should have had official news and been in London by now. And why was *Hastings* telling us? He was Lord Chamberlain, but it was for the Chancellor – for Parliament – for the Council – to advise the new Protector. Trouble in London, indeed.

I handed the messenger over to the Middleham steward, asking them to keep silent on the matter until I had told Richard. Then I went to a quiet room downstairs and opened Hastings' letter. I felt no compunction about this piece of prying: I had to be sure there was no mistake.

What I read made my blood run cold. The King had died on the ninth day of April from a chill, stomach trouble and fever. He had indeed named Richard Protector, and on his deathbed he had made Hastings and Dorset and the Queen clasp hands and swear to honour his authority. No more factional feuds: had he believed that? I wondered, especially as I read on. Sir Edward Woodville had tried to take the fleet to sea – Rivers was bringing the new King up from Ludlow – the Woodvilles were pushing for a coronation on May the fourth! Oh, they were in a hurry to seize power and no mistake. Incredulously I turned the letter over, holding it to the window to make out Hastings' frantic writing. It had come near to open fighting among the Council (Hastings wrote) and he was doing his best to keep things under control and restrain the Woodvilles, but he had to threaten to take all his men back to Calais if the King's escort was not limited to two thousand. *Limited!* Two thousand is an army – what did the Woodvilles have in mind? But of course the answer was clear: an armed take-over. The only spark of hope was that, according to Hastings, there were enough moderates and sensible men on the Council to block the Woodvilles. But it sounded like a close-run thing – Dorset and the Queen were winning people over every day and acting as if they controlled the government. The letter ended: 'Get you to London as fast as you can. I have proclaimed your authority as Protector throughout London, and people look to you to stop the Woodvilles and establish good government for the new King. Come in strength and secure the King. Get you here as fast as you can.'

Grimly I folded the letter away into my shirt and went to find the others. Maddeningly, I learnt that Richard and Anne had gone out riding alone, shortly after I had taken the children out. I knew what that meant. In our world you are never alone except in bed with the curtains drawn, and even then, even at night, you can never be sure you won't be woken for some emergency. So Anne and Richard had crept out to a certain place by the river, a pretty spot hidden by trees, for a few hours' precious privacy. Knowing what they might be doing with that privacy, I hadn't the heart to send someone after them. An hour or two's delay would do no harm, and meanwhile we others could do what was necessary.

Of course the Middleham household was used to urgent departures. We sent messages to the stables and the men-at-arms' quarters, warned the kitchens to prepare journey-food, sent the servants to pack. Richard's secretary, John Kendal, began to prepare letters for the gentleman and towns of the North; it was in all our minds that Northumberland was touchy enough, and if he thought Richard had had the news for half an hour without telling him there'd be trouble. Bringing me a draft letter for approval Kendal said, 'If Duke Richard has had no official advice, would the London people have told the Duchess of York? And his sisters?'

'Oh, surely!' But Kendal raised a sceptical eyebrow. 'No, you're right – had they known they would have sent messages to Richard. No doubt he will want to write to them himself.'

Word came then that the sentry had spied Richard and Anne

returning. Taking a deep breath I went down to the courtyard and waited for them inside the gate.

They looked so happy; peaceful and content, rather smug. They smelt of wine, and there were a few betraying bits of grass and leaves on their clothes. When they saw me standing there, clad in black, their smiles faded and they exchanged a glance of great fear. As Richard dismounted I lifted Anne down, and she gripped my arms, saying,

'Martin – not Edward …'

Jesu, for a dreadful moment I almost said yes. 'Don't fear for your son, hinny, he's safe and well and having his supper. But there is bad news for you. From London.' Richard's eyes met mine, and I saw him pale. 'I am so sorry. The King is dead.'


After the couriers had galloped away with the letters, after Richard had approved our preparations and we had supped in silence and heard Mass, Richard simply disappeared. He was needed for all manner of last things, for the business of ruling the North could not be left at a moment's notice; forty people were demanding him.

'Leave him alone!' Anne snapped distractedly at the people besieging her with questions. 'His brother is dead. Give him some time alone. And no, I do not know where he is.' But she shot me a meaning little glance as she spoke. We both knew where he would be, and Anne knew that just then he would want me, not her; as indeed I wanted him, not Innogen. I had had no time for grief and Richard was the only one who could comfort me.

When I came through the door onto the roof I saw him at once, where I had known he would be, leaning on the battlements staring out at the dales. This quiet place on the roof had been our bolthole when as boys in training here we had been homesick or miserable or the Master of Henchmen had beaten us.

Hearing me, Richard swung defensively about. He recognised me and his shoulders slumped in relief. 'Good. I couldn't stand anyone but you.' He turned back again. I went to stand beside him, leaning my forearms on the wall. It was full dark now. I could see only a light or two from the village, and the dark shape of the hills against the sky. The breeze was fresh and sweet. I could hear the river purling below us.

'I've been standing here looking out. I love this country, and I have been wondering if I will ever see it again.' I said nothing. Empty reassurances were pointless. 'I've been thinking of the past. Of Ludlow. I always loved Edward. I didn't forgive him for putting George to death, and I despised him at the end, but I loved him. Now all my brothers are dead.'

I put my hand gently on his shoulder. 'I loved him too. I remember the first time I saw him. My world had ended, all in a few days – parents dead, house burnt, no home, no family, no future. Until Edward put me on his lap and let me cry. Odd to think he was only eighteen; he seemed fully a man, I thought him a god, yet he was only a boy. Eighteen seems very young, now, doesn't it?' Richard nodded, his hair brushing my hand. 'I detested and rather feared him at the end, and nor did I forgive him. I loved him, though, and now I know it.' I gave a great childish snuffle as I spoke. Richard put his arms around me, and suddenly we were hugging each other and weeping. We sank down, our backs to the battlements, and as we huddled together our tears mingled.

If you think after all I have said of Edward that mine were false tears, or that I spoke hypocritically to Richard, you are wrong. I wept, as Richard did, not for the gross whoremonger Edward had become, but for the golden boy who had taken me under his wing, the glorious young king in his victory laurels, our guardian, the man who had loved us, teased us, taught and protected us, who had made us warriors. We wept for our hero, friend, bulwark and our safety. Richard's last brother. We wept for our past and for our youth. Also, the end of a reign, of an era, is a stunning thing, and Edward had been King for twenty-two years.

And trouble lay ahead.

I had brought a flask of wine up with me, and when we had cried ourselves out we dried our faces and leaned again on the battlements, passing the flask back and forth. The air was growing cold; April in the North is no time for standing out on a roof. But we didn't go in; we wrapped our cloaks tighter and drank the wine, reluctant for any other company.

'I spoke before of Ludlow,' Richard said at last. 'And I will not see my children standing in Middleham courtyard waiting for a Woodville army to take them. Or another Lancastrian one. Nor will I allow civil war to spring up again.' I thought of the way my mother had died; thought of Innogen, Anne, my daughters. 'I will not be the first to provoke trouble, but nor will I allow the Woodvilles to take over this kingdom. I have written as much to Hastings, to the new King's Council, and to Rivers.' I nodded, for I had seen these letters. They were intended for public sight, so Richard had written plainly of his loyalty to the late king, saying he would be no less loyal to the new king and all his late brother's issue. His only desire was that the new government be settled according to justice and law, and due regard given to his legal authority as Protector. He added one warning note: nothing contrary to law and the late king's will could be decreed without harm. To Hastings' letter he added a brief personal note thanking him and saying he was on his way.

'I must make all due haste,' he mused on; he was speaking more to himself than to me, 'but nor will I seem to sweep down with an army. I am Protector and the new King's uncle; no more. I come to London only to take my rightful place. If the Woodvilles have acted in good faith ...' we both laughed cynically '... then we shall deal cordially together. But Lord, I wish I knew my nephew! Edward was wrong to send him to Ludlow so young, he can know nothing of London, or a king's business. Or of me.'

'True. And probably the Woodvilles have primed him with their own version of facts. But you have the Protector's authority, they can do nothing about that.'

'They can kill me.'

It was nothing I had not already faced, but for a moment it seemed the wind had grown colder.

'I am a threat to the Woodvilles,' he went on without expression.

'Plainly they are desperate to seize power and get the new King crowned as fast as they can. And plainly they know I will never be content to let them. Christ, have the country run by the Woodvilles! Margaret of Anjou all over again!'

'A Protectorate lasts until the King's of age. Eighteen – sixteen at the earliest. Four years. Crowning him will make no difference.'

Frowning, Richard said, 'Trouble is, there's no actual *law*. Precedent, yes, but no law. My father was Protector when Henry VI went mad … but look back to Henry's childhood! Duke Humphrey – also Duke of Gloucester, not the best omen – was named Protector by his late brother Henry V, and what happened? He ended up with nothing but nominal power while the Beauforts and their cronies ran things. And made a right pig's breakfast of it. Same will happen again, give the Woodvilles an inch and they'll take a mile. And even if I stayed here doing nothing, asking no power and keeping the Scots off, how long do you think I'd be allowed to go on doing that? They would have my lands off me and all my authority, they'd render me powerless then trump up some charge of treason and that would be the end of me.'

'No,' I objected, 'you're too powerful for that. You are the one person they cannot afford to harm. The Londoners would tear them limb from limb, the country would be up in arms in a flash. Louis of France is rampaging all over Europe, he might have a go at England any minute. The Scots are lying low but that won't last, and with the sniff of a chance the Welsh would be up in arms. If Louis isn't hand in glove with the Beauforts and old Lancastrians my name's not Martin Robsart. And who would England need? You. And anyway, as I say, the Woodvilles simply wouldn't dare. You are too popular, you're a by-word for good government and the keeping of the peace.'

He thought about it and was halfway persuaded. 'They probably fear exactly those things. I'm too strong. And that is why I am taking no more than my usual riding household; no northern army, no show of power.' He shivered, tugging his cloak closer. 'It's time to go in.' But as I pushed off reluctantly from the wall he seized my arm.

'Martin, my mother must not hear of Edward's death from a stranger. I cannot go – will you?'

Somehow I wasn't surprised. 'Of course.'

'Good. Thank you. And I want you to take John with you.'

'A good idea. He'll be comfort for your mother.'

'Yes. But also I can't help fearing – some convenient accident; an ambush … Think how often Margaret of Anjou tried to capture my father. Well, if that happens, it happens; but I won't risk John. Yet if I leave him behind Anne will know I'm worried and she is already afraid. Sending him to Mother makes a good excuse. And Martin, if anything should happen to me, look after Anne and my children. Do whatever is necessary: go over to the Woodvilles, flee abroad, anything. But protect my family.'

I couldn't tell him he was being fanciful or morbid. We were both children of the civil wars, we had seen what could happen. 'I promise. And you will do the same for me?'

'Of course.' He released my arm. We exchanged a final, rather desperate hug, then went inside.


It was fine weather, and we made good time to Berkhamsted. This was a neat little property with a flourishing home-farm and good stock in the fields. It had handsome orchards, a kitchen garden and a knot-garden laid with brick paths. Although it was a fortified manor and much grander than my home, somehow it always reminded me of that childhood home, but here the memories were pleasant ones. As we rode in I looked over the rose-garden the Duchess had planted nineteen summers ago, and recalled eavesdropping on Margaret and John Neville. Odd that it should be here that we heard of Edward's foolish marriage, and here that I came with news of the fruit of that action.

The arrival of a group of men-at-arms caused a flurry in a peaceful nunnery. The sisters working outside carried on, their eyes on their work after the first anxious glance, but one of them, a tall woman, strode towards us, rolling down her sleeves. A nun's habit is little different from the ordinary dress of a widow, but I was surprised to see that this weather-beaten woman was the Duchess; I suppose I had never pictured her joining in the mundane domestic activities. Her long sight was still excellent, and she had recognised my banners. 'Martin! My dear boy, how good to see you. And is that John?' She held out her arms.

He scrambled down from his horse and ran to meet her. He was as tall as she now, and could have swept her off her feet. 'Grandmama, good day to you.'

'And to you, darling ... But you're in black ...' She looked along the line of my horsemen, desperately seeking Richard's banner. 'Is Richard ... What has happened?'

She had aged a great deal in the last five years – well, she was nearly seventy – but her back was as straight as ever, and after that first moment her blue eyes showed courage. Forgetting all the etiquette of rank I took her in my arms and kissed her.

'Richard is safe and well, but there is bad news.'

'The King?'

Since the night we heard of George's death she had never called her elder son by his name. 'Yes, dear madam. The King is dead.'

She took one sharp breath. Her hands began to shake, and with my arms around her I guided her into the house and made her sit down. Some of the nuns had come out, and John sensibly asked them to bring wine. Then, simply, he hugged the Duchess and said, 'I'm very sorry, Grandmama.'

She laid her head on his shoulder. 'So am I, John. Sometimes it is very hard to say: "God's will be done". When his father died Edward was my only worldly comfort and strength.' The wine came and gratefully she drank it. 'How did he die?' I told her the little I knew, and waited until she had scanned Richard's letter. 'Yes, he lived unwisely these last years ... But he was only forty-one! And I had not heard, you know; he is dead and buried and no one has thought of telling me, his own mother!' Again I held the cup for her. 'I'm glad it was you who came. Richard always was a thoughtful boy. And what happens now? Because don't tell me there isn't Woodville trouble.' I told her what I knew, Hastings' information. 'Exactly what I would have expected. That woman and her family were trouble from the start. I daresay Edward thought he could control them, but what boy of twenty-two can manage people like that? And now it all falls on Richard's shoulders. As usual.'

'Yes.'

Fiercely she said, 'Tell him to be careful. I will write to him, but tell him to take care. It was the Woodvilles who pushed Edward into executing George, and I will not lose another son to them. Tell him too to beware of the Beauforts and their cronies. A king's minority is a dangerous time.'

'I'll tell him.'

'Where is he? What is he doing?'

'Riding to meet with the King on his way to London. Lord Rivers is escorting the King.'

'Rivers! Oh yes, I'm sure. I always thought well enough of him, but he will be neck-deep in whatever Woodville plotting is going on. May God help us and not see us plunged back into the trouble we thought was over twenty years ago.'

'Yes indeed.' A silence fell. I watched her tanned, aged hand twining in John's.

At last she rose, saying, 'This is poor hospitality to show you. I must see our priest, to arrange Masses for the King – but you will stop with us? We live plainly, but you shall have a good supper and a night's rest before you travel on.'

'If you wish it, madam, we would be glad to stay.'

'Well, I do wish it. Here, my life is given to God and I am never alone, but yes, it would comfort me if you stayed with me tonight.'


In London, the moment I had seen John safe at Crosby Place – and forbidden him to leave the building – I went around to Hastings' house.

He was in his fifties, and it showed, but unlike the King he'd kept himself in trim, although the deep drinking of the last few years had riddled his face with broken veins. He was glad to see me, but at the same time oddly on edge in some personal way. 'Fact is,' he said sheepishly after we had stumbled through a few of the preliminaries, 'you caught me asleep. It's been a busy time.'

Murmuring an apology I thought: in bed, yes; asleep, no. But his private life was no concern of mine.

'Tell me just how things lie here in London.'

'Richard isn't with you?'

'No.' I had already explained. Yawning, he apologised and gathered his wits.

'Can hardly think straight. God's teeth, Martin, it has been a business here and no mistake! I'm Lord Chamberlain and Captain of Calais, and I've had to act like Julius Caesar and Solomon all in one! You should have seen me up on my hind legs before the Council and that mincing fool Dorset and the Queen, yelling that if they didn't see sense I would take myself off to Calais and all my men with me.' He chuckled at the memory. 'Wouldn't have gone, of course – Edward Woodville would have had the fleet at sea and kept me stranded in Calais. But the threat frightened the idiots who were for the Woodvilles, and the moderates nearly had kittens, they knew they needed me here. Howard and Stanley supported me, of course.'

'Howard – yes, it is "of course" with him, but do you trust Lord Stanley?'

Hastings gave me a sidelong, cynical look. 'Not usually, but he is no friend of the Woodvilles. The Bishops are mostly sound, of course – though there is so much feeling against clerics at present that the Crown's their only hope. I fear they would go with whoever has the power – which so far means the Woodvilles. That blithering old idiot Rotherham gave the Queen the Great Seal.'

'Never!' I cried, appalled. With the Great Seal, signet of the royal authority, any order could be enacted. No one had any business touching the Seal except the King or his Lord Chancellor. Archbishop Rotherham was elderly and none too clever, but this action was close to treason.

'He did,' said Hastings. 'The Queen seems to think that if she acts as Regent, people will either believe she actually is, in law I mean, or overturn the King's will and make her so. For instance, she and Dorset have re-appointed all the judges and they're collecting taxes.'

Now, this might sound innocuous, even sensible, but the point is that they had no right to do it. Groping to remember the law thrashed into me as a boy I said, 'I think the Council isn't even a legal body yet, is it? Only the King can call it. Edward's Council so to speak died with him, it is up to the new King to re-convene it. Until he does, it has no power, there *is* no Council.'

'Right, but try telling them that.' Hastings yawned again, stretching irritably. 'Let's have some wine, I should have offered before.' He shouted for a page, and when the wine came he snapped at the boy to leave, and banged the door clumsily shut. A huge swig of wine seemed to pull him together, for he went on, 'I had Richard's letter proclaimed at Paul's Cross, I made sure the whole city heard it. That calmed things down. People trust him, they're anxious to have him here. God's teeth, I told you, didn't I, that Dorset wanted Rivers to bring the King down from Ludlow with an army of five thousand? If you stared in one of Dorset's ears you'd see daylight coming the other way – there is so much goodwill for the new little King, but if he marched down on London at the head of an army ...'

'It was to be the complete armed take-over.'

'Yes. That's why Richard must get here. The people want him. Let Richard only arrive, with all the Protector's authority, and the thing's done. Did I tell you the Woodvilles wanted the King crowned at once? Fourth of May, they decided; they were getting everything ready.'

'But,' I objected, 'the Protector's power doesn't end when the King is crowned.'

'No, but then no one would look too closely at what the Woodvilles have been up to.'

Agreeing, I glumly drank my wine. Hastings sat turning his jewelled gold cup between his fingers. In the silence I identified the sound that had been at the edge of my mind. Upstairs, a woman was singing. Light feet pattered down the stairs, and the door opened.

Hastings jerked upright, blood suffusing his face.

'Will, has he gone? Come back to – oh.'

It was Jane Shore.

Her hair was loose – and a different shade of gold from when I'd last seen her – and her face was heavily painted. The wrapper clutched about her was so diaphanous it emphasised rather than concealed; damned erotic it was, too.

She and Hastings both stared at me, then Hastings sank his head in his hands.

'Good day, Lord Robsart,' says Jane, curtsying in a way that makes the most of her bosom. 'I am sorry to intrude; I heard the door bang and thought you had gone. Forgive me.'

'Of course, madam,' says I with all the worldly grace at my command, and she grinned at me. I couldn't help smiling back, and in that moment I knew I could have had her for the asking. Then she retired demurely upstairs.

'I know how it looks,' Hastings mumbled. 'She and Edward loved each other, they really did, and he was my friend, yet not a month after his death she's in my bed.'

'It's not my business, Will.'

His bleary eyes blinked painfully at me. 'I love her, you see. Always did. Jealous of the King. And of Dorset, he's had her too. He's young and handsome and I think she wants him ... she won't stay with me. But I love her! I can't help it that I love her!'

The lover's cry down through the ages. 'Of course not,' I said, more embarrassed by the confession than by the sight of the near-naked Jane. 'And it is none of my concern.'

'She'll go to Dorset sooner or later. But I think she's a little bit fond of me.'

'I'm sure she is. Will, it's not my business. I don't care. Now tell me what else I need to know about the situation here. The Woodvilles.'

'Yes ...' His mind was upstairs with Jane, but he said, 'I dislike and resent Dorset, but everything I have told you is true. People are getting nervous, the Woodvilles are being altogether too blatant about grabbing power. When I had Richard's letter proclaimed, people started swinging back away from the Queen's party. Richard is Protector, he has the rightful authority. But Dorset said, first, that that would end with the King's coronation, then, second, that it only made Richard another member of the Council – *primus inter pares*. That of course was going much too far for even the Dorset party. But Richard has to get here, Martin! He has to seize the King and bring him here – and soon! Where is he?'

'He should be about at Northampton now, meeting up with the King and Rivers.'

'And only three hundred men with him? Not enough.'

'But he cannot be seen to sweep down with an army, Will.'

'No, s'pose not. Well, as long as he secures the King and gets here fast.'

Seeing me to the door Hastings muttered, shamefaced, 'About Jane – don't tell Richard. He wouldn't understand.'

'Wouldn't he?'


I gathered news on my own account. I did this by putting on nondescript clothes and leaving off my jewels, and hanging around the markets and inns at the busiest times. I took John, and taught him the art of eking out a drink and looking gormless; it's amazing what you can pick up, besides fleas.

It was as Hastings had said. People mourned Edward and feared the reign of a child-king. No one trusted the Woodvilles or wanted them in power. Hastings' proclaiming Richard's letter had had good effect; some people said, 'What do we want with a fellow who's spent all his life up with the barbarians?' But most said, 'He's the late King's brother, the hero of the Scottish war, and if King Edward wanted him to look after things that's good enough for us.' In one inn a tall fellow was holding forth, saying he had heard Gloucester was bringing down an army of twenty thousand men to kill all the Queen's family and take power for himself – 'And the Queen should be Regent, she's got the right.'

Never! – was the general reaction, but the fellow went on, 'She were Regent when the King went to France back in 1475.' He wasn't quite right, but it was a sophisticated argument for a grubby nobody. I took another look at him, and knew I was in luck.

Putting on the almost forgotten rustic accent of my youth I said, 'Here, you was with Dorset when he visited the siege at Berwick.'

'I was not!'

'You was. I were with Lord Howard an' I see you there. Not that your master 'ung around too long. Didn't like war. No wonder you're all for 'im and 'is sister.'

Mocking cries came from the other drinkers. 'And I 'eard,' I went on, 'that your master and the Queen didn't even tell the old Duchess of York the King was dead, nor the King's sisters neither. I've got a cousin over that way and 'e told me.'

Cries of *Shame!* or ruder equivalents.

'Well, if Gloucester comes,' argued this Demosthenes of Deptford, 'it'll be King Dick before you know it. Mad for power, Gloucester is.'

'Better than King Tom,' I quipped, 'with the poor little King shut away in his schoolroom while his mother's family ruins the country like old Margaret of Anjou did with poor King Henry. Gloucester is Protector by the King's will, and what's good enough for King Edward's good enough for me.'

On the principle of quitting while you're ahead, I finished my drink and took John away.

Next day I received Richard's letter. It was a triumph. He had peacefully secured the King and was on his way to London.

After he had left Middleham a letter had come from the Duke of Buckingham saying, roughly, that this was a time for the men of the old royal blood to stick together and he was Richard's man in everything – where and when could they meet? Richard had replied saying, Meet me at Northampton where Rivers has agreed I'll meet up with the King's retinue, and bring no more than three hundred men.

Richard arrived at Northampton at the agreed time, but there was no sign of the King. He and his party had ridden on to Stony Stratford – fourteen miles nearer London, giving Richard the slip. However, back came Earl Rivers with a mouthful of excuses about there not being enough room in Northampton for the two parties. (This would have surprised the proprietors of Northampton's many large and excellent inns.) However, Richard put a good face on it, and invited Rivers to dine with him, and while they were at dinner Buckingham arrived.

'I had forgotten what good company Harry is,' Richard wrote, 'and he is well-read and witty, and the three of us found much in common. It was a lively and cordial evening, odd though this may sound in the circumstances. However, there was clearly fishy business afoot, and when Rivers agreed we would leave for Stony Stratford at dawn to meet the King, we were up earlier and surrounded Rivers' inn and kept him under guard. He acted bewildered, wondering that we could think anything wrong, but of course could do nothing but accept it. Harry and I then rode on to Stony Stratford, where it was no surprise to find the King's party already on the road and apparently believing that I had been 'dealt with'. I did not enjoy explaining to the young King what I had done – of course he can think no wrong of his uncle Rivers. Nor did he know the late King had appointed me Protector; this had of course been carefully kept from him. And nor could he understand for a long time that his mother and Dorset have been acting improperly. However, he accepted my authority and we returned to Northampton. I had to place Sir Richard Grey, the King's half-brother, and old Vaughan under guard also, for they were evidently deep in the plot to hurry the King to London and overthrow my authority. But in the end all passed off peacefully, without the trouble or bloodshed I feared. The young King neither likes nor trusts me, but this was to be expected in the circumstances and I hope we will soon be on better terms. We expect to be in London on the fourth day of May.'

There was more, of course – thanks for conveying his letter to his mother, and a good deal about Harry Buckingham, but the above is all that matters. It was very late when I received the letter, but I hurried around to Hastings' house. He was at Westminster, a servant told me, so off I went.

'You've heard from Richard too?' he greeted me. 'Yes, I had his letter, and so has the Council. Martin, what a relief! We're safe now.' Relaxed and less tired – less of Mistress Jane, I imagined – he was the Lord Hastings I remembered: lively, assured, confident. 'We have done the thing, Martin! The King's safe and so is his government. And good for Richard, not that I ever doubted he would do it properly – why, if you cut your finger there'd be more blood shed than over this business! Though – do you hear that din?'

Of course I did. 'What is it?'

'It's our innocent, well-intentioned Dowager Queen and pretty-boy Dorset scurrying into Sanctuary.'

'Sanctuary! Why, for heaven's sake?'

'Guilt. And they know they've lost. Played – and played dirtily – and lost. The minute they heard Richard had secured the King they were off. The Queen is taking all her goods and chattels with her, they've had to break down a wall to get it all in.'

We looked out at the scene: scurrying men bent double under loads of goods; a bed being carted holus-bolus; servants with chests and carpets, bolts of cloth, furniture, boxes – all in the flare of torches. I saw the Queen once, her face twisted with fear or fury, shouting with no regard for dignity to hurry the servants on. Dorset even had his doublet off, working in his shirtsleeves.

'They're stripping the Palace bare! Can't you stop them?'

'How?' Hastings said simply. 'Not without a standing fight between my men and theirs. I did go and see the Queen, I tried to talk sense to her but she gibbered at me and fled.'

'What about Prince Richard and the girls?'

'Being bundled in with Mum. Martin, I know it's not right but what can I do? Everyone has the right to take Sanctuary without hindrance. They'll come out again when they realise they've made fools of themselves.'

I could only agree – but the Woodvilles made fools of us in one way. Dorset somehow got access to the Tower treasury, and stole the Royal treasure. Worth, you may note, hundreds of thousands of pounds. And he gave a third of it to his uncle Sir Edward Woodville, who promptly took the fleet out to sea with it. The rest the Queen and Dorset divided between them. Most of it was never seen again.

Early the following day John and I set out to meet Richard. It was May Day. The Maypoles were up and girls were coming in from the woods and fields with armfuls of May flowers. In St Albans we watched the Morris Men, hailed Robin Hood and Maid Marian, then rode on to the King's inn. John slid off to watch the merry-making, and I looked for Richard.

The first person I met was Buckingham. To my pleasure he remembered me and greeted me kindly. He was full of high spirits. Richard looked tired, I thought – well, no wonder – and he was content to sit with a cup of ale and let Buckingham talk. Born to talk, was Harry Stafford, or perhaps he had picked it up from living among the Welsh – his lands lay in Wales and he had lived at Brecknock much of his adult life. But he was entertaining and witty, and he obviously thought the sun shone out of Richard.

I told them about the Queen scuttling into Sanctuary. Richard swore, but admitted there had been nothing anyone could do to stop it. 'Is all the Tower treasure gone?'

'Afraid so.'

'Will they stop at nothing! Because I don't suppose they'll meekly hand it back to the King when he arrives.'

'Hardly. Richard, where is the King? I should greet him.'

Richard's face closed over. 'I believe he is resting.'

'Sulking,' Buckingham translated, 'for he loathes us, doesn't he, Dickon? Sulks and spite and sullen silence are all we get from him.'

Smiling gently at Buckingham Richard said, 'It's to be expected. He loves his Uncle Anthony, and he has met me, what, twice in his life. I arrive out of nowhere, throw my weight around, and hustle his uncle and half-brother into prison. He doesn't know who to trust any more.'

'Yes but Dickon, he could be civil!'

Now, Richard didn't like being called Dickon. He tolerated the old family nickname from his sisters, but it always reminded him of being three years old. None of his close friends used it, yet here was Buckingham Dickoning away like, well, the dickens. Still, Buckingham was his cousin, which perhaps made a difference. As we talked on, they describing the action in Northampton and Stony Stratford, I elaborating on my visit to the Duchess and what I had seen in London, I realised Buckingham was more and more reminding me of someone. When he made a rude but very funny joke about Rivers, and Richard laughed aloud, I had it – George! Oh, there was no great physical resemblance, or no more than you'd expect between cousins – in profile he and Richard were alike, and they shared a certain bearing and even some mannerisms. No, he was like George in the indefinable things: the glancing humour that often had a sting to it, the eagerness, the confidence – and, to be fair, in his obvious affection for Richard. For I think I have made it plain that despite everything there was great affection between George and Richard. Losing his last brother so suddenly, Richard must have felt, even yearned for, the similarity and the easy family liking.

But I found that a little of Buckingham went a long way – and so, to judge from their expressions, did Rob and Francis. The horrid thought occurred to me: were we actually jealous? We had known Richard so long, yet in comes this new friend … I took my drink over to the window and looked idly down into the garden. Butts had been set up and two boys were shooting.

'Richard,' I said over my shoulder, 'what does the King look like?'

'Tall, very fair, thin …'

'Like two yards of pump water,' laughed Buckingham, and Richard couldn't quite suppress his own laugh.

'Then it's he John is shooting with in the garden.'

'*What?*'

'Having the time of their lives, it seems.'

Everyone rushed to look. Happy as you like, evidently on the best of terms, the two boys were engaged in some impromptu contest. The King's shot went wide, and John shouted as he might to any of the Middleham boys, 'Ha ha, missed! My turn!'

'You think you're so clever ... '

'And that's *my* orange you're eating. Watch this!'

But John also missed. The King jeered companionably and they clapped each other on the back as they retrieved their arrows.

Richard came away from the window. 'I wouldn't have believed it! The boy's human.'

'Richard, he *is* a boy. He's twelve. His father is recently dead, everything has changed.'

'I know,' Richard sighed. 'But I keep thinking, if it were one of my boys ... I've tried being friendly, remote, crisp, submissive, paternal, gentle, authoritative, avuncular, humble – nothing works. He sees me as an enemy.'

'That's inevitable.'

'I know, and it's foolish of me but it hurts. I wanted to love Edward's son. And he knows nothing of his father's family. I bet he knows every detail of Alexander or Julius Caesar but nothing of Mortimer's Cross or Barnet.'

'Yes, well, that's probably inevitable too, for his mother's family made no great contribution. Give it time, Richard. Perhaps John will do the trick – for I bet the King is the most learned boy in England but he's never *been* a boy, a child, never played with friends in an ordinary way and so Innogen said that if one more consignment arrives ...' Just in time I had heard the two boys coming in, and we rose for the King. 'Oh hello, John, dear. Your Grace, God's greeting.'

The two boys were flushed and sweaty from their games. The King lost his smile and stiffened up at the sight of us, although he acknowledged our bows. 'Edward, I mean Your Grace,' John prattled, 'this is my stepfather, Lord Robsart, and he's a really good shot. Papa, the King needs a longer bow.'

'To draw at a venture? Well, there's no difficulty. Shooting, were you? A contest? Who won?'

'I did,' both boys said. Everyone laughed, and suddenly things were easier.

'The best thing,' Richard said, 'is to ask your armourer to make a bow to fit you. We shall see to it in London; meanwhile you could borrow Lord Robsart's, he's about your height. You take after your father, and even as a boy he had to have all his weapons specially made for him.'

'I keep just missing the gold,' the King confided. His voice was still a child's, high, rather soft and husky. I guessed that this was the first personal remark he had made to Richard; certainly the first admission of a fault or difficulty.

Richard nodded seriously. 'If your bow's too small, that will do it. Or if you aim too directly, not allowing for wind or the way the arrow drops in flight.'

'Papa, could we use yours?' John asked.

'Of course. Though you may need to adjust the pull.'

And soon we were all out in the garden happily competing as we had so often done at Middleham. When at last we went inside the easier feeling continued, and John's eager chatter led to talk of battles. The King was genuinely interested, and we refought Barnet and Tewkesbury on the tablecloth, with knives and bits of bread standing for the different positions. The King's eyes shone whenever we talked of his father. Clearly Edward had been, although a remote figure to him, a heroic one, and he couldn't hear enough about him. That a hero, a king, can do inglorious or ordinary things was a surprise to him; he laughed until he cried at the story of our escape to Burgundy in 1470, with Edward having to sell his cloak to the ship-masters, and he listened enthralled when Richard steered the conversation to Ludlow and his first meeting with his big brothers.

'That reminds me, Father,' John broke in. 'Edward, I mean His Grace, wanted to ask you something, there's a tutor he had at Ludlow and he wonders if he could have a rectorship he wants?'

Disentangling the pronouns Richard said, 'A rectorship for your tutor? Your Grace, of course.' Risking a smile he added, 'You have only to say, you know. You are the King. What is the man's name?'

'John Geffrey. He was chaplain at Ludlow.'

'We'll see to it in the morning, I'll show you how such instruments are drawn up. Does Master Geffrey want any particular place?'

'He said, Pembrigge.'

'Then you write to the Bishop of Hereford.'

'As simple as that?'

'As simple as that. Of course there's a customary form of words for these things, and it's as well if you know that kind of minutiae, but it's straightforward. I remember your father told me once that when he and Edmund were boys at Ludlow they loathed their tutor, they wrote to our father complaining bitterly.'

The King laughed, yawning. It was after nine o'clock, and he had been kept to such a strict regime at Ludlow that to him nine was the middle of the night. Saying goodnight – and of course he had perfect manners – he called Richard 'uncle' for the first time, and asked if John could share his room.

'Of course, Sire.' As he would to any of John's friends Richard added with mock severity, 'But no talking all night, mind!'

'We *know*.' John rolled his eyes. The King looked shocked (and rather interested) at the impertinence, and although Richard raised an eyebrow he couldn't repress a smile. 'Sorry, Father. Goodnight. Goodnight Papa, Your Grace, gentlemen.' John flung his arms around Richard then me for his usual goodnight kiss.

'Goodnight.' Richard kissed him, then with a hesitation only his friends would notice, he gave the King a kiss. 'Goodnight, Edward, my dear boy. Sleep well.' The King liked it, he flushed with pleasure. I'm sure Anthony Rivers loved his nephew and took great care of him, but I wondered if he had ever given the boy a hug or kissed him goodnight. His father would have.

The next morning Richard made sure they wrote out the order for Whatsisname's rectorship. I think the King had believed he would forget, or had only been indulging him with a promise he never meant to keep. Dipping his pen in the ink the King said, 'You have very neat writing, Uncle.'

'Years of doing this sort of thing.' The King was still holding his pen uncertainly in the air. Understanding, Richard said, 'First time? Practice first,' and slid over a spare sheet of paper. Gratefully the King tried out his signature: *Edwardus Quintus.* The writing was a child's: large, unpractised. Looking at him, Richard inked his own pen and wrote his signature on the paper, adding below it his motto: *Loyaulté Me Lié.* 'Loyalty binds me,' he said gently. Their eyes met. The King smiled.

Buckingham had been watching intently. 'Me too,' he said, and seized the pen from Richard's hand to scrawl his own signature and motto: *Souvente me souvene.* 'Remember me often'. The King gave him rather a cool smile, then signed the rectorship order.

We left for London the next day. A London reception was something new to the King, and at first he seemed aloof, looking around unsmiling. Then suddenly he relaxed and waved at the crowds, grinning about at the aldermen in their ceremonial violet gowns and the burgesses in their scarlet; all the ordinary people in their best clothes to see the new King. A woman ran alongside his horse to push a bunch of flowers into his hand, and with an air he tossed one of the blooms back to her and blew a kiss after it. It was his city, his people, and he enjoyed it.

At the back of our retinue were the wagons full of arms and harness seized from the Woodville men-at-arms. The badges on them were enough, coupled with the news that had already gone around, to make the point about Woodville intentions.


Richard's first action was to take and administer to the people of London a public oath of fealty to Edward V, as he had done at York on his way south. Then it was down to business. A child when Edward IV took the throne, I had had no idea just how much business there was at such a time. The coronation was set for the twenty-fourth day of June, and writs were issued for the Parliament. Of course the most important thing was to confirm Richard's Protectorship and determine his powers. Once the King was crowned this was a matter for Parliament, but for the time being the Council of Lords could give him sufficient power to act in the King's name.

One of the first things was to deal with the Woodvilles. The Marquis of Dorset had managed to escape from Sanctuary, and his uncle Edward Woodville had the fleet at sea. That made Richard's mind up, and he pressed for treason charges against Rivers and Grey and old Vaughan. However, this was difficult, for Richard had not been formally proclaimed Protector at Northampton, and their actions, although highly suspicious, were not provable as treason in law. Richard withdrew his proposal, but it was agreed to let the conspirators stew in their own juice in prison for the time being.

As for Dorset and Sir Edward, it was simple. They were proclaimed traitors, and pardons offered to any man who deserted them. Promptly, many did. And now Lord Howard came into his own, for there never was a better man of the sea than Jock Howard – in my view, there never was a better man. Had Edward IV not secured the Mowbray dukedom for his son Richard by marrying him to Anne Mowbray, Jock Howard would have become Duke of Norfolk when the little girl died. Many men would have devoted their lives to getting that dukedom back; Howard had more sense. He said he had enough money for his needs, and better things to do – as indeed he had, for ever since he had joined the young Edward back in 1461 with his sword in one hand and a bag of gold in the other, he had been the mainstay of the English crown. Remember how, recently, he had sailed coolly into the Firth of Forth and made the Scots look silly? A typical Howard action in its daring and its cool competence. So now, having sized up the new reign, he put himself at the Protector's disposal. Winkle out the traitors and get our ships back? Nothing to it. He suggested a couple of good men, old shipmates: a fellow called Fulford and Edward IV's great friend Sir Edward Brampton, a converted Jew, and sent them after the

Woodvilles. Dorset and his uncle got away, however, to Brittany, the holds of their ships clanking with the King's treasure.

Howard was very friendly with Hastings, having been his deputy at Calais. They were much of an age, I think, and bound by having served the late King and been his friends ever since he first came to the throne. These were the sort of good, solid, experienced men the new King would need around him – and, for the present, it eased things that both knew Richard so well and had fought with him. There were other good men a-plenty: Suffolk and his son John of Lincoln, Howard's son Thomas, Northumberland, Lord Stanley, Bishop Stillington, Bishop Langton, Hastings' protégé the lawyer William Catesby. Bishop Russell was appointed Lord Chancellor; Doctor Gunthorpe, Dean of Wells, was made Keeper of the Privy Seal; John Wode, who had been Speaker of the Commons, became Treasurer. They were all sound fellows who had worked for Edward IV and knew the ins and outs of government to its last detail.

Maximilian of Burgundy wrote in the friendliest of terms, greeting the new King. But the French fleet was prowling the Channel raiding our shipping, and what old Louis might get up to was anyone's guess. Brittany and Scotland, likewise. However, for the moment there was no sign of international trouble, we could get on with domestic affairs.

## Fourteen

## *June-July 1483*

Crosby's Place had a cat. A lost and starving kitten, the animal had wandered in a year or two ago and decided this was home. The steward tolerated him because he was a good mouser, and somehow he had acquired the name Tiddles. Now a plump, sleek patriarch, he took a great interest in Richard's Council meetings, sauntering up and down the table sniffing the ink and sitting with feline skill on precisely the one document that was needed. From time to time he turned kittenish and chased the ends of our quills, causing many a blot and spoiled paper, or stole our pencils to chew them. Kendal hated him and wouldn't allow him in the clerks' room. At night he shared his favours around – Tiddles, I mean, not Kendal – and tonight he was lying on my stomach, paws tucked under, purring loudly. Innogen was almost asleep, her head on my shoulder, and absently I stroked both wife and cat, pondering the day's incidents.

Late in May things had seemed so settled that Richard had sent for Anne. She and the other Middleham ladies had arrived two days ago, on June the fifth, and today Anne had paid a ceremonial call on the King. Richard being busy, I had escorted her, taking John for the King's sake, and Innogen, Katherine and our two oldest children for theirs.

Recently moved from the Bishop's Palace to the pleasanter surroundings of the Tower, the King had been pleased to see us. He was lonely, poor lad, and bored with business. Charmed by Anne, whom he had met only once, but a good deal more interested in Katherine and Cecily, he gave us wine and sweetmeats then suggested we look at the Tower menagerie. To be frank, this wasn't all that exciting – some exotic birds, several of whom talked; a dromedary remarkably like Doctor Morton; hunting cats; turtles; monkeys and apes of different kinds.

'I wish the elephant were still here,' the King said, 'and it would be interesting to have a camelopard – I saw a picture of one once in a Bestiary. But perhaps they are not real.'

'What's a camelopard?'

The King turned eagerly to Katherine. 'In the book it had a body a bit like a horse but much longer legs, and a neck at least ten feet long, and a little head rather like a cow's but with little stubby horns. And its body was covered with great spots.'

'A neck that long? Wouldn't it fall over? Surely they can't be real?'

'I believe they are,' Innogen said. 'My father owned several ships and he traded all over the Mediterranean Sea. He said he had been in Africa and had seen a camelopard. Twenty feet high, he said, and they run very fast and gracefully.'

'I would like to see one,' the King said wistfully. 'I wonder if they are easily found? And I've heard of all sorts of other beasts in Africa and the Indies.'

'You can fund explorers and send ships to all sorts of places,' Anne suggested. 'They could bring back beasts for your menagerie.'

'I could.' His eyes lit up. 'There must be all kinds of marvels. Of course I've read Pliny and Herodotus, and although many of the tales cannot be true, one still wonders. Alexander the Great used to send back plants and strange beasts to Aristotle. And I once heard a tale that the Vikings sailed westward, oh, about a thousand years ago, and found a new land! And they say that in Africa people are black all over and go about naked, and some have their heads sunk beneath their shoulders. I wonder if any of it is true.' Boyish, he cried, 'I'd like to go to sea!' The last word echoed as he spun about, his arms out-stretched.

'Become one of the Merchant Adventurers, Sire, and send out explorers. There are even stories of a great land in the south below the Indies – but sailors' tales grow taller with every voyage. Ask Lord Howard to take you out in one of his ships.'

I suppose it is still the same, but in my day several hundred people lived in the Tower, the keepers and soldiers, the gardeners and animal keepers, the men in charge of the various Crown departments. In the warm June weather Tower Green was as busy as any country town. Women were hanging washing in the sun, others were enjoying a gossip while their children played. Looking at these simple occupations the King said suddenly, 'I would like my brother for company, even though we don't know each other well. And my sisters; I like Bess. But ...' We were on delicate ground here. The Queen-Dowager still refused to leave Sanctuary, and nor would she permit any of her children to leave. It had caused ill-feeling between Richard and the King.

'Ask your lady mother,' Anne suggested. The King looked at her in surprise. 'Why not, Your Grace? Visit her or write to her and say you want your brother and sisters for company; her too, of course.' Though I doubted Elizabeth Woodville had seen her elder son more than four times since he was sent to Ludlow at the age of three.

'But – she fears ...' The King was too well mannered to say to Richard's wife that the Woodvilles feared her husband. Anne walked on for a moment in silence.

'Let's be blunt,' she said at last. 'Your mother acted unwisely. Indiscreetly. Of course she was distraught at your father's death, and it is hard to think clearly at such times. And, to be even blunter, after wielding great power for twenty years your mother had no mind to step back to the lesser role of Queen Mother. That's very natural. But she and Lord Dorset let themselves be persuaded into rash and even illegal actions. In short, they thought of you not as King and their master, but as a little boy who couldn't think for himself and whose government they could control.'

Clever Anne – that brought the King's head up, and a mulish look very reminiscent of his father to his face.

Pretending not to notice she went on, 'My husband was your father's choice for Protector, not your mother or Lord Dorset or even your uncle Rivers. You have made it plain you are content to trust your father's judgement, and I believe Richard's actions since

April prove that judgement was not misplaced. He is prepared to let bygones be bygones. Your mother knows she has nothing to fear, but no doubt she feels rather foolish. Let them only come to your Court as your family should, and no one will refer to the past.'

'But – would my uncle ...'

'He would welcome them in your name,' Anne said smoothly, 'and make it plain they were to be treated with honour.'

'I see. I'll think about it.'

We were back at the State apartments and making the phrases of farewell when the King blushed again and asked if John and Martin – and Katherine and Cecily too if they'd like – could stay on for a little.

'Of course, Your Grace.' So the King was old enough to take an interest in pretty girls. 'And why not make up a party one day to go on the river, or ride out in the country? By the way, isn't that Lord Stanley over there with Rotherham and Doctor Morton?' I had first noticed them when the King had spun happily about as he talked of going to sea.

'Oh yes,' the King said indifferently, 'they often meet here.' The Council had split into different groups that met here, at Westminster, at Crosby's Place, each group managing a different branch of the royal business. 'Lord Hastings is usually with them. Lord Stanley's wife Lady Margaret Beaufort came to see me the other day.' His tone suggested it had been no meeting of minds.

'I see. Well, good day to Your Grace. Children, don't be late for supper.'

A pleasant little occasion, and the children had come home chattering of the fun they had had feeding the Tower ravens and exploring some of the buildings; to them, being King was a fine thing because it meant being able to command any game you wanted. But what stuck in my mind, and kept me awake, was that brief sighting of Morton and Stanley. Something about it had been wrong.

The problem nagged at me. Asleep, Innogen turned over with her back to me. I did the same, making the cat growl crossly. He settled down beside me, however, purring away. Purring. Yes, that was it. Stanley and Morton had been too much at ease, too casual. They had looked less like colleagues than conspirators. Colleagues parting after a routine meeting have no need to stand so studiedly in public view to say goodbye.

And the King had said Hastings was often with them. There should have been nothing in that to make me uneasy – except that Hastings had never liked Morton or Stanley, he tried to avoid them. But Hastings had changed these last few weeks. I believe he had expected Richard and Buckingham to act for him and take the King, and then hand over to the older man. Hastings had been the late King's closest friend; he had stood firm and averted trouble in the first days. Yet once Richard arrived Hastings found himself only one among many. And perhaps it had always rankled that Edward had not named him Protector. So yes, he had changed lately.

Perhaps he was jealous of Buckingham. Hastings had known Richard since he was a child, he had twenty years' experience at the late King's side, yet suddenly there was this new man claiming Richard's friendship and confidence. Claiming great rewards.

Buckingham had already been made Chief Justice and Chamberlain of Wales, and given powers of supervision and array in five counties, in which he was also Constable of all royal castles and steward of all royal lands. Doesn't sound very great? But these were the sort of powers Edward had given Richard himself, and they made Buckingham overlord, ruler in fact, of Wales and the West Country. And Richard had earned his honours. Oh yes, Buckingham was the great man now, and put beside the grants to him, those made to other men of longer loyalty seemed modest. It was as if Buckingham had such a hold on Richard that he had only to ask and he received. And Buckingham's more flamboyant personality made it seem that he, not Richard, was ruling the roost.

But that was another matter. My mind still ran on that oddly furtive little meeting in the Tower. Morton had detested Richard since the business of the French treaty back in 1475. Rotherham's stupid games with the Great Seal had made it plain where his loyalties lay. No one could count the times Stanley had turned his coat in the past twenty years, and he was married to the arch-Lancastrian Lady

Margaret Beaufort, who in turn was thick as thieves with Morton. No, I didn't like it. Little to go on except a pricking in my thumbs, but I didn't like it. 'I had better tell Richard, hadn't I?' I asked Tiddles, but the cat only flicked his ears irritably.

Richard did much the same when I told him. He questioned me in the sternly gentle way he used with witnesses in law cases, until I ended up shuffling my feet and admitting that all I had seen was three councillors going about their rightful business. 'And what is there in that, Martin?'

'Nothing. Except it didn't feel right.'

'Duly noted.' He looked impatient. I felt a fool.

'But if Hastings is often with them?'

'So?'

'So nothing.'

'Very well. Now if you'll excuse me, I am to play tennis with Harry.'

'Enjoy yourself,' I said, but I doubt if it really stung.


To my fury, the next day Richard solemnly told me that Buckingham was uneasy about things he was hearing about Morton, Rotherham and Stanley.

'That's what I said.'

Richard had the grace to laugh and apologise. 'But Harry has a little more to go on than merely seeing them leaving the Tower. Hastings is more and more often with them, and Lady Margaret Beaufort has been visiting the Queen – and so has Jane Shore. Interesting?'

'I imagine any conversation she has with the Queen would be interesting, yes. Jane Shore. Visiting the Queen. And she is still with Hastings.'

'Oh yes. So it does begin to look as if there's a rat in the wainscoting.' He glanced up, amusement warming his eyes. 'I didn't entirely disregard what you said then listen panting to Buckingham. But he's better than you at picking up gossip.'

'Perhaps,' I couldn't resist, 'he's hearing things from the Woodville end?'

'Possibly,' Richard said thoughtfully.

'I'd have a word with William Catesby if I were you,' I suggested.

'Why?'

'A bit of gossip. He's always been Hastings' man, but now he's uneasy. Find the time to have a quiet word.'

For there was definitely something afoot, no mere figment of my imagination – or Buckingham's. Once alerted, we heard more and more hints, until it became clear it was some Lancastrian-Woodville plot to overthrow the Protector. Dick Ratcliffe, who was married to Catesby's wife's stepsister, took Catesby aside, but if Hastings was involved, Catesby was no longer in his confidence – a fact suspicious in itself. For once thoroughly in accord, Buckingham and I – and Richard's other friends – guarded him more closely, and sent out our own spies.

Only the last item on the agenda paper remained: the list of gentlemen to be knighted after the coronation. Kendal put a neat tick, and we pushed back our chairs, stretching with relief. It was a stuffy, hot night. Even with every window open we were sweating.

'Bishop Stillington is waiting to see you, Richard. He says it is urgent and important.'

Shuffling his papers together, Richard made a little grimace. He and I had planned to go on the river tonight, taking our wives and making merry. In our minds we were already out in the cooler air, trailing our hands in the water and listening to the minstrels while we drank cool wine. Stillington was a decent old boy, but long-winded. 'Has he waited long?'

'Sir, all day. He says he will wait until you see him.'

'Oh, very well.' Richard tugged at the laces of his shirt, vaguely trying to make himself tidy. 'Bring us something cool to drink, but drop a hint that I would be glad to be finished soon.'

Age had shrunken and stooped the Bishop. His rings hung loose on his knotty fingers, and he gazed short-sightedly about as he made his way to the table. Kendal held a chair for him, and he sank down, peering at Richard.

'Your Grace, I have some information for you. It is of the first importance. I have sinned in keeping secret what I have to tell you.'

'Sinned, my lord? Surely not.'

'Oh yes,' the old fellow said sadly. '*Mea culpa, mea maxima culpa.* Your Grace, the late King Edward's son cannot be crowned. He cannot inherit the throne. He is illegitimate. When he married Elizabeth Woodville, King Edward was already married.'

# Fifteen

The words meant nothing at first. People were hardly listening. Then one by one every head turned towards the Bishop.

Frowning, Richard said, 'Bishop, there was always gossip about my brother the King. Perhaps you have merely heard …'

'Oh no, Your Grace. You see, I married them.'

The silence held and held. Suddenly Richard slammed his hand hard down on the table and said, 'Speak plainly, man. Married who? And when?'

'In 1461 I married your brother the late King Edward to Lady Eleanor Butler.'

Now you could have cut the tension with a knife. We had all expected some nonsense story about Elizabeth Lucy or another of Edward's known mistresses. The name of one of the highest-born ladies in the land stopped us flat. *Lady Eleanor Butler…*

Lord Howard said incredulously, 'Can you be serious, man? Lady Eleanor? Eleanor Talbot? The *Earl of Shrewsbury's* daughter?'

'Yes. Edward was eighteen. She was a widow and nearly ten years older.'

His face the colour of parchment Richard said, 'You cannot expect us to believe this.'

'I have proofs, Your Grace. It was a binding trothplight. '

Richard let out a breath, relaxing. 'You said marriage, before!'

'It comes to the same thing, sir. A formal trothplight, a pre-contract of marriage, before witnesses, is as binding as marriage.' Several men around the table nodded. Such a promise was binding, test cases in courts of law had established that; not even witnesses were necessary if a promise was solemnly made. 'And,' the Bishop added, his voice twisting, 'it was consummated.'

Of course. Knowing Edward, that was the object of the exercise.

'Are you saying,' Richard asked, 'that the late king was contracted in what the church and civil law consider the equivalent of binding marriage, to Lady Eleanor Butler, three years before he married Elizabeth Woodville? That the later marriage was invalid? Bigamous, in fact?'

'Yes, Your Grace.'

I thought Richard would faint. I snapped my fingers at the pageboy for wine, and had to hold Richard's hand around the cup, he was shaking so much.

'But that means,' Buckingham said shrilly, 'that the new King is a bastard!'

'Yes.'

'Now steady on.' Howard's calm East Anglian voice was a breath of sanity. 'Let's not get ahead of ourselves. Lady Eleanor went into a convent, didn't she, and she died when? '68, if I remember rightly?' After a moment's thought, Richard and the Bishop both nodded. Lady Eleanor had been some sort of cousin to Richard; she was certainly Anne's cousin through her mother. 'Well then, we'll find the late King went through another and a legal marriage with Elizabeth Woodville after Lady Eleanor's death. That would mean all but the two eldest girls are legitimate.'

'Yes.' Colour was returning to Richard's face; too much colour. His eyes shone like a fever victim's. 'Yes of course he must have done that. The Queen would have insisted.'

'If she knew,' said Buckingham.

'Oh, she knew. There must have been a second marriage and she will have proof of it. Doctor Russell, you and Lord Howard and the Archbishop go at once to Westminster Sanctuary and see the Queen. Tell her what Bishop Stillington has revealed. Assure her on the Cross that if she produces proofs of her second and valid marriage to my brother, and her sons are legitimate, the tale will not be made public. Go now. Gentlemen, none of you may leave until they return.'

No one spoke when they left. Awkwardly we drank wine, stood

about. Waiting. Richard said suddenly, 'Doctor Stillington, did my brother George know of this pre-contract business?' Willing him to say no, to leave him something of Edward to respect.

But the Bishop bowed his head and said, 'Yes. Clarence knew.'

I saw understanding work like yeast in the other faces. Buckingham said, 'So, Bishop, do I recall correctly – you were imprisoned at the same time as Clarence?'

'Yes.'

'For the same reason? I mean, for this reason? Because you knew this secret?'

Again the Bishop's head bent in a nod. 'Yes, Your Grace. I should have spoken out then.'

'Before then!'

'Yes. I was weak. I've done penance … I was weak and venal. Prison and a crippling fine frightened me … I could bear no more. I would not risk the king's wrath. I am not the stuff of martyrs.'

Oh shut up, shut up, I silently begged him. Again it was Buckingham who said the unsayable. 'Why didn't Clarence speak out in '78? Think – he was tried before Parliament, no one ever believed much in those treason charges – why did he not tell this story then?'

'He loved his children.'

Silences can have their own character, and I'd not live through that moment again. No wonder Edward had refused to let Richard see George. No wonder he had refused to listen even to his mother's pleas. I remembered that weird secret audience I had had with him – *this* had been in his mind. He had nearly weakened, but the Queen had persuaded him. He had put his brother to death to protect this old secret. He had threatened his brother's children.


It was nearly two hours before Howard and Russell returned. We had sat in silence so profound that a sigh, or the cat scratching, had the power to make us jump and feel instinctively for weapons. For the last hour Richard had stood at the window, hands stretched high on the embrasure, staring out sightlessly into the courtyard. I think he was praying.

We knew at once from Howard's expression. Still no one spoke. Richard turned very slowly, and his nephew Lincoln went to his side. 'No second marriage,' Howard said. 'She knew at once why we had come. She tried to lie, then broke down and admitted the truth. It is as Bishop Stillington says. The late King told her the truth in '77.'

'Poor woman,' Richard said. Buckingham smothered a grin, but I knew Richard meant it. He had never liked Elizabeth Woodville, but he could feel for her. To marry in good faith, to bear a string of children, to glory in your power as Queen: then to find your husband had made a whore of you and bastards of your children ... Poor woman indeed.

'Yes,' said Howard, for he too had imagination and compassion. 'There was no way for the King and Queen of England to re-marry in secret; the story would have got out. They would have needed witnesses, it would not have been enough to have, say, Stillington, perform the marriage in secret. And there were the children. They preferred to gamble on the Butler pre-contract never coming out, they thought Stillington had been sufficiently frightened to keep silence.'

'People always did say the Woodville woman bewitched Edward into that marriage,' said Buckingham. 'It's the only explanation.'

'Perhaps,' said Richard. 'No wonder they were in such a hurry to crown the new King. They would have made a bastard King of England. And blamed their rush on me, saying they feared me. I w-wondered why th-they sh-should fear me, all I've ever w-wanted is to live in the n-north and s-serve the king as I've always d-done, I've h-hated everything that's happened since Edward died, since G-George died ...'

'Easy, lad,' said Howard, and under his breath to Francis and me, 'For God's sake get him out.'

'But we have to settle this!' cried Buckingham. 'Don't you understand what this means?'

'It means nothing until we decide it does.' A burly man, Howard crossed the room and took Richard's arm, half-lifting him. 'You go along now, lad, you've had enough for the night. Leave this to us.' Unceremoniously he bundled Richard to the door. Francis and I took over, hustling him along the corridor to his room.

We dismissed his servants and sat him on his bed, took off his boots and outer clothing. He let us do it, moving when we told him, stiff as a child's wooden doll. Rob had stayed to obtain wine. 'Drink it,' he said sternly. Richard obeyed. Rob turned the bed down and we swung our unresponsive lord about and tucked him in. His favourite wolfhound Ludlow leapt up onto the bed beside him, licked his face, then curled up. Richard patted him, and in a moment they were both asleep.

'That's done it,' Rob said in satisfaction. 'Valerian in the wine. Else he'd've been awake all night. I'll stay with him, you two get rid of everyone. And better tell the women.'

All but Howard had gone. He sat with Kendal at the table, tickling the cat under the chin. 'Threw 'em all out,' he said simply. 'Even that chatterbox Buckingham. Told them if one word of this gets out they're for it, duke or commoner I'll fix them personally. Put the fear of God up them. I've sent to double the guard on Sanctuary and the … the King.'

'Good.' I felt as tired as after a battle. 'Richard's asleep. Lord Howard, what will happen now?'

'God alone knows. It's a matter for the full Council, for Parliament.' He rose wearily. 'I'm for my bed. Guard Richard. We'll meet tomorrow. Goodnight.'


We told the women, and again I'd not go through that twice. At first Elizabeth of Suffolk flatly refused to believe it, then, convinced, she said, 'So my brother Edward was nothing but a … a conscienceless … No wonder he went to pieces after he put George to death. But why didn't he marry Elizabeth properly once Lady Eleanor died?'

We repeated what Howard had said: impossible to keep it secret; any doubt would cloud their children's rights.

'And they had two more children after George died. Even then.'

White to the lips Anne said, 'Does the pre-contract necessarily invalidate the Woodville marriage? Is there no way out?'

'Stillington says it was a binding pre-contract of marriage, *verba de praesenti*, witnessed and consummated. It is the same as a marriage. And Edward married Elizabeth Woodville in secret, remember all the talk at the time? We wondered then if a clandestine marriage was legal.'

'No wonder it was clandestine,' Innogen snapped. 'But how *could* Edward? And why didn't Lady Eleanor speak out when he married Elizabeth Woodville? She was a high-born woman with a powerful and influential family, she had proofs of the pre-contract – why didn't she speak out?'

Wearily, my head throbbing, I said, 'She had gone into a convent. She told Stillington she believed she had sinned in yielding to Edward. Same pattern as with Elizabeth – older woman who wouldn't lie with him without marriage. Stillington thinks Edward convinced her the pre-contract wasn't binding. And ... many people feared the Woodvilles.'

A long silence fell. At last Anne said, 'They will try to make Richard king now, won't they?'

'It hasn't come to that, not ...'

'They will, won't they?'

'Probably.'

She swung around to stare at us. 'Probably – certainly! Who else is there?'

'George's son,' Suffolk said. 'Little Warwick.'

'God help us, we'd be no better off! He's, what, eight? And – George's son! Even if the country accepted him – which it won't – George died under attainder, a traitor.'

'Well then,' said Anne in a voice I'd never heard her use before, 'it must be you, Lincoln. The late King's nephew, son of his eldest sister; of age; no taint of any kind on your birth or background. It must be you.'

'No,' Lincoln whispered in horror. 'I don't want it. I won't.'

'No, he will not,' said his mother, standing and looking down at Anne. 'Not my son.'

Anne looked right back at her. 'Not my husband.'

'It must be Richard,' said Elizabeth in the implacable voice of truth, 'because the protection of the Crown is all that can save him and all of us from the Woodvilles and the Lancastrians. Be queen, Anne, or be a widow in a week.'


She was right. Elizabeth Woodville told her cronies of Howard's night visit, and either she told the truth of its reason, or made it seem Richard was making some bid for the throne. Suddenly Hastings's men were everywhere, armed and wearing brigandines. The Stanley-Morton-Rotherham group was always together. Lady Margaret Beaufort and Jane Shore were in and out of the Woodville rooms in Sanctuary like mice. And finally Catesby came to Richard's council and spilled the beans. Hastings had trusted him with the whole story. Hastings was deep in conspiracy with the Woodvilles, the Stanleys and Morton. They planned to overthrow Richard, crown young Edward, make Hastings Protector. Not two months before Hastings had used Richard to overthrow the Woodvilles; now he would use the Woodvilles to overthrow Richard. Warwick had once deserted all his old loyalties to make a compact with Margaret of Anjou; now Hastings would do the same and join the Woodvilles.

Every day more proofs came in. People talked. Secret papers were secret no longer. Things were moving quickly. Richard wrote desperately to York for men. And on Friday the thirteenth of June, ill-omened day, he called a full Council meeting at the Tower.

Everyone assembled, pretending fellowship and ease, Morton talking of the fine strawberries he grew at his Holborn house. The doors were locked. Richard rose and addressed us.

There were those, he said, who cared nothing for good government and the old royal blood, those who for their own ends would overthrow his rightful authority as Protector and return the country to the days of civil war and bloodshed. 'These people,' he said, 'are guilty of treason.'

The word was a signal. Armed guards entered. The doors were locked again. 'I name these conspirators guilty of treason,' Richard said. His voice was cool and very clear. 'I name the Dowager Queen Elizabeth Woodville. I name her brother Lionel Woodville, Bishop of Salisbury. I name her son the Marquis of Dorset.' He took a breath. He could not, I noticed, bear to look at Hastings. Bleakly he continued, 'I name you, Doctor Rotherham. You, Doctor Morton. You, Thomas, Lord Stanley. I name Mistress Jane Shore. And I name you, William, Lord Hastings.'

'No!' cried Hastings and leaping to his feet he drew his sword. At once the guards seized him and disarmed him.

'Yes,' said Richard very quietly. 'Yes, Lord Hastings. I name you.'

'Richard ...'

'Catesby told us everything. We have the proof, there on the table.'

Hastings slumped against the men holding him. He began to cry. None of the other conspirators had spoken since Richard named them.

'Richard,' Hastings whispered, 'we were friends once.'

'Yes. We were. Once. And you betrayed me. You betrayed my brother. You betrayed the House of York. You would have brought this country to murder and civil war ...' He looked at the guards. 'Take him out. Get a priest. Have him shriven. Then execute him.'

Hastings broke. Weeping, shouting, struggling, he begged, he repented. He thrust his fellow conspirators deeper into the mire of blame. He screamed as they took him away.

It was over in five minutes. I daresay it was only in our imaginations that from that distance we heard the blow that beheaded Hastings down on Tower Green.

'Bury him at Windsor,' said Richard, 'beside my brother Edward. It was the wish of both of them.'

'And the rest of us?' Doctor Morton asked coolly; no blubbering or pleas from him. 'Are we to die also?'

'No. Prison. For all of you. For now.'

They had hardly been taken away before a guard burst in to say that the news had got out. The city was in uproar. Treason – executions in the Tower – Hastings dead – plots and conspiracies – many-tongued Rumour was loose in London. Men were putting on their armour.

Richard sent for Mayor Shaa, and soon a royal herald was proclaiming the news in the streets that a plot to destroy the Lord Protector and the Duke of Buckingham and overthrow the King's rightful government had been detected, and dealt with. The conspirators had been taken, there was nothing to fear.

And, with juicy gossip to enliven the evenings, the city settled down again.

There was a full Council meeting that night. There was some censure of Richard's peremptory execution of Hastings; surely, men said, he had been entitled to a trial? But when the proofs of the conspiracy were tabled there was no more than quiet censure. Richard's action had prevented an uprising; no one wanted armed bands fighting in the London streets. Nor did anyone argue when Richard called for Rivers and Grey to be executed for treason.

We had almost finished for the night when Buckingham said, 'I think the time has come to get the little Duke of York out of Sanctuary.'

The Archbishop of Canterbury looked aghast at Buckingham. 'Get him out? Violate Sanctuary?'

'No one is talking of violating Sanctuary rights. Anyway, has a child, who is sinless, such a right?'

It was a fine point of ecclesiastical law. The Archbishop pursed his lips.

Buckingham continued, 'And the little boy has no need of Sanctuary,' he argued. 'It is purely his mother's doing, she took Sanctuary for fear of retribution for her scheming against us. That does not affect her children. The … the King wants his brother's company; Prince Richard must be at the coronation. While I respect your arguments, my lord Archbishop, I would argue in return that it is the Queen who, in holding her children needlessly there, makes a mockery of the holy right of Sanctuary.'

The argument went on for some time. Richard took no part in it, I think he hardly knew what was being discussed. In the end the bishops and temporal lords overcame the Archbishop's objections: little Prince Richard should be brought out of Sanctuary.

On the Monday, June the sixteenth, the Archbishop went himself, with Lord Howard and others of the Council. Howard told me later that Elizabeth Woodville enacted a fine old scene, clutching her son to her breast and screeching that he was going to his death. 'She even managed a few tears,' Howard said in disgust. 'But she could hardly argue that the Archbishop was going to encompass a child's death, and the boy himself couldn't wait to get out of the place. In the end she gave in quite quickly. I felt sorry for the girls, though – poor Lady Bess begged me to get them out too.'


Did we, his friends, urge Richard to take the Crown? Of course we did.

Much as we all liked Lincoln, he genuinely did not want it, sensible man, and there would always be those who would argue that although England has no Salic law, his descent through the female line made his right inferior to Richard's. Also, he was barely twenty-one. Richard had the experience, the skill, the trust of the people; he had a growing son as his heir.

Also we thought Richard had no real choice. Probably when his brother's children came of age the rebellions and uprisings would begin again – well, let 'em, we thought; let the Woodvilles try to put a bastard on the throne. By then Richard would have reigned for several years, his sensible rule would have shown the people they were well off, his son, too, would be almost of age.

And we, his friends, would rise or fall with him. No one could turn time back. The late king had left this situation; his children were bastards. Richard had never schemed for the crown, but now it was his for the asking. Let him take it.

But O for the gift of foresight! Had we known, we would have put Lincoln or little Warwick on the throne, even concealed the truth that Edward V – never, in fact, to be Edward V – was a bastard, and let him rule, and gone quietly back to the north. But I daresay things would have fallen out as they did whoever was king.

So the pre-contract story was revealed to the full Council, Stillington gave witness on oath and produced his proofs. Now there was no more doubt. No child of Edward IV's could rule. It must be Richard.

On Sunday the twenty-second of June, Friar Ralph Shaa, brother of the Lord Mayor, proclaimed the truth from Paul's Cross. He preached the Biblical text: *Bastard slips shall take no root*, then revealed the story of the Butler pre-contract. The late King's marriage to Dame Elizabeth Grey, née Woodville, had been bigamous, no true marriage, and all their children were therefore illegitimate. The Duke of Clarence's son, the Earl of Warwick, was debarred the throne by his father's attainder. Therefore, Richard of Gloucester …

I doubt it surprised anyone. The story had got about by then. To those cynics who thought Richard had trumped up the tale as a cover for his own ambitions, the name of Lady Eleanor Butler came as a shock. Her family was too powerful for her name to be so used unless the tale were true. And Edward had always been lecherous, and no one had ever liked the Woodville marriage. Pity about the children, but there you are. And here is Richard of Gloucester, the late King's trusted and loyal brother, the hero of the civil wars and the saviour of England in the Border wars … Let it be Richard.

Buckingham had a wonderful time in those few days. He was ubiquitous. Speaking to the session of the Lords, addressing the chief citizens in the Guildhall, addressing Parliament again when Richard's claim was formally put and accepted; leading the Lords and Prelates when Richard appeared before the citizens of London at Baynard's Castle.

And when Buckingham finished his silver-tongued oratory and

formally called upon Richard to accept the petition of Parliament and assume the throne, a great cheer went up from the people. They were in no doubt. They wanted Richard.

My childhood friend, my kinsman, the man I loved most in my life, that day rode to Westminster Hall and seated himself upon the marble chair of King's Bench. By that simple action he became King.

King Richard III of England.

## Sixteen

## July-November 1483

The coronation was on the sixth of July. The King goes barefoot to
his coronation, walking in solemn state up the red carpet to the
Abbey. We were all in crimson, blue or white; the King and Queen in
purple, white and gold. Northumberland carried the blunted Sword
of Mercy, Stanley the High Constable's Mace, Kent and Lovell the
sharp Swords of Justice, Lincoln the Sceptre, Surrey the Sword of
State, Norfolk the Crown. (Richard had given the Norfolk dukedom
to Lord Howard a few days before, at the same time making
Howard's son Thomas Earl of Surrey.) And, train-bearer to the King,
and High Steward for the day – a post which traditionally belonged
to Norfolk, the Earl Marshal – was Buckingham. Then came all the
nobles and the lords who carried the Queen's regalia. Train-bearer to
the Queen was none other than Lady Margaret Beaufort. This had
caused a quarrel between Richard and Anne. Carrying the King or
Queen's train is a great honour, and Anne thought it should go to
someone more worthy – more loyal – but Richard was hell-bent on
starting his reign with a clean slate, old enmities forgiven; note that
he had pardoned Stanley for his admittedly minimal part in the
Woodville plot, and given him a position of honour at the
coronation. Behind the Queen, Elizabeth of Suffolk walked in
solitary state as befitted the King's sister; behind her came the
Duchess of Norfolk leading the group of noblewomen, and all the
knights and squires and gentlemen.

Playing my part, clad in my crimson, I wept when the Archbishop
put the Crown on Richard's head. Twenty-two years earlier I had

wept, a rescued child, when his brother was crowned. I mastered myself for the sacred moment when the King and Queen were anointed with the Chrism, but the glorious music of the *Te Deum* undid me again. I saw Innogen crying too, beautiful in her blue gown among the Queen's ladies, and most of the Mass passed in a haze of tears.

From the Abbey we went to Westminster Great Hall for the banquet. I, together with Rob and Francis and some of the highest lords in the land, served the King from gold and silver dishes; and once when Anne gave me a little secret smile I remembered that kiss-and-make-up feast here back in '69 – that Christmas, when Warwick had plotted to make his daughter Queen. There is a traditional challenge at coronation banquets; the King's Champion, Sir Robert Dymmock on this occasion, rides into the hall in white armour and challenges anyone who disputes the new King's right to the Crown to do combat with him. Up went the cry from everyone present, 'King Richard!' and the Champion drank the traditional wine and rode out again. Then, with our formal obeisance to our new sovereigns, it was all over.

Two weeks later Richard began a formal progress around the southern parts of the country. From Windsor he travelled to Reading and Oxford, where he lodged at Magdalen College. I think I have made it plain that Richard was a learned and a scholarly man, but I wonder if Bishop Waynflete, founder of Magdalen, quite expected that the new King's idea of entertainment was to hear two Latin debates in moral philosophy and theology?

I was not with him for that part of the progress. Officially I was with my wife in attendance on the Queen, who was resting at Windsor. London never suited Anne, and the last few weeks had exhausted her. Unofficially, or at least out of the public eye, I had quite other business.

At various times in Richard's reign, malcontents put it about that he had murdered his brother's two sons. Now, Richard could be naïve, over-trusting, dogmatic, arrogant and so stubborn you wanted to kick him, but he was never a fool. Idiotic rumours didn't bother him, but he knew that what could ruin him was not being able to produce those boys at need. Nor did he believe for a moment that the Woodvilles – and others – had given up plotting against him – or against other Yorkists. He wasn't going to have those boys 'rescued' and used as focus for rebellion. Or murdered by other claimants. Therefore, he quietly removed them from the Tower and sent them north. Well, it does no harm to tell it now, and many people knew it at the time: he sent them to Sheriff Hutton.

So that is what I was doing when I was officially attending upon the Queen at Windsor: conveying the boys north.

I always liked the younger boy, little Richard. He had common sense, and the merry nature he'd inherited from the York side of his family. Bewildered and hurt by recent events, he still trusted his namesake uncle and was willing to make the best of things. But of course, he had not been Prince of Wales from birth, he had not grown up expecting to be King. The elder boy had retired into a carapace of sulky resentment, believing Richard had all the time been plotting to usurp his throne. Natural enough, and I pitied him, but by the time we reached Sheriff Hutton I would have paid to put my boot up his bum. I restrained myself, however, and with relief handed the boys over to the Earl of Lincoln, who had charge of the King's household in the north. Lincoln had recently brought the Clarence children to Sheriff Hutton, and my two eldest children and some of the King's wards were also to make their home there. If the two Lords Bastard, as they were now officially known, couldn't settle down among their cousins and make friends, bad luck to them.

A good thing Richard sent those boys away when he did.

I caught up with the royal retinue at Minster Lovell, Francis's home. That same night, the Chancellor's letter reached Richard. There had been an attack on the Tower of London.

'Doctor Russell says,' Richard looked back and forth from us to the letter, 'that fires were started in the city near the Tower. I suppose the idea was that in the confusion men would get inside and seize my nephews.' In London, that conglomeration of wooden buildings jammed hugger-mugger along narrow streets, fire is as great a fear as plague. Each ward is compelled by law to keep fire-carts ready stocked with the fire-fighting equipment of buckets, and hooks to pull down burning buildings. But passing regulations is a different thing from being able to enforce them. And people *will* come out to stare at a fire – getting in the way, panicking, blocking the way of the fire-carts. The Tower's stone buildings have withstood every threat of the past five hundred years, but fire inside its walls is a terror.

'Either,' Richard read on, 'the Tower gates were innocently unlocked for men to help fight the fires, or someone inside let men in – the fires were a signal, of course. Armed men were apprehended near my nephews' rooms.'

'Woodville's behind it, of course,' said Francis.

'Oh, certainly. Will that woman never learn sense! What was she going to do, launch a rebellion against me to put her bastard son on the throne?' He broke off, thinking, tapping the letter against his teeth. 'Or if it wasn't the Woodvilles ... Beaufort; the Lancastrians. A good thing I sent Doctor Morton to Brecon, or this business might have been more serious; without him they're not much at plotting. Wouldn't it be convenient for them to brand me a child-murderer, King Herod *de nos jours*, and rise up against me?'

'How embarrassing for them to find the boys gone,' I said. 'Much wailing and gnashing of teeth.'

'Yes. I'll write to Sheriff Hutton to strengthen the guard. And I must write to Russell. Send for my secretary, will you?' The man came, sleepy and bothered, and I listened as Richard dictated his letter to the Chancellor. *Whereas we understand that certain persons be attached and in ward, we desire and will you that you do make our letters of commission to such person as by you and our Council shall be advised to sit and proceed to the due execution of our laws ...* Etcetera and so on, obliquely put for the sake of discretion. We later learned that the four men arrested were all old servants of Edward IV: his Groom of the

Stirrup, a London Serjeant, an Officer of the Wardrobe. Either they had been well chosen for their ability to keep their mouths shut, or they truly knew little of the real plot, but the Woodville connection was plain.

When the letters had been despatched and the secretary had gone yawning back to bed, I said, 'Richard, has His Grace of Buckingham reported to you on this matter?' Buckingham was still in London, and since he was Constable and Lord High Everything these days, an armed attempt on the Lords Bastard should have sent him galloping to Richard – at least, sent his courier with a full report.

'No,' Richard said tonelessly. 'I wonder why that is?'


It was twelve years since I had been to Gloucester. Once, we had expected to fight there, or to rescue the town from Queen Margaret's siege. You can imagine how the people preened themselves that their own duke was now King. Everything was dancing, pageants, glory, and they nearly burst with pride when Richard gave the town its Charter of Incorporation, putting it on equal basis with York and Bristol, with the right to elect a Mayor and Sheriffs. In thanks for its brave stand against the Lancastrian army, Richard remitted forty pounds of the town's annual fee-farm rent, and he refused the usual payment for granting the Incorporation. He also, most unusually in a King, declined the traditional gifts of money from the town, saying he would rather have their love than their money.

And it was at Gloucester that the Duke of Buckingham once more shed the light of his countenance upon us. He breezed in just before dinner, giving Richard a token bend of the knee and throwing himself into a chair. 'Well, Dickon, you're certainly Gloucester's favourite son today! I could hardly force a way through the crowds out there, cheering and dancing in the streets. What have you done, made the place the capital?'

'Hardly that.' Richard looked him up and down thoughtfully.

'Has it been like this all the way? A right royal progress? What's the matter? Why are you looking at me like that? Aren't you glad to see me?'

'I am extremely glad to see you. I have been awaiting your report on the attack on the Tower – on my nephews.'

All of a sudden I realised he had not confided in Buckingham about moving the boys.

'Oh, that business!'

'Yes. That business. You were there and –'

'Meaning?'

'My lord duke?' said Richard, and Buckingham would have been wise to take warning from his tone.

'Just what do you mean by saying I was there, and asking for my 'report'? What's it to do with me? I am not some common servant, Dickon. I don't care for your tone.'

'Do you not?' Richard said so mildly that Francis, Rob and I nearly shat ourselves. But Buckingham didn't know him as we did.

'No, I do not. But … Oh, I see! You think I should speak more formally to you now you are King? But we're friends! You never care what your other friends say to you.' He looked over at us. 'If I've offended, so have they every time they open their mouths!' Petulantly he gazed at Richard, giving him the smile that had never failed before. But now Richard saw only the petulance, and the practised confidence of that smile.

Very quietly he said, 'No, in private, from my old friends, I do not expect formality. But nor have I ever tolerated insolence. You have offended me, my lord duke; you have offended me by not accepting that you as much as any of my other officers must report properly to me on matters of importance. You were in London at the time and you are Constable of England; surely Brackenbury reported to you?'

'Brackenbury's an old woman.'

'Really,' murmured Richard, who had appointed Sir Robert as Constable of the Tower, among other posts, precisely because of his hard sense and long experience.

'Yes. He came flapping along with some muddled story – Dickon, it was nothing! A fire; a lot of confusion; a few misguided fellows taking advantage.'

'Indeed? And you have no idea – there is no indication – of who was behind it?'

Buckingham shrugged. I think Richard damn' near hit him.

Lounging to his feet Buckingham said casually, 'Well, since that's dealt with, and I've had a long day on the road, have I permission to retire and prepare for dinner? By the way, where do you plan to stop next? And when do you leave?'

'Tewkesbury, Worcester, Warwick, then north. Leaving tomorrow. Will you be joining me?'

'If it's your wish, of course I will. But I did rather want to get home.'

'Of course. Your wife must miss you.' Of her own choice, or at her husband's command, Buckingham's Woodville wife had not come to London even for the coronation.

'Of course,' Buckingham agreed, bowed and swept out.

None of us dared speak. 'Has he,' Richard asked, 'always been like that?'

'No,' we said in the tone that means yes.

'Now I know how Edward felt about Warwick. And I have to face the fact that I've put a great deal of power in the hands of a man unworthy of it.'

'Not necessarily,' Rob said. 'He was insolent, yes, and too high-handed by half, but he's always had a high opinion of himself.'

'Too high.'

'Well, yes.'

'Thinks himself a king-maker? Like Warwick? And I've created an over-mighty subject?'

'Perhaps.'

'Oh, damn it,' Richard said with a sigh, 'I liked him, that's all! I miss my brothers, and suddenly there was Harry, royal like me, my cousin … And he arrived at Northampton with his men precisely when I needed him, openly loyal to me, competent, helpful.' He rubbed his hands over his face. 'It's not quite the same as ordinary friendship. You three are my closest and dearest friends, and your loyalty is unwavering, but Harry Stafford is royal, one of my family, of my blood. That counts, you see. But I won't have another Warwick. So I had better learn to manage him, hadn't I?'

Edward had said that about Warwick.


This time we took the road to Tewkesbury at our leisure, in luxury. Same route, but only the sunny weather reminded us of that boiling May day we had slugged along in the desperate race against the Lancastrians. People say battlefields are haunted, but I sensed no ghosts on Bloody Meadow or in the Abbey. Not even the ghosts of Clarence and poor Isabel, buried there behind the altar.

From Tewkesbury we travelled to Warwick, and here Anne and her ladies joined us. Not only her ladies – Anne had an admirer in tow. Graufidius de Sasiola had been sent by Queen Isabella of Spain as an ambassador; missing Richard at Windsor, he was obviously more than content with the Queen's company.

'Should I be jealous?' Richard enquired. 'Planning a happy life in sunny Spain? Remember I can't afford to ransom you back if the Spanish ambassador steals you away.'

'He is merely being courteous and deferential to the Queen,' smirked Anne.

'Oh yes, and how much courtesy and deference would we see if you were a fat, middle-aged boot? If he makes sheep's eyes at you once more there'll be an international incident.'

'He merely admires the English style of looks.'

'We've noticed, thank you. Well, at least the old greaser – I mean the dear gentleman – has brought good news from Queen Isabella. Peace with Spain – ideal. Though I'm not getting England dragged into war with France.'

'De Sasiola told me privately that Queen Isabella has never forgiven the late King for slighting her by marrying Elizabeth Woodville when he'd been offered her hand. And he hints that

Isabella would like to secure peace between England and Spain by a marriage between her daughter Catherine and our son.'

'What a good spy you make,' Richard said approvingly. 'Keep up the good work.'

'Even if it means letting the ambassador kiss my hand?'

'Hand, yes. Anything else and it's war with Spain.'


A change of monarch always sets the cat among the international pigeons. Neighbouring countries were eager to be on terms with Richard; perhaps wary of his military reputation they hastened to send their good wishes. Scotland was keen for a truce, hinting at a full peace treaty. Probably they thought that if Richard could do so much damage as Lieutenant-General, what could he do as King? Even Louis of France wrote. If you ask me, Louis and Richard had secretly taken something of a liking to each other back in 1475; they had corresponded several times and, oddly, with Richard Louis never stood on ceremony in his letters. Even now that Richard was King, Louis wrote in typical style:

*My Lord and cousin, I have seen the letters you have written to me by your herald Blanc Sanglier, and thank you for the news of which you have apprised me. And if I can do you any service I will do it with very good will, for I desire to have your friendship.*

*And farewell, My Lord and cousin.*

*Written at Montilz les Tours,*

*The twenty-first day of July.*

*Louis.*

This effusion was brought by one of his dog-handlers.

'Which from Louis is probably a compliment,' said Richard, 'knowing how fond of animals he is.' And he wrote back in the same off-hand style. He had no intention of breaking current truces, he wrote, but Louis had better take steps to stop his subjects pirating English shipping. He closed, 'And farewell to you, my cousin.' He sent it by hand of one of his stable grooms. After all, Louis liked horses.

Speaking of letters, it chanced that I saw a letter Bishop Langton was writing to the Prior of Christchurch. Well – 'chanced': I had been looking after Richard for twenty years, so if someone leaves a letter open while they duck to the privy ...

*He contents the people where he goes best that ever did prince; for many a poor man that hath suffered wrong many days have been relieved and helped by him and his commands in his progress. And by many great cities and towns were great sums of money given him which he hath refused. On my truth I never liked the conditions of any Prince so well as his; God hath sent him for the weal of us all.*

I couldn't have put it better myself. Richard was popular, and these people of the south were learning that he genuinely had their welfare at heart. His first concern was always for justice and the rule of law, and at every stage of this progress he had sat with his Lords and Justices to hear cases at law. Even the lowest, most ordinary person could come to him with complaint or query or some old grievance. And, used to a legal system manipulated by the rich and powerful, the common people soon learnt that nothing was too trivial for the new King's attention. Better still – he got things done.

While I'm speaking of letters: another Bishop wrote to Richard that August. Opening the letter Kendal began to read it through, stopped, choked, read on, and near pissed himself laughing.

'Share the joke?' Richard glanced up from his work.

'It's – well – your Solicitor-General begs your permission to marry.'

Gazing in wonder at his spluttering secretary Richard said, 'Thomas Lynom? Well, he has my best wishes – thought he was a confirmed bachelor – but what's so funny?'

'He wants to marry Jane Shore!'

Richard's jaw dropped. Everyone's did. Thomas Lynom was one of those good men, solid, salt-of-the-earth, honest as the day is long – but strait-laced, moral and dull.

'Thomas Lynom and *Jane Shore*? The same Jane Shore?'

'Yes,' William Catesby looked up from the letter, 'and oh yes, screamingly funny, but Lynom is a good man, too good for this.

Your Grace, you won't allow it? I mean – Jane Shore!'

Taking the letter Richard said, 'He's exactly the type who goes through life uninterested in women, then falls for a tart. Oh dear. Yes, the Bishop of London writes that they've made a contract of marriage ... Then why is he asking my permission? For a lawyer he's remarkably vague about details. Huh, met her in prison in the course of his duties ... hmm, hmm ... And no doubt nature took its course.'

After Hastings' execution Richard had sentenced Jane to do public penance as a whore through the streets of London – and very fetching she looked in her shift and striped hood, carrying her penitent's candle – then popped her into prison. In my opinion he would have done better to turn a blind eye. Janey was popular with the Londoners, and they thought Richard a hypocrite for kicking up such a fuss about her whoring with King Edward and his friends. Of course he held them to blame for Edward's ruin, but *que voulez vous* ...

'Nature did not take its course, not with Thomas Lynom,' said Catesby crossly. 'Marriage or nothing. And of course he has to ask your permission, Sire, she is a prisoner. Don't allow it, I beg you. Lynom is too good for her, and she'd have horns on his head before they'd been married a week.'

'Isn't that for him to worry about? He knows what she is. And she has enough sense to know which side her bread's buttered. Besides, I owe Jane a favour.' Catesby's face was a study. Grinning, Richard said, 'Not what you may be thinking.' Catesby tried to look as if he was thinking nothing at all, never had and never would. 'She did her best to stop my brother George's execution.'

'If so, she cancelled the debt when she plotted with Dorset.'

'Oh, maybe, maybe. No, I'll allow the marriage. Write to the Bishop – Jane is to be released into her father's custody and they can wait till I am back in London. Give them both time to think. Then, if they're set on it they can marry with my good will.'

And, if anyone is interested, they did, and Jane mended her ways and faded from public view into faithful matrimony. Well, faithful so far as one can tell.

And now we were back in the north. York.

Richard asked me to bring the Prince of Wales and the other children to York, and on my way with Lancaster Herald I carried Kendal's letter to the Mayor. I knew Kendal had dropped a heavy hint about the southerners who would be in the King's train, with their beady noticing eyes and their conviction that civilisation stopped at the Trent, so I watched the Mayor's reaction with interest.

'So the King is bringing foreigners,' said the Mayor.

'Well, a Spanish ambassador.'

'Aye. Spain. What's a Spaniard eat?' It sounded like a riddle.

'Don't know.'

'Well, he'll get our good northern food and like it, especially if he's been eating that southern shite. But Master Kendal says our King is bringing *southerners*.'

Ah – real foreigners. 'Yes, many of them.' My own southern birth had long since been forgiven.

'And we don't want them looking down their long noses and saying we're savages, now do we? Not in front of our King Richard. There will be pageants,' he said in the tone of the Creator decreeing light. 'And dancing. And the Creed Play, perhaps. And Kendal says to hang the streets with arras and tapestry as they do in the south. Not enough, my lord, not for King Richard's York!' I think if I had hinted that the King would like to see the Ouse flowing with milk and honey they would have done it. 'Children to present the Queen with flowers – eh, our little Anne Queen of England! The streets will be cleaned. Gold and silver given to their Highnesses. Food. New costumes for the actors. New scarlet for the Aldermen. Music, of course – the King's own minstrels, and I'll send for his lady mother's. Paint the houses. And wine. Eh, York will show them how to treat the King!'

I left him scribbling lists, and rode on to Sheriff Hutton. This was always one of my favourite places, with its double moat and nine great towers. The village was preparing for its annual fair, and I couldn't resist stopping to buy some sweetmeats and little fairings for the children. The moment my retinue entered the courtyard my children were scrambling to meet me. I was always soft with my children; many parents would be horrified not to be greeted with formal bows from offspring who speak only when addressed, but I would rather the hugs and kisses and clamour of questions. Even the baby, little William, not yet two, toddled eagerly along with the twins holding his hands.

Behind my horde came three quieter children, strikingly alike in their blonde and fragile looks. Shy in his new dignity, the Prince of Wales held out his hand. Bowing, I kissed it and said the formal words of greeting, and his gap-toothed grin widened.

'Uncle Martin!' In private this honorific had been allowed from the time he could speak. I kissed him, and he flung his arms around my neck. 'Uncle Martin – I mean, my lord – you're taking us to York to my parents, I mean the King and Queen – oh!' Remembering his manners, he drew the other two children forward. Shyly George's children bowed to me.

After George's death King Edward had made Dorset their guardian – well, I don't say he mistreated them, for although I never liked him he was no monster, and he was a father himself; but it was a frightened, almost cringing pair of children who came to London once Dorset was out of the way. The boy, little Warwick, couldn't remember his mother, but they had been three and five when George died, and for all his faults he had loved them tenderly. I think they had known neither love nor interest under Dorset's care, for they were bewildered by the open affection that surrounded them once they were under Richard's wing. Lady Margaret, ten now, had a grave, sweet manner that hid a lively intelligence. The little boy, young Warwick, was a different matter, so shy and young for his age I had wondered if he were quite normal; wondered, too, what he had heard of the circumstances of his father's death and how deeply it had wounded him. However, he greeted me sensibly, and was watching my entourage and listening to the din of arrival with interest, and he didn't cower away from me as he had done in London.

These greetings over, and a thousand questions about the King's progress to York answered, I went to call upon Sheriff Hutton's other two junior inhabitants: the Lords Bastard. I sent in my compliments as formally as I would in the past – no need to cause offence – and while I waited I inspected their quarters. Certainly they couldn't complain they were ill-housed. They had two rooms for themselves, and one for their body-servants, and I remembered the bleak dormitory in which Richard and I had nursed our chilblains at Middleham. Here all was luxury, thick new hangings on the walls, fur rugs, cushioned chests, a livery cup-board holding some splendid plate, an inlaid chess set. The long table under the windows showed two distinct personalities. At one end a pile of devotional works, paper and ink and a Greek grammar were stacked with painful neatness. At the other, heaped with a boy's untidiness, were an unstrung bow, a knife in a nest of wood-shavings, a battered copy of *De Re Militari*, a pair of grubby gloves.

A servant brought a message that the elder boy asked to be excused on grounds of imperfect health, but after a moment young Richard came shyly from the inner room. 'Lord Robsart, how do you do. Um, my brother's not very well.'

'So your man told me. Is it serious? You have good doctors, of course?'

'Oh yes, everyone looks after us very kindly.' He looked up through his lashes. 'He really isn't very well, though it is none too serious. A summer cold, and he gets a lot of toothache. And he – he – It is different for him, you see.'

'I understand. My lord, your uncle asked me to see that you have everything you need. He is coming to York, the other children are to meet him there. Would you care to come too?'

Looking wistful, he shook his head. 'My brother could not, so I won't either. He's my brother, you see. But please give our uncle my – our good wishes.' Staring anxiously at me he said all in a rush, 'Ned doesn't know Uncle Richard very well, you see. But I remember him, I saw him more often, and I remember that my father trusted him. So – so can you explain that we can't come to York, and say all the right things from us both?'

Touched, I said I would. 'And you know that if you need anything you have only to ask? You like it here well enough?'

'Oh yes!' he said, relieved that we were back on more neutral ground. 'Yes, I like it. We've good tutors; Ned's very bookish, you know, much more than me, he reads a lot with our cousin Margaret. And we ride and hunt and all that sort of thing, and I like the other children. And I'm getting some good training, because if I can't be a prince I'll be a soldier. The food's very good. I miss my sisters, though. Are they still in Sanctuary?'

'I'm afraid so. But the King hopes your mother will soon come to terms with him, and then perhaps your sisters could live up here too. Look, Lord Richard, things are still rather dangerous. You're old enough to understand that; I suppose your father used to talk of political troubles?' He nodded earnestly. 'When things have settled down perhaps you and your brother could live with your mother – we'll see – but at present your uncle is concerned to keep you safe. There was an attack on the Tower not long ago, on the rooms you used to live in.'

He was a sensible boy, and he must have absorbed from his father a good deal of the political realities of royalty, for he saw the point at once.

'It could have been people trying to – to save us, or – or something quite different. Lancastrians or French.'

'Quite right. So for now we have to keep you safe. And listen, Richard, I've been your uncle's friend for more than twenty years, so I know he can be trusted. Well, that's the sort of thing his friend would say, isn't it; but remember your father trusted him too; he named you for your uncle. Cling to that, and be patient.' I gave him a hug, because he was only a little boy of ten, and lonely.


With my group of children, with the Mayor and Aldermen and citizens, I stood near York's Mickel Gate awaiting the King and Queen. An outrider galloped up the road, shouting that the King was not a mile away. A sigh of anticipation went up; everyone made last-moment adjustments to their clothes. Then there was the sound of trumpets, and we could discern the banners and the matched greys that had been Richard's last anniversary present to Anne. The cry of welcome that went up nearly split the heavens. I will never forget how they looked that day, Richard and Anne, the King and Queen of England, riding on a wave of pure happiness. Richard wore crimson and cloth of gold, Anne blue with diamonds. Above them blazed the royal arms of England, the banners of St George, of York, of Gloucester. Behind them in glorious pageant rode the nobility of England, the bishops, the ambassadors, the Knights of the Household, Anne's ladies in their jewel-like colours.

They rode into York on solid noise – cheers, weeping, whistles, battle cries, clapping, trumpets and drums. The first northern King was home. And you never saw anything so fine as York that day. A rich and beautiful city at the best of times, now it outshone every legend in the world.

The royal retinue halted. Richard dismounted and himself helped Anne down. In front of everyone, they kissed. On the din that simple action produced, I urged the Prince of Wales forward. He stared, half-afraid I think, but he had practised this with me and after that first moment's awe he went forward with great aplomb and kissed his parents' hands. I heard Richard whisper, 'Well done!' then he and Anne moved as one to sweep their son into their arms. The townspeople loved that, and I saw a couple of hard-bitten southern lords blow their noses.

The Mayor made his speech – and nothing provincial here, it was as graceful and able as any London Mayor could manage – then out came the gold cup holding a hundred marks for Richard, and the hundred gold pounds on a gold plate for Anne. And here there was no thought of refusing the loving gift.

In thanks for past and present loyalty, Richard remitted half York's annual taxes to the crown. Also, he hit on the idea of investing his son as Prince of Wales here. One in the eye for London, eh? It was a rush to prepare everything, of course, but who cared. It was so splendid an occasion that word went around that Richard had held a second coronation at York – I think he was tempted to do just that; but only tempted. He knighted many men after the ceremony of investiture, including George's son Warwick, and the flattered Spanish ambassador. And including his son John Plantagenet, for illegitimacy is no bar to knighthood. And when the King and Queen and seven-year-old Prince of Wales left the Minster to walk among the people again, York proved it knew how to celebrate.

But that was York, and the north. In the south, trouble was brewing.

In hindsight, you could say it began with that damned impudent letter from Duke Francis of Brittany. Georges de Mainbier, the Breton ambassador, had taken a lively interest in the York celebrations, and nothing could have exceeded his proxy demonstrations of amity and friendship. Richard had made it discreetly clear that he would be obliged if Brittany refused to harbour Sir Edward Woodville and his treasure ships, but of Woodville Duke Francis had nothing to say. Plenty to say, however, about Henry Tudor.

Ever since Edward IV regained his throne in '71, Tudor had been lurking in Brittany, eking out a living on the scraps from European royal tables, bitterly aware that his only value lay in the nuisance he represented to the English king. I counted it up once, and made Tudor twenty-ninth in line to the English throne, and that only if you ignored the fact that on both sides he was descended from bastards. Remember his father Edmund was one of Queen Katherine's bastards by her Welsh lover Owen Tudor? And, for all her vaunting airs, his mother Lady Margaret was from the illegitimate Beaufort line, and they had been expressly debarred from the royal succession. So as a pretender to the English throne Henry was as shabby as the tattered old Lancastrian banner he held aloft. But a nuisance, just the same. Louis of France had a few times waved him threateningly at Edward IV, and now Duke Francis was playing the same old game.

And so de Mainbier regretfully told Richard that for love of his ally England, Duke Francis had refused Louis' many offers to take Tudor under his wing – but now, alas, for this recalcitrance Louis was threatening Brittany with war. And dear me, Francis could only hold out with English help. Therefore, unless Brittany promptly received at least four thousand archers – at English expense – Duke Francis would have to hand over Henry Tudor to France, who no doubt would promptly outfit him with an army with which to invade England.

It was blackmail, of course, although Richard dressed his refusal in fair and loving terms. He wasn't about to give Duke Francis, or any other European ruler, the idea he was afraid of Henry Tudor.

Then at the end of August King Louis of France died, and France was plunged into such chaos it was for the time being removed from the international game. Just as well, for we had our own worries.

We were still in the north when word came that the men of Kent were rioting. Kent always was a hotbed of Woodville sympathies; Lord Rivers had had lands there. It seemed that the prime movers were men who had held offices under Edward IV and lost them under the new regime. I doubt if the aims of the uprising were very clear even to the conspirators; certainly we never unravelled them. As far as we could discover, the plot was to send Edward IV's daughters abroad; 'rescue' his sons from the Tower; overthrow Richard; and march gloriously to Westminster to set a discredited, bastard, under-age king on the throne and restore the Woodville domination. Not surprisingly, few people found this tempting. However, there was another strand woven into this uprising: the Beaufort-Lancastrian one. Henry Tudor had somehow raised enough cash – no doubt from the irritated Duke Francis – to muster some sort of army. As soon as the southern parts of England had overthrown Richard, or provided enough trouble to keep him busy, Tudor would sail to England and march gloriously to Westminster etcetera etcetera. Presumably the restored Edward V and the brand-new Henry VII would then toss for the crown.

Richard had already appointed commissions of oyer and terminer, and the Duke of Norfolk and the Council were on the alert against action in the south. Rather enviously we sent our wives and children up to Middleham, and set out southward. News came in at every halt. Lionel Woodville, Bishop of Salisbury, had somehow escaped from Sanctuary and was stirring trouble in his diocese, aided by Dorset who had been hiding heaven knows where. Sir Richard Woodville and the Stonor family were mixing it in Berkshire. Fomenting trouble down in Exeter was Richard's brother-in-law Sir Thomas St Leger; and one wonders what it was about Anne of York that made her husbands so consistently rebel against her brothers. *Quelle galère.* Then, better news. The south had risen too early to suit the rest of the conspiracy, and with his usual efficiency Norfolk quashed the rising before it spread to make real trouble. However, rumours were going around, wrote Norfolk in disgust, that Richard had murdered the late King Edward's sons …

We were at Lincoln, on the eleventh of October, when we heard that the rebellion had spread to Wales and the western counties. And it had a new leader.

The Duke of Buckingham.


Richard said nothing when he heard. I think that interview at Gloucester had — I don't say prepared him for this, but it had stripped away much of his affection for his cousin. But Buckingham had made him look the most almighty fool, and Richard never forgave any betrayal of loyalty. From the moment he heard, it was as if Buckingham were a stranger, he referred to the man as impersonally as to any other traitor. The only sign of his feelings was when he wrote to the Lord Chancellor to send him the Great Seal. His secretary finished the letter and gave it to Richard. He inscribed his signature, then snatched the letter back and began to write a postscriptum. In the silence the scratching of his pen was as loud as a call to arms. He wrote on, filling the page and running up the side:

*… Here, loved be God, is all well and truly determined, and for to resist the Malice of him that had best Cause to be true, the Duke of Buckingham, the most untrue Creature living; whom with God's Grace we shall not be long till that we*

*will subdue his Malice. We assure you there was never false traitor better purveyed for ...*

Buckingham who, yes, of all men had best cause to be true, glutted with honours and wealth, trusted, perhaps even loved, had betrayed his king and his friend. No forgiveness. Buckingham was not Clarence.

The proclamations naming the traitors had put prices on their heads: a thousand pounds for Buckingham, a thousand marks for Dorset and the other Woodvilles, five hundred marks for the lesser men. By the twenty-fourth Richard's army assembled at Coventry, and we began the fast, hard slog south to intercept Buckingham.

They say Henry V had bad weather on his French campaign before Agincourt. Well, it was nothing compared to the weather that bitter autumn. They also say the weather always favours the House of York. It pissed down. It rained, poured, sleeted, drizzled, spat and misted. Roads were flooded, fords impassable. Storms lashed the coastal towns. Winds the like of which I've never seen brought down trees, even whole houses; at times men dared not stand out in the open for fear of being blown away. Still, campaigning in bad weather was nothing new to us, so even if this was worse than usual we put on our leathers and oiled-wool cloaks, and endured.

And perhaps that filthy weather did favour York, because if it was bad for us, it was worse over in Wales. Worse for Buckingham, and he had no campaign experience at all. Nor had he loyal supporters. Almost before he was out of Brecon the Vaughan family were snapping at his flanks, blockading his way, attacking his men, destroying bridges ahead of him. Behind him the Stafford brothers (no close relation, I believe) cut off his lines of retreat. His men, reluctant recruits from the start, began to melt away. By the time he reached Weobley in Herefordshire he had only a handful of men left, including the egregious Doctor Morton, a wizard called Nandik, a London man and one knight. Twice, Edward IV had found himself in a similar position, but he had always been lucky. No luck for Buckingham. Morton fled in the night, the other men vanished, and Buckingham slunk in peasant's disguise into Shropshire. He made the mistake of trusting an old servant of his, one Ralph Bannaster. Bannaster turned him in for the reward.

'I'll not see him,' Richard said.

'Of course not.' We were at Salisbury, enjoying a rare night's rest. Our clothes steamed as we huddled around the fire in Richard's room.

Through chattering teeth Francis asked, too cold for any finesse, 'Do you fear you might forgive him if you see him?'

'Oh no. But – I do wonder *why*?'

'Back in Gloucester you called him a king-maker like Warwick. He thought he had made you king; he thought that therefore he could unmake you. Not for Henry Tudor; for himself.'

A page brought mulled wine. Drinking it hot and thick with ginger and spices Richard said, 'I imagine they were all at cross-purposes, knowingly or not. It was a right pig's breakfast of a rebellion; the Woodvilles for Edward the Fifth, Buckingham for King Harry Stafford; the Beaufort lot for King Harry Tudor. And I suppose Morton and Margaret Beaufort were using them all. And defaming me by putting it about I had killed my nephews.'

'They can't have it both ways,' Rob objected. 'They can't say you've killed them yet ask people to rise to restore them to the throne.'

'The Woodvilles wouldn't have seen that, they never did have any wits. Or, once they'd got rid of me, oops, made a mistake, he didn't do it after all, still, never mind, while the throne's vacant … Defame me to whip up Woodville support, talk Buckingham into joining them – Buckingham thinks he's using Henry Tudor while all the time the Beaufort lot are using him. Buckingham was very expendable.' Coldly he added, 'He always did remind me of George.'

We had more wine and, warmer, at last dared peel off a few layers of clothes. 'I wondered,' Francis hesitantly spoke my own thoughts, 'if Buckingham planned something like this from the start. Clearly he had heard of Edward's death through his wife's Woodville connections. He must have known something about the Woodville plans. He might even have known about the Eleanor Butler pre-contract. At least he might have known there was *something* – some secret. He might have suspected all the time that Edward's son would never be crowned. Which would mean a chance for Buckingham. He was too subtle to put himself forward at first – far more effective to let you do the dirty work, then he'd come along afterwards and reap the reward.'

'Me as Buckingham's John the Baptist? It sounds too subtle for Buckingham.'

'But not for Doctor Morton.'

'True.' Sitting down, Richard began to tug his boots off, waving away our attempts to help. 'I wondered if Buckingham was involved in that attempt on the Tower, that fire. How puzzled was he that those boys weren't there? And why did he not come as fast as possible to *tell* me they weren't there?'

'Is that why you didn't tell him you'd moved them?' I too pulled my boots off, quite surprised to find my feet still there; I hadn't felt them for the last six hours.

'I didn't suspect him, if that's what you mean. The best-kept secret is the one everyone knows – but not in this case. No, it was simply a feeling that the fewer people who knew, the better. What I wonder is whether Buckingham was involved with the Lancastrians from the start – if that's why he suggested I send Morton to Brecon back in June. Because it *was* his suggestion. And he was very anxious to get home from Gloucester.'

'Ask him, when they bring him in.'

But Richard's face closed over again. 'No, I will not see him.'

I did, however. I didn't recognise this shambling, filthy wreck. I remembered him blazing at Richard's coronation in blue velvet embroidered all over with golden cartwheels. I remembered him riding gloriously through London with his men in the badge of Stafford knots – and I remembered him once boasting that he would soon have as many men in that badge as ever Warwick had in his Bear and Ragged Staff. In a sorry semblance of his old eloquence

Buckingham begged to see the King, and could not believe the refusal. Did he think, even then, that he might win Richard round? He demanded, implored, screamed, grovelling on his knees with tears and snot smearing his face. I had had some idea of talking to him, trying to penetrate the plot he'd thought he was leading, but by the time I got to him he was raving. His mind cracked when he understood his failure, and it was a shrieking madman they took away to execution. They found a knife hidden in his sleeve; perhaps he had meant to kill Richard.

And the other conspirators? Morton escaped to Flanders, the Woodvilles to Brittany. Henry Tudor sailed bravely into Poole, where he was greeted by men in Buckingham's livery shouting assurances that the rebellion had been a roaring success, come ashore and take your throne, Sire. Canny devil, Tudor sailed on to Plymouth, where he learnt the truth and promptly upped sails and fled for home. A few minor rebels were taken and executed, including St Leger. Lady Margaret Beaufort was stripped of her lands and titles. We begged Richard to execute her, but he only put her into her husband's custody. Stanley was being so diligently loyal that I think Richard had no mind to set him thinking of turning his coat again by mistreating his wife. Also York never took vengeance on women. Should have, in this case, but didn't.

Richard rode on through the south and west, but there was no more resistance. By the end of November we were back in London. As rebellions go, it had been – almost literally – a washout. No town had been taken by the rebels, or had gone over. No nobleman had deserted Richard. No area but the southeast and far west had risen.

Richard's reign was secure.

## Seventeen

## 1484

Watching Anne as she read through the documents, I wondered if Edward IV ever discussed the Acts of his Parliaments with his wife. Probably not. I think even William Catesby, whom the Commons had chosen as their Speaker, and who by now knew Richard well, was shocked to see him refer such business to the Queen. But no son of the Duchess of York could ever think women incapable of understanding affairs of state, and from the moment they married Anne had been in Richard's confidence.

This Parliament, sitting January to February 1484, had been largely concerned with mopping up the business of the late rebellion – passing bills of attainder on the chief rebels, protecting the rights of their wives, that kind of thing. But the first Bill passed had been the *Titulus Regius*, which settled Richard's right to the Crown and made his son officially his heir. There were the usual private Bills to do with land claims, and one annulling the old attainders against the Percies. Many Bills concerned trade, import and export: protecting English-made goods against foreign competition and ensuring that foreign merchants spent their profits in England, on English goods, rather than shipping them off home. Only books were exempt from restrictions, for Richard wanted no hindrance to the spread of learning.

But the main business of that Parliament was matter dear to Richard's heart. He was determined to look after his subjects, the common people who had such little redress under law. He outlawed 'benevolences' so that the monarch would never again be able to demand money from the people. He overhauled the messy system of land titles, making it illegal for land vendors to conceal previous sales or transfers. There was a statute reforming the Piepowder Courts, which although originally permitted only to hear cases arising at fairs, had sneakily extended that traditional jurisdiction. Another Bill, perhaps prompted by memories of Clarence, reformed the method of jury selection so that powerful men could no longer subvert justice by stacking juries with their own supporters. Perhaps the most important statute of that parliament was the one granting the right of bail in felony cases, and prohibiting the seizure of accused men's possessions before conviction.

'There will be many lords who won't like all this,' Anne commented.

'Bad luck.' Richard had that mulish look. 'Times are changing. The old systems are wearing out. No one who treats his tenants or neighbours justly has anything to fear from this legislation. But I'll have no more stacked juries, and no more people acquitted by courts only to find everything they own has been snatched by their accusers.'

'Oh, I agree with you; I'm just pointing out that a lot of men will see this as eroding their powers.'

'High time too. And,' he said proudly, 'I am having all my statutes printed in English. From now on every Parliament will. I want everyone to be able to read the laws that govern their lives. And I am going to institute a Court of Common Pleas that any person, however humble, can take any injustice to. I saw when I was on progress last year how many people thought they had no redress until they were able to see me. Justice for the common man, not just the rich. It is one of the reasons I took the Crown. If it makes me unpopular with some of the nobles, at least I will have the support of the ordinary people.'

'You'll certainly be remembered as a king who made good laws.' Anne smiled over at Catesby. 'The Commons think it's wonderful, they're more or less dancing in the streets.'

Catesby grinned at the picture this called up, but he agreed. 'But Sire, I wondered if we could discuss Dame Grey?'

Richard sighed. 'Is there anything to discuss?'

'Well yes, Your Grace, I think there is. Last time your men went to see her there were definite signs of weakening. There was a little set-back when she realised Parliament had passed that Act taking away her property and annulling her letters patent.'

'What did she expect!'

'Well, yes. But of course she didn't like it. But Norfolk has been again to see her, just yesterday, and he says she is willing to negotiate.'

'And just what,' Richard said sarcastically, 'does my dear sister-in-law think she has to negotiate? She can rot in Sanctuary the rest of her life for all I care. She has conspired against me, most of her family are lurking in Europe plotting heaven knows what, and she promised her daughter Bess to Henry Tudor in the rebellion last year. I've made it plain time and again that I'll take no action against her, I will provide for her and her daughters – what, pray, does she wish to "negotiate"?'

'I daresay she knows,' Anne put in, 'that it's embarrassing for you, her staying in there as if she's afraid of you. And we both want at least the girls to come out.'

'Yes, well … What did she tell Jock Norfolk?'

'It was more Lady Bess,' Catesby said. 'Though I think it was a message from her mother. The girls have had enough – more than enough, poor lasses – and they've told their mother straight. And if I may say so, Your Grace, Dame Grey genuinely believed you had her sons put to death.' He held up a hand as Richard began to speak. 'I know, I know – the woman's a fool. But she was cleverly worked on, Lady Margaret Beaufort in particular had her so she didn't know if she was Arthur or Martha. The recent letters from her sons have made her see how stupid she's been.'

I knew about those letters. Sending Christmas gifts and new clothes for the Lords Bastard, Richard had asked Lincoln to get the boys to write to their mother, including the sort of private family references that would prove the letters were genuine. I could imagine the effect upon a mother who had believed, however foolishly, that her children were dead. Perhaps Richard's patient care in providing for the widows of Buckingham and Hastings had also had its effect.

'If you were to make some sort of official arrangement,' Catesby said hopefully, 'perhaps some public statement or written agreement of terms for Dame Grey and her daughters?'

Richard considered a moment. 'Oh, very well. Draft something up for me. Say they shall be in surety of their lives, no manner of harm at my hands, marriages and dowries for the girls, provision for Elizabeth herself – say, seven hundred marks a year, and she can live wherever she wants. And say that if there's any report of trouble, or any accusation against them, I'll give it no credence unless it is proved in court. But make sure she knows I'm not grovelling to her, she's the one in the wrong. Silly woman. Tell her to take it or leave it.'

She took it. On the first day of March Richard swore an oath, much as he had put it to Catesby, before all the lords and the Mayor and Aldermen of London. Two days later Elizabeth Woodville came out of Sanctuary and submitted herself and her daughters to Richard's care.

It was just over a year since I had seen Elizabeth. On that occasion, bidding us a cool farewell after we had been honoured for our part in the Scottish war, she had been glorious in cloth of silver, diamonds and sapphires. Now merely Dame Grey, she wore brown velvet with fur at the hem and wrists, and a small piece of jewellery – the sort of thing that, say, a prosperous merchant's wife might wear. The gown was cut in the new style, square-necked and with the waist where nature intended, and no train. Her headdress, also in the new fashion, framed a face innocent of the heavy paint she used to wear; unexpectedly, this made her look younger. She was nearly fifty and probably at the difficult time of life, for she had gained weight. Still handsome, she was an elderly woman now, and you would pass her in the street with hardly a second look.

Behind her came her daughters, lined up in order of age: Bess, turned eighteen, a hazel-eyed blonde with her father's height and a heavier version of her mother's face; Cecily, fifteen in a few days' time, with the darker York colouring. (Mary, the baby I had cuddled when I first came to Westminster, had died two years before of one of those sudden fevers). Then came Margaret, almost twelve, pale and pretty; Anne, eight, another darker one; Katherine, at five very like Bess; and Bridget, the smallest; not yet four, all curls and big eyes. The girls were neatly dressed, but their gowns had a made-over look (or so my wife later told me).

Walking timidly with the girls was Elizabeth's sister, Catherine, Dowager Duchess of Buckingham. I think Richard had felt some reservations when last December she asked permission to join her sister in Sanctuary, but he had allowed it; he always was generous with wives of traitors. I hardly knew Catherine Stafford, for Buckingham had so furiously resented being forced to marry her that the moment he came of age he whisked her off into the wilds of Wales and kept her there, far from the Court and her family. She was a pretty woman, as pale of skin and hair as her sister. The black of mourning didn't suit her. I wondered how old she was.

Elizabeth kept her eyes levelly on Richard as she came in. She curtsied and kissed his hand, waiting to see how he would address her. He said, 'Elizabeth, dear sister,' pleasantly, and her eyes (just a touch of careful paint there) widened in relief – for legally she was *not* his sister-in-law. Gracefully she motioned the girls forward. As they curtsied like a row of dolls, I caught Bess's eye and grinned; she smiled back, hiding it with a duck of her head. Katherine tripped making her bow, giggled, said, 'Uncle Richard!' and flung her arms around him. 'Oh. I forgot. You're King now.'

Laughing, he kissed her and lifted her onto his lap. 'I'm still your uncle, darling, and I am very glad to see you again. Ladies, you remember my friend Lord Robsart, and Doctor Alcock.'

'Of course,' said Elizabeth, bowing. Richard had been clever to have Doctor Alcock, Bishop of Rochester, at this meeting. A man whose integrity no one ever doubted, he had been tutor to the ex-Prince of Wales and President of his Council. He was devoted to the boy, yet had gladly taken a place on Richard's Council. His presence was a guarantee of good faith.

'Perhaps,' Richard suggested, 'the younger girls might like to go through to the Queen's room to meet their cousins. Bess, Cecily, I would be glad if you would stay. And, ladies, please be seated.'

Thus the business part of the meeting was declared open. As a page brought wine I noticed Elizabeth looking around the room. Leaving on his progress the previous year, Richard had given orders for Westminster Palace to be cleaned from rooftops to cellars (long overdue, I may say), and he had over-hauled the household management to cut some of the waste and extravagance. A lot of noses were out of joint when he put in his own servants. No doubt Elizabeth had heard of this, and perhaps she, like others who didn't know Richard well, thought it meant he was a dull, strait-laced fellow, quaintly faithful to his wife, as bad as old King Harry in his dislike of frivolity. Well, I don't say he was ever frivolous, but like all his family he enjoyed magnificence; for years he had been the richest man in the kingdom, and he knew what people expected of a king. For his private suite he had taken different rooms from those his brother had used, and Elizabeth looked around at walls hung with gorgeous Flemish tapestries, ceilings new-painted and gilded, brocade cushions embroidered and tasselled with gold, priceless plate and glass on the shelves. I wondered if she also noticed, as I recently had, that eight months' monarchy had aged Richard by as many years.

A past master at getting people to talk, Richard sipped his wine in silence. Putting down her cup (gold, with a band of emeralds), Elizabeth said, 'Your Grace, what do you mean to do with us?'

'I made it plain in my public oath that I will look after you. I thought the girls would like to live at Court. I daresay they could do with some fun.' Bess and Cecily nodded vehemently. After a year in Sanctuary they were pasty and spotty for lack of air and exercise, and I daresay they had been bored rigid.

'Will we wait upon Aunt Anne? I mean, upon the Queen?' Bess asked.

'If you would like to, I know she would be very pleased.'

'Well, we would like it. But, er, we wondered – perhaps now, er, we are not suitable.' She blushed furiously. Bess never was capable of dissembling, but the thing had to be brought out in the open sooner or later.

'Let's be plain,' said Richard. 'Your father did an unforgivable thing, and he robbed his children of the positions they had been reared to expect. I wish it were otherwise, but it is past praying for. However, at my Court you will be treated with respect. The law says you are bastards, but you are still the children of a king, Bess – and my nieces and nephews. You will still be addressed as "Lady".' He smiled swiftly. 'If you get any cheek from anyone, tell me or someone like Martin here, we're quite good at dealing with that sort of thing. My own bastard son and daughter, John and Katherine, wait on me and the Queen. Like my Katherine you can join the Queen's maids of honour. We plan to move north soon, probably to Nottingham, and I hope you'll enjoy travelling with us. The Queen's Wardrobe Master will see about clothes and so on for you, and I'll see you have allowances. Good marriages, too, when the time comes.'

'And me, Your Grace?' Elizabeth asked. I think she dreaded that Richard would expect her too to live at Court, perhaps attending on the Queen, all the last twenty years turned to mockery.

'That is up to you. Of course you will always be welcome at my Court, but you may prefer some private household.'

'Catherine and I thought of living together.' It made a touching picture, the two widowed sisters rearing their wee ones in a cottage and passing the evenings knitting. 'Would you permit that, Your Grace?'

'Have you anywhere in mind?' No they hadn't. Queen and Duchess, it was twenty years since they had had to think of providing for themselves. Trustingly they gazed at Richard. 'I know Sir James Tyrell would be glad to rent his house at Gipping,' he suggested. 'It's large and pleasant.'

'Very well.'

There was a pause as we all drank wine. Elizabeth said, 'May I have my sons to live with me?'

'Later, perhaps.'

Elizabeth put down her cup. 'They told me you had murdered them.'

Richard gave her a long, level look. 'In the twenty years you have known me, what have I done to make you think me capable of that?'

'You killed my brother and my other son!'

'I executed traitors.' Under his cold blue gaze Elizabeth's eyes fell. 'Who told you I had killed your sons?'

'Lady Margaret Beaufort. Doctor Morton. My son Dorset. They were very convincing.'

Quite gently Richard said, 'Didn't you stop to think it would do me no good to murder my nephews, but that the mere accusation would do me great harm? And that it is the Lancastrian party, led by Lady Margaret, who have every reason to want those boys dead? Did you never realise they were working to the sole end of putting Henry Tudor on the throne?'

'No!'

'You did, Mother,' Bess said, and I've never heard such simple dislike expressed in three words. 'It was why you agreed to marry me to Tudor.'

'That was after ...'

'... after they'd told you a lot of lies a child wouldn't have believed.'

Catherine Buckingham spoke for the first time. 'Harry told Doctor Morton he had killed those boys on your instructions, Sire. I didn't believe him. I thought it would be a stupid thing for you to do, and I never believed much of what Harry said. He thought Morton would make him king.'

'And did Doctor Morton believe this convenient story?'

She spread her hands in a shrug. 'I do not know. Although I do know he put it about that you were responsible for the deaths. He was always writing letters.'

'And who,' Richard asked, 'was behind that attack on the Tower last July?'

Colour surged patchily up Elizabeth's face. 'We were. My son

Dorset. And me. All of us.'

'Why? Did you really think people would rise to restore your son to the throne?'

'I did then. You cannot understand. All those years. Everyone thinks I only married Edward to be Queen, but I would have married him whoever he was. He said that if I truly loved him I would be his mistress. He never understood that a woman can be chaste. So in the end he had to marry me because that was the only way he could have me and he was mad for me, and when he insisted on a secret wedding he said it was because of Warwick and I believed him.' The words were gushing from her; I think she had forgotten where she was and who she was speaking to. 'I don't suppose he loved me for very long, soon I bored him and always, always there were other women. I had to suffer that. Then in '77 Clarence found out about Eleanor Butler and Edward had to tell me, and yes, I urged him to put Clarence to death, but you know Edward, if he had not wanted to do it nothing I said could have swayed him. And he did it, and ever since I have lived in fear of the secret coming out – and with the knowledge of what the man I had loved and married really was. And you, you men, ask your wives how they would feel if you made them bear two children after they knew their marriage was invalid and they were nothing but whores and their children bastards! So yes, I tried to get my son crowned before anyone could stop it, I thought it wouldn't matter then if the pre-contract story came out, and yes, I went on trying to regain his throne because it was not his fault! It was all your brother's doing, and after twenty years …'

Suddenly she realised she was on her feet, haranguing the King. She broke off, half crying. Her sister took her hand and put her gently back on her seat, giving Richard a look that begged him to understand.

'Elizabeth,' Richard said, 'I have already said I think it unforgivable of Edward. I have not enjoyed discovering what he was capable of. And of course it is not your son's fault. But do you understand now that all those schemes are finally over? That rebellion last year – no one wants your son as King. The people trust me. History has shown time and again how unpopular – and dangerous – royal minorities are. I hope your sons won't rise against me when they are of age; but certainly they have no hope now. Nor do people want some unknown Welshman as king, married to Bess or not. Did you never stop to think that he could not marry her and make her Queen? She is illegitimate. By marrying her he'd be declaring her legitimate – which would also make her brother legitimate and therefore the rightful king. That scheme was merely to involve you, to use you.' He too broke off as if realising he had said more than he intended. Wearily he said, 'Do you understand? All of you? I am prepared to overlook the past, but if you become involved in rebellion again I will not be lenient. Do you understand?'

'Yes.' Elizabeth hesitated, then went slowly on, 'If you will believe in it and accept it, I give you my word.'

There was a long silence. At last Richard said, 'Very well.' Elizabeth sank to her knees and kissed his hand.



'And do you think she's really learned her lesson?' Innogen asked me one night soon after this.

'Oh, I think so. At the very least she has decided to cut her losses. I think she realises the Beaufort-Morton crowd made a fool of her, and no one enjoys that.'

'Hmm, well, I hope so. But Richard must be careful.'

I knew Innogen. 'What does that, in that tone, mean?'

'Little, I hope. But have you noticed Bess lately?'

'Noticed her? What do you mean?' Bess and Cecily had settled happily enough into life at Court. They had new clothes and pleasant rooms; all I had noticed was two pretty, well-dressed girls enjoying a life of parties and young men.

'She is in love with Richard.'

This flat statement left me gasping. I reared up in the bed to stare at Innogen, who crossly tucked down the bedclothes I had disturbed. 'That's nonsense! He's her uncle!'

'And when did commonsense have anything to do with love? Lie down, the cold air's getting in.'

I lay down. 'You're mistaken. Bess misses her father. They were very close, she was his pet. Naturally she looks for the same with Richard – whom she has also admired and loved all her life. No, Jenny, it is nonsense.'

'Is it? Power can be very seductive. She looks at him not as a fond niece at her uncle, but as a woman seeing a man she desires. And the fact that he's interested in no woman but Anne only makes it worse. To a woman, that can be a challenge. Katherine has noticed it too, she spoke to me about it.'

'Yes, but Katherine's seeing love everywhere just at present.' The day before we left London William Herbert, Earl of Huntingdon, had tremulously asked Richard for his daughter's hand in marriage; no great surprise to anyone. Looking glumly at the prospect of being a grandfather at thirty-two, Richard had given his consent, for he had a good opinion of Will Herbert and wanted Katherine to be happy. Which she radiantly, delightedly was.

'Maybe, but she has sense. So Richard must be careful. You know how easily gossip starts. And Bess might take after her father.'

'Oh dear, yes. Although,' I tried to look on the bright side, 'she may take after her mother, and Elizabeth Woodville was always chaste. Bess is a good girl, I think.'

'I think so too, but both her parents were clever at getting what they wanted. And scandal starts from little things.'

'So what's to do? Should someone speak to Bess?'

'Probably that would be the worst thing. To do her justice, she tries quite hard to hide her feelings. No, I think I'll take her north with me next week.' We had decided that from Nottingham Innogen would continue on up to Middleham to see our children. As well, Anne worried about her niece and nephew, George's children. 'Bess can hardly refuse the chance to see her brothers. Best thing would be for Richard to marry her off as soon as possible – but for the time being she can come north with me. I'll keep her there for a while. I could do with a rest.'

'Why? Aren't you well?' For answer she put my hand on her stomach. 'Jenny! Really? Oh my love ...' I had always wanted more children. 'When?'

Her hand covered mine. 'I've missed twice, though you were too busy with Parliament to notice.' She giggled. 'Not too busy all the time, it seems. I think it was that night you were so proud of yourself going off to Parliament in your Earl's robes for the first time.'

'Ah yes, that night. So you must rest. Yes. Go home to Middleham, see the children, take care of yourself. No rushing over to Sheriff Hutton all the time.'

'I'll send Bess to do that.'

That conversation took place in Cambridge, where Richard had paused on his way north; from memory, he was discussing the most suitable men to send as envoys to Pope Sixtus VI. Both keen to encourage learning, Richard and Anne took a great interest in universities, and they liked Cambridge. Anne took the chance to endow Queens' College, while Richard founded scholarships and poured out money for the building of a chapel at King's College. From the plans it promised to be the most beautiful in England.

In those few days there, and on the journey north, I observed Bess. Reluctantly I concluded that Innogen was right. In private Richard and Anne never hid their feelings for each other; lovers as well as husband and wife, they would hold hands, kiss at every parting and meeting. Once, discussing that King's College Chapel, Richard absently lifted Anne's hand and kissed her palm then the tips of her fingers, and her answering smile held all the romance in the world. Bess blushed an ugly red and turned away. A minor incident, but it made me watch her, and yes, she could hardly keep her eyes off Richard. And she didn't like it when Innogen put forward the plan that Bess should accompany her north.

Puzzled, Richard said, 'But surely you want to see your brothers? I know your mother would like to hear that you have seen them.'

'Oh yes of course, but ... I don't know the north, you see. How long must I be away?'

'As long as it takes,' said Anne with such a sweet smile that I realised she knew too. Well, in twelve years she had become used to women taking too much interest in her husband. 'Lady Robsart will be glad of your company, Bess. So will your cousins.'

To give Bess credit, she was doing her best. Smiling, she said, 'Yes of course. And my brothers, as Uncle Richard says. I've never been further north than York.'

'You'll enjoy it,' said Anne.

After one night in Nottingham Castle, perched high on its rock, Innogen set out for the north, Bess smiling valiantly beside her. And I didn't know as I kissed them farewell that it was the end of all our happiness.

# Eighteen

Whispering voices. Someone crying. A candle being held too close to my eyes. I struggled up from the clinging mists of sleep. 'Invasion?'

'No. Martin, wake up.' Francis Lovell was shaking my shoulder. The candlelight shone on the tears falling down his cheeks.

'O Lord, is it my wife? What has happened?'

'No, Martin. I'm here.' She came forward from the shadows at the end of the room, Joyce Percy with her. Sheet-white, tears in her eyes, dishevelled and travel-stained, Innogen was clad in black. So it was one of the children. 'Martin, there is terrible news.'

'Which one is it?'

She pressed her hand to her head as if it ached. 'No, darling, not ours. It's Edward.'

Stupidly I said, 'Which one?' and then I remembered Francis's tears, and saw the cold, still horror in Innogen's face. And I knew. 'No! O dear lord, no!'

'Yes. Richard's son. Anne's only child. The Prince of Wales.' Innogen sank down on the bed. I shoved a pillow behind her back. It was still full night, she must have ridden hard to get here.

'What happened?'

Joyce shut the door. Innogen said, 'Among us, the truth. He complained of pains in his stomach, low down.' She laid her hand against her groin. 'We thought he had been eating green apples again. We gave him the usual medicines. The pain didn't go. It got worse. He had a fever. Soon he was screaming with agony. His abdomen swelled up, it was hard as a rock to the touch. He was delirious. His breath smelt of shit and he had such pain. Nothing we did was any help, the doctor didn't know what to do. He was screaming for his parents. In the end all we could do was to dose him until he was unconscious. After three days he died. That little boy.'

'O Christ. No. It's too cruel.'

'Yes it is. Don't appeal to Christ, Martin. There is no God, no loving Virgin who understands a mother's love. For this will break their hearts.' She didn't cover her face as she wept, rocking back and forth. 'Why should a child suffer like that? Why was there nothing we could do? And why that child? The King's heir, Anne's only child. *Why him?*' Struggling to master herself she said, 'And you and Rob must tell them, Martin. Their oldest friends.'

Yes, of course it had to be us. I didn't think I could do it but I had to. 'What do we tell them? They mustn't know the truth.'

Drearily Innogen said, 'The nursery mistress and Lady Warwick and I swore everyone at Middleham to silence. Because no, his parents must never know the truth. You will tell them – a sudden fever. Sweating fever. It was quick, all in a day. He soon fell unconscious from the heat of the fever. He hardly suffered. That is all Richard and Anne must ever hear. Get up, Martin, for you must go and tell them.'

'Let them sleep, tell them in the morning ...'

'They would never forgive it. Besides, it's hardly an hour to dawn, and word will get around the castle, I had to wake the doorkeeper and servants to get in, they know I wouldn't come like this in the night for nothing. Wake them now and tell them before they have time to think it is a normal day.'

'Yes.' I began to pull on my bed-gown, realised it was a gay affair of green and gold, and found a dark, plain one. 'Innogen, come with us, they will want to hear it from you. You were there, you must tell them.'

'Oh, Martin. No. Don't you see, I am the last person they'll want to hear this from, the last they'll want near them. I'm pregnant, I've got a clutch of healthy children, I'm the mother of Richard's great flourishing bastard son. They won't want me.'

Richard and Anne always shared a bed. They looked so sweet, so young, curled up back to back, Anne's hair coming loose from its night-time plait, Richard lying with his cheek on his hand. Gingerly I shook his bare shoulder. Years of campaigning had given him the ability to wake instantly, his thoughts collected. He swung over and sat up, pushing the hair out of his eyes. Like me his first question was about invasion.

'No, Richard. No, my dear.' He stared at me, then at Rob and Joyce. All the colour drained from his face. Beside him Anne blinked awake, murmuring a sleepy question. Joyce slid her arm under her, lifting her.

There was no easy way to do it.

'I have come to bring you the worst news in the world. I have come to break your hearts.'

Anne cried out, then shoved her knuckles in her mouth. 'No! No … Richard!'

'No,' he echoed her. 'No …'

'Yes. I am so very sorry, but yes, it is your son. The Prince of Wales. Your son Edward is dead.'

Anne screamed, not a hysterical shriek but a deep primeval wail that held all the grief of every bereft mother since time began. So must the Virgin have wailed, so must Hecuba and Niobe.

Richard gazed at us, ashen, desperately hoping it was not true. 'Martin?'

'Yes, my dear friend.'

He let out a long breath, not a sigh, not a sound, then turned and grabbed Anne, pulling her hard against him. She clung to him, so tightly her knuckles shone white.

'Tell us how. What happened. When. Who told you?'

Cleverly we told our lies, and they were bad enough. Tears began to seep from Richard's closed eyes. 'I see. Thank you. Thank Innogen. Later we will … Please go away now. Thank you, but go away, all of you. Do what is necessary. Leave us alone.'

I didn't think we should, but Joyce caught my eye and nodded. 'I will stay in the outer room,' she said. 'Call me at need. No one will disturb you.'

And that was all we could do for them at first: leave them alone with their grief.

And there was more grief, for me. My wife miscarried. She should not have ridden down from Middleham.

But when later that day Richard and Anne sent for her, she did what was necessary, she drank a cup of that smoky spirit the Scots call *uisquebagh*, and she stayed on her feet while she told them of their son's death and answered all their questions.

'Of course we had a doctor. Yes, I was always with him, and Mistress Idley and Lady Warwick. He died in his grandmother's arms. No, not the sweating sickness, I don't think, it was not like that. Fever. It burnt him up. Very quick, too quick. No, no pain after the first onset, he was unconscious so soon. He didn't suffer. Of course the Mass, the vigil, and he lies in the chapel at Middleham, his grandmother with him. He didn't suffer.'

Joyce had slipped a sleeping drug into the wine when she finally persuaded them to take drink. They were in that half-dreamy state where although they took everything in, nothing was quite real or had the power to hurt. Anne said vaguely, 'It was kind of you to come yourself, Jenny. We had to hear from someone who was with him. Kind. But you shouldn't have ridden, aren't you having a baby?'

'No, love.' With a fine pretence of embarrassment in front of men she said, 'I wondered, back in London, but it was merely – you know.'

'Oh yes, I see. Thank you for coming to tell us. You and Mother were with Edward all the time?'

'All the time. I loved that little boy. I was with him. So was his grandmother. He had people with him who loved him.'

'Mmm.' Anne's eyes drifted shut. Richard picked her up and carried her back to the bed.

Quietly, intensely, he asked, 'Is all that true? Innogen? It wasn't a ... a bad death for my son?'

'It's true, Richard. His suffering was short.'

'God be thanked for that at least.'

'Amen,' said Innogen, and kissed him. I made an excuse to get her out of the room before our structure of lies fell apart.

I had no sooner closed the door behind us than Innogen said,

'Martin …' in a strange little voice, and I was just in time to catch her as she collapsed. I swept her up in my arms and hurried to our bedchamber. There I shouted desperately for her waiting women, yelled for a doctor, for help. Much as I liked Anna Lovell I had always thought her too timid to say boo to a goose, but it was she who stepped up to me and said, rolling up her sleeves, 'Martin, be quiet! Innogen needs rest, you must go away. This is women's business.'

'But she's unconscious! Anna, look, there is blood on her skirts!'

'That's normal. It means little. I was with her this morning when the miscarriage happened. Of course she should have stayed in bed, but there is nothing to fear. Martin, I know.' The pain in her honest black eyes reminded me that, yes, poor Anna knew; she had never carried a child to full term. 'Now go away, Martin. Leave Innogen to us.'

I let her push me towards the door. Innogen's voice stopped me. 'Martin. Don't worry. Only tired. Martin – John. John 'n Kath'rine. No one's thought …'

Ashamed, for I too had forgotten about Richard's other children, I went back to the bed. Innogen was ashen pale and too weak even to lift her head. Softly I kissed her limp hand. 'I'll find them, I'll look after them. But my darling … '

'I'm all right. Tired. Don't worry. Find John.'

Then Anna and the other women bundled me out of the room.


The castle was at sixes and sevens, of course. Servants stood in whispering knots, all normal business suspended. Women wept – and not only women. I passed Rob Percy sitting at the foot of a stair, tears flooding down his face. He was cursing aloud and hitting his fist against the stone wall beside him. I left him, for I had no comfort to spare. No one knew where John and Katherine were; when I asked for them, people stared as if I had spoken in a foreign language. At last I had the sense to try Will Huntingdon's rooms.

He opened the door a crack, as if to protect what was behind it. 'Oh, it's you.'

'Yes. I'm looking for Katherine and John.'

'I wondered when someone would remember their existence. They're here. I suppose you'd better come in.'

Will had a fine, big room with a windowed bay at the end. On the seat under the window John and Katherine huddled together like puppies. Two pairs of sodden blue eyes stared at me with hostile, defiant grief. I had never seen much likeness between them, but sorrow had hollowed their cheeks and defined the strong York bones. They were Richard's children, and they had been left alone to mourn their brother.

Helplessly, I said, 'Your father has to stay with Anne.'

'Oh yes, of course. We understand.' John looked away as he spoke, and I did what I should have done at once. I knelt down and put my arms around them.

'My darlings, I'm so sorry. I loved that little boy too, but he was your brother, it is worse for you two. Worse for you than for anyone but Richard and Anne. Poor Anne, at least Richard still has you.'

'We know he won't want to see us. Everyone must be thinking, why couldn't it be me who died? A king needs a legitimate son. Now he has no heir.' John tried so hard to say these things flatly, without rancour, but his voice was breaking and the swoops from childish treble to a man's baritone gave his words unintentional pathos.

I tried to think of something to say, and could not. Will Huntingdon said, 'And since that's the flat truth, we might as well look it in the face. Martin, sit down. You'll have a drink?' He kicked a stool towards me. It was the first time he had called me by my name, and it reminded me that he was not much younger than me. He poured four cups of wine and sat down beside Katherine, trying to smooth the tear-stuck curls from her face. He had a little daughter, I remembered, from his marriage to Mary Woodville. Odd to think that he would have been a king's uncle-by-marriage, and soon would be son-in-law to another. 'Come, sweetheart, drink the wine. You need it.' Katherine shook her head, but gave in to his coaxing. I noticed she had bound her hair with a black ribbon and tied another around the sleeve of her blue gown; probably she had no black dress, and had not wanted to put herself forward by asking for one. Poor little lass, she had done her best. John had found a black jerkin, but it was old, and his wrists stuck out below the cuffs.

I had a crashing headache, the kind that starts at the back of the neck and sinks iron claws right through your head. The wine helped a bit, it cleared my fogged mind enough to think what to say.

'I've no brothers or sisters, but when our son Peter died we wanted you, John, and all the rest of our children. Give your father time. I'm sorry it seems no one has thought of you, but ... John, there is something I have to tell you. Your mother was expecting a child, and she miscarried this morning.'

A sudden flush of red mantled his pale face. Back at Christmas I had caught him with a girl – oh, it was innocent enough, just a kiss, but we had had to have a very frank talk; but one's parents' lusts are another matter.

'I'm sorry. Is ... is Mother all right?'

'She is in no danger, but she's weak and very tired. Richard and Anne asked to see her, to ask about – about Edward. Now she's in bed. That's why she couldn't come to you. Nor could I, till now. By the way, your father and Anne don't know about the miscarriage, and they mustn't know.'

'Indeed no,' Katherine was quick to understand. 'My lord, how did Ned die? No one has told us.'

Glibly I rattled off the agreed story. The children believed it, but I caught Will Herbert's eyes fixed on me in a doubting half-frown. I met his look with a commanding one of my own, and he nodded and slid his arm around Katherine.

'I'm glad it was – wasn't bad,' she said. 'But oh, poor little Ned.' Her fingers were pleating a fold of her skirt. With a sorry little look up under her lashes she said very quietly, 'We wondered ... It's what John said: now the King has no heir ... There are so many people who would like to overthrow him, there are plots and rebellions all the time ... We wondered, we thought ... the old Queen and her daughters leave Sanctuary and come to terms with Father, then his son dies …'

The same thought had been in the back of my mind. But Innogen had said it seemed a natural death. Still, how could we be sure? Could a poison simulate the illness she had described? Was the timing of Edward's death pure happenstance, or something far more evil? John and Katherine were fourteen, and in our world they were adults, yet they were too young to have to face the idea that their beloved brother, a child of not yet ten, had died for political advantage.

I was glad when Will said robustly, 'Come now, Kate, that has to be sheer fancy! Oh, I understand why you would think it, but ask yourself who? How? Ned was Prince of Wales, he was protected and well cared for.'

One name was in all our minds. Katherine gave it voice, only to dismiss it. 'Not Bess, of course. I never thought that. I don't know her very well, but well enough to know she never, never would. She's good, you know, and kind. Besides, she didn't go to Middleham. But other people might think what we did. Could one of the Lancastrian lot, someone who's for that man Tudor …?'

'Hard to see how,' Will said, and it crossed my mind that he must know a good deal of what the Woodvilles were capable of. 'No, Kate. Don't burden yourself with fears like that. This dreadful thing has happened, and it's not only heartbreaking but a dire political blow … That's enough. Of course,' he assured me, 'this is only among us. We would speak of it to no one else. And I hope no one is wicked enough to suggest it to the King.'

In silence we finished our wine. Will re-filled our cups. Staring down into the drink John said, 'We weren't sure what to do. We want to tell Father and Lady Anne that … you know. But they probably won't want to see us. We don't know what is right to do.'

'Give them a little time,' I repeated. 'Later, send in a message.'

I stopped, because John was staring past me with a look that made the hairs on my neck stand up. I spun around, and I crossed myself, because I give you my word I thought I was seeing the old Duke of York's ghost.

Then Katherine said, 'Father!' and got to her feet.

Richard came silently towards us – silently, because he had only bedroom slippers on his feet. He wore a long gown of black, crookedly buttoned. His pupils were wide and dark from the drugs they had given him. He had left the door open, and outside people clustered, whispering, uncertain what to do. Will slipped past him and shut the door.

'I couldn't find you, then I thought of coming here.' Richard sat raggedly down on the end of the bed. 'Anne's asleep, you see. I couldn't sleep. I wanted my children. Poor Anne. At least I have you. That helps, I find.' Katherine and John went to him. He put his arms around them, drawing their heads down on his shoulders. 'I know you loved Edward too. I've lost so many of my brothers and sisters. Poor children. I'm sorry I couldn't come to you before. Where's Innogen, I thought she would be with you, John?'

Will and I exchanged a glance. It was hard to tell, from his vague and dragging talk, how much Richard was really taking in. Smoothly Will said, 'I gather she is resting.'

'Oh yes. She had a long journey down from Middleham. She always did travel fast and hard. Remember, Martin, after Tewkesbury, at Coventry? We didn't even know she was in the country, and she had heard you were dead or was it wounded and came to find you. I remember how she came bursting in with her hair flying and the baby under her arm – that was you, of course, John – and no attendants but one groom because she'd travelled too fast for them. When was that, Martin?'

'After Tewkesbury. Thirteen years ago.'

'Oh yes of course. Back when all we had to worry about was winning a battle. And telling Mother about John. Oh and the Scots, of course. Always the Scots. And telling Edward I wanted to marry Anne. Poor Anne.' He started to laugh, weirdly and harshly, then broke off as if by an effort of will. 'So many deaths. And now my son. But at least I still have my other son, and my daughter.'

'If we can do anything,' John hesitantly began.

'Oh, just *be*. Stay with me. For there's no other comfort now.'

Katherine wound her arms around him, and over his bent head gave Will and me a look. In silent signal she jerked her head towards the door. We rose, and John nodded. We left. There was nothing else we could do.

I still cannot bear to think of that time. Of the rest of that first day I remember only Kendal weeping as he wrote the official letters, and Anne collapsing during Mass. Poor girl, she went suddenly from icy control to convulsive sobs, crouching helplessly back on her heels, weeping as if her heart would break again. In front of everyone Richard held her in his arms, but his attempts at comfort went for nothing. She hardly seemed to know he was there. After an agonised moment the choir's training held, and they sang valiantly on while Anne's sobs battered against the walls. We carried her away to bed, and there she curled up with her knees hard against her chest and her arms wrapped around her shoulders, and nothing could stop that dreadful weeping. Joyce said to let her cry, that it was better now than later. But she cried all night, slept a few hours at dawn and woke to weep again. For all my love and pity I would have given anything to stop that crying – and if I could not bear it, what was it doing to Richard? For he never left her, he lay beside her on the bed, enduring it and suffering his own grief.

After two days Anne seemed better; at least, Joyce reported that she slept all night without drugs, and she rose up next day pale, haggard, shaky, but resolute. Not for nothing was she the daughter of Neville and Beauchamp, not for nothing was she Queen of England. But she had changed, oh, she had changed. Poor Anne. And poor Richard. Without a woman's easy release of tears he simply endured.

At the end of the month we moved north, making our way to Middleham. The north had always been home, but now it brought no comfort. Anne, who had always ridden, always been a superb horsewoman with no patience with invalidism or self-indulgence, had to travel in a litter. She kept the curtains drawn as if to shut out all reminders that this journey, always before undertaken with joy, led only to misery. At Pontefract she could hardly walk up the steps of the castle, and Joyce and Innogen put her immediately to bed.

I think Richard needed the same, but no sooner had we arrived than outriders galloped in with news of a foreign visitor come to see the King.

'Ambassadors?'

'No, Your Grace – a private visit from a Bohemian gentleman.'

'From Bohemia?' For the first time since his son's death some faint interest crossed Richard's face. 'Who is he?'

'Sire – his name is Nicholas Von Poppelau.'

It meant nothing to anyone, but Richard said, 'Well, I daresay I'll see him. Yes. Have him brought to me.'

It was an extraordinary figure that entered. The only Germans any of us had ever seen were of the Hanseatic League who in London skulked behind the regimented walls of the Steelyard, and a few mercenaries in Edward's army in '71. This man was something quite different. Not tall, but immensely strong in the body and richly dressed in the German style, he strode forward, beaming, and made his bow to Richard. He had letters of introduction from his Emperor, and he delivered a formal address in Latin, speaking of the amity between our two peoples and his delight at being received by the English King. Richard replied formally in Latin, to the visitor's evident pleasure – but it soon became apparent that Von Poppelau had only a few words of English and had pretty much shot his bolt when he had said 'Good day'. It seemed the whole thing would have to be conducted in Latin, but we discovered French was another common language, and Innogen did wonders with her smattering of German. Von Poppelau was rich enough to travel where he chose, for interest alone, although the Emperor Frederick had used him as ambassador to Russia. Hard though it is to tell in a foreign language, he seemed a likeable fellow: educated, travelled, interesting.

'You will stay here with us?' Richard asked.

'*Avec beaucoup de plaisir, Monsieur le Roi.*'

'It would give me great pleasure,' said Richard, and asked Francis Lovell to show the guest to his lodgings.

Anne said, 'A Bohemian gentleman? Richard II's Queen Anne was from Bohemia. What's he like?'

'Seems pleasant. Thinks England beautiful. Shall you see him?'

'How could I resist.' Like Richard, it was the first interest she had shown in anything. Richard had the distraction of work, and he had driven himself hard these last weeks because after twelve or fifteen hours of business he could sleep. Anne, I think, found it harder, because she had nothing to occupy her except the trivial pastimes for which she had no heart. So Von Poppelau had unwittingly come at the perfect time.

And Anne bowled him over. He stared at her, murmured something about *Quelle beauté!* then dropped to his knee and kissed her hand. *'Madame la Reine! Votre serviteur!'* Anne's Latin was nothing wonderful, but she had spent part of her childhood at Calais when her father was Captain there, and her French was impeccable. Too thin and very pale, she was beautiful in her black gown, and Von Poppelau couldn't take his eyes off her.

He came to Mass, of course, and here he found another beauty. As we left the chapel he turned to Richard with tears in his eyes. 'The music! Never have I heard anything so lovely! Your minstrels are famous, and we have nothing so fine in all Europe. I have heard English people singing for pleasure on my travels, the music of the people, you understand, and of course I have taken Mass, but this is something extraordinary!' He could have said nothing to delight Richard more, for he loved music. The only sign of low cunning I ever saw in him was the way he 'poached' minstrels for his troupe, stopping at nothing to hire the best. And, as von Poppelau said, his musicians were famously the best in England, which is to say the best in the known world.

Later that morning, while Richard attended to business, Francis and I were set to entertain the visitor. The moment we were alone he said, 'Please tell me – the King and Queen, they are in mourning?'

'For their son, M'sieu.'

'Their son?' Poor man, he was stricken. 'But I had not realised! Perhaps the news has not travelled fast, for no one told me on the way here? They cannot want a guest at such a time? Was it recent?'

'Less than a month ago.'

He crossed himself, murmuring in his own tongue. 'A young child? And was he your Dauphin, your Prince of Wales?'

'Eight, sir, and yes, he was the Prince of Wales.'

'The King's heir. What a sorrow.' Indeed it was, and more than a sorrow. A king without a natural heir is vulnerable. We had tried not to imagine the delight Edward's death must have given Henry Tudor and his friends. 'Have they other children?'

'No. Well, that is, the King has; from before his marriage, you understand.'

'Ah yes. All kings have bastards, it seems. The young gentleman Sir John Plantagenet and the Ma'mselle Katherine. But I should not stay at such a time? I will go away again?'

'No, sir,' said Francis, 'the King and Queen are enjoying your visit, they would be sad to see you go. It would have been made clear if they did not want you here. So please stay. Now, tell us something of your travels. Do you like England?'

'Very much.' His eyes twinkled. 'The ladies are very beautiful, more beautiful than in Europe, I think. But bold! Free, I mean.' He didn't seem displeased about it. 'And I confess I do not like the English cooking so much, but that is because it is strange to me. And prices are high, I find. But England is beautiful, and so wealthy! Everyone seems much richer than comparable people would be in Europe. And I admire your King and Queen. She is beautiful and brave, and he has a great heart. I am honoured to meet them.'

Later he showed us the enormous lance he took everywhere, and challenged us to lift it. To his clear amusement, none of us could. It was heavier than an English lance, and we couldn't imagine the horse that could bear the weight of it with an armoured rider. At dinner Richard and Von Poppelau had a lovely time talking of weapons and warfare, comparing English campaigns with European ones. Von Poppelau spoke of the wars against the Turks, telling of the King of

Hungary's victory over the Unbelievers the previous year.

'I wish,' Richard said intensely, 'that my kingdom lay upon the borders of Turkey – with my own people alone and without the help of other princes I should like to drive away not only the Turks but all my foes.'

'Indeed – France sees England as an enemy; King Louis left, I think, a legacy of hatred between the two countries.'

'Since the peace treaty back in '75, particularly. And yes, the new French Regent, the Lady Anne, does not seem to think we can come to terms. Although I try. And Brittany blows hot and cold. Spain is well-disposed to us, but they would like me to make war on France so they can get on with their campaign against the Moors. And Maximilian would also like me to make war on France so he can get on with his own plans.'

'But you will not be tempted into foreign wars, I think.'

'No. I want peace. You may have heard, M'sieu, that there is a half-Welsh gentleman called Henry Tudor who pretends to my throne, and Brittany and France have both tried to use him against me.'

'I have heard of him. His grandmother Katherine de Valois, wife to your Henry V, was King Louis's cousin? Sister? But he is of no importance, Monsieur le Roi. You are a famous warrior, Monsieur, and a great king. You will brush this pretender aside and be secure.'

Richard smiled. 'M'sieu, I trust so indeed, but your words are comforting. Let me thank you. Martin ...' I went to him, and with a wink he took the gold chain from my shoulders and hung it around Von Poppelau's neck; in mourning Richard wore no jewellery but the Coronation ring. Von Poppelau was enchanted.

He stayed on another week. He was with us when we moved on to York – and the poor people of Richard's favourite city were at a loss what to do for their beloved King and Queen. In the end they simply lined the streets, every person clad in full black, and held a gentle silence as their monarchs passed.

Middleham was the worst, of course. There Von Poppelau left us, and without the distraction of his company Anne and Richard had to face their home without their son. They had to face his funeral. I thought Anne would faint as they rode in and she looked instinctively for Edward running to greet them. Her mother came stiffly down the steps – she had aged dreadfully – and in silence took them in her arms, then went inside with Anne.

Prince Edward lies buried in the chapel at Sheriff Hutton. The Abbey, or Windsor, would have befitted the Prince of Wales, but his parents could bear no prolongation of their grief for the sake of ritual. I think too that they knew they would come no more to Middleham, whose happiness was as distant now as Camelot. Anne could bear very little then. There was no question of her attending the funeral, and when the cortège wound down the dales from Middleham she was in her room with her mother, her cousin Anna, and Innogen. Twelve years ago, to the day, we had ridden into Middleham, on a spring day like this, our hearts glad to be coming home.

The entire Sheriff Hutton household lined up to greet us. Dismounting, Richard paced through the men of the garrison and over to where his nephew Lincoln headed the line of children. The two men embraced, and I saw tears in Lincoln's eyes as he spoke quietly to his uncle. Richard moved slowly along the black-clad line, which dipped like a runnel in the wind as they bowed. He spoke to all of them, here and there stopping to hug a child like little Warwick or my children. Side by side Bess and Cecily curtsied gravely, and I kept an eye on Bess, just in case, but either she had got over her silly crush or her beautiful manners hid anything but proper condolence.

Next to their sisters stood the Lords Bastard. I had wondered if the elder boy would attend his cousin's funeral, and how he would conduct himself. Lord Richard took his uncle's hand and said something that made Richard smile faintly and thank him, ruffling his hair. Then he moved on to the Lord Edward.

Neither spoke. The boy did not bow or offer to kiss the King's hand. Even at twelve he was, though very thin, taller than his uncle, and I wondered if he enjoyed that small physical advantage. For a long moment they stood looking into each other's eyes, the king who never was and the king not meant to be. It seemed to be sheer curiosity that held them so, an adult exchange of some silent message. Then the boy bowed his head, and whatever he said made Richard reply, 'Thank you, Edward,' in the tone you use when someone has surprised you. That was all, and we made our way into the chapel.

I knew Richard's self-control too well to fear he would break during the funeral. I watched him, though, for one's body can overcome all the efforts of the mind. Once, during the Mass of the Holy Trinity, he lifted his face to the music as if it were sunshine on a winter's day. That was the only sign of his desperate need for comfort; in fact, it was he who took John's hand when the boy wept. Beside me Francis Lovell was weeping too. Childless himself, he had been deeply fond of young Edward. Well, so had I, and lest I seem unfeeling, let me say that a child's funeral breaks your heart by reminding you of your own children's mortality. They were with me that day, my children, all but the very little ones, and, looking at them, I knew that desperate pain familiar to every parent: that you are impotent to protect your children.

Something else, too, occupied my mind when I should have been praying. A glance around that chapel showed nearly all the royal family. Which of them would now be Richard's heir? Lincoln, I supposed, and after him his brothers. For Richard to name his nephew Warwick would be a confession that his reign was bankrupt. I wondered again if the Prince's death had been mere coincidence. I had asked Innogen again about the way he died, without of course mentioning my fears, and she had been sure it was no more than it seemed, some affection of the internal parts, perhaps some blockage. Yet still I wondered. Such a convenient death for Richard's enemies. How easy, now, for rumours to go about that he was under the displeasure of heaven; was being punished. Next we would be hearing again that he had murdered his nephews. How easy, when simple folk so quickly believe such stuff, to make him seem an unlucky king. Even damned. Tudor was still said to be planning an invasion. No one would rise for an unknown man, half-Welsh, with his heritage flawed by bastardy; a man who hadn't even lived in England these past thirteen years. Yet now, when Richard had no son, and it could seem God had turned his face from him …

If only Anne had given him more children. Her sister had borne four, yet Anne had conceived only the once.

As I knelt, and fingered my beads, and mouthed the responses, I was chilled with foreboding. This was the end of our security. And all our enemies would know it.

The Scots were the first to strike. Of course. Master Tudor seemed to be lying low, but there were plenty of other troubles. Brittany was playing with us, their fleet marauding wherever it could; and the same was true of the French and the Scots. English pirates had done so much damage to foreign shipping that demands for compensation, and threats virtually of war, poured in with every messenger.

Richard dealt with the pirates by making ship owners and their captains post bonds agreeing they would attack no foreign ships, and town magistrates who let unbonded ships out of port were made liable for any damage. He sent embassies to the Pope, to Spain and Portugal, he brought Maximilian to understand that England could not afford to be drawn into in his troubles with France. He buttered up Spain and Brittany and secured a truce with the latter, and in the summer he gathered a great fleet off Scarborough to deal with the Scots. A brilliant soldier on land, he proved as good a naval commander – reduced to helpless spewing by the mere sight of the sea at Scarborough, I left him to it and did my bit by working with the northern commands who were patrolling the borders against the Scots.

We all did well. Richard's fleet thrashed the Scottish one, while we up on the border made mincemeat of the Scottish army. Honestly, you would think they would have learnt. Well, eventually they did. In July King James sent Lord Lyle to discuss a peace treaty, and in September we welcomed the Scottish embassy to Nottingham. They were in good earnest this time, though I daresay their pleasant smiles and smooth phrases of adulation masked the same loathing for Richard they had felt the past four years when he so regularly thrashed them. They had called him 'The Reiver', and no doubt less repeatable things, but now all was sweetness and light, we were all friends. The Scottish King's secretary, Master Whitelaw, made a Latin oration ringing with praise for the English king, and the peace treaty was signed. One provision of this was that Richard's niece, Anne de la Pole, the Duke of Suffolk's daughter, was to marry the Duke of Rothesay, heir to the Scottish throne. There is nothing like a marriage for securing a treaty. It was thirteen years since Richard had first taken command against the Scots, four years since he had begun that dedicated campaign, but at last it was done, and we had peace with our unruly northern neighbour.

By late November we were back in London, and it was time for Katherine's wedding. First Lent, then mourning for her brother, had made the marriage impossible earlier, and Katherine herself was prepared to wait until the next year. But Will Herbert was impatient, and through me he sounded Richard out. I think he put the matter to Anne, fearing she would have no heart for a wedding, but the thought cheered her. Of course Katherine should have her wedding, she said, and why not on her fifteenth birthday? So it was settled, and from international politics we were plunged into the feminine to-do of wedding preparations. I doubt we once managed to sit down to dinner without some vital question coming up, usually to do with clothes. Glumly I began to calculate: I had three daughters, and Cecily was thirteen. In a year or two all this fuss would be for her. Well, she wasn't a king's daughter, but I would see my girls married magnificently or not at all, even if it meant selling off land. Marrying Innogen so quickly, and in such odd circumstances, I simply had no idea what a wedding involved. Innogen must have a new gown, of course. So must all my daughters, and what was Cecily, as one of

Katherine's bridesmaids, going to wear? And John must of course have a full new outfit. What would the Queen wear for her stepdaughter's wedding? Should the other girls be dressed the same as one another? What was suitable for Will's little daughter Elizabeth? And then there was the matter of wedding gifts. Innogen and I gave a set of bed-hangings and two tapestries. The Duchess of York sent a Book of Hours and a service of silver plate. From Margaret in Burgundy came a timber of sables and lengths of violet velvet in grain. John conferred anxiously with us, and gave Katherine a saddle and a set of gilded red leather harnesses. Richard dowered Katherine generously with lands and tenements worth a thousand marks a year, and an annuity of a further hundred and fifty pounds, but his more personal gift was a matched pair of magnificent bay horses.

Anne moved briskly through all this to-do, organising everything with the expertise of one used to managing a great household. She had everything at her fingertips, down to the vexed question of who was to be wearing what. I think she enjoyed it, for she loved Katherine and it was a distraction from grief. I noticed she had lost flesh lately, but thought little of it.

Katherine was a pretty girl, but on her wedding day the traditional bridal glow made her into a beauty. She wore sapphire-blue velvet with cloth of gold, and gold and sapphires binding her lovely curly hair. Will, looking as thoroughly filleted as any other groom, was also in gold and blue, and the bride's maidens wore yellow with white York roses. Richard managed his part well, saying, 'I do,' clearly when asked the question who gave Katherine away to be wed? Then, it was noted, he and I both burst into tears. Women weep sentimentally at weddings, but we were remembering the youthful year of Katherine's conception, the Christmas we heard of her birth, the fight we had had soon after I had been to see Innogen. We were crying, in fact, for our youth.

We kept Christmas magnificently, the Court blazed with all the colour and glory of Edward IV's days, we had all the usual games, the gifts, the music and the mumming, the pleasant nonsense of the Lord of Misrule. Richard spent lavishly on clothes and jewels, on presents for everyone. It should have been wonderful.

But Anne was ill.

# Nineteen

## January-June 1485

I first noticed because of Bess's *faux pas* at the Twelfth Night banquet. I have mentioned that styles in women's gowns had changed lately; I remember paying the bills as my wife and daughters had new clothes made. For Christmas everyone naturally wore their best and newest things; there is nothing in that. But because of the new style it caught everyone's eye that Bess seemed to be wearing the same as the Queen. In actual fact the two gowns were not all that similar – they were the same colour, but Anne's of course was far the richer, and trimmed with cloth of silver and bands of ermine – but it was enough to set people murmuring. Richard looked furious when he noticed, for it is the custom for the Queen's ladies to ensure they don't wear the same as their mistress, and Bess of all people should have remembered that. But Anne said calmly, 'Oh, good, you're wearing the cloth I gave you. It's very becoming, Bess.'

And so it was. That was the trouble. The blue-green colour suited Bess, and the gown's cut made the most of her handsome young figure. Beside her Anne looked drab and washed-out, almost elderly. No, worse: she looked ill. I couldn't understand why I had not noticed before. She had always been slenderly made, but even in the worst grief after her son's death she hadn't been gaunt. Now there was nothing of her, she was skin and bone. Her skin was chalky, and shadows lay deep around her eyes. What I had thought was face-paint highlighting her cheeks was the flush of fever. Even her pretty hair, worn loose for the occasion under her crown, was dull as straw.

I turned to Innogen, a question on my lips, and met a glare that stunned me to silence. Pasting on a smile I reached for my wine cup.

It was at that moment that a messenger came to Richard and bent over him, murmuring. Richard's brows lifted, and his lips thinned to nothingness. The messenger talked for several moments more, then Richard pitched his voice to carry along the high table.

'Our friend Master Tudor has taken a solemn vow, in Rennes Cathedral, to marry my niece Elizabeth of York when he "regains" the throne of England from the usurper Plantagenet. What have you to say to this, Bess?' Hot colour surged up her face then ebbed, leaving her sickly pale. Helplessly she shook her head. Richard stared coldly at her. 'You did not know?'

'Of course not. How dare he!'

'Indeed. Lord Stanley, what have you to say of your stepson's genius?'

Looking honestly shocked Stanley said, 'Sire, he will do anything to give his pretensions the colour of legitimacy.'

'And he thinks promising to marry a bastard will help his cause?'

I noticed Bess blush and pale again. Stanley said, 'I am not privy to his thoughts, Your Grace. I have neither spoken to him nor communicated with him for more than a decade.'

'Does your wife not confide in you?'

'No, Your Grace. I believe she has given up ideas of aiding her son.'

'Do you? Tell her, Lord Stanley, that she had better do so. I will not be lenient again.' He spoke without emotion, but his tone was enough to set Stanley sweating and pulling at his shirt-band. Richard gave him a glance, and went on, 'I will not be provoked into taking action against France. The French Regent can welcome Tudor as warmly as she likes; fortunately, the French government is so divided against itself it can give Tudor little help. No doubt he thought Oxford's escape would help his cause, but he would be well advised not to trust that gentleman too far.'

A couple of months earlier the Earl of Oxford, whom we had fought against at Barnet, had escaped from Hammes Castle where he had been imprisoned since 1474. His gaoler James Blount had gone with him, and for a while it had looked as if Oxford and Tudor would mount an attack on Calais, but it had come to nothing; Richard had replaced the garrison, offered a pardon to Blount's wife, and put James Tyrell in as Lieutenant. He had also put the Cinque Ports on alert, and issued proclamations against Tudor and his followers, and I knew he had renewed his offers to the Continental rulers to have Tudor captured. Really it was all more of the same, it posed no great threat, but Tudor was like the canker in a sore tooth, nagging away until the tooth is rooted out.

'What will you do, Sire?' Stanley asked.

'Tudor cannot try invasion again until spring at the earliest. I am well prepared. Tudor can make all the high-flown vows he likes. None of it matters.'

In bed that night, with the bed-curtains drawn and the door shut, I said to my wife, 'Anne is ill.'

'Yes.'

That one syllable said everything. I said: 'Oh no, not Anne! Lord, not Anne! Of course, she hasn't got over her son's death yet; she ...'

'It's more than that. Has Richard said anything?'

'Nothing. But he must know?'

'He knows, I think, but he's not admitting it. Soon he will have to. We have done everything we can, and Anne has consulted doctors secretly. There is nothing they can do. It's the lung disease, consumption. She is coughing up blood. We have known for the last month, but this loss of flesh has come suddenly.'

'So she knows?'

'Oh yes. She knows. She was ill through the autumn, but she put it down to grief and thought little of it. She enjoyed the planning for Katherine's wedding, but once that was over ... At first she thought it was just the let-down after the fun of the wedding, but soon she knew. She has been using up her strength trying to pretend there is nothing wrong, trying to keep Richard from worrying. Poor Richard, why must he bear this? His son, then his wife.' She rolled over and put her arms around me, hugging me tightly. She was trying not to cry. 'Of course people will say he's being punished, and they'll ask what his sin is. People fear to be ruled by an unlucky King, a King under God's displeasure.'

'And it will give Tudor and his cronies a fillip.' Remembering my doubts the year before, I said, 'Innogen, Anne isn't ...' Even in the secrecy of our bed I whispered the word into the shell of her ear '... it's not poison?'

'Can a poison counterfeit the lung disease? No, I think it's simply the disease. No one would poison her, what is there to gain?' In the darkness I felt rather than saw her eyes widen. Her lashes brushed my cheek as we both thought of a silly but perhaps callous girl who loved Anne's husband. Or of that girl's ambitious mother. 'No,' Innogen said, and I agreed.

After a time I said, 'Jenny, is Anne really so ill? There is no hope?'

'None.' She was weeping openly now. I remembered her saying at Coventry in '71 that she liked Anne; over the years they had become dear friends. Anne's mother had at first taken a dim view of Richard bringing his mistress to live in his wife's household, but even she had seen that my marriage to Innogen was as strong as Richard's to Anne, and that the fact of that old liaison had somehow bound the two women in a fierce female loyalty. 'There's no hope. I love her dearly and there is no hope at all. The doctors think she has only a few months to live.'


Soon everyone knew. Anne dwindled away, and at the end of January she suffered a massive bleeding from the lungs. The doctors spoke now of weeks rather than months. Still Richard never spoke of it, not even to me or Rob.

I made a point of calling on Anne every day. One afternoon in February I was on my way to see her when I saw Richard leave her room. The moment the door closed behind him he slumped back against it as if all his strength had gone. He was nearly as pale as Anne herself, and his whole body shook. I drew back, but as I moved Richard heard someone coming from the other way. He recoiled, looking panic-stricken, and bolted past me into a nearby room. He slammed the door behind him, but not even two-inch oak could keep the sounds of his grief private. I had never heard weeping like it, not even when Anne keened for her dead son, and I knew he should not be alone.

He was huddled on the floor, his head down on his arms. When he heard me he turned on me, snarling like a cornered animal, and swore at me in words culled from army camps. Even so, I crouched down beside him and took him in my arms. He hit me, but I had taken worse than that in his service. I held him, and suddenly he flung his arms round my neck, and soon the worst of it was over.

'Anne is dying.'

'I know.'

'Yes. Everyone knows. I've pretended it's not true. If I didn't talk about it, it might not be true. I was with her just now and all of a sudden it was as if I really knew and understood. It became a real thing. She is dying. My beloved is dying. And for a moment I felt as if it was her fault, as if she had chosen to leave me, I hated her for leaving me. Don't say you understand, because however kindly you mean it you don't understand, you cannot.'

'No I cannot, but I love her too. She is very much loved.'

'Oh yes.' He gulped, snuffling, and wiped his nose on his sleeve. 'But still people will say she has been done away with. That I poisoned her or something. Because that's the way people think. Or they'll say her death is to punish me. God's will. People always say that, they say it's the will of heaven. And perhaps it is, but I wish I understood why. What have I done, what is my sin? I have prayed for understanding, but I get no answer. Do you believe in God, Martin?'

'I believe in Christ; in His teachings. I don't believe in much of what we have made of those teachings. I don't want to believe in the petty, vindictive, irrational God of the Old Testament.'

'Perhaps that is the only one there is. Perhaps there's no benevolent Creator. Or perhaps St Augustine was right when he said that the Divinity is either benevolent or omnipotent, because events prove He cannot be both. For why must I within two years lose my brother, whom I did love despite everything, and my son and my wife? What have I done to deserve it? What has Anne done to deserve the death of her son? I took the Crown because it was mine for the taking. No doubt many people believe I concocted that pre-contract story because I knew that if Edward's children were bastards I would be offered the Crown – but I didn't. I had no idea, I never suspected. If I had done what people say and put Edward's sons to death then I would deserve retribution. But I didn't. So why must I be punished? What is my sin? If I could understand I could bear it, but all the priests can say is that God's will is not for us to understand, He is inscrutable and we should not seek to know. But why must I lose my wife?'

'I don't know. Richard, I have nothing to say. There's no comfort. I don't know.'

I doubt he heard me, for he went on, 'If taking the Crown was a fault or a sin, what else was I to do? Allow a bastard to reign? Well, I suppose it would not have been the first time. Or someone else, Lincoln for instance? But he didn't want it, and everyone wanted me, they wanted the soldier, the man who had kept the Scots out of England, the man who ruled the north justly and sensibly. They wanted a strong, adult King. It had to be me. So was my sin in wanting it? Because I did, Martin, as soon as Bishop Stillington told us about the Eleanor Butler pre-contract I knew the Crown was mine for the asking, and I wanted it. I thought I could be a good king. Partly it was because I would not see England torn apart by the Woodvilles and the Lancastrians. But all I've done is strengthen Tudor's pretensions. When I thought I could be a good king!'

This was close to hysteria, but I answered him sensibly. 'And you have been a good king, and the people know it. Richard, think! Calm down and think: Peace with Scotland; good terms with France, with Brittany, with Portugal, with Burgundy; and perhaps good lasting peace treaties yet to come. And all the legislation of your Parliament – good laws and justice for the common people, their rights protected in law; women's rights protected, traitors' wives protected. The Court of Common Pleas; the College of Heralds; all your gifts to charities, to universities, to hospitals; trade looked after; the building you have done. No one rose for Tudor or Buckingham. There will always be malcontents and people pushing old claims; that went on all through your brother's reign and the ones before him. It will always go on but it means nothing. The people love and trust you, the nobles are mostly content. You have been a good king. Even if you had waded to the throne through the blood of every Lancastrian in England it would have been worth it for the good you've done.'

Weary now, he heard me out, a faint smile on his lips. 'Yes, I've done some good things. I knew I could. But I doubt it would have been worth it at the cost you speak of. But I know what you mean. Oh, God, perhaps I should have been a good deal more tyrannical. Ruthless. Perhaps I will have to be in the future.'

'Perhaps, yes,' I said, thinking that he should have sent Morton and Lady Margaret Beaufort – to name only two – to the block when he had the chance. He had been ruthless only with William Hastings and with Buckingham, who had been his friends and betrayed that friendship.

'I will, perhaps.' He fished for his handkerchief and ingloriously blew his nose. 'Leniency and mercy don't pay, perhaps. Justice, always. But not leniency. People take it for weakness. I thought I could only act according to my beliefs. But even honour is a luxury for a king. Now I can see why Edward put George to death. Well, I am luckier, I don't have to face putting my brother to death – but now I can see why he did it.' He blew his nose again. 'They'll make me re-marry, won't they?'

'Yes. I'm afraid so. It is necessary, Richard.'

'I know. There have been a few hints already. No more than hints, nothing to offend. Though even the idea offends. But I must, to protect my country.' All this time we had been crouched together on the floor. Now he stood up, trying to tidy his clothes. 'The doctors told me yesterday I mustn't share Anne's bed any longer. Of course we haven't been able to make love for a long time, but being together has been some comfort. We've slept together ever since we married. Thirteen years. It's nearly our wedding anniversary. But now

I am forbidden. The doctors fear I might take the disease. The King must be protected. Today, when I saw Anne, I had to tell her. Well, she already knew, of course, the doctors had told her. She tried to make it easier by saying she's so uncomfortable at night now that she would rather sleep alone – if she does ever sleep. And perhaps that's true. But just her presence is a comfort to me, and mine to her. Gone, now. And no doubt my subjects will occupy themselves wondering who is sharing my bed now.' Since that was true, there was nothing I could say. He gave me a wry smile and put his hands on my shoulders and kissed me. 'You've comforted me today, Martin. You're good at that. You've a gift for friendship, and that is all I have left. I will need it, to get through this.' He kissed me again, and abruptly went out.

I sat there for a while, staring at the closed door, then quietly I wept for Anne and for Richard, my friends.

I didn't go to Anne that day, but the following day I paid my usual visit. She was nothing but a skeleton in a pretty gown – heartbreakingly, she still took stubborn pride in holding the indignities of disease at bay with lovely clothes and scent. They had cut her hair recently, for she could no longer bear the weight of the hip-length fall and having it dressed tired her too much. The short little curls clustering round her face made her look like an adolescent boy. I told her so to amuse her, and she giggled and said it was not an idea that would appeal to Richard. Even the light little laugh made her cough, and I saw the blood on the handkerchief she pressed to her mouth.

'It won't be long now.'

I looked up with the usual reassuring phrases on my lips, and saw that things had gone beyond that. 'I know, hinny.'

'I'm not afraid. Interesting, isn't it? Because however much we believe, we still fear death, although it comes so commonly. And mine is the easier part, I couldn't bear it if Richard died and I was left without him. I've faced that so many times over the years, ever since I first knew I loved him.'

'Which was in 1469. That Christmas feast.'

'Yes. He says that's when he fell in love with me too, but I doubt it.'

'It's certainly when he first noticed you had become a woman, and a beautiful one. So perhaps it's when he fell in love with you – but one has to notice one's in love. And that happened in '71, when William Stanley brought you into Coventry. Remember?'

'Yes. Richard suddenly appeared from nowhere.'

'Actually his bedroom, we were watching – and he stormed down into that yard and read Stanley his fortune.'

'Yes.' She laughed again, and broke off, her hand pressed to her side. 'Hurts. Martin, tell Richard not to trust the Stanleys. Not to trust Margaret Beaufort. I think he can trust the Woodvilles now. He doesn't know about Bess.' She saw the question in my face. 'Oh yes, I know all about Bess mooning love-struck after Richard. Who'd understand that better than I? Though I never made sheep's eyes, I hope! And Martin, my dear friend, look after Richard for me?'

'Always.'

'Make him face his duty and marry again and have sons. I failed him there, didn't I? Make sure he does it. The moment the King of England is back on the marriage market every foreign country will rush to offer him their Infantas and duchesses; he must marry as soon as possible or else he might as well abdicate and give the throne to Lincoln, or restore Edward's son. In a year there could be a new heir to England. A king can't afford the luxury of private grief. Make him understand that, Martin, and do it. And look after him.' She was running out of strength. It was time for me to go.

I was bending to kiss her when the bells began to ring – the Westminster Abbey bells, the Passing Bells. Anne's eyes stared horrified into mine. She screamed.

'Anne! No! Ssh, it's all right!'

'No! It's the Passing Bells! For a Queen! For me! They're saying I'm dead! *They are saying I am dead!*'

I clutched her, trying to soothe her, to keep her in the bed, but she fought me with frenzied strength. I could hear the breath whistling in her tortured lungs, and her brittle bones felt as if they would break in my hands. She was screaming for Richard, screaming protests as those bells rang on. I thought she had lost her mind with terror, and all I could do was hold her and try to make her hear my futile reassurances. Innogen and Joyce and her other ladies had come at the first sound, but none of us could do anything. She broke from my grip and ran to the door, screaming Richard's name like a woman demented.

He came. He had heard her – or he had heard the bells and thought he read their message. He had been in a Council meeting, and in terror he had run the length of Westminster Palace, half the Council behind him. Shoving everyone aside he swept Anne into his arms, kissing her frantically, calling her darling, lovey, hinny, sweet.

'The bells! They're saying I am dead! The bells are for me! Richard! Richard!'

Richard shouted at the top of his voice, 'The bells mean nothing! Anne, be quiet. It's stupid boys ringing the bells, the bells are not for you! Be quiet! Darling, I'm here, I love you, it's all right, be quiet, hush, I love you, I'm here.'

'Richard!' Her voice broke, she coughed, then blood gushed from her mouth, bright scarlet frothy blood from the lungs. Richard lifted her onto the bed, and her blood stained them both. Doctor Hobbes came then, and between them they made Anne quieten down, they made her understand. Someone had got the bells stopped, and Anne lay limply against her pillows.

'Damn all bell-ringing fools!' Hobbes grumbled. 'Would you believe it, a couple of apprentices made a fool bet they could ring the Westminster bells and get away with it! Boys today, I don't know, no discipline. Sore bums tonight. Now drink up your medicine, Your Grace, there's a good girl.'

His matter-of-fact explanation, and his way of mixing formality with endearments, soothed Anne. Eyes closed, her hand clutching

Richard's, she drank the draught he gave her, and a moment later was asleep.

That was the last time I saw Anne alive. Terror, the strength with which she had fought, the bleeding – they were the end of her. She died a day later, on the sixteenth of March. She was only twenty-eight.

I can write no more of it, for I loved her – except to say that as she died the skies darkened as if in sorrow and the sun ceased to be. It was what they call an eclipse of the sun, and for all that learned men say such things have a natural cause, it seemed that the very heavens shared our mourning. People who know less than the learned men said it was an evil omen, and who can say they were wrong? Call it sin or call it chance, we were under Fate's displeasure.

Barely a week later the scandal broke. I was leaving a Council meeting when a hand hooked around my arm and I was swept deftly into a side corridor. 'My lord,' said Richard Ratcliffe, 'a word with you, please. In private, and quietly. It concerns the King.'

'He'll be looking for me.'

'It is taken care of. Sir Robert is with him. Please, Lord Robsart, this is very urgent.'

Dick Ratcliffe was far from a panicky sort, so, puzzled and alarmed, I followed him to his room. There I found Sir William Catesby and Francis Lovell, and irreverently I thought of Colingbourne's rhyme:

*The Cat, the Rat, and Lovell our Dog,*
*Rule all England under a Hog.*

I'm ashamed to say I had been amused by it when Colingbourne pinned it up on the door of St Paul's Church the previous year. I had thought it witty for all its cruelty; Francis's badge was a hound, while the 'hog' was Richard's White Boar. (Either the conspirators couldn't work my hart's head badge into the rhyme, or they knew my utter lack of interest in influencing government.) None of the principals had been amused, and of course while the rhyme itself was harmless, the malice behind it was quite the opposite. Colingbourne was one of Tudor's agents, and in December he'd been executed for treasonable correspondence with the Welshman – advising him where to land when he invaded England, if you please, and, more dangerously, telling him to tell the French government that Richard intended to make war on France.

The Duke of Norfolk came in behind me. Dick shut the door. 'Lord Robsart,' Catesby abruptly began, 'have you been aware of any rumours circulating? About the King?'

'Rumours? You mean something particular? Or new? Because there are always rumours. Has he murdered his nephews again?'

'No. This is much more serious than that nonsense.'

'More serious than murder? No, I'm aware of nothing, but I've hardly left the Palace since Anne's death, I have been with Richard most of the time. You'd better tell me.'

'The rumours say the King is going to marry Lady Bess.'

I stared stupidly. 'Marry Bess! What nonsense! She's the last person ... You're not taking this rubbish seriously?'

But they were, and as I looked at their grave faces I knew this was real trouble. Catesby said, 'The story's everywhere. It is being put about deliberately; we are not sure by whom. Go into any inn and you'll hear it.'

The first shock over, I had got my mind working. 'And of course people are saying the Queen was ... hurried to her end. That Bess has been Richard's mistress.' They nodded. I felt sick. 'But it's such arrant nonsense! Very well – people who don't know the King as we do would believe it; a King with a barren, ill wife ... But he couldn't marry Bess without legitimating her, and that would legitimate her brothers – same problem Tudor apparently can't see he would have. Oh but I'm forgetting, Richard's murdered those boys. This story must have originated with Tudor's cronies, they're afraid Richard will marry Bess and they're getting in first by slandering him with the story.'

'To look at both sides of the matter,' said Catesby the lawyer, 'I think the story might have begun with the Archbishop of York. Apparently the King said something to him in his dry way, and old Rotherham has no sense of humour ...'

'Silly old fart,' muttered Francis.

'Indeed. And, having no humour, he took the King's remark seriously and passed it on. He mentioned it to me, and although I laughed it off and tried to explain, he was worried. He's a fool, of course, but fools do more damage than clever men. After all, it was Rotherham who blabbed to Doctor Morton about the King's plans to capture Tudor with the aid of Duke Francis of Brittany last year. If he'd kept his mouth shut the Welshman would never have escaped to France.'

Jock Howard stirred, wrapping the skirts of his gown over his knees. 'There is more to it, unfortunately. Martin, it's Bess herself. She has been – indiscreet. I suppose you're aware she fancies herself in love with the King?'

'Yes. That was why my wife took her north last year. What do you mean, indiscreet?'

'She's been writing to me about it.'

'*Writing* to you?'

'Yes. A most unpleasant, foolish letter. Jesu, Martin, I've been fond of that girl from the day she was born, I was her father's good friend ...'

'What did she say in this letter?'

With a grimace of distaste Jock said, 'She dared to write asking me to intercede for her with the King. She wrote that she loves him – I won't quote her actual words – and wants to marry him, and that the Queen – she wrote this in February – that the Queen was a long time dying. Words to that effect.'

None of us cared to break the silence his words produced. We were all friends of Richard's, most of us had loved Anne, had seen Bess grow up and been fond of her. Vaguely I recalled someone – Innogen? – saying that perhaps Bess had inherited from both parents the bull-headed determination to get her own way. Sick, I recalled

Anne's kindness to the girl, her gentle sympathy, her gifts, her affection.

'What do we do?' I asked.

'Richard will have to know, and soon.'

'Don't ask me to tell him!'

'No,' Jock sighed, 'that's how we all feel. We'll tell him together. I've talked to Bess, of course; in fact I tore a strip off her. Damn near put her over my knee. I think I've shut her mouth. Richard should marry her off, of course, doesn't matter to whom, get her married.'

'He won't, of course. It would look as if he were taking this seriously. Look, give it a day or two. I'd like to get a feeling for myself of how far this thing's gone.'

That evening I repeated my actions of two years ago. I put on plain clothes and my childhood country accent and went out into London, doing the rounds of the principal inns. In each place I sat and listened, struck up mildly drunken conversations, bought a few rounds of drinks, and by the time I reeled home I had well and truly plumbed the London gossip. The story was everywhere, and most people blindly credited it. The King was a man – and remember his brother, eh, and he's got all them bastard children – and Bess was a young and pretty girl, and she's probably as randy as 'er dad, eh? *Quod erat demonstrandum.*

I told Innogen when she was sarcastic about her husband stinking of cheap ale and cheaper perfume (I'd been well and truly propositioned by a couple of London whores). She said, 'So that's it.'

'You've heard things?'

'More a matter of the odd look. I was one of Anne's ladies-in-waiting and known to be her friend, so no one would dare repeat the slander to me. But yes, I think it is all through the Palace.'

'And all through the city. I hated London tonight. Petty, small-minded, smug people. In the same breath they admire Richard as King, they talk about his good laws and his efforts to bring peace, yet credit every filthy rumour about him. Few could care whom he took as a mistress, but they don't see what it means that it's Bess they talk about. I don't think many believe Anne was – was hastened to her death, but they believe the gossip, and they repeat it. And it's too widely spread not to have been deliberately put about.'

'So what will you do?'

'We have to tell Richard.'

The following day we did so. At first he refused to believe us. He kept saying, 'Marry Bess?' until at last he absorbed it, and all its filthy implications. Only if you knew him very well would you have seen how angry he was, and what effort it took to control that anger. Sick with disgust he said, 'I'll deny it. Publicly deny it.'

'No one believes anything until it's officially denied,' said Norfolk. 'Best let it die of its own accord.'

Yes, we all urged, that's sense, don't fuel the fires of gossip. But Richard saw it otherwise. It was the insult to Anne he minded, the smear on his love for her and his fidelity; and, I think, although he didn't admit it, he resented being taken for such a fool.

And on the second last day of March, exactly a fortnight after Anne's death, he assembled his Council, the officers of his Household, the lords spiritual and temporal, the Mayor and Aldermen and chief citizens of London, and in the Hall of the Hospital of the Knights of St John, in Clerkenwell, he spelled out to them the rumours, and formally denied them. In the voice with which he addressed armies he charged the gathered men to pay no credence to any part of the slander, and to take all steps to deny it on his behalf and to arrest anyone heard spreading the gossip.

That same night he wrote to the Mayor of York to publish his denial; he knew his northerners would be loath to believe it, but it's the sort of dirty story that sticks in people's minds, and the people of the north would be sorely offended at the slight to their Anne.

And then he had to deal with Bess. In vain did I offer to speak to the girl – and Norfolk, Francis, even Innogen did, too – no, Richard had to do it himself. And when I saw her come glowing and starry-eyed to his audience chamber, I knew he was right. I don't know what passed between them. I lingered only long enough to hear her say,

'Richard?' and to hear his cold reply that she could call him *Uncle Richard* or *Your Grace*. Then I made myself scarce until I saw Bess run sobbing from the chamber.

I found Richard slumped over his table, his fists pressed against his temples as if his head ached. Seeing me he said drearily, 'Well, it's done. I came close to hitting her. There's nothing so disgusting as being offered love you don't want. And she did offer. Offered me everything. Why did none of you tell me what she thought she felt for me?'

'I'm afraid we thought a childish infatuation could do no harm.' He laughed harshly. 'Innogen talked to her, so did her sister and Katherine, we got her out of the way last year. I'm afraid we thought it was over. Or that she'd have the grace and the guts to suffer in silence.'

'I was shocked that she could believe it was possible. Do you suppose she put the story about? With some stupid idea of forcing me into marrying her?'

'I think she stopped at confiding in Jock Howard. But of course people knew how she felt. I think it was the Tudor lot, trying to discredit you. Or perhaps they believed it. They've got nothing else they can use against you. What will you do?'

'Pack the wretched girl off up to Sheriff Hutton.'

'Marry her off to someone, Richard. Doesn't matter who.'

'No. It would look as if I took the business seriously.' He saw my expression. 'I know, I know, I did take it seriously, I proved that by denying it publicly. I suppose that was a mistake. But I will not have my wife's memory discredited like this. Martin, I was glad when Anne's suffering ended, but O Lord, I miss her! I miss her company, and her love, her friendship; I miss the past. I would give anything for the power to turn back time, to make time stop so we could live forever at Middleham: Anne and Edward, all of us, happy. It's not two years since my brother died, and in those two years I have lost everything. Sometimes I wonder if I have the heart to go on.'

'You have to.'

'I know. But I wonder how. Anne had a special prayer, before she died she gave it to me so I could take the same comfort from it she did. And for a while it did comfort me. No longer.'

'Perhaps it will again, with time. Because that's all that can help you. Time. And it will help. I wish I had more comfort for you.'

'I know. I said to you before, didn't I, that at least I have your friendship. I've many friends.' He rubbed his hands over his pallid face and said wryly, 'Oblivion would help. Even sleep would help. I can't sleep, or only briefly and with such dreams that I wake … I dream of the past, I dream Anne and my son are alive and well and happy, that we're at Middleham and the worst trouble is the Scots. And then I wake, and for a moment the dream holds and I reach for Anne. Then I remember, and I don't sleep again. They offer me drugs, but they don't help; the dreams are worse and I walk around dazed. And there is no respite when you are king. No respite.'

'I can help there, a little. Come on.' And against his will I gathered Rob and Francis, had our horses saddled, and took him out into the country, into the fresh spring air and made him ride as we had done in the north, for hours, until he was so tired he could hardly sit his horse. Then we took him back to Westminster, fed him, and poured so much drink into him he staggered off to bed three-quarters drunk. And that night at least he slept. It was a prosaic remedy, but it worked.


With the spring came definite news of the lurking Henry Tudor. Somehow he had scraped together enough cash to outfit an army, though a sad little rabble it was by all reports: some Breton or French archers; mercenaries, prisoners who would rather serve under Tudor's banner than stay in gaol. Without the French government's hysterical conviction that England would any moment declare war on their old enemy, Tudor would not have received the time of day, let alone the small amount of active aid he did get. But there, old Louis had rooted that conviction into his descendants' minds and nothing would shift it.

This positive threat was something Richard knew how to deal

with – just as he did not know how to counter the creeping fog of slander and misinformation. Briskly he set about disposing his forces. Francis Lovell went to Southampton to oversee the refitting of the fleet and to lead the men of the southern counties if Tudor invaded there. Norfolk and Surrey made their preparations over in East Anglia. Wales, which seemed a likely entry point for a man who boasted of his Welsh descent, was strengthened, and Richard's son-in-law William Herbert held the Chief Justiceship there. Also, the Crown's York and Mortimer lands, Richard's possession now, lay along the Welsh border: a firm barrier. The Stanleys held the area from Wales to the north. Everything seemed secure, and in May Richard left London and moved to Nottingham again.

Spring wore on into summer, and we didn't know whether Tudor was deliberately delaying his invasion to fray our nerves, or whether he had had second thoughts. One huge second thought must have been given him when the Marquis of Dorset took his mother's advice and tried to come back to England to submit himself to Richard. Someone blabbed, of course, and he was captured, but we grinned at the thought of what a blow his attempt was to the conspirators. We heard, too, that Tudor had given up on Bess and was angling to marry Will Herbert's sister. So much for his high-flown oaths about healing the old 'divisions' in England.

Still, as time went on, it seemed he had not given up altogether, and by mid June Richard had taken what steps he could. Through the summer heat of 1485 we waited at Nottingham.

# Twenty

## Summer 1485

Lord Stanley was ill. Or so he said. Certainly he didn't look well as he faced Richard to ask permission to go home.

'Is it so unreasonable a request?' he said when Richard looked stonily at him.

'Not unreasonable. Untimely.'

Stanley wiped sweat from his face. 'Your Grace, I have been with you constantly since your coronation. In two years I have not been home. This weather disagrees with me, and I would not infect you or your men with some disease.'

'No, we would not want that.' Richard threw down the pen he had been pulling to pieces. 'My lord, Tudor is your stepson.'

'And therefore you doubt my loyalty.'

'I have not done so.'

The words seemed to hang in the air between them. At last Stanley said, 'You need not do so now.'

'What of your brother Sir William?'

'I feel no doubt of his loyalty.'

'A two-edged answer.'

'Not meant as such.'

'But this is a time when loyal men should be with me.' Richard picked up the mangled pen, stared at it, threw it down again. 'I am sick of this Tudor's pretensions and his vaunting claims to my throne. He is nothing and he has none of the rights he claims, but for the two years of my reign he has been a thorn in my side. I am going to end his menace once and for all and then I will be able to rule this country as I should, for the benefit of my people. If Tudor does in fact invade it will no doubt come to battle. I have never been defeated in battle and I doubt Tudor and his ragbag army will manage it. Treachery could overcome me, of course. Anyone in doubt of his loyalty should consider his prospects under an unknown Welshman whose rule would be unacceptable to the people of England. You and your brother have been loyal to me and I have made it plain I reward loyalty. I have been lenient with traitors, as your wife Lady Margaret has cause to know. I may in future be less lenient.'

Pale, Stanley said, 'You need not doubt my loyalty, Your Grace.'

'Good. But consider well that your request to go home now makes you suspect in men's eyes.'

Almost inaudibly Stanley said, 'I do consider that. I wish to – to consult with my brother.'

'Very well. You may go. But so greatly will I miss your presence that I must have some substitute. Send your son Lord Strange to join me in your place.'

'Sire, I shall. The moment I arrive home I …'

'Oh no, my lord. You may not leave until Lord Strange is here.'

'Then I will send for him at once, Your Grace.'

When Stanley had bowed himself out I said, 'Do you think he means to turn against you, Richard?'

'I don't know. How many times have the Stanleys turned their coats in the past thirty years? Five? Ten? But on the whole I think self-interest will keep Stanley loyal to me. And I will be holding his eldest son and heir as a safeguard.'

'The Stanleys between them could put as many as ten thousand men in the field. They are probably the biggest single factor. And our sweating friend is married to Tudor's mother.'

'I know. But what am I to do, Martin? Arrest them all on suspicion? That wouldn't uncover all their agents, but it would give Tudor cause. I suspect Stanley's brother. And I think he wants to go home to discover precisely how deeply his wife is implicated. I think – I hope – that self-interest will prevail and he'll stay loyal. Now send for Kendall, would you? It's time I wrote to London to have the Great Seal brought here.'

And nothing more would he say about Stanley. Lord Strange arrived, and to my surprise I found him a modest, likeable fellow. Edgy, though, and no wonder. He knew he was hostage for his father's loyalty, and I think he was none too sure of that loyalty. Nothing was said, of course; we were all on the best of terms.


In the second week in August we moved for a couple of days to Beskwood Lodge, out in Sherwood Forest. No sooner had we arrived there than John came running to find me. 'It's Mother! She's here!'

'Here? Whatever for?' Of course I thought at once of our other children. Martin was safe here with me – thirteen, he had begged to be allowed to come as my page, and over Innogen's disapproval I had allowed it – but the others were at Middleham, and we had heard there was sweating sickness in the north.

'She said she has to go to Bruges, there is something wrong in her wool business.' John shrugged; trade was a dreary matter to a lad of fifteen when England was in arms against an invader.

'Perhaps she has come to ask my permission to go. Wonders will never cease.' John laughed, for he knew I was soft as butter with my wife, I don't have it in me to be a domestic tyrant.

I found Innogen drinking cold ale with Richard, Martin attending upon them. 'Darling!' she said, kissing me. 'Martin, it's so tedious, it seems I must go to Bruges.'

'So John tells me. What's the matter?'

'Oh, so annoying! I've thought for a while my agent there wasn't being quite honest, and now I've had a letter – the agent has absconded with six months' takings, there is no one competent in charge. Martin, I have to go, it's not something I can deal with by letter. You don't mind, do you?'

'Of course not. I'm surprised you didn't simply go.'

'Oh well, it seems it might take some time to settle matters there,

I may be away a month or more. I wanted to see you, darling.' Butter wouldn't have melted in her mouth. 'And to see my boys. Are they behaving themselves?'

'Mo-ther,' Martin groaned, as boys do at this sort of maternal remark.

'They're being splendid,' Richard said. 'And no, Innogen, if it comes to battle they'll be left well behind, I won't see them in any danger. Have you seen the new book from Master Caxton?'

'*Le Morte D'Arthur*? Not until now.' She picked up the volume lying by Richard's hand. 'By Sir Thomas Malory. Is the book good?'

'Excellent so far as I've read.'

We chatted on like this, of literature and the wool trade, until time for supper.

We were going inside when a messenger crashed his sweating horse to a halt in the courtyard and ran up to Richard.

'Your Grace – news. Tudor has landed at Milford Haven in Wales.'

Richard held still, his face expressionless. 'Ah. So it has come. In Wales? So, we will see.'

'See what?' Martin asked as we followed Richard indoors.

'See how reliable are all the Welsh promises of loyalty to the King.'

But Martin was too young to conceive of the sort of treachery we feared, and he ran inside scoffing.

It was late by the time we chased the boys off to bed and could be private. It was a warm night, and close, so no one thought anything of it when Richard suggested we ride in the forest. He adroitly dismissed the usual attendants, and only the three of us went. When we were away from the Lodge, in a clearing deep into the forest, Richard reigned in his horse. 'Martin, I wrote to Innogen asking her to come.'

'I thought there was something. All that chatter about Malory … what's wrong?'

'I want Innogen to take my nephews abroad.'

'Ah …'

'Yes. She can easily do it, you see, without arousing suspicion; she is often back and forth to Bruges. Will you allow her to do it?'

I glanced at Innogen. She nodded thoughtfully.

'Of course. But Richard, how?'

He looked about as if suspecting spies lurking in the trees. By tacit consent we rode on, our horses' hooves and the jingle of the bridles covering our words. 'You know Sir Edward Brampton?' Again I nodded. He was Portuguese, a Jew who had converted to Christianity, and he had been a close friend of King Edward. As is the custom in such cases the King had stood godfather, and Brampton had adopted the King's Christian name. I knew him as a thoroughly reliable fellow. Clearly Richard thought so too, for he went on, 'Brampton is in my confidence about this matter. He's an experienced seaman, and clever. I trust him. And he has a vast acquaintanceship in Europe. As we speak, there is a ship about to put in down the Yorkshire coast. Brampton will get my nephews to the ship; Lincoln is in on the secret, of course. No one else knows. If you two agree, Innogen can hurry off to Bruges to see about her business there. She'll take a servant and a couple of apprentices: Brampton and the boys. No one will wonder at her going, it will seem an ordinary business journey.' He pulled off his hat, rubbing fretfully at his forehead. 'It's not a perfect scheme, but it's the best I can think of. The boys will go to my sister Margaret, of course.'

I thought about it. 'Yes. And of course we agree.' But the import of the plan battered at me. 'Richard, you don't believe – do you think this is necessary?'

He looked straightly at me, smiling a little. 'I hope it is not. I haven't given up, Martin; I haven't despaired. I've never yet lost a battle. Who knows, Tudor might turn tail and flee again. But I've been too trusting in the past, I've left too much to chance and my faith in other people. But if Tudor should defeat me, or if I should die, those boys are at risk. Tudor will have to marry Bess to shore up his claim to the throne. The moment he marries her, her brothers are dead. I'm taking no chances.'

'I see. Shouldn't you send Bess away too?'

His face went quite blank. 'If Innogen can convince her to go: certainly. But I doubt she will. We did not,' he said with pain, 'part on good terms.'

There was nothing to say to that. We turned our horses' heads about and began the ride back to Beskwood. 'I'll do it, of course,' said Innogen, 'and gladly.' None of us spoke the rest of the way back.

In bed that night, Innogen asked me, 'Sweetheart, what of the Stanleys? Richard told me of Lord Stanley needing so urgently to visit his home.'

'I don't know. We suspect Sir William, we're in doubt about Lord Tom. The thing is, of course, their lands run from Wales to the north. They could raise the whole west for Tudor.'

'Hmm. Who has Tudor got with him?'

'His uncle Jasper Tudor, of course, and the Earl of Oxford. Barkley and Arundel, I believe. Our friend Tom Grey, Dorset, was left behind in France as surety for Tudor's French loans.'

'An interesting reversal of fortune. Will Tudor pick up much support in Wales?'

'Some, of course. Rhys ap Thomas has vowed Tudor will have to pass over his very belly to get by him. The Vaughans and the Herberts are blocking the northeast ways out of Wales. Tudor might yet give up. Though I doubt it. Darling, since you must leave tomorrow, must we spend tonight talking of Tudor?'

'Why, no,' she said, and began to kiss me.

I remember that night's lovemaking so clearly. Innogen was thirty-five and had had seven pregnancies. It showed in the fine lines around her eyes, in the slackened flesh of her breasts and belly, in the grey strands in her hair; but to me that night she was as beautiful as the girl I had first made love to sixteen years before. I loved her, and I told her so as I wound my hands in her hair to pull her hard down on top of me. I loved her forever.

She had to leave early in the morning. Richard left Kendal frantically scribbling letters to Norfolk and Surrey, to Northumberland, Sir Robert Brackenbury, Francis Lovell, all the men who would bring troops to him, and strolled out into the courtyard with us.

'I hope your business in Bruges prospers, Innogen. Safe journey.'

'It will be. And yes, my business will go well, have no fear.' She turned away to kiss Martin and John. 'God keep you safe, my dear boys. I will see you soon.' Abruptly she turned back to Richard. For a moment she stared hard into his eyes, then she took his face between her hands and kissed his mouth. 'I love thee, Richard Plantagenet. May God have thee in his keeping.'

'And thee, my dear.'

It was time for her to go. We embraced, and I helped her up into the saddle. She said a sweet farewell, but as she turned her horse's head towards the gateway I saw that tears were streaming down her face.

We returned to Nottingham Castle that day. There was no telling which direction Tudor would take out of Wales, or how quickly he might advance. Richard ordered his commanders to muster at Leicester with all haste. One of the men so commanded was Lord Stanley, who was stationed with his men to the east of Shrewsbury, his brother a little further north. If they held loyal to Richard, they alone should be able to prevent Tudor penetrating far into England.

On Monday the fifteenth, the Feast of the Assumption of Our Lady, Lord Stanley sent a message that the sweating sickness prevented him joining Richard. And that night Lord Strange tried to escape.

It was Richard's nephew Lincoln who told us, and took us to the room where Strange was being held. The man drooped between two guards, his hands bound and blood drying at the corner of his mouth. He was dressed in the clothing of a lower servant, with one of the King's badges on his jerkin. Richard's lips thinned at the sight, and he lifted a knife from the table. Strange's eyes widened with fear as his King walked towards him with the knife in his hand, but Richard only looked at him in contempt and said, 'We'll have that off, for a start,' and slid the point of the knife under the stolen badge, cutting the hasty stitches and flicking the badge to the floor. Strange sagged with relief.

'Explain yourself,' Richard said.

'Need I?' Strange asked wearily.

'Probably not. You have somehow had word that your father and uncle have gone over to Tudor. Or did you know it all the time?'

'No!' cried Strange, and they stared at each other. 'Your Grace, yes I have had a message ... My uncle Sir William is for Tudor. Sir John Savage too. You know Sir Gilbert Talbot is also?'

'Yes. Who else?'

'Rhys ap Thomas.'

That cut Richard; he had trusted ap Thomas. 'He said Tudor would have to pass over his belly ... I daresay he meant it literally.'

'Yes. He submitted himself to Tudor. Lay down and invited Tudor to walk over him.'

'Which is something I have never asked of any subject. Go on.'

Strange hesitated, then almost defiantly burst out, 'Tudor is through Shrewsbury.'

'Right into England without let or hindrance. Who else is for him?'

'That's all I know of, Your Grace. Tudor has been advised not to try for London.'

'I see. And your father?'

'Is loyal to you. I swear it.' There was a long silence. Richard's eyes never left Strange's face. 'What – what will you do with me?'

'I don't know. But you will write to your father, my lord, here and now. Tell him that you tried to escape and were apprehended. Tell him that you have told me what you know. Tell him that by tomorrow his brother and Savage and the others who have aided Tudor will be proclaimed rebels and traitors. Tell him that if he is loyal to me he must prove it by coming to me with every last man he can raise, at once. And tell him that you are hostage for his loyalty. Tell him that your life is in his hands. Write, my lord.'

For some time there was no sound in the room but quickened

breathing and the scratching of Strange's pen. At last he held out the letter to Richard, who read it through, nodded, and said, 'I'll send it with some token your father will trust. Your ring, perhaps.' Trembling, Strange tugged the ring off his finger. Closing his hand over it Richard said, 'You realise your life goes with this letter?'

'Yes.'

'Very well. You'll be kept under guard.' He signed to Lincoln to take the man away.

Francis Lovell arrived next day. Coming up from the south he had gleaned a little news about Tudor's advance. 'Marching under the Red Dragon banner of Wales. The heir and hope of Cadwallader. Brutus and Arthur are mentioned often, even Uther Pendragon. Most glorious. A new identity for every area. Outside Wales he's the last hope of Lancaster.'

'Perhaps I should remind people,' said Richard dryly, 'that I am not only Duke of Lancaster but a good deal more Lancastrian by birth than Henry Tudor. Come to think of it, I'm Earl of Richmond too.'

'So you are. Can you muster some Welsh blood too?' Then Francis's brittle levity drained away. 'Richard, I have to tell you this. Tudor is issuing proclamations.'

'I know.'

'But do you also know he is styling himself King of England? His proclamations are headed "By the King" and he signs them Henricus Rex.'

It was the only time in those days I saw Richard angry. Angry – he lost his temper more violently than I had ever seen, as violently as ever his brother had done. It was Tudor's casual impertinence that did it, that meaningless assumption of rights he had done nothing to earn. You do not become King by saying so. By right of victory in battle, yes, but not even then is one truly king until the anointing with Holy Chrism. Not by vaingloriously saying so.

And all at once Richard received another blow. We were at

Beskwood again, trying to keep cool in the open air of the forest, when two riders approached.

'It's John Sponer from York, and John Nicholson, I think. I have sent for men from York, but ...'

'Your Grace.' The two men tumbled wearily from their horses and knelt before Richard. 'Your Grace, we've ridden as fast as we could from York – the city sent us.' Sponer's thick Yorkshire voice was sorely puzzled, even hurt. 'Your Grace, we are sure you have good reason, but the York Council is worried ... Your Grace, we heard days ago that this Tudor has landed and you are gathering men: so why haven't you sent to York for men?'

Richard turned so white I thought he would faint. I gripped his arm. He said, 'I always turn to my men of the north, before all others. Has York had no word from – from anyone?'

'No, Your Grace.' I think Sponer understood at once, from that hesitant question. 'Of course there's this sickness about up there, but it didn't prevent us ... No. No word.'

Tonelessly Richard said, 'I sent to Percy of Northumberland some days ago, telling him to bring in his own men and a contingent from York. I had trusted him to do so. I need my men from York.'

'We are ready, Your Grace,' said Nicholson. 'The Council has issued orders, every man is to get his weapons and armour ready to move at an hour's notice. It was all put in hand after yesterday's Council meeting. They only need the word. I'll ride back at once.'

'Please. I leave for Leicester on Friday. Could the York contingent be there by, say, Monday?'

'We'll be there Friday,' Nicholson promised. Richard smiled faintly.

'Monday will do. God bless you. Heaven bless my men of the North.'

Later Francis said, 'So Northumberland's turned traitor too.'

'Perhaps.'

'*Perhaps* – Richard!'

'Yes, all right. He has always resented me. But what can I do? He'll plead the sickness in the north, say his message to York inexplicably got lost or delayed – Sponer told me Northumberland's wife died only a couple of weeks ago, he'll plead his bereavement. I can prove nothing. Unless he simply fails to bring his men to me.'

'He wouldn't dare. He has to live in the north.'

'Yes,' said Richard, 'there is that, isn't there.'

Stanley and Northumberland had probably turned traitor. Yet that was the worst: Tudor raised little enough support on his blustering march into England, and all the other men Richard sent for came, in strength. When on the Friday we rode into Leicester we saw the banners of most of the great nobles of England: an army of some fifteen thousand.

We lodged at the White Boar inn in Guildhall Street, and there to greet us were the Howards, father and son, and Sir Robert Brackenbury with the London contingent. A message also awaited us, that Northumberland was on his way. He arrived that night when we were at supper. Clad in black for his wife, he listened wearily to our condolences, then asked to be excused.

'One moment,' Richard said. 'Harry, how many men have you brought?'

'Around three thousand. Lucky to have that many, there's this sickness all through the north.'

'So I gather. What about the York contingent?'

'On their way.' But he couldn't meet Richard's eye. They say in the north, 'No Prince but a Percy' – but in the past decade and a half he'd learnt the bitter lesson that he would always come second to a Neville.

'Brackenbury tells me,' Richard said carefully, 'that Hungerford and Bouchier slipped away on the march and joined Tudor.'

'Aye? Well, they're of little account. No one else has been beguiled by this Welshman.'

'I trust not,' said Richard, and Northumberland glowered for a moment, then asked again to be excused.

We set out from Leicester on the Sunday morning, the twenty-first of August, starting early so as to have the greater part of the march over before the heat of the day. There was just enough breeze to make the banners snap in the summer air, and as I paced to my horse I made note of them. Richard was riding out today with the full panoply of King of England. Seasoned campaigner though I was, I could yet thrill to the stern message of those banners. The Royal Arms of England. Richard's battle standard with the Cross of St George. The badge of York and his own Blanc Sanglier. In a calculated sting to the slinking invader, the banners of Lancaster and Richmond. Then in every colour created under heaven, the arms of England's nobility: the silver lion of Norfolk, my own rose and harts' head, Lovell's hound, Stanley's eagle's foot, Northumberland's crescent moon; oh, I can't list them all. The arms of the earls of Lincoln, Surrey, Kent, Nottingham, Shrewsbury, Westmorland; Lord Zouche and Lord Ferrers, Lord Dudley and Lord Maltravers, Francis's kinsman Lord Fitzhugh, Lord Grey, Sir Henry Bodrugan from Cornwall, the twenty or so Knights of the Household, the northern lords and knights, the Spanish knight Juan de Salazer, and all the others.

The people of Leicester were enjoying the show, but they wanted the King. At eight of the clock they got him, and cheered to see him. He was in full armour, of course, with the tabard whose red, gold and blue again displayed the Royal Arms. He carried his helmet, and on his dark hair was the crown. Not the coronation crown, of course; this was the coronet of red-gold trefoils with diamonds and a single great ruby. Another ruby flared on his hand as, smiling, he saluted the crowd.

John and Martin stood by Richard's stirrup, the epitome of military smartness – the previous night they had made the mistake of begging to march with us today, and had nearly been packed off back to Nottingham. Richard said, 'Very impressive,' in an amused voice, and gave Martin a hug. We had said our farewells privately, at breakfast, but now Richard embraced John and kissed him. All the bystanders cooed; somehow people never expect a monarch to do anything so ordinary as kiss his son farewell.

Then Richard mounted. With a last kiss for Martin I swung up into my saddle. Trumpets blared the signal. Richard lifted his hand, said, 'Ride on,' as casually as he always did, and on a swelling cheer from the townspeople we left Leicester.

It was a typical August day: high summer, the sun blazing from a clear blue sky. As we made our way down the Kirkby Mallory road I thought of that May march to Tewkesbury fourteen years earlier. Common soldiers could strip off against the heat, but this time we had to swelter in our armour. My head aching with heat, I tried to count up the number of times I had marched with Richard under the White Boar banner and the Lilies and Leopards of England – '69, when Warwick had taken Edward prisoner; in Wales; pursuing Clarence and Warwick down to the coast; down from Ravenspur; at Barnet and Tewkesbury; all the years we had kept the north; the campaigning against the Scots; mopping up after Buckingham's abortive rebellion. I couldn't make a total, there were too many patrols and skirmishes besides the major campaigns. It was only the heat beating down from a sky like baked blue enamel, but it seemed I heard Edward cheering his men on to Tewkesbury; saw George of Clarence riding beside us trying to joke with his little brother. It seemed I heard again John Milwater saying 'I'll follow the White Boar till the end of my life,' and morbidly I wondered if this time I was riding to the end of mine.

We halted at Kirkby Mallory to eat and let the men get at the ale barrels. Trying to wipe the pouring sweat from his eyes Richard said, 'The scurriers say the Stanleys are holding their positions, they're at Stoke Golding and Shenton. Tudor is said to be moving, he might still think of trying to give us the slip and head for London. What's the next village, Sutton Cheney? It's on a ridge, from there we can keep them in view. The nearest large town is Market Bosworth away to the northwest.'

As he spoke a scout galloped up to say that Tudor was moving – not for London but up towards us, heading for an area called Redemore Plain.

'Send to Lord Stanley to bring his men to join me at once.'

Wearily Richard pulled his helmet on again, and gave the signal to move on.

We camped that night with our army strung out north-south in three wings, Richard's, Northumberland's, Norfolk's, running from the eastern end of that ridge they call Ambien Hill. Lord Stanley was to our south, and looking to the west we could see Sir William Stanley and Tudor's army. The ground between was marshy and low-lying, tilting westward. The configuration of the ground would protect our flanks if Lord Stanley moved against us, and in the morning we would occupy Ambien Hill, from where we could strike downwards to the northwest or southwest.

It was an ordinary commanders' conference Richard held that night. He was confident, and calm; but we all knew that if Northumberland declared for Tudor, or simply failed to fight with us, we would be hard-pressed to match the enemy numbers. What either or both Stanleys would do was anyone's guess, but their numbers would be decisive.

The bustle of the camp at night was comforting because it was familiar and normal. Campfires twinkled as the men began to cook their meals, there was the usual singing and the hum of gossiping voices. With night had come blessed coolness, and as we did the rounds of our troops it could have been the eve of any battle.

Yet I could not sleep. Never before had I been so aware of the stink of treachery. I kept futilely going over and over the numbers: if Northumberland turned traitor, if Stanley did ... We had perhaps fifteen thousand men. Tudor had only half that – therefore he was depending on the Stanleys. On one at least of the Stanley brothers. Richard had reigned two years and a month, and he had done it well, yet in the first real test it seemed we were surrounded by a fog of doubts. Looking down towards Northumberland's camp I noticed his banners with the Crescent Moon, and with a chill I remembered an incident on the march here. At the bridge where the road turned sharply we were crammed briefly against the stone wall, and I'd seen

Richard's mailed foot strike sparks from that wall. An old man had leapt up from nowhere behind the wall, a rustic old idiot in rags, cackling and mowing and bleating some nonsense about 'the foot becomes the head'. Meaningless nonsense, but then he had cried 'Beware the moon when it changes.' Nonsense again, it was the time of the full moon – but now I looked at that Crescent Moon of Northumberland, and wondered.

About to go to my tent and try to rest if not sleep, I walked slap into a man similarly patrolling.

'Richard.'

'Martin. Can't sleep? Nor can I.'

'Battle fears?'

'Battle fears. Remember before Barnet? I was shitting myself with terror.'

'*You* were! I couldn't leave the latrines for hours!' We laughed ruefully together.

'Edward said he was afraid too, though somehow I've always doubted it. Remember how he talked that night, about the King's duty, responsibility … A good thing we can't see the future, isn't it. Martin, I'm so afraid. God help me, I'm so afraid!'

Inadequately I said, 'We all are.'

'Yes – yes. I never wanted it to come to this. I should have done things differently, so many times. Martin, there is so much I want to do, so much to achieve. Two years, and I've done so little. Two years of niggling threats and uprisings distracting me from my real work. I want this over. I want to be free to rule. Yet – if it goes against us tomorrow, Martin, I won't retreat. This matter will be settled tomorrow, with my death or this Welshman's.'

'Richard …'

'I don't expect to die. I don't want to. But nor am I afraid to. Yet I can see no future.'

Frightened, I said, 'There is a future, Richard! So much work to be done, so many things to achieve. Your daughter is married, you might have a grandchild soon.'

'Yes, I might. I'd like that. Remember how we said I would have to marry again? I've had the offer from Portugal, they are offering me Princess Joanna, and Manuel of Bega for Bess. Even Spain is casting out lures. There could be more children, I suppose. An heir.' He was talking to himself rather than to me, but suddenly he said, 'I don't want to leave my country to this unknown Welshman. He knows nothing of England, nothing of what it means to be King. Without right of blood, he would rule by tyranny, the country would be back in the civil wars and bloodshed of thirty years ago. So I must win tomorrow.'

Suddenly we both yawned. Richard said, 'Get some sleep.'

'I won't sleep.'

'Nor will I. Rest, though. Martin, I have known you all my life, only those two years in our childhood we were apart. Thirty-three years of friendship. I've been lucky in that, in friendship; lucky in my friends. You are my best friend and I love you.'

'I too have been lucky in my friends. Lucky in your friendship. You are my dearest friend, Richard. I love you.'

We tried to laugh at all this intensity, then suddenly we were hugging desperately. I felt his slight body shivering, or trembling. Battle fears, or something more.

'God have you in His keeping, Martin.' He kissed me and traced the Cross on my brow. 'God keep you safe, my friend.'

'And you, Richard my dear friend.'

Sunrise was at five. Armed, I went to the King's tent. I knew at once that Richard hadn't slept, any more than I had. He looked deathly pale, and although he said he wasn't hungry, to please us he ate some bread and drank a little watered wine. Someone said something about Norfolk, and Richard spun about.

'Norfolk? What?'

'It's nothing,' said Norfolk himself, striding in with his son behind him. 'A stupid rhyme pinned to my tent in the night.'

'Saying what?'

Reluctantly Norfolk held out the ragged paper. 'Jockey of

Norfolk, be not so bold, for Dickon thy master is bought and sold.'

Richard raised an eyebrow, his sole comment. Norfolk crumpled the paper and threw it away.

There was some trouble with the priests, with Mass; first the wine was ready but not the bread, then by the time they found the bread the wine was missing. Our men were muttering that it was an ill omen so Richard said, 'Any man who wishes to will find he can take Mass. But either our cause has God's blessing, or it has not.' There were some shocked faces at that, and he raised his voice to carry to all the leaders now grouped around his tent. 'Any man who fears to fight for me today can go; so be it. For you should all know that I have tried to rule this country as a just prince, for my people's good, and sometimes I have turned men against me. I have been lenient, but I will be no longer. There will always be justice where I rule; mercy may be harder come by. If I sinned in taking the crown, that sin is on my head and none other, but I have not committed the sins my enemies accuse me of. Yet I have been beleaguered throughout my reign by this Welsh milksop who covets my crown and my realm, and who comes with his rabble of beggarly Bretons and faint-hearted Frenchmen to try to seize it.

'This battle today is a symbol of the creeping treachery that has surrounded me since I took the Crown. Let me say, therefore, that there will be no more of it. This battle is to the death, mine or Tudor's. Should he win, then I weep for England, for Tudor will have to rule by fear and by force, and he will find the Crown rests uneasy on his head. You are my friends and I have trusted you all. If you cannot find it in your hearts to trust me and fight for me with whole hearts, then consider what I have said. And like valiant champions, advance your standards and see if your enemies can try the title of battle by dint of sword.'

For a moment not a man moved or spoke, then, as one, we cheered. Richard's stern face broke into its swift, sweet smile. 'Thank you,' he said simply. 'Now finish arming, get ready. We move out within the hour.'

As he turned away a messenger said nervously, 'Sire, Lord Stanley sends his answer. He says — he says he has other sons.'

A shocked murmur went up. Richard was perfectly still for a moment, then he said casually, 'Then it shall be as he wills. Now we know. Take Lord Strange and execute him. Anywhere. Now.'

'Richard ...' Francis said. 'Richard, don't.'

'I ... Very well — one more message to Lord Stanley. He is to bring his men up *now*, and his son's life depends on his conduct in this battle.' The messenger went away, looking backward over his shoulder.

It was time. Just before we went to mount up, Richard's squire handed him his weapons, then knelt before him holding out a square wooden box. We looked on, puzzled, as Richard put on his helmet then reached into the box.

'Richard, no!'

'Your Grace, you cannot ...'

'Man, you're mad!'

For it was the Crown. Ignoring us all Richard bent his head and the squire fitted the circlet around his helmet.

'Richard,' I cried, aghast, tugging at his arm, 'you cannot wear that in battle! Christ, man, it'll mark you out, you'll be every man's target! Don't do it!'

In silence he mounted his horse. Then, looking down at me, he said, 'I am King of England. Whether I live or die today, I do it as the anointed King of England. God keep you safe, my friends.'

Norfolk and Surrey led the van, some fifteen hundred archers flanked by spears-men and artillery, the cannon chained together; I wished we had brought more guns from the Tower arsenal. Slowly they went forward to the western extremity of that ridge, then down onto the edge of the plain. Under Richard's command the centre, thousands strong and with a large mounted contingent, moved forward along the ridge. Northumberland moved the rear-guard into position.

We could clearly see Tudor's force, and Sir William Stanley to the north. There was quite a large force of Scots fighting for Tudor, I noticed. The Earl of Oxford was leading the enemy vanguard, we could see his banners with the Star with Streamers that had caused so much havoc at Barnet. He was forced to attack on a narrower front than he would have liked, with the marsh constricting his right flank. He was having to attack upwards, looking at an angle into the sharp morning sun.

Our archers fired, then the enemy's. The two vanguards met, and it was hand-to-hand fighting all along the line. Oxford had formed his men into solid wedges around the standards; provided the men hold, this is one of the most difficult formations to attack. Ominously, Norfolk's line was bending, giving way in the centre. Richard ordered more men down in support. Norfolk spread his line further, trying to swing the flanks round upon the enemy centre. He needed more men. Richard despatched them, and I knew he was thinking of the thousands whom the Stanleys held motionless, joining neither side. We needed them, but would they fight for us?

Norfolk and Surrey were in trouble. About to dispatch yet more men Richard suddenly lifted his arm in the signal and galloped down into the fray. Desperately we pelted after him. I noticed the man beside me was John Kendal, Richard's secretary, and I knew he'd never fought before. His armour didn't fit him well; I wondered who he had borrowed it from. That was my last conscious thought for some time, it was like every other battle, act and react and do what damage you can. The enemy lines were giving way before our assault. We fought on, and I saw Richard by that damned conspicuous crown. His tabard with the Royal Arms was solid red now, his right arm was blood-soaked to the shoulder. So was mine, I had used both axe and sword, and my lance. How long we fought I don't know, as usual in battle it could have been a very short time or many hours, but then Richard was leading us back up onto that ridge.

Frantically we yelled for water, and I snatched the chance to take my helmet off and wring the sweat out of my hair. A runner seized Richard's arm and shouted news – Norfolk was down. Killed. Richard said, 'Jock!' in a tone of great grief, then, 'Surrey?'

'Holding.'

'Send down more men. Tell Northumberland to move his men down now.' The runner scurried away. Richard grabbed a water bottle, drank deep, then poured the rest over his head. 'The Stanleys?' he asked anyone who could hear.

'Have not moved. Richard, look. Down there.' I turned to follow Francis's outflung arm. Richard's eyes narrowed.

'Tudor. Right down there behind his lines. Not going to dirty his hands with battle. All alone with his little bodyguard. Right.' He stood up in his stirrups, pitching his voice to carry to all of us, the Knights of his Household. 'Tudor is back behind the main force, only a small guard. Take him and the day is ours. It's a risk because it means riding right across the face of Sir William Stanley's force, but they've not moved yet. Five minutes, gentlemen; less, with luck. A few minutes and it is over. Who's with me?'

It was a mad risk, but none of us hesitated. The cry went up. Richard grinned and snapped his visor down. William Parker his standard-bearer moved to his place and the trumpets blew one short command. Then we were off, down the slope of the hill and across that plain, riding straight for Henry Tudor. I heard the ancient battle cries, the galloping hooves. I swear I even heard the small crack of the banners in the wind. It was a risk, it was dangerous, it was wonderful.

I swung my sword in my hand, and felt myself smiling as I took the first of Tudor's guard. I laughed at their terrified, disbelieving faces. I wanted to shout, Yes, this is the King of England fighting for his country, not your bedraggled Welsh pretender. A man moved forward: Tudor's standard-bearer. Richard rode straight at him, and took his head off with one blow. The Red Dragon banner was down. I saw a skinny man backing away, and knew by the tabard it must be Tudor himself.

I urged my horse forward, my sword avid for blood. One of Tudor's men leapt in front of me, and my horse reared so that I had to clutch the mane not to be flung off. I fumbled for the reins, but they were useless, cut through. My horse turned again, blood pouring from a gash across its neck. Desperately I tried again to urge it forward, but it was dying, and panicking as it died it carried me back away from Richard. I screamed, and my horse went down. I screamed again, for my right foot was trapped under the horse and pain was spearing through my head.

I saw red, and thought it blood or the rage of battle. No. It was the red of Stanley's men, a great wave of them galloping down on Richard. Someone grabbed me, and I freed my arm and thrust with my dagger.

'No! Martin!' I had nearly killed Francis Lovell. 'Come on!'

'I'm trapped – my foot – Francis, go to Richard, leave me, go to Richard!'

'No, Martin!' He got his hands under my shoulders and heaved, and with blinding pain I was free. I tried to stand, and fell.

'Ride to Richard!'

But Francis was crying, he wouldn't listen. He manhandled me up onto his horse, and I saw why we could not go to help our friend. I knew Richard by the Crown and by the fury with which he fought to his death, a figure red from head to foot. I saw him cut down an enormous man and by his size thought he was Edward come to aid his brother, then knew him for Sir John Cheney. Cheney was down and Richard had Tudor within his sword's length.

But the Stanley men were on him, hundreds of them. All after that one valiant fighting figure. I heard the last word he spoke, I heard him cry, 'Treason! Treason! Treason!' as the Stanleys overwhelmed him. I heard the other cries of hatred and blood-lust, and I saw the blades cut into my friend. I heard the axes and hammers as they smashed into his armour. I saw and heard Richard die.

Lovell put his horse's head about and spurred it into flight.

# *Twenty-one*

Of course we were not the only ones fleeing. All around us dazed survivors – incredibly, the vanquished – were limping, running, riding away. There was no organised pursuit yet, and soon we halted and secured a second horse. We looked back then. Tudor's banner was up again, and I dared not think what kept Stanley's men so horribly busy underneath it. Northumberland, who had not moved during the battle, was leading his troops down Ambien Hill and across the plain towards Tudor. So too was Lord Stanley. It was still very early, and they cast long shadows across the red earth. No one had begun to collect the dead, and you could trace the battle's progress from the concentration of the bodies.

'Shouldn't we look for …'

'They are all dead, Martin. All our friends are dead.'

It was incomprehensible. 'Rob?'

'I saw him die. And Jock Howard, John Kendal, Robert Brackenbury, Dick Ratcliffe, Fitzhugh, Scrope … They are all dead.'

I had fought only for Edward IV and Richard III, so defeat bewildered me. I didn't know the rules. 'What are we to do?'

'We must get to Leicester and get those boys safely away.'

It shows you what state I was in, that I had forgotten their existence. My son and stepson. Richard's son. 'But where shall we go? What do we do?'

'We'll go to the Duchess of York at Berkhamsted. After that, I don't know.'

We halted past Market Bosworth to strip off our armour. At a well we drank, and washed as best we could, then in a wide circuitous route we made for Leicester.

On the stairs of the White Boar we ran into the landlord, and

God knows what we looked like, for he recoiled, flinging up his crossed arms.

Quickly Francis said, 'It's Lord Lovell and Lord Robsart. We have to fetch those two boys away, and no one must know they were here.'

'My lords, what's happening? People are saying ...'

'The day is lost. King Richard is dead.' The man sank down on the stairs, crossing himself. 'Sir, if you were loyal to the King, saddle the boys' horses and provide us with two more mounts and some food.' Francis tugged the jewelled cross from around his neck. 'Here's payment for your help and your silence.'

'I don't want paying! But my lord, who – who is king now?'

'Tudor.' Francis led me upstairs.

We were only just in time. John and Martin were leaning from the window to peer down the street. 'They're coming!' John said in excitement. 'My father's coming, hear them cheer? He's – Martin, they are the wrong banners! They're dragon banners, not my father's!'

I grabbed him and spun him around into my arms, pressing his face against my breast. I was only just in time, for indeed his father was coming.

They had stripped King Richard's body naked, without the decency even to cover his privy member. They had flung his body over a donkey, and they must have broken his spine to make the body hang there. Between his trailing arms his beautiful hair hung down to the ground, clotted with mud and blood and brains. Not an inch of his body was free from breaks and gashes, for they had taken their vengeance long after he was dead. They had put his herald, Gloucester Herald, up on the donkey before him, making the poor beaten weeping boy display his king, a felon's halter around his neck. Thus did King Richard come to his last resting place.

They flung Richard's body down onto the cobbles of the market square. After the first massed gasp of shock the townspeople watched in silent disbelief. Some Stanley men and their camp-followers kicked the body, spat, threw a few things. The thin man wearing Richard's crown watched, perhaps meditating on kingship.

John was shivering in my arms. He kept saying, 'Is my father, is my father ...'

'My dearest boy, I am sorry, so sorry. Your father is dead. He died fighting most valiantly, like a soldier and a king, and only treachery overcame him. Now you must be brave, a king's son, for we must get you away, your father charged me with your care.' But shock had turned him useless, and it was left to Martin, sickly green and weeping, to gather their belongings and wrap him in a cloak. Francis put things together for himself and me, and he took some of Richard's possessions: a bag of coins, jewellery, the two books he had brought to Leicester, a gold collar of York white roses with the White Boar pendant. They were John's now, and perhaps his only inheritance.

True to his word the landlord had four horses saddled and bridled, and as we mounted he gave us water bottles and a bundle of food, and wished us Godspeed. As we rode mildly out of the street, Stanley men were converging on the inn.

Then we rode hard. It's, what, fifty or sixty miles from Leicester to Berkhamsted, and for fear of pursuit we dared not take the main roads. I suppose it took us three days, but I remember little of the journey, I was ill with shock and in such pain and near blind from that head wound. I do remember that in my rare lucid moments I tried to plan how to break the news to the Duchess – but the news had outrun us, and when at last I stumbled down from my horse at Berkhamsted the Duchess took me in her arms, and it was she who comforted me. Not that there was, for a long time, any comfort.

The nuns put me to bed and tended me, but it was another three days before I could string a coherent sentence together. It must have been the seventh day after the battle, for the nuns were singing the Requiem Mass for Richard. I should have gone to the little church, but instead I sat in the garden with my son Martin to wait for the Duchess.

I had last seen her in June, when I had accompanied Richard here on his way to Nottingham. Grief had diminished her, and I was aware as never before of her great age. I didn't know what to say to her. I heard myself stammering an apology for the way I had acted when we arrived. Taking my hand she said, 'You were Richard's friend and you loved him. Martin, the others have told me everything that happened, and we will not refer to it again, please. It is a bitter thing to outlive one's children; I've only Margaret and Elizabeth now. I have outlived all my sons. None of them lived long, Richard was not quite thirty-three. I was against my husband claiming the crown back in '59, for I knew it would be his death warrant. I never foresaw that it would be his sons' also.

'Now, the Mother Superior has had official news of the battle, and there is something I must tell you. You and Francis have been attainted as traitors.'

'Traitors!'

'Yes. This Tudor is dating his reign from the day before the battle. Thus, he can call all the men who fought for the King traitors, and attaint them.'

I didn't believe her, for it was unbelievable, it ran counter to every law and precept. I thought grief must have unhinged her, or she had turned senile. But Francis nodded, saying, 'It's a typical usurper's trick. Having no right, he has no regard for law. And it's a neat way to fill his coffers, all those sequestered estates; at the least, hefty fines. You and I are attainted traitors with a price on our heads. It is a new world, Martin.'

His words made me realise that everything I had known was gone. Richard, Anne, my friends, Middleham, London, Westminster, the north, the House of York. All gone.

But I had my wife and children, and Richard's son. 'We must leave England. We'll go to Bruges. Innogen is there. She took Richard's nephews the Lords Bastard there.'

The Duchess's eyes sparked. 'Ah. Yes, I thought Richard would do something like that. Very sensible. Tudor says he will marry Bess. Yes, go to Bruges. Soon Tudor will remember my existence and send to see if a harmless old nun is harbouring traitors.'

'But madam,' I interrupted her, 'what of Richard's burial, his funeral ...'

She bent her head over our clasped hands. 'The Grey Friars in Leicester have taken his body. They have given him burial.'

I couldn't understand. 'But he was King! He must be buried in the Abbey or at Windsor, there must be the proper rites ...'

'Martin,' said Francis, 'it is done. Tudor calls Richard a traitor, too, with no right to the throne of England. Burial in a little church in Leicester is all he deserves, in Tudor's eyes. And – and his soul is with Our Lord.'

There was a long silence. At last the Duchess said, 'It is time for you to go. Go to Colchester; I have friends there who will see you onto a ship, there will be no difficulties. You will be a pair of foreign merchants, I think, here on a matter of trade. Leave it to me.' She rose and laid her hand gently on my head. 'Richard was lucky in his friends, Martin. Unlucky in much else. But he was a good King, although God granted him little time to prove himself. I doubt we will meet again, my dear. I have loved you. Go with God, Martin.'


It was as she said, and her immaculate planning saw two Flemish merchants and their apprentices safely to Colchester and thence aboard ship for the Low Countries. Fellow passengers observed that one of the merchants was a martyr to seasickness and had recently sustained injuries. His partner explained the latter of these ills as due to a misunderstanding in a Southwark tavern.

Two weeks after Richard's death we entered my wife's house in Bruges. All my family was there. Innogen had known, you see. That day at Beskwood Lodge she had somehow known beyond doubt that Richard would lose the battle and die, and that I would survive. She had therefore taken all our children, and all the gold and portable possessions she could manage. And a good thing she did, for I was under attainder – still am, so far as I know – and Tudor seized my estates, from the rich lands Edward IV granted me with my earldom to the little family manor I left in 1461 to begin this story. He also seized Innogen's Beauclere and Shaxper estates, and the English end of her wool business; so much for the Yorkist ideal of protecting the rights of womenfolk.

I suppose that is almost the end of my story. It has taken me two years to write, it's 1507 now. And for the years between 1485 and now?

We lived in Burgundy, with Margaret, from 1485, but times changed and although Margaret did her best for us, Tudor's treaties negated her influence and it was safer for us to leave. No one wanted a group of embittered exiles dedicated to the overthrow of England's king; in fact, Tudor wanted us handed over to him. He wanted me in particular.

And why, you might ask, did we come to Scotland of all places? Well, our son Martin offered us a home with him in Venice, but Italy seemed too foreign. Our son Richard came to Scotland with Prince Richard – who, I fear will be known to history as the impostor Perkin Warbeque – and like his namesake married a Scottish girl. When the Prince's ill-starred invasion failed and he was captured, my Richard managed to make his way back here. He is on good terms with the new King, James IV, and with his permission offered us a home. So here we are. Perhaps if I ever look back over these writings I should excise some of my comments about the Scots and their late king, for Scotland has been kind to us in our exile. I like King James, who in return for snippets of political information and military advice has granted us an island in the west. I say granted, but I insisted on paying for it in hard cash, with the deeds of sale properly witnessed; I have seen what can happen to property granted at a king's pleasure. Besides, four years ago the King married Tudor's daughter Margaret – she reminds me of her mother, my little Bess – but although the younger generation are safe Innogen and I feel it wiser to live discreetly. I have even learnt to speak a little Scots and Gaelic, enough to know what a curiosity I am: the old English Earl who once led an army against his new home.

For the rest – well, I have largely kept out of English politics, for it is no longer my country. Francis Lovell felt differently, and as soon as he had conferred with Duchess Margaret he returned to England and set about fomenting rebellions against Tudor. He did quite well on the whole, there was the '86-87 business of the boy they pretended was the Earl of Warwick, and Tudor was badly rattled by the degree of support they won.

John of Lincoln, who had initially come to terms with Tudor, in '87 tore off the mask and joined Francis, and they brought Tudor's forces to battle at Stoke. Again Tudor owed his victory to the Stanleys, and Lincoln died in the battle. Francis disappeared after Stoke – officially disappeared, that is. He was declared dead, but for a corpse he was pretty lively when he visited me in Burgundy. Later he was involved in the Prince's rebellion, and later he came to Scotland. He is dead now. I miss him; I would like to have one friend from the old days.

Bess too is dead. She died in childbed four years ago. For all I had not seen her since that last summer, '85, it was a bitter blow. I loved her, that little girl who kissed me the first time she met me. Poor girl, I fear she never knew much happiness with Tudor. He married her in January of '86, and by September she was the mother of a son, grandiloquently called Arthur. He married Catherine of Aragon, daughter of Isabella and Ferdinand of Spain, the same girl who was once tentatively offered as bride to Richard's son. Arthur died a year or two ago, of what cause I never heard, but there is another son, called Henry, and the two daughters Mary and Margaret. For all his cant about uniting the white rose of York with the red rose of Lancaster, Tudor was loath to have Bess crowned; not until '87, and he had his son, did he yield to popular indignation. He didn't bother to attend her coronation, however, and he kept poor Bess in the background breeding heirs, and the real queen was his mother Margaret Beaufort. People have to address Tudor as 'Your Majesty' now. 'Your Grace' was good enough for every king in England's history, but not for this usurping upstart.

Bess's sisters were mostly married safely off, although Bridget is a nun somewhere in Kent, I believe.

To marry Bess, Tudor repealed Richard's *Titulus Regius*, and he repealed it unread so the issue of her bastardy quietly lapsed. But as Richard foresaw, that made Bess's brothers legitimate – and I have informants at Westminster who tell me Tudor's rage was a wonder to behold when he realised those boys were nowhere to be found. What sort of fool does he think Richard was? Tudor threatened Lincoln with the Tower, with torture, with the block; Lincoln looked him in his cold grey eye and stolidly repeated that he knew nothing of the Lords Bastard.

What did happen to them, you ask? Well, Innogen and Sir Edward Brampton got them smoothly to Burgundy, and their aunt Margaret took them under her wing and housed them discreetly out of sight. The elder boy, Edward, came much under the influence of Margaret's friend the Bishop of Cambrai, and decided to take holy orders. He went to Germany, and perhaps Italy would have been a better choice for its warm climate, for his health was never good. He died some years back. Even now I would be wiser not to write down his place of burial, or the name on his headstone. We had to keep moving the other boy, Richard, around Europe as Tudor got wind of him and redoubled his efforts to capture him. Brampton took him to Portugal, then he lived in Tournai with the de Warbeques, Portuguese friends of Brampton's, later in Bruges and in Malines with his aunt. It goes to my heart to remember him, for he was so unmistakably Edward's son, six feet tall at eighteen, strongly built, with Edward's eyes and his dark blond hair; and his determination. From his sixteenth birthday he worked with Duchess Margaret to reclaim the throne of England. In the end I helped, though in a luke-warm way because his bastardy stuck in my throat; but yes, I helped. Of that business I will say nothing more, for it is not my story and I hesitate to commit what I do know to paper. Some surprising people were drawn into the web of conspiracy around the Prince – his mother Elizabeth Woodville exchanged letters and tokens to be sure it was indeed her son, then she was one of the most active plotters.

Tudor found out, and with loving care for his mother-in-law stripped her of all her possessions, even the modest pension Richard gave her, and clapped her into that Bermondsey nunnery, a prisoner. She died there in 1492. Another one, much more astonishing, was Sir William Stanley. Disaffected with the man he had made king, he was prowling about Europe asking questions. Thinking him a Tudor spy we made sure he learned nothing, but he picked up enough snippets to tell a friend that if the Prince were indeed the son of Edward IV he would not fight against him. That was enough for Tudor, and it was off with Stanley's head. Others died too, and many sympathisers turned out to be spying for Tudor, but there was much support for the Prince. Much good it did him. Prince Richard wasn't one-tenth the soldier his father and uncle were, and although I did my best to advise him otherwise he insisted on leading an army of Scots down into England. I think that damned his cause, for people looked askance at a King-pretender who came with our traditional enemies. He didn't even die in battle, poor boy. Abandoned, he was captured and given over to Tudor. He was beheaded in 1499. I wonder if he met his sister Bess again before he was put to death? I wonder too what passed between him and Tudor. Did he tell the truth of who he was? I think he did, for not even a child would believe the garbled story Tudor put about, that the Prince was merely another 'feigned boy', some common lad cleverly coached to pass himself off as royal. And it was not until the Prince was safely dead that Tudor dared openly to accuse my poor Richard of murdering King Edward's sons. Not that Tudor could even do it thoroughly – James Tyrell died a handful of years ago, and Tudor let it be known that Tyrell had 'confessed' to performing the murder on Richard's behalf. But was the 'confession' ever published? No. Was Tyrell brought to trial for the alleged deed? No. Was there ever any public enquiry into the matter? No. But of course the tale is becoming common currency, another nail in the coffin of Richard's reputation. The good king who cared for his people and passed good laws has become a usurping tyrant and murderer of innocent children. Soon he will be accused of murdering everyone who died in his lifetime, and Tudor will be England's saviour.

Speaking of the Stanleys and other traitors: Thomas Lord Stanley was quickly made Earl of Derby and loaded with rewards; but I wonder how far his stepson trusts him. Doctor Morton flourished, of course: Bishop of Ely and Tudor's closest adviser. The Earl of Northumberland won little trust from Tudor by his betrayal of Richard, and in 1489 Tudor sent him north to gather taxes (could the man possibly have a sense of humour?) The men of the north have not forgotten their good lord Richard, nor would they forgive the man who betrayed him. Northumberland was set upon and murdered.

The sweating sickness Tudor's men brought to England claimed many victims. One was Richard's daughter Katherine. She outlived her father by barely a month.

George's son the Earl of Warwick was kept a prisoner in the Tower since Tudor's accession. In '99 Tudor executed him, allegedly for supporting 'Warbeck'. His sister Lady Margaret is married to Sir Richard Pole, a friend of Tudor's and a man of no account. At least she is safe.

Duchess Elizabeth of Suffolk also died in 1503; odd, that the last women of Richard's family, his sisters and his niece, should die in the same year. Elizabeth's sons do their best to keep the White Rose alive, but it will come to nothing. Too much has changed, and like Tudor in his time they live on sufferance, useful pawns to the monarchs of Europe.

The Duchess of York died in 1495. She was eighty. Anne's mother Lady Warwick died in 1492.

And my own family? Innogen still owns her business in Burgundy, and is famous for a rich, exquisite type of cloth. She bought a ship, too, and trades all over the Mediterranean. She sailed to Venice once, and on to Cyprus and even Turkey. My two elder children are married, and I have five grandchildren. Richard took his degree from the Sorbonne at sixteen and is a Doctor of Laws; or was, for he seems to do little here in Scotland but hang around the Court.

His twin, Alison, is almost as learned, and was Duchess Margaret's lady-in-waiting and protégé. Against my will, she is a nun now. Philippa married one of Innogen's Shaxper connections, the nephew of her first husband. Widowed now, Philippa lives in Warwickshire, and we hear little from her. William inherited Innogen's stomach, not mine, and went to sea at twelve. He has his own ship now.

My stepson John also went to sea, but not so willingly. He turned intractable and hard to manage – who can blame him – resenting the promises that bound him to stay out of trouble; resenting too the bastardy that prevented him raising his father's banner as the true heir to England. In the end we indentured him to a ship's master and bundled him off on a year's trading journey around the Mediterranean. He jumped ship at Alexandria and we heard nothing for three years, then one day he strode into the house, brown, grown-up, with an earring and stories that grow taller with every telling. He says he fought as a mercenary for the Emperor, was the lover of the Doge's wife, sailed down the Nile, made money trading in Ireland. Certainly he has money, and certainly he is again the dear, gentle boy I loved. My informants in England wrote that Tudor had Richard's illegitimate son imprisoned in the Tower, and executed him for some part in the Prince's invasion. But the story is muddled; if there is any truth to it, perhaps there was another son, born perhaps to some girl in the north or over on the Welsh border. I don't know. But John is downstairs as I write this; he is safe.


So there you are. I was a boy of little account until friendship, and fate, raised me high. Now I am of no account again, a tired old English exile. Sometimes I hardly remember that I am an Earl, a Knight of the Bath and of the Garter, and was the friend of two kings. To my heart's sorrow I have outlived most of the people I have written about in this chronicle; although I am luckier than most in that I still have my beloved Innogen and our children. May God protect them.

I miss Richard so much. He was my friend and I loved him. So did others. I had word from a man of York, who wrote quoting, for my comfort, the words the York City Council entered in their records when they heard of Richard's death:

*King Richard, late mercifully reigning upon us, was through great treason piteously slain and murdered, to the great heaviness of this City.*

They valued him and they do not forget. But I wonder if in fifty years anyone outside Yorkshire will remember him?

## Author's Note

*Treason* is fiction, but it is firmly based on fact. Readers have the right to know which is which.

My narrator Martin and his family are fictional, but all the other characters existed. ('Innogen' was the form of the name until Shakespeare or his typesetters made it 'Imogen' in *Cymbeline*.) Dialogue, private incidents, and characters' motivations are, of course, my own invention although wherever possible I have based conversation on recorded fragments (for example, von Poppelau's record of his meeting with King Richard). The main incidents are a matter of record, although I have had to omit a great deal. The letters quoted in this novel are genuine, except for those to and from fictional characters and Edward's of 1461 and Hastings' of 1483.

No one knows what became of Richard III's son John. There is a vague reference to a 'base-born son of Richard III' being executed in the Warbeck rebellion, but there is no definite record. In fiction, of course, the author can keep John alive. Similarly, no one knows precisely when Richard's daughter, Katherine, died, but by the time of Elizabeth of York's coronation, Katherine's husband was recorded as a widower. It seems a reasonable supposition that Katherine died of the sweating sickness brought to England by Henry VII's army.

Even among the nobility, dates of birth and death were often only recorded incidentally; at other times such records have been lost. The *Rous Roll* gives 1476 as the year Richard III's son, Edward, was born, and the *Croyland Chronicle* tells us he died in April of 1484. No other details are known. Nor is there any information about Richard's illegitimate children, John and Katherine, except that they existed; that Katherine was old enough to be married in 1484 (which tells us little since child marriages were not uncommon), and that

John was knighted and made Captain of Calais in 1483 (which again tells us little, for children could be knighted and given honorary positions). Since Richard III's private life after his marriage was approvingly noted as a model of decorum I have assumed his bastard children were conceived before that marriage. Their mothers are my own invention, since nothing is known of them.

No one would dare invent the eclipse of the sun when Anne died. It happened.

The English of the fifteenth century were a xenophobic, insular lot who believed they were better than the rest of the world put together. My narrator Martin is a cynical, partisan man of his times, and his views on England's neighbours, and other characters, are not always my own.

For the sake of clarity I used the most well-known modern spellings of names, for example, Tudor not Tidder or Tydr; Woodville not Wydeville. I have used a plain, modern vernacular throughout the novel, because once you start being 'medieval' where do you stop? Moreover, the real speech and writings of the fifteenth century would be all but incomprehensible to the average modern reader. Also, for clarity I have treated dates as if the medieval year began, like ours, on 1st January.

Battle details are as correct as I can make them. I am not entering into the recent controversy about whether Richard III's final battle took place at Bosworth or Dadlington or somewhere entirely different: I have stuck to Bosworth, which is familiar to everyone and at least has alliteration in its favour.

No one knows with certainty what became of Francis, Lord Lovell. He fought in the battle of Stoke in 1487, and later was given a safe conduct by the King of Scotland, but his eventual fate is unknown.

Lady Margaret Pole, Clarence's daughter, was for a long time about the only Plantagenet to escape the Tudors' policy of removing anyone with a better claim by birth to the throne. She survived to become one of Catherine of Aragon's ladies in waiting and her friend and staunch supporter, and was created Countess of Salisbury in her own right. In 1541, when she was 67, Henry VIII had her executed for alleged treason.

The two things everyone 'knows' about Richard III, thanks to Shakespeare, are that he was a hunchback with a withered arm, and that he murdered his nephews, 'the Princes in the Tower'. Despite the efforts of unbiased historians over the past five hundred years, it is still necessary to emphasise that the first is definitely not true and the second highly unlikely and certainly not proven.

No one in Richard III's own time noticed any deformity (particularly Nicholas Von Poppelau, who as a foreigner writing in his own country had no need to be flattering). Richard was a warrior from the time he was seventeen, and a half-paralysed cripple could not have fought in medieval conditions.

No one knows what happened to 'the Princes'. Rumour is all. And for every rumour that Richard had them killed, or that they died during his reign, there is another that they survived and were taken abroad. Nicholas Von Poppelau, whose reminiscences of his visit to England are included in Armstrong's translation of Dominic Mancini's *The Usurpation of Richard III*, heard but didn't believe the rumours of their death; he also recorded hearing that they were alive and kept in some safe hiding place. And if all England had been ringing with the scandal of the boys' known murder at their uncle's behest, Von Poppelau would surely have recorded the fact. Instead, he chats about his pleasant visit to a king he clearly admired.

After five hundred years it is still a mystery, and a subject that seems to make some people lose all grip on reality. But unless any proof ever turns up, we must at the very least say that Richard is innocent until proven guilty. *Cui bono?* – who benefits? – is as valid a question when dealing with history as with present-day events. Murdering his nephews would have been an outstandingly foolish thing to do, and there is no evidence that Richard was a fool. One currently popular theory is that the Duke of Buckingham killed the boys to further his rebellion, and handed Richard the *fait accompli*. Many people at the time, apparently including King James of Scotland, who would surely have been loath to give his kinswoman in marriage to a nobody, believed that 'Perkin Warbeck', whose 'confession' is patently rubbish, truly was Richard Duke of York. No one knows. My version of the boys' fate is of course fictional, but it is as good as any.

Henry VII soon realised that he would face rebellions (as indeed he did, right through his reign) and had set a dangerous precedent by backdating his reign and attainting Richard III's followers as traitors. Most of the attainders were reversed, and Parliament rapped their new king over the knuckles by passing legislation to protect men who fought for the ruling monarch. Henry VII did eventually cough up ten pounds for a tomb for his predecessor. It was despoiled during the Dissolution, and Richard III's remains were apparently thrown into the River Soar. Or else they lie under a carpark in Leicester; no one is too sure. A King of England, he had to wait another four hundred years for a memorial to mark his possible burial place.

Meredith Whitford

Adelaide, South Australia

# Also Available from BeWrite Books

*Crime*
| | |
|---|---|
| The Knotted Cord | Alistair Kinnon |
| The Tangled Skein | Alistair Kinnon |
| Marks | Sam Smith |
| Porlock Counterpoint | Sam Smith |
| Scent of Crime | Linda Stone |

*Crime/Humour*
| | |
|---|---|
| Sweet Molly Maguire | Terry Houston |

*Horror*
| | |
|---|---|
| Chill | Terri Pine, Peter Lee, Andrew Müller |

*Fantasy/Humour*
| | |
|---|---|
| Zolin A Rockin' Good Wizard | Barry Ireland |
| The Hundredfold Problem | John Grant |
| Earthdoom! | David Langford & John Grant |

*Fantasy*
| | |
|---|---|
| The Far-Enough Window | John Grant |
| A Season of Strange Dreams | C. S. Thompson |
| And Then the Night | C. S. Thompson |

*Collections/ Short Stories*
| | |
|---|---|
| As the Crow Flies | Dave Hutchinson |
| The Loss of Innocence | Jay Mandal |
| Kaleidoscope | Various |
| Odie Dodie | Lad Moore |
| Tailwind | Lad Moore |
| The Miller Moth | Mike Broemmel |
| The Shadow Cast | Mike Broemmel |
| As the Crow Flies | Dave Hutchinson |
| The Creature in the Rose | Various |

*Thriller*
| | |
|---|---|
| Deep Ice | Karl Kofoed |
| Blood Money | Azam Gill |
| Evil Angel | RD Larson |
| Disremembering Eddie | Anne Morgellyn |
| Flight to Pakistan | Azam Gill |
| Removing Edith Mary | Anne Morgellyn |

### Historical Fiction

| | |
|---|---|
| Ring of Stone | Hugh McCracken |
| Jahred and The Magi | Wilma Clark |
| The Kinnons of Candleriggs | Jenny Telfer Chaplin |

### Contemporary

| | |
|---|---|
| The Care Vortex | Sam Smith |
| Someplace Like Home | Terrence Moore |
| Sick Ape | Sam Smith |
| A Tangle of Roots | David Hough |
| Whispers of Ghosts | Ron McLachlan |

### Young Adult

| | |
|---|---|
| Rules of the Hunt | Hugh McCracken |
| The Time Drum | Hugh McCracken |
| Kitchen Sink Concert | Ishbel Moore |
| The Fat Moon Dance | Elizabeth Taylor |
| Grandfather and The Ghost | Hugh McCracken |
| Return from the Hunt | Hugh McCracken |

### Children's

| | |
|---|---|
| The Secret Portal | Reno Charlton |
| The Vampire Returns | Reno Charlton |

### Autobiography/Biography

| | |
|---|---|
| A Stranger and Afraid | Arthur Allwright |
| Vera & Eddy's War | Sam Smith |

### Poetry

| | |
|---|---|
| A Moment for Me | Heather Grace |
| Shaken & Stirred | Various |
| Letters from Portugal | Jan Oskar Hansen |
| Routes | Twelve poets. A road less traveled. |
| Vinegar Moon | Donna Biffar |
| The Drowning Fish | John G Hall |
| listen to the geckos... | tolulope ogunlesi |

### General

| | |
|---|---|
| The Wounded Stone | Terry Houston |
| Magpies and Sunsets | Neil Alexander Marr |
| Redemption of Quapaw Mountain | Bertha Sutliff |

### Romance

| | |
|---|---|
| A Different Kind of Love | Jay Mandal |

The Dandelion Clock          Jay Mandal

**Humour**
The Cuckoos of Batch Magna          Peter Maughan

**Science Fiction**
Gemini Turns          Anne Marie Duquette

**Adventure**
Matabele Gold          Michael J Hunt
The African Journals of
Petros Amm          Michael J Hunt
The Stones of Petronicus          Peter Tomlinson

**Coming Soon**
The End of Science Fiction          Sam Smith
The Adventures of Alianore
Audley          Brian Wainwright
Treason          Meredith Whitford

## All the above titles are available from

**www.bewrite.net**

Printed in the United States
115008LV00003B/5/A